THE COLLECTED
SHORT STORIES
OF LOUIS L'AMOUR

Bantam Books by Louis L'Amour

NOVELS

Bendigo Shafter
Borden Chantry
Brionne
The Broken Gun
The Burning Hills
The Californios
Callaghen
Catlow
Chancy
The Cherokee Trail
Comstock Lode
Conagher
Crossfire Trail
Dark Canyon
Down the Long Hills
The Empty Land
Fair Blows the Wind
Fallon
The Ferguson Rifle
The First Fast Draw
Flint
Guns of the Timberlands
Hanging Woman Creek
The Haunted Mesa
Heller with a Gun
The High Graders
High Lonesome
Hondo
How the West Was Won
The Iron Marshal
The Key-Lock Man
Kid Rodelo
Kilkenny
Killoe
Kilrone
Kiowa Trail
Last of the Breed
Last Stand at Papago
    Wells
The Lonesome Gods
The Man Called Noon
The Man from
    Skibbereen
The Man from the
    Broken Hills
Matagorda
Milo Talon
The Mountain Valley
    War
North to the Rails
Over on the Dry Side
Passin' Through

The Proving Trail
The Quick and the Dead
Radigan
Reilly's Luck
The Rider of Lost Creek
Rivers West
The Shadow Riders
Shalako
Showdown at Yellow
    Butte
Silver Canyon
Sitka
Son of a Wanted Man
Taggart
The Tall Stranger
To Tame a Land
Tucker
Under the Sweetwater
    Rim
Utah Blaine
The Walking Drum
Westward the Tide
Where the Long Grass
    Blows

SHORT STORY
COLLECTIONS

Beyond the Great Snow
    Mountains
Bowdrie
Bowdrie's Law
Buckskin Run
The Collected Short
    Stories of Louis
    L'Amour
    (vols. 1–7)
Dutchman's Flat
End of the Drive
From the Listening Hills
The Hills of Homicide
Law of the Desert Born
Long Ride Home
Lonigan
May There Be a Road
Monument Rock
Night over the Solomons
Off the Mangrove Coast
The Outlaws of
    Mesquite
The Rider of the Ruby
    Hills
Riding for the Brand
The Strong Shall Live
The Trail to Crazy Man

Valley of the Sun
War Party
West from Singapore
West of Dodge
With These Hands
Yondering

SACKETT TITLES

Sackett's Land
To the Far Blue
    Mountains
The Warrior's Path
Jubal Sackett
Ride the River
The Daybreakers
Sackett
Lando
Mojave Crossing
Mustang Man
The Lonely Men
Galloway
Treasure Mountain
Lonely on the Mountain
Ride the Dark Trail
The Sackett Brand
The Sky-Liners

THE HOPALONG CASSIDY
NOVELS

The Riders of High Rock
The Rustlers of West Fork
The Trail to Seven Pines
Trouble Shooter

NONFICTION

Education of a
    Wandering Man
Frontier
THE SACKETT
    COMPANION: A
    Personal Guide to the
    Sackett Novels
A TRAIL OF MEMORIES:
    The Quotations of
    Louis L'Amour,
    compiled by
    Angelique L'Amour

POETRY

Smoke from This Altar

LOST TREASURES

Louis L'Amour's Lost
    Treasures: Volume 1

THE
COLLECTED
SHORT STORIES
OF
LOUIS L'AMOUR

ADVENTURE STORIES
Volume 4, Part 1

Louis L'Amour

BANTAM BOOKS
NEW YORK

The Collected Short Stories of Louis L'Amour, Volume 4, Part 1, is a work
of fiction. Names, characters, places, and incidents either are the product
of the author's imagination or are used fictitiously. Any resemblance to
actual persons, living or dead, events or locales is entirely coincidental.

2015 Bantam Books Mass Market Edition
Copyright © 2006 by Louis & Katherine L'Amour Trust
Excerpt from *Law of the Desert Born, A Graphic Novel,* by Louis L'Amour
copyright © 2013 by Beau L'Amour and Louis L'Amour Enterprises, Inc.

All rights reserved.

Published in the United States by Bantam Books,
an imprint of Random House, a division of Random House LLC,
a Penguin Random House Company, New York.

BANTAM BOOKS and the HOUSE colophon are registered trademarks
of Random House LLC.

Originally published as part of *The Collected Short Stories of Louis
L'Amour, Volume 4,* in the United States by Bantam Books, an imprint of
Random House, a division of Random House LLC, in 2006.

ISBN 978-0-8041-7974-4
eBook ISBN 978-0-553-90307-2

Cover design: Scott Biel
Cover art: Gregory Manchess

Photograph of Louis L'Amour by John Hamilton—Globe Photos, Inc.

Printed in the United States of America

www.bantamdell.com

9 8 7 6 5 4

Bantam Books mass market edition: March 2015

CONTENTS

Beyond the Great Snow Mountains   *1*
May There Be a Road   *15*
By the Waters of San Tadeo   *40*
Meeting at Falmouth   *57*
Crash Landing   *67*
With These Hands   *75*
The Diamond of Jeru   *89*

Death, Westbound   *139*
Old Doc Yak   *145*
It's Your Move   *153*
And Proudly Die   *159*
Survival   *167*
Show Me the Way to Go Home   *185*
Thicker Than Blood   *190*
The Admiral   *195*
Shanghai, Not Without Gestures   *201*
The Man Who Stole Shakespeare   *207*
The Dancing Kate   *214*
Off the Mangrove Coast   *228*
Glorious! Glorious!   *244*
By the Ruins of "El Walarieh"   *257*
Where There's Fighting   *260*
The Cross and the Candle   *272*
A Friend of the General   *283*
Author's Tea   *300*
Afterword   *305*

THE COLLECTED
SHORT STORIES
OF LOUIS L'AMOUR

BEYOND THE GREAT
SNOW MOUNTAINS

WHEN THE BURIAL was complete, she rode with her son into the hills.

The Go-log tribesmen, sharing her sorrow for their lost leader, stood aside and allowed her to go. Lok-sha had been a great man and too young to die.

Only in the eyes of Norba and his followers did she detect the triumph born of realization that nothing now stood between him and tribal control. Nothing but a slender woman, alien to their land, and Kulan, her fourteen-year-old son.

There was no time to worry now, nor was there time for grief. If ever they were to escape, it must be at once, for it was unlikely such opportunity would again offer itself.

It had been fifteen years since the plane in which she was leaving China crashed in the mountains near Tosun Nor, killing all on board but herself. Now, as if decreed by fate, another had come, and this one landed intact.

Shambe had brought the news as Lok-sha lay dying, for long ago the far-ranging hunter had promised if ever another plane landed, he would first bring the news to her.

If the fierce Go-log tribesmen learned of the landing, they would kill the survivors and destroy the plane. To enter the land of the Go-log was to die.

It was a far land of high, grass plateaus, snowcapped mountains, and rushing streams. There among the peaks were born three of the greatest rivers of Asia—the Yellow, the Yangtze, and the Mekong—and there the Go-log lived as they had lived since the time of Genghis Khan.

Splendid horsemen and savage fighters, they lived upon their herds of yaks, fat-tailed sheep, horses, and the plunder reaped from caravans bound from China to Tibet.

Anna Doone, born on a ranch in Montana, had taken readily to the hard, nomadic life of the Go-log. She had come to China to join her father, a medical missionary, and her uncle, a noted anthropologist. Both were killed in Kansu by the renegade army that had once belonged to General Ma. Anna, with two friends, attempted an escape in an old plane.

Riding now toward this other aircraft, she recalled the morning when, standing beside her wrecked plane, she had first watched the Go-log approach. She was familiar with their reputation for killing interlopers, but she had a Winchester with a telescopic sight and a .45-caliber Colt revolver.

Despite her fear, she felt a burst of admiration for their superb horsemanship as they raced over the plain. Seeing the rifle ready in her hands, they drew up sharply, and her eyes for the first time looked upon Lok-sha.

Only a little older than her own twenty-one years, he was a tall man with a lean horseman's build, and he laughed with pure enjoyment when she lifted the rifle. She was to remember that laugh for a long time, for the Go-log were normally a somber people.

Lok-sha had the commanding presence of the born leader of men, and she realized at once that if she were to survive, it would be because he wished it.

He spoke sharply in his own tongue, and she replied in the dialect of Kansu, which fortunately he understood.

"It is a fine weapon," he said about the rifle.

"I do not wish to use it against the Go-log. I come as a friend."

"The Go-log have no friends."

A small herd of Tibetan antelope appeared on the crest of a low ridge some three hundred yards away, looking curiously toward the crashed plane.

She had used a rifle since she was a child, killing her first deer when only eleven. Indicating the antelope, she took careful aim and squeezed off her shot. The antelope bounded away, but one went to its knees, then rolled over on its side.

The Go-log shouted with amazement, for accurate shooting with their old rifles was impossible at that range. Two of the riders charged off to recover the game, and she looked into the eyes of the tall rider.

"I have another such rifle, and if we are friends, it is yours."

"I could kill you and take them both."

She returned his look. *"They,"* she said, indicating the others, "might take it from me. You would not, for you are a man of honor, and I would kill you even as they killed me."

She had no doubt of her position, and her chance of ever leaving this place was remote. Whatever was done, she must do herself.

He gestured toward the wreck. "Get what you wish, and come with us."

Her shooting had impressed them, and now her riding did also, for these were men who lived by riding and shooting. Lok-sha, a *jyabo* or king of the Go-log people, did not kill her. Escape being impossible, she married him in a Buddhist ceremony, and then to satisfy some Puritan strain within her, she persuaded Tsan-Po, the lama, to read over them in Kansu dialect the Christian ceremony.

Fortunately, the plane had not burned, and from it she brought ammunition for the rifles, field glasses, clothing, medicines, and her father's instrument case. Best of all, she brought the books that had belonged to her father and uncle.

Having often assisted her father, she understood the emergency treatment of wounds and rough surgery. This knowledge became a valuable asset and solidified her position in the community.

As soon as Anna's son was born, she realized the time would come when, if they were not rescued, he would become *jyabo,* so she began a careful record of migration dates, grass conditions, and rainfall. If it was in her power, she was going to give him the knowledge to be the best leader possible.

Lok-sha was sharply interested in all she knew about the Chinese to the east, and he possessed the imagination to translate the lessons of history into the practical business of command and statecraft. The end had come when his horse, caught on a severe, rocky slope, had fallen, crushing Lok-sha's chest.

She had been happy in the years she'd spent as his wife, certainly she was better off than she would have been as a refugee in the civil war that gripped much of China or as a prisoner of the Japanese. But as happy as she had learned to be, as safe as she had finally found herself, Anna never forgot her home, nor ceased to long for the day when she might return.

Now, her thoughts were interrupted by Shambe's appearance. "The plane is nearby," he said, "and there are two men."

Shambe was not only Lok-sha's best friend, but leader of the Ku-ts'a, the bodyguard of the *jyabo,* a carefully selected band of fighting men.

They rode now, side by side, Kulan, Shambe, and herself. "You will leave with the flying men?" Shambe asked. "And you will take the *jyabo* also?"

Startled, Anna Doone glanced at her son, riding quietly beside her. Of course . . . what had she been thinking of? Her son, Kulan, was *jyabo* now . . . king of six thousand tents, commander of approximately two thousand of the most dangerous fighting men in Asia!

But it was ridiculous. He was only fourteen. He should be in school, thinking about football or baseball. Yet fourteen among the Go-log was not fourteen among her own people. Lok-sha, against her bitter protests, had carried Kulan into battle when he was but six years old, and during long rides over the grasslands had taught him what he could of the arts of war and leadership.

Her son *jyabo*? She wished to see him a doctor, a scientist, a teacher. It was preposterous to think of him as king of a savage people in a remote land. Yet deep within her something asked a question: *How important would baseball be to a boy accustomed to riding a hundred miles from dawn to dusk, or hunting bighorn sheep among the highest peaks?*

"We shall regret your going," Shambe said sincerely, "you have been long among us."

And she would regret losing him, too, for he had been a true friend. She said as much, said it quietly and with sincerity.

When she heard of the plane, her thoughts had leaped

ahead, anticipating their homecoming. She had taken notes of her experiences and could write a book, and she could lecture. Kulan was tall and strong and could receive the education and opportunities that he had missed.

Yet she had sensed the reproof in Shambe's tone; Shambe, who had been her husband's supporter in his troubles with Norba, a chief of a minor division of the Khang-sar Go-log.

Over their heads the sky was fiercely blue, their horses' hooves drummed upon the hard, close-cropped turf . . . there were few clouds. Yes . . . these rides would be remembered. Nowhere were there mountains like these, nowhere such skies.

When they came within sight of the plane, the two men sprang to their feet, gripping their rifles.

She drew up. "I am Anna Doone, and this is Kulan, my son."

The older man strode toward her. "This is amazing! The State Department has been trying to locate you and your family for years! You are the niece of Dr. Ralph Doone, are you not?"

"I am."

"My name is Schwarzkopf. Your uncle and I were associated during his work at the Merv Oasis." He glanced at Shambe, and then at Kulan. "Your son, you said?"

She explained the crashed plane, her marriage to Lok-sha, his death, and her wish to escape. In turn, they told her of how they had seized the plane and escaped from the Communist soldiers. Their landing had been made with the last of their fuel.

"If there was fuel, would you take us with you?"

"Take you? But of course!" Schwarzkopf's eyes danced with excitement that belied his sixty-odd years. "What an opportunity! Married to a Go-log chieftain! So little is known of them, you understand! Their customs, their beliefs . . . we must arrange a grant. I know just the people who—"

"If it's all the same to you, Doc," his companion interrupted, "I'd like to get out of here." He looked up at Anna

Doone. "I'm sorry, ma'am, but you mentioned fuel. Is there some gas around here somewhere?"

"Several months ago my husband took a convoy bound for an airfield in Tibet. He captured several trucks loaded with gasoline. They are hidden only a few miles away." She paused. "I can drive a truck."

Yet, first she must return to the Go-log encampment to meet with the elders and the fighting men of the Khang-sar. Kulan, as *jyabo,* must be present. It would be improper and even dangerous if she were not present also, for a decision was to be made on the move to new grazing grounds, and there might also be some question as to leadership.

The time had come for the Khang-sar to return to their home in the Yur-tse Mountains, and the thought brought a pang, for these were the loveliest of mountains, splendid forests and lakes in a limestone range near the head of the Yellow River.

"Whatever you do," she warned, "you must not leave the vicinity of the plane. Start no fires, and let no metal flash in the sun. When our meeting is over, Shambe will remain near you until Kulan and I can come."

She swung her horse around. "If you are found, neither Kulan nor I could protect you."

"Kulan?" The younger man looked at the boy in surprise.

Kulan sat straight in the saddle. "I am now *jyabo,*" he replied sternly, "but our people think all outsiders are the enemy."

When they had gone some distance, Kulan sighed and said, "The machine is small. There will be no room for Deba."

She knew how much he loved the horse. "No, Kulan, there will be no room, but you would not wish to take him away. He was bred to this country, and loves it."

"I love it, too," Kulan replied simply.

She started to speak, but the horse herd was before them, and beyond were the felt yurts of the camp. Tsan-Po awaited them before their own tent. With Lok-sha gone, the Khang-sar Go-log would have need of the old man's shrewd advice.

Kulan waved a hand at the encampment. "How would we live in your country?"

"Life is very different there, Kulan, and much easier. You might become a fine scholar and lead a good life."

"If that is what you wish. I shall do my best, for both you and my father have taught me obedience. Only sometimes," his voice tightened, "sometimes I shall think of Deba and these grasslands, and of Amne Machin, the God Mountain."

For the first time she felt doubt, but quickly dismissed it. Of course she was doing the right thing. Once he was adjusted to life in civilization, he would be as happy there. True, he was mature for his years, as boys were apt to be among the Go-log. It was natural that he would miss Deba, and he would miss Shambe, as she would. Shambe had been a second father to him, even as Tsan-Po had been. The old lama had taught Kulan much that was beyond her.

Yet, how long she had dreamed of going home! Of luxuriating in a warm tub, conversing in English for hours on end, and the good, fireside talk of people who were doing things in the larger world of art, science, and scholarship. She longed for a life where she did not have to live with the fear that her son might die from something as silly as a tooth infection or as serious as the bullet from the rifle of a Communist soldier.

She was thirty-six, soon to be thirty-seven, and if she ever wanted a relationship with another man, it could not be here, where she had once been the wife of a king. Nor could she wait for too many years after the rough life on the steppes, a life that had been good to her so far, but was bound to leave her a windburned and arthritic old woman.

What Dr. Schwarzkopf had said was true. Her experience was unique. A book might sell . . . she could make a contribution to anthropology, and even to geographical knowledge. As for Kulan, he would do well in America. He was tall and wide-shouldered, and would be a handsome man with his olive skin, his dark, curly hair and truly magnificent dark eyes. There was a touch of the exotic about him that was romantic, and at fourteen he was already stronger than most men.

As SHE ENTERED the yurt, she sensed trouble in the air. Shambe was beside her, but when had he not been present when she needed him?

All of the Khang-sar Go-log chieftains were there. Tsemba was the chief of two hundred tents and an important man whose opinion counted for much. Beside him were old Kunza, Gelak, and of course, Norba.

Norba was a towering big man with one muscular shoulder bare, as was the custom, his broad-bladed sword slung in its scabbard between his shoulder blades. His coterie of followers was close around him, confident now that Lok-sha was dead.

Norba had both hated and feared Lok-sha, but had no heart for a fight with the *jyabo*. Yet had Lok-sha left no heir, Norba would have become chief.

The impending shift to new grazing grounds promised trouble. A faction of the Khang-sar led by Norba wished to go to Tosun Nor, but Lok-sha had decided, under the present circumstances, it was better to graze far from the caravan trails and let a season go by without raids. The new soldiers from the east were not the undisciplined rabble of old. Something was afoot in China proper, and Lok-sha had thought it best to gather more information before testing fate. Moreover, there had been rumors of serious drought around Tosun Nor, and drought meant losses from the herds.

She seated herself beside Kulan, with Tsan-Po beside her, and Shambe seated on the other side of her son. Norba had moved to take the seat of *jyabo*, but Kulan was before him. Norba's face flushed angrily when he saw the boy take the seat where he wished to sit.

"Move, boy. Go play with the children."

Kulan sat very straight. "Unless it is decided otherwise, I am *jyabo*," he replied. "Until then, take your place."

For an instant there was utter stillness, then a mutter from the followers of Norba, but Kulan ignored them. Glancing at her son, Anna Doone was astonished. Truly, he looked every inch the young king. There was strength in him, of that there would be no doubt, strength and courage.

Norba hesitated, then reluctantly took a seat. Anna could see his repressed fury and knew there was trouble to come. It was well that they were leaving. The thought of escape from all this sent a little tremor of excitement through her, excitement tinged with relief.

The yurt filled and the air was stifling. Anna studied the faces of the chieftains, but they were expressionless. Would they follow Kulan, or would they demand an older, more experienced leader?

Tsan-Po whispered to her that most of those within the tent were supporters of Norba, and Anna Doone felt inside her coat for the pistol she was never without.

Their very lives might depend on the selection of Kulan as *jyabo,* for if Norba were able to take power, he would at once seek to rid himself of his rival. It would not be without precedence if Norba attempted to kill Kulan here, now. Her hand on her pistol, Anna suddenly knew that if Norba even moved toward her son, she would kill him.

She accepted some tea, drinking from a bowl that had come to Tibet from India in the dower of a princess, more than a thousand years before. In those years, Tibet had controlled most of western China, as well as part of India and Kashmir.

Abruptly, without waiting for the others to assemble, Norba declared himself. "Tomorrow," he said, "we will move to Tosun Nor to pasture upon the old lands."

There was silence as he looked around the yurt. That silence held for a slow minute, and then Kulan said one word. "No."

The word was definite, the tone clear, the challenge accepted.

Norba's face flushed with anger, but Kulan spoke before Norba could frame a word.

"There is drought at Tosun Nor. The grass lies yellow and dead, the air is filled with dust. The beds of streams are cracked earth. We must go to the mountains, to the Yur-tse."

Again Norba prepared to speak, but Kulan interrupted. "My father is dead, but I am my father's son. We rode upon the high grass together and he taught me what I must do."

For the first time, he looked at Norba. "You are *deba* of two hundred tents. You may ride with us or go to Tosun Nor. I would advise you to come with us."

Norba looked around at his followers. "We are men, and not to be led by a boy. It is I who shall lead the Khang-sar. When you are of an age to lead," he added slyly, "you may lead."

Tsan-Po spoke. "The boy is his father's son. Leadership falls upon him."

Norba got to his feet. "Enough! I say that I shall lead. I say it, and my men say it."

Kulan arose, and Shambe and Anna arose with him. Anna held her gun in her hand. "The Ku-ts'a stand without," Shambe said, "and they follow Kulan . . . Unless all the chieftains say otherwise."

Norba's lips flattened against his big teeth, and for an instant Anna thought he would strike Kulan despite the fact that the bodyguards surrounded the tent. The Ku-ts'a numbered fifty-eight chosen men, the hereditary guard of the *jyabo*. Norba had not expected the Ku-ts'a. With the *jyabo* dead, he had believed they would accept the situation.

He slammed his sword back into its scabbard. "We will go to Tosun Nor," he said. "You are fools."

"Go, if you will," Kulan replied, "and those who survive are welcome to return. Our herds will be fat upon the long grass of the limestone mountains."

With a pang, Anna realized that Kulan was no longer a boy. The discipline had been strict and the training harsh, but he was every inch a king. Yet she was impatient, for their time was short, and if the plane were discovered, the fliers would be killed and they would be condemned to more fruitless, wasted years.

Alone at last, she said to him, "What was all that about the drought at Tosun Nor?"

"It had been rumored, so while you talked to the old man of your people, I asked the other. He spoke of dense clouds of dust high in the heavens, and of sheep and horses lying dead from starvation and thirst."

He paused. "It is well that Norba goes, for when he returns, if he returns, his power will be broken."

He glanced at her slyly, his face warming with a smile. "My mother taught me to listen, to question when in doubt, and to keep my thoughts until the time for speaking."

After Kulan was asleep, she went outside the yurt and stood alone under the stars. There was moonlight upon the snows of the God Mountain, reflected moonlight that seemed born from some inner glory within the mountain itself.

She thought of home, of the quiet college town and the autumn leaves falling. It had been almost twenty years, but tomorrow they would fly over the mountains to India. To a fine hotel, a room of her own, a hot bath, and a real bed . . . it was impossible to imagine such things still existed.

For fifteen years she had been virtually a prisoner. True, Lok-sha had treated her well, and she had been respected among the Go-log, but their ways were strange, and her nights had been given up to dreaming of home.

The thought of Norba returned. If Kulan was gone, he would be in control, and would probably lead the Khang-sar Go-log to disaster. Lok-sha had always said he was a stubborn fool.

No matter. It was now or never. It was impossible that another opportunity would occur, for travel was restricted. No Europeans or Americans would be flying over this country. It was her last chance.

She looked around at the sleeping encampment. She would miss it. Lok-sha, despite their differences of background, had been a superior man. If he had been slow to appreciate her feelings, there had been no cruelty in him.

The icy peak was austere in its bath of moonlight; it was taller than Everest, some said, yet it gave an impression of bulk rather than height. It was no wonder the Go-log called it the God Mountain.

Tsan-Po was walking toward her. "Do you go tomorrow?"

She had ceased to be startled by his awareness of things. "Yes."

"You have been long away . . . does someone await you there?"

"No."

"We will miss you, and we will miss Kulan."

"He goes to a great land. He will do well, I think."

"Here he is a king. Ours is a small king, but even a small king is still a king."

She felt the reproof of his tone, and together they watched the moonlight on Amne Machin. "He will make a strong man," the lama said, "a stronger man and a better leader than Lok-sha."

She was surprised. "Do you really believe that?"

"You have taught him much, and he has character. We Go-log face a trying time, for as the world changes, even we must change.

"Kulan has a sense of the world. You taught him of your land and of Europe, and I have told him of India, where I worked as a young man. He is schooled in the arts of war and statecraft, and I believe it is in him to be a great leader."

He was silent, then added, "Your country could use a friend here."

"Do you believe I am wrong to take him away?"

"We need him," Tsan-Po replied simply, "and he needs you. For several years yet, he will need you."

The lama turned away. "It is late." He took a step, then paused. "Beware of Norba. You have not finished with him."

When morning dawned, they rode swiftly to the hidden trucks. What Lok-sha planned to do with the trucks, she did not know, but presumably he intended to use them as a trap for Chinese soldiers.

She started the truck with difficulty for the motor was cold. There was no road, but the turf was solid, and she had driven on the prairie during her childhood in Montana. The old Army six-by-six was no problem.

Kulan followed, holding off to one side and leading her horse.

Keeping to low ground and circling to avoid gullies or patches of rock, she needed all of an hour to reach the plane.

The pilot and Dr. Schwarzkopf rushed to the tailgate and started to unload the cans. As soon as the truck was empty, Anna drove back for a second truck, and by the time she had returned, the cans of the first had been emptied into the tanks of the plane.

Yet they had scarcely begun on the second load when Shambe came down off the ridge where he had been on watch. Kulan, also watching from a quarter of a mile away, wheeled his mount and raced back at a dead run, drawing his rifle from its scabbard.

"Norba comes," Shambe said, "with many men."

Schwarzkopf dropped his jerry can and started for his rifle, but Anna's gesture stopped him. "Finish refueling," she said, and when he hesitated, "Doctor, put that gun down and get busy!"

Kulan swung his pony alongside her as she mounted, and Shambe drew upon the other side. They sat together, awaiting the oncoming riders.

Norba's horse reared as he drew up, a hard pleasure in his eyes. "So . . . you are traitors. I shall kill you."

Anna Doone's heart pounded heavily, yet she kept all emotion from her face. Her son's life, as well as her own, was at stake.

"These men are our friends. We help them on their way," she said.

"And I shall decide who is and is not a traitor," Kulan added.

From behind them the pilot said, "One more can does it."

Anna's heart lifted. Behind her was the plane that could take her home, the rescue of which she had dreamed for fifteen years. The time was here, the time was now.

The sky beckoned, and beyond the mountains lay India, the threshold to home.

"Go with them, Mother." Kulan's eyes did not turn from Norba. "I cannot, for these are my people."

Her protest found no words. How often had she taught him that kingship was an obligation rather than a glory?

Her eyes swung around the semicircle of savage faces, and then for one brief instant the dream remained, shimmering before her eyes: a warm quiet house, a hot bath, meals prepared from food from a market, life without fear of disease or crippling disfigurement, life without war.

"Dr. Schwarzkopf," she said, "you will leave your rifles and ammunition, they are in short supply here."

"If you are going," Kulan said, "you must go now."

"If these are your people, Kulan, then they are my people also."

The winding caravan of Norba's people appeared, heading north toward Tosun Nor. She should have remembered they would come this way.

Dr. Schwarzkopf brought the weapons and the ammunition. "You will not come with us, then?"

"I can't. This is my son."

"You will die," Norba said. His eyes flickered over the three he hated—the wife of Lok-sha, the leader of the Ku-ts'a, and the boy who stood between him and the kingship.

Norba's rifle started to lift, and Shambe's started up with it, but Kulan put out a hand to stop the movement, then stepped his horse toward Norba and looked into his eyes.

"I am *jyabo*," he said. "I am your king."

For an instant Norba's rifle held still, then slowly it lowered. With an oath, Norba whirled his horse and dashed away, followed by his men.

Behind them the motors broke into a roar, and throwing up a vast cloud of dust, the plane rolled off, gathered speed, then soared up and away, toward India, toward home.

"You should have let me kill him," Shambe said.

"No, Shambe," Kulan replied, "many go to die, but those who remain will remember that I spoke truth."

Three abreast, they rode to the crest of the ridge and halted. The caravan of Norba's followers moved north toward the great lake known as Tosun Nor, moved toward drought and death.

Anna Doone, born in Montana, looked beyond them to a bright fleck that hung in the sky. Sunlight gleamed for an instant on a wingtip . . . then it winked out and was gone, leaving only a distant mutter of engines that echoed against the mountains.

MAY THERE BE A ROAD

T OHKTA LOOKED AT the bridge suspended across the gorge of the Yurung-kash. After four years, the bridge hung again, and now, at last, he could go to his betrothed, to Kushla.

At this point the gorge was scarcely a hundred feet wide, but black cliffs towered into the clouds above it, even as they fell sheer away hundreds of yards below. Down those cliffs came the trails that approached the bridge on either side. From where the bridge came into view from above, it seemed the merest thread . . . a thin line for which the eye must seek and seek again.

Scarcely four feet wide, the bridge was built of their hand-made rope, of slats cut from pine forests, and of thin planks laid across the slats. With every gust of wind the bridge swayed, but those who had built it hoped that it would be their lifeline to the outside world.

Tohkta's people were of the mountains, yet once each year they had descended to the oasis towns at the desert's edge, taking the furs, the wool and hides, for which they were known. The gold they sometimes took was a secret thing. In the timeless kingdom of their mountain valleys the bridge was their link to the future.

Only once in all the years their tribal memory encompassed had the bridge not been there, hanging five hundred feet above the tumbling white water. And for too long had Tohkta's people been isolated by its loss.

Four . . . almost five years before there had come a great shaking of the earth when the mountains raised higher, and steam and hot water gushed from newly made cracks. There had been a grinding of rock when the teeth of the earth were gnashed together. In the midst of it, the pinnacle that supported their bridge had toppled from the far side of the Yurung-kash into the gorge below.

There followed years of struggle against the high rocks and the torrent, years of terrible work to replace their bridge. Fields still had to be tilled and flocks tended, but two men had been dashed to death on the jagged rocks below when they fell from their ropes. Yet now the bridge was done.

The Kunlun Mountains rim the northern edge of Tibet, hanging above the deserts of Sinkiang, and are among the loneliest of the world's mountain ranges. Long, long ago when Tohkta's grandfather was a boy, a rare caravan still ventured along the ancient track that led from Sinkiang across Tibet and through the Himalayas to India itself, passing close to Mount Kailas, sacred to Buddhists.

For centuries that ancient track had been almost abandoned. Only yak hunters, as wild and strange as the creatures they hunted, used it now, or an occasional herdsman taking his flock to secret pasturage in the high mountain valleys.

Tohkta sat his horse beside his grandfather, Batai Khan, chieftain of their small tribe of fifty-six tents. This was a proud day, for today Tohkta rode to claim his bride from her father, Yakub, a wealthy Moslem trader. He glanced at his grandfather with pride, for the old man sat his horse like a boy despite his almost one hundred years. Fierce and fiery as always, the Khan was the oldest among a people known for their great age and their great strength.

Few outsiders ever came to know the mountain Tochari, remnants of a proud, warlike race that had ruled most of eastern Turkestan and much of western China. In ages past they had carried their banners against Mongol and Chinese, against Tungan and Turk, against the Tatar and Hun.

Slowly the column of twenty riders and their pack animals crossed the swinging bridge, and Batai Khan did not start up the trail until all were safely across.

"Yol Bolsun!" he called out, waving to the people of the village who lined the switchback trail on the other side of the gorge. It was an old greeting to those who rode the mountain trails: "May There Be a Road!"

And now, for the first time in four long years, there was a

road. The home of the Tochari was an island in mountains, cut off by the deep gorges of the Yurung-kash and the Keriya, and at its ends by impassable slopes. Within there lay more than one hundred square miles of grassy valleys, forest glades, waterfalls, and grass-covered mountain pastures. It was an isolated paradise among the snow-covered peaks, but now it was isolated no longer.

———

TOHKTA WAS IMPATIENT. Kushla awaited in the ancient oasis town of Kargalik, and how many were the nights he had remained awake to dream of her? Batai Khan and Yakub had arranged the match, but since their eyes first met, neither Tohkta nor Kushla had thoughts for another.

Yet four full years had gone by when no word could be received from her, nor sent to her.

"She will have forgotten me," Tohkta said gloomily. "It has been forever."

"She was a child," Batai Khan replied, "now she will be a woman, and so much the better. You are not forgotten, believe me." He glanced around at his handsome grandson. "I, who know women, say it. You have been a dream to her, and who can forget a dream?"

In the days that followed the finishing of the bridge Tola Beg, an ancient yak hunter, had been the first to cross, and he brought strange news. Chinese soldiers of a new kind had come to Sinkiang and to Tibet. The Dalai Lama had fled to India, and soldiers were in Khotan and Kargalik as well as Lhasa. People had been driven from their farms and their flocks to work upon a new road, harnessed like yak or camels.

"Do not go, Batai Khan." Tola Beg peered across the fire from his ancient, rheumy eyes, his skin withered and weathered by wind and cold, darkened by wind and sun. "They will imprison you and seize your goods."

"It is the time for the marriage of Tohkta."

"There is danger. The Chinese seek the ancient track to India but it is not India they want; it is the men of our mountains they would enslave." Tola Beg gulped his yak-butter tea noisily, as was the custom. "They respect nothing and they have no God. The mosques and lamaseries are closed and the lamas driven to work in the fields. The prayer wheels are stilled and there is a curse on the land."

"I can go alone," Tohkta said. "I will take the gold and go for Kushla."

"We are Tochari." Batai Khan spoke with dignity. "Does a khan of Tochari go like a thief in the night to meet his betrothed?"

They were Tochari. That was the final word among them. Tohkta knew the history of his people, and much more had been told him by an Englishman. In ages past it was said some of his people had migrated from Central Asia, going westward to become the Greeks and the Celts. Others had gone into northern India, to settle there, driven by the Hiung Nu, known to western nations as the Hun.

The Englishman had dug in ancient refuse piles along the ruins of the Great Wall, searching for bits of wood or paper on which there was writing. He had told Tohkta these fragments would piece together the history of the area, and of the Tochari. He glanced at Tohkta's dark red hair and green eyes, a coloring not uncommon among these people of the mountains, and said the Tochari were a people who made history.

Batai Khan had rebuked him gently. "We know our past, and need not dig in dung piles for it. If you would know it, too, come sit by our fires and our bards will sing for you."

And now they rode to claim the bride of Tohkta, for a khan of the Tochari must ride with warriors at his back and gold to consummate the union. Raw and cold was the weather, for the season was late. Soon the high passes would be closed, and the mountain basins would brim full with snow.

IT WAS MIDNIGHT on the third day when they reached the outskirts of the ancient town, crossing the road by which silk had once been carried to Greece and Rome. They drew up in a grove of trees and waited as the moon set beyond the desert hills. Tohkta was impatient to push on to the town, for eagerness rode his shoulders with sharp spurs. But Batai Khan had the caution of years.

Old as he was, he sat erect in his saddle, and the broadsword he carried slung between his shoulders was a mighty weapon in his hands. "The town has a different smell," he said, "there is trouble here."

"I must go to the house of Yakub," Tohkta said. "Tola Beg can come. If help is needed, he can return for you."

The Khan paused a moment, then nodded.

The house of Yakub was the largest in the oasis, and Tola Beg led the way on foot. Wind rustled among the tamarisks as they skirted an irrigation ditch. Beside Tohkta the old yak hunter moved, silent as a *djinn.* Tohkta, who had stalked wild sheep upon the highest peaks, was hard put to keep pace with the old man.

Outside the nearby *Ya-men,* which was the government house, stood vehicles that smelled of greasy smoke and petrol. Tohkta had seen them before, in Khotan. There were soldiers there also, reflected light gleaming from their gun barrels. They were fine rifles that filled Tohkta's mind with envy.

"The old wolf was right," Tola Beg breathed in his ear, "the town stinks of danger."

The town was different, very different. The fires in the foundry were out and the alley of the bazaar was dirty and neglected. Everywhere there were horses and trucks and soldiers and supplies. Even in the violent days after the murder of the old governor, when the fighting between the Nationalists and the Moslem generals was at its worst, there hadn't been this many armed men in Kargalik.

"The forces of history are at work here," Tola Beg mumbled. "And that is something to avoid." They moved on through the darkness and then drew up.

Tohkta crouched in the shadows, listening. Before him was the wall of the compound of Kushla's father. Soon he would see her. His heart pounded with excitement.

Creeping like wild dogs to a sheepfold, they came into the yard. Here, too, they heard the language of the Han Chinese, and one voice that made Tohkta's hair prickle on his scalp . . . a voice with the harsh tone of command. Neither of them spoke Mandarin, for Sinkiang is a land of many tongues, Chinese the least of them, but both knew its sound.

The house of Yakub, yet filled with Han soldiers. Tola Beg tugged at his arm. They must steal away while they had the chance.

But where then was Yakub? And where was Kushla?

"We must go. They have taken it for their own use," Tola Beg whispered in his ear.

Tohkta moved back into the darkness, his thoughts racing over possible alternatives. Then it came to him, and he knew where they would be if they were alive and still in Kargalik.

———

IT WAS AN ancient Buddhist temple, fallen to ruins, rebuilt, and ruined again. Sometimes Yakub had used it for a storehouse, and Kushla loved the ancient trees around it. There was shelter there, and a good spring nearby. They made their way through the dark town and approached with caution.

"Look!" Tola Beg caught his arm. "The spotted horse . . . it is the old one the girl loved. At least they left her that."

Why not? The horse was almost as old as Kushla herself, who would be eighteen this year.

Leaving Tola Beg, he moved swiftly, glancing each way, then listening. Like a wraith, Tohkta slipped past the yak hide that hung over the door.

In the vague light from the charcoal brazier he saw her, and on the instant he entered she looked up. She stood swiftly, poised like a young deer, ready for flight. And then she looked into his eyes and came into his arms without shame.

Yakub got to his feet. He was in rags. The one room of the temple that still possessed a roof held only a few sacks and some bedding. Yakub had been a proud and wealthy man, but was so no longer.

"Go, Tohkta! Go, quickly! If you are found here—!"

From his shirt, Tohkta drew the sack of gold. "The marriage price," he said. "I claim my bride."

How lovely she was! Her dark eyes glowed, her figure

under the thin garments was so lithe and eager. The years he had waited had brought her to womanhood, and to a loveliness he could scarcely believe. He tried to say all this.

"If you think I am beautiful after all that has happened, then our parents have chosen well," she said.

"Please go!" Yakub seized his elbow. "For the sake of my daughter, take her and go. The gold also. If they find it they will take it, anyway."

"What has happened here?"

"The Red soldiers, the ones that we heard of but who never came, they have come at last. They take everything and say it is for the future. Whose future? What future? I do not understand them, for until they came, we were happy. All we wished was to tend our flocks in peace. Now they are moving into the mountains, more soldiers arrive every day."

"Batai Khan awaits us. Come, we will gather your flocks as we go, and you can live among us. I would not have my bride mourning her father on her wedding night."

Kushla handed him her bundle and they turned swiftly to the door. Then Kushla caught a cry in her throat, and Tohkta felt rage and despair crowding within him.

The man who stood in the doorway was small with square shoulders and a neatly perfect uniform. Slender, he seemed to have that whiplike strength that resists all exhaustion. His cold eyes inspected Tohkta with careful attention.

"Greetings." He stepped into the ruins of the room, and behind him were two soldiers armed with submachine guns. "Greetings to Yakub and his lovely daughter. Greetings to you, hillman. That is what you are, am I correct?" He spoke Tungan, and spoke it well. Tohkta said nothing.

"Answer me . . ." He pulled a small automatic from a holster. "Or I will shoot Yakub in the foot." He flicked the gun's safety off.

"Yes," said Tohkta. "I am from the hills."

"Very good. I am Chu Shih." He said this as if it were a fact that explained itself. "We have been waiting for you. Waiting quite awhile. We knew that this woman was betrothed to a young man from the Kunlun. I could have sent her and her father to a labor camp, but I wanted to meet you.

Our destinies are intertwined, you see. Would you like to know how?"

Tohkta quietly assented. He was listening, listening to Chu Shih and listening for sounds from outside the building. There were more men out there, but how many he didn't know.

"You can have the opportunity of serving the people of China. I'm sure you do not care . . . but you will. There is a secret track over the mountains to India. It is the track used by Abu Bakr in the sixteenth century when he fled from Khotan. It is also my gateway to the mountain people. Do you know this track?"

"It is idle talk . . . bazaar talk. There is no track. There are only a few mountain pastures and fewer people. All you will find in the mountains are granite and ice, glaciers and clouds."

"If you were to show me the track, which is important to my future plans, I might permit you to keep your bride, and would let her father go free."

"Such stories are the talk of fools," Tohkta said. "They are the idle talk of goatherds."

To know men, Batai Khan had taught him, is the knowledge of kings. Tohkta looked into the eyes of Chu Shih and saw no mercy, only ruthless ambition. To refuse would mean torture and death. Torture he could stand; what he feared was torture for Kushla, or for her father.

"I do not believe," Chu Shih said, "that stories of the ancient route are talk. If you wish to go free, you will show me the track. If you do not show me, another will."

"I will show you what is there, but it may not be to your liking."

This man, Tohkta told himself, must die. I must kill him or return to kill him. If he lives our mountains will never be free. If need be Tohkta's people could wait for years before they came again to the oasis towns, and by that time, these might be overthrown, or their ideas changed. Young though he was, Tohkta had learned all things change; the Tochari had learned patience from their mountains.

Chu Shih's command brought in two more soldiers. Tohkta

had a moment of sharp panic when he saw them, wanting to plunge at the door and fight his way free, but he fought down the feeling. He must think of Kushla and her father, who might be killed. Escape they must . . . somehow.

Out upon the street, the bridge of his wishing fell into the gorge of despair, for they had Tola Beg also. Two soldiers gripped the arms of the old yak hunter, and there was blood welling from an ugly cut on his cheekbone.

Turning, the Chinese colonel strode away. Kushla and Yakub being pushed ahead, Tola Beg and Tohkta followed surrounded by the six soldiers.

The Chinese who had searched them were coastal Chinese, unfamiliar with the customs of mountain Tochari. It was the custom in the hills to wear their hair long and their beards also. Tohkta's hair was wound about his head under his sheepskin hat, and into the hair was thrust a thin-bladed knife, as was also the custom.

Soldiers loitered before the *Ya-men,* several hundred yards away, but the street led through a narrow avenue of darkness bordered by a double row of tamarisks. In this darkness, Tohkta halted, and when the soldier behind him ran into him, Tohkta turned and drawing his knife, struck upward into the softness of the man's stomach.

Tohkta's hand drew Kushla behind him. Yakub, with more courage than Tohkta expected, seized the rifle of the soldier next to him, and then with a rush like a sudden gust of wind, Batai Khan and his riders swept through the tamarisks.

The horses were among the soldiers and all was confusion, pounding hooves, and flashing blades. Several of the soldiers had their rifles slung and Chu Shih was knocked sprawling by the shoulder of the horse of Batai Khan.

Lifting Kushla to the saddle of a lead horse, Tohkta leaped into his own saddle. A soldier slipped a rifle to his shoulder, but Tohkta rode him down, grasping the man's weapon as he fell. Then they were away in the darkness and riding hard for freedom and the hills.

There was shouting and a wild shot, but the attack had been sudden and with broadswords, the ancient Tochari way of fighting. In the darkness the soldiers had no chance against the charging horses and flashing blades. And it was only now that the force at the *Ya-men* was alerted.

Tohkta glanced back. Behind them there was confusion but no roaring of motors coming to life, yet remembering the eyes of Chu Shih, Tohkta knew pursuit would come soon, and it would be relentless.

FALSE DAWN WAS cresting the peaks with gold when they reached the Valley of Rain where Yakub's last herd was held. This was the only one the Chinese had not seized, for, as yet, they had not discovered it. The people of the oasis were secretive about their pastures, as his people were about the mountain tracks.

Tohkta checked his captured rifle in the vague light. How beautiful it was! How far superior to their ancient guns! Six rifles had been captured, and two men had even taken bandoleers of cartridges. They shared them among the others.

"We must go," Batai Khan said. "The flock we drive will cause us to move slowly."

Tohkta watched the yaks and fat-tailed sheep bunched for the trail. The Tochari were men of flocks and herds, and could not easily leave behind the wealth of a friend.

He looked up at the mountain peaks, and in the morning light, streamers of snow were blowing like silver veils from under a phalanx of cloud. Now fear seized at his vitals. They must hurry. If snow blocked the passes, none would escape.

Hours ago they had left the desert and the threat of pursuit by trucks or cars. Only mounted men or those on foot could follow them now. But the Chinese had horses; Tohkta had seen many of them in town and they would follow, he knew that as well. Whether they liked it or not they were leading Chu Shih into the mountains, just as he had wished.

Hunched in their saddles against the wind, they pushed on, skirting black chasms, climbing around towering pinnacles, icy crags, and dipping deep into gorges and fording streams, until at last they came to a vast basin three miles above the desert. Here they rested into the coming night.

Far away to the west lay a magnificent range of glacier-crested mountains, their gorges choked with ice, splendid in the clear air that followed the snow of the morning and afternoon. Though the setting sun lit the peaks and ridges, close over them hung a towering mass of cloud like the mirror image of the mountains below.

Long before dawn they were moving again. Batai Khan pushed onward, fearful of the storms that come suddenly at high altitudes where there was no fodder for man or beast. Pushing up beside him, Tohkta noted that the old man's face was drawn by cold and weariness. Batai Khan was old . . . older even than Tola Beg.

"Batai Khan," Tohkta asked, "now that we are among our mountains we must fight the soldiers. They must not be allowed to return with knowledge of this trail. Their leader, most of all, must be killed." He explained what Chu Shih had wanted.

"Tohkta," the old man paused, "you will await them in the pass. You are right and the beasts move slowly; we must have time. These fifty yak and many fat-tailed sheep will mean wealth to your wife's father and food and comfort for our people. But do not fight so hard that you do not return to us. Let the mountains do their work and if these soldiers come to the Yurung-kash we will be waiting for them."

"I shall remain with him," Tola Beg spoke up.

All those with modern rifles stayed beside Tohkta, eager to test them on their former owners. Two others remained, hopeful of obtaining more rifles for themselves. The pass was a natural point for a surprise attack, and so the Tochari set their trap where it would be unexpected, in its narrowing approach.

Though they had little ammunition, each fired several ranging shots to check the sights of their new weapons. They then concealed themselves, all but two, along the walls of rock before the deep cleft that was the pass. There they waited, waited for their enemies to come.

———

AND THEY CAME, the Chinese soldiers did. But they came slowly because of the great altitude, which bothered horses as well as the men.

Tohkta watched them from far across the elevated basin, and it began to snow once more. One of the horses slipped and fell, but the soldiers helped it up and came on.

How many were there? A hundred or more. But they were not dressed or provisioned for the high mountains. Tohkta could tell this because, though all were mounted, they had few packhorses, and these seemed to carry only weapons and ammunition.

At three hundred yards Tohkta and his hidden men opened fire. Instantly there was confusion. A milling of horses and men. For a moment only sporadic fire was returned, then Chu Shih rode into the midst of them on a tall gray horse and suddenly there was order. Soldiers dropped to the ground and sought cover, the bullets striking the rocks around Tohkta and his men were no longer random; it now seemed that the fire was seeking out each of them as separate targets.

"Be ready!" Tohkta called out as under the covering fire a group of soldiers swarmed forward. "Now, run!"

Tohkta turned and ran himself. Before him, Basruddin spun and fired one last shot before entering the pass. The others followed as rifle fire cracked and whined off the rocks around them. Tohkta had known that they couldn't stand off a concerted attack, but he also knew that in the thin air of the mountains he and his men could outrun any lowland soldier.

Chu Shih's men paused in their rush to fire at the fleeing Tocharis, but their breath came too hard at fourteen thousand feet and their shots went wild. At a signal from their leader, soldiers on horseback charged into the pass to pursue the retreating tribesmen, but this was exactly what Tohkta had been planning for.

Tola Beg and a strong young boy had made their way up the steep walls of the pass and together they had found a precariously balanced boulder that the yak hunter had spotted years before. With their shoulders braced against the cliff behind them and their feet on the huge rock they waited. They waited until they heard the sound of firing stop and the sound of horsemen entering the pass. Then they pushed.

Nothing happened.

They eased up and Tola Beg looked at the boy and they pushed together then released and pushed again. Suddenly the boulder was rocking and Tola Beg pushed hard, pushed with all the strength he had in his old body and with all the strength he had in his mind. Something gave inside of him, something in his back, but he pushed on through the blossoming pain and then the boulder was rolling. It dropped from sight, and Tola Beg could feel its impact further down the mountain, then he heard the roar of other rocks falling with it and the screams of men and horses.

———

TOHKTA, IBRAHIM, AND Basruddin turned and threw themselves back into the maelstrom of dust and flying rock that now choked the pass. They had seen little of it, for they had been running for their lives not only from the soldiers but from the landslide that nearly took them as well. It had only been the fast thinking of Ibrahim that had saved them, for as soon as they cleared the pass he had forced the running tribesmen into a corner of the hillside protected from the crashing torrent of rock.

Now they pushed their way back through the slide, and while Ibrahim mercilessly stripped the dead and wounded soldiers of guns and ammunition, Tohkta and Basruddin poured fire into the oncoming Chinese. Their lines wavered and fell back, the impact of this double ambush overcoming even Chu Shih's leadership. As soon as the soldiers had taken cover Tohkta and his followers fled back through the pass to where the others had brought up the horses.

Under a sky dense with cloud they started down the rocky slope. The men were excited by their victory, but Tohkta saw the look on the face of Tola Beg and knew that he was in pain. In the trees far below the pass they waited to see what the Han Chinese soldiers would do.

Chu Shih was taking no chances. After some time had passed there was activity around the mouth of the pass: a scouting party who had, no doubt, worked their way carefully through the rockfall alert for additional trouble. Then they watched as a squad moved into position on the hillside beside the entrance to the pass and set up a position with a machine gun unlimbered from one of the packhorses. Then, the area totally secure, mounted troops began to file out into the area controlled by the gun. Soon they would be ready to continue the pursuit.

Tohkta and his men filtered silently back into the trees. They had been very successful, counting many enemy dead or wounded, and Tola Beg was their only casualty. The old man had torn something in his back and could barely ride, being in constant pain.

———

By AFTERNOON THEY were back up out of the trees and on a vast tilted plateau of snow and barren rock. The trail left by Batai Khan and his party was easily visible. The old warrior was pressing along as quickly as was possible, but Tohkta could tell that they were not far ahead. At the far edge of the plateau, just beyond their sight lay the beginnings of the trail down to the bridge. Remembering that trail and the bridge itself, Tohkta was suddenly frightened. However quickly his grandfather had been able to move the animals, once on the narrow trail their pace would slow to a crawl, and at the head of the bridge the beasts must be carefully managed or they would balk and panic. It might have been better to have turned them out into one of the mountain valleys on this side of the river, but as Tohkta galloped his horse along the path left by the horsemen and animals, he could see that was not the course that the old chieftain had taken.

Batai Khan was counting on the gorge of the Yurung-kash to protect the village. Since the beginning of time the approach to the bridge had been their village's greatest defense. The descending trail was exposed in every way, while the trail to the bridge from the side of the village wound between trees and rocks, the cover allowing the tribesmen to pour rifle and arrow fire into any attacker unlucky enough to start down the path.

Even though Tohkta had managed as successful an am-

bush as he could imagine in the pass, Chu Shih's management of the situation had been impressive. He had acted with courage, and once the officer had realized the danger he had carefully covered his men with the machine gun and then organized his column before proceeding. Even on the exposed approaches of the bridge trail Tohkta feared the effect that the rapid firer would have. Chu Shih must not be allowed to cross the gorge to their village and pastures, but he must not be allowed to return to report of this mountain route either. Something had to be done and it had to be done soon.

At the edge of the plateau the dark canyon of the Yurungkash became visible in the distance. Looking back, Tohkta could see the first of the Han Chinese scouts fanning out as they discovered themselves facing open ground. There was one more thing that the young Tochari could see and it was this that gave him hope. The high ridges behind the soldiers were invisible . . . invisible because of falling snow. The storm was headed toward them, but what was more important was the amount of snow that would build up in the pass. At fourteen thousand feet it wouldn't take long for the way back to Sinkiang to be closed for the season. Perhaps the weather would take care of one of their troubles.

He reined around and whistled to his men. "The invaders must not be allowed to return to the desert," he told them. "God brings a storm to answer our prayers, but they will try to reach our village. Even now Batai Khan may be crossing with Yakub's herds. We must hold the Chinese here to give our men time to clear the bridge, and we must hold them here to give the father of storms time to fill the pass."

They tied their horses where the trail dipped into the gorge. The bridge was a long way down and beyond a bend, but through the trees and rock Tohkta could see animals straggling up the trail on the other side. Good. If they could hold out for an hour Batai Khan would have the resistance organized and the trail to the bridge would become a trail of death for the Chinese. All Tohkta would have to do is get down the trail and across the bridge with fourscore soldiers at his heels.

Tohkta called for the boy who had helped Tola Beg and one other. He gathered up the nine rifles that Ibrahim had taken from the fallen troops in the pass; he weighed them heavily with ammunition also.

"Go to Batai Khan," he said. "Have him give these rifles to the best marksmen among our people. We must guard the bridge like in the stories of old, he will know what to do. Now go!"

He turned to the remaining men. "Go with them and prepare.

Basruddin, Ibrahim, and Loshed; these I would keep with me."

"And I," said Tola Beg. When Tohkta began to protest he raised a hand. "Do not tell me I am hurt. It is only pain, I can still shoot farther than any man here and my hands are steady."

"All right." Tohkta shook his head but smiled. "Let us go see at what distance your lightning can strike."

———

BASRUDDIN AND IBRAHIM crawled, flat to the ground, into the plain of ice and boulders. Tohkta, Loshed, and Tola Beg found their way to a group of rocks and carefully prepared a shooting position for the old hunter. Just over a hundred yards behind them they set up another position at the head of the Yurung-kash trail.

Though the plateau was flat, it angled downward away from them. The oncoming Chinese were clearly visible, and while they had some cover available, they could not use it and advance at the same time.

When they were nine hundred yards off, Tola Beg squeezed off his first shot. It struck at the ground just before the first horse, which reared and panicked.

"It was low. Six or seven feet." Tohkta, watching through the hunter's spyglass, advised him.

The rider had fallen from the horse even as the others scattered out, dismounting. As the fallen rider got to his feet, Tola Beg shot him through the thigh.

"The leg . . . two feet low."

The fallen rider, the man shot through the leg, was lucky, for Tola Beg now had their range. The yak hunter's next three targets died instantly, felled by bullets they didn't even hear.

Soldiers dove for cover; in moments the top of the plateau was empty but for standing horses. Tohkta had spotted where Chu Shih had gone to ground, and from that shallow depression he saw a flicker of movement and, a moment later, could hear the distant sound of a barked order. The hand of Chu Shih went up and gestured right and left. Instantly, six soldiers moved the one way, and six the other, advancing to flank Tohkta's small party.

But Tohkta had planned for this. He opened up on the men to the right and Loshed joined him. While they lacked the practice of the old hunter, both had good eyes, and soon they forced their targets further off down the top of the plateau, out of range.

Occasionally shots clattered in the rocks around them, but their cover was good and the range extreme. Several of the main party had pushed the advance and were struggling to set up a machine gun. "They have come far to die," Tola Beg said, and squeezed off two shots.

Out upon the granite a man screamed and died. And then the six flankers to the left ran into Ibrahim and Basruddin, belly down in the snow. Tohkta could not see all that happened, but within a moment five of the Chinese were dead; the last shot down as he ran panic-stricken back toward the main body.

Tohkta and Loshed cheered . . . and then the machine gun opened up. Tracers flew, like flickering meteors, the snow and earth around Basruddin shredded, the bullets throwing up gouts of mud then blood as the gun crew expertly worked their weapon. The heavy throbbing of shots ended, then the bullets were striking around them!

Tracers flashed toward the rocks. Loshed howled, a bright red line appearing on the back of his hand. Tola Beg twisted out of the way, grimacing as his back spasmed. Three times dust jumped from his heavy sheepskin coat and then there was blood on his lips. Tohkta dropped behind a rock trembling. He glanced at Loshed.

"The old hawk is dead." Scattered flakes of snow drifted from the dark sky.

"Basruddin, too, and maybe Ibrahim," Tohkta said. Behind them the machine gun lashed the rock, and ricochets whined off into the clouds like banshees. Then the fire tore high into the air to drop down and the end of its arc spattering like heavy rain inside their fort of rock. The gunner worked the falling bullets back and forth.

How can you fight this weapon? Tohkta damned himself for a fool. You couldn't raise your head, you couldn't even take cover. It took the random inaccuracy of rifle ammunition at long range and used that to its advantage, peppering a whole area with fire. Under its protection Chu Shih's soldiers would be advancing.

"Run to the horses," Tohkta commanded. "Our other position is useless. Get to the bridge. We will put our trust in God and Batai Khan. Let us hope that one or the other is ready for us."

They ran. First Loshed, then Tohkta, who paused a moment to scoop up the ammunition of Tola Beg and to touch his cold form once on the back. They ran with bullets hitting all around them, but the light was going and with the oncoming storm, snow filled the air. Then a rifle opened up seeking out the oncoming soldiers from the rocks at the head of the trail, covering them as they ran. They came to the horses, sliding down the hillside, landing in trampled snow. Ibrahim was waiting for them. He grinned. "I killed two more. They will be Basruddin's servants in heaven!"

Stepping into the saddle, Tohkta could clearly see the advancing Chinese, spread out in a skirmish line. The squad with the machine gun was struggling forward with the heavy weapon, the altitude weighing them down as much as the ammunition and tripod. Behind them, almost hidden by the swirling veils of snow, Chu Shih was bringing the horses up.

They came on, relentlessly. They had passed the point where they could retreat through the pass; in the time it would take to get back to that notch in the mountains it would be too late. Chu Shih's only hope for either victory or survival was to press on, find the Tochari village with its warm felt tents, its supplies of fuel and food. Nothing could survive upon the high plateaus. Tohkta knew then that he hated them, hated them with a wild hatred mingled with fear, for that slender, whiplike man was relentless as a hungry wolf, fierce as a cornered tiger. His men might whimper and wish to go back, but he drove them on.

A group of mounted soldiers thundered forward, through a gap in the line of advancing troops. Tohkta wheeled his horse, and the three of them plunged down the switchbacked trail. The horses skidded on the icy gravel; Ibrahim's mount slid and its shoulder struck Tohkta in the leg, sending both horses and riders into a painful collision with the rock wall.

Then the firing began from the head of the trail. With a wild glance thrown back up the slope Tohkta saw a knot of soldiers gathered there, rifles aimed almost vertically down at them. Flame stabbed from the gun muzzles, but then the soldiers were pushed aside and a squad of Han horsemen with Chu Shih in the lead took to the trail.

Tohkta, Ibrahim, and Loshed clattered through a straight stretch. The bridge was only one hundred yards off to their right, but it was still far below them. A bullet snapped past him and, looking up, Tohkta saw the first switchback lined with kneeling soldiers all firing down at them. Closer still, Chu Shih and his band of horsemen came on, less than a halfdozen switchbacks above.

Bullets ricocheted off the rocks. One caught Loshed across the top of the arm and he laughed, smearing his wounded hand with blood and waving it at Tohkta as they turned their horses into another level. Then a bullet caught him in the side and another pierced the spine of his horse and he was falling, the horse was falling, from the narrow trail and disappearing into the rocks hundreds of feet below.

At that moment a fusillade of rifle fire exploded from concealed points along the trail leading up to the Tochari village. Soldiers fell from the top of the trail, and in a moment the

Chinese and the villagers were pouring volley after volley into each other in the thundering confines of the gorge.

Reaching the shelf where the bridge stanchions had been fastened to the rock, Tohkta dropped from his horse and was met by Batai Khan and four warriors armed with old rifles. Ibrahim turned his horse tightly in the narrow space.

"They follow us closely, Grandfather!" Tohkta pointed up the trail. But the four men had pressed forward, and as the first of Chu Shih's horsemen came into sight they fired, sending the first horse screaming over the cliff edge, its rider still astride, and collapsing two more in a struggling mass, blocking the trail.

Above, the machine gun opened up, forcing the defenders on the trail to cover and allowing soldiers to crowd their way onto the trail again. In the gray light of the gorge tracers whipped like hellfire, streaking in all directions as the burning bullets bounced from the rock and whirled away into the oncoming night.

The nearest soldiers were advancing again; using the dead horses as cover, they rained fire on the shelf, leaving few areas of even partial safety. Chu Shih was, whatever else he might be, a leader. Yet better than any of them he knew how desperately he must cross the bridge and take the village.

Tohkta nestled the stock of the rifle against his cheek, measuring the distance. He squeezed off his shot, and the man at whom he fired froze, then fell. The snow fell faster. Blown particles stung like bits of steel upon their cheeks. The Chinese above moved in. One paused to crouch against the rock wall. Ibrahim shot him, and he rolled down the trail to their feet.

At the top of the trail more soldiers made their way down the switchbacks, covered by the machine gun. They came in short, quick dashes, utilizing the slightest bits of cover. Ever they drew closer. Occasionally there would be the crack of one of the captured rifles or the dull boom of a muzzle-loader from the villager's side of the gorge and often a soldier would fall, but always this would instantly attract a lash of resumed fire from the machine gun.

"WE MUST GO, Batai Khan," said Tohkta. "We cannot hold out here."

"Yes," agreed the old man, and motioned to his companions to cross the bridge. He dropped into their place and, as they ran into the open, dropped the first soldier to raise a rifle. Ibrahim shot and Tohkta was beside him firing and reloading, but the second Tochari on the bridge was down and as the others bent to pick him up another was shot and fell into the crevasse. Then Ibrahim ran, pounding across the swaying bridge.

The old man put his hand on Tohkta's arm. "Go," he said. "Go, Tohkta Khan. I will stay."

It was not lost on Tohkta that Batai Khan had used the leader's title. He shook his head.

"No," Tohkta protested. "Our people need you."

"Go, I say!" He glared at Tohkta from his fierce cold eyes. Then in a softer voice, he said, "Would you have me die as an old horse dies? I cannot stop them," he said, "but the bridge can."

Tohkta stared at him, uncomprehending. Then it came to him, and he was astonished. For an instant he was filled with despair as he realized what tremendous cost had gone to the building of this bridge, the long struggle with the mountain and the river, the backbreaking toil. "You would destroy our bridge? It cost four years to build!"

"What are four years of work against four thousand years of freedom. In time, you can build another bridge." Even as his grandfather spoke, he knew it was what they must do. The despair left him.

Together they knelt and fired, retreated a few steps, then fired again. An icy wind roared down the tunnel of the gorge, and the bridge swayed before it. Down the cliff trail they could see them coming now, many dark figures, blossoming with fire. Bullets struck about them.

Batai Khan was hit, and he fell, losing his grip upon the rifle, which fell into the void. Tohkta bent to lift him but there was a gleam in the old man's eye. "Leave me here! You must destroy the bridge and silence the devil gun."

"Yes, Grandfather."

"Tohkta Khan, go with God!"

Batai Khan tore loose and fell to the stone. Snow drove down the gorge, obliterating all before them. And Tohkta ran though his heart was crushed.

On the bridge the howling wind caught him. The ropes flexed and jumped with every step and bullets tore through the rope and wood around him. Soldiers depressed the muzzle of the machine gun, holding the tail of the tripod high, and tracers tore at him. One left a smoldering hole in his sheephide jacket, another left a slice like that of a knife upon his calf.

Then he was across, he fell, and was struggling to rise when he felt small hands lift him. It was Kushla. Ibrahim was there, reloading his Chinese rifle.

"Go!" He grabbed her by the shoulders. "Have men bring axes. We must cut the bridge!"

Ibrahim was next. "Come on!" Tohkta said. "We must stop the machine gun!"

The three of them ran. They ran up the narrow trail, and though there was cover it was scant enough. Bullets flew. Tocharis fired back from behind rocks or trees. Men on both sides of the gorge died.

As he went Tohkta gathered up the few men with stolen rifles, and when he could wait no longer they took cover behind a boulder. There were five of them.

"We must destroy the devil gun!" Tohkta ordered them. "We must kill those who use it and any who are close, we must keep firing though we all may die. With that gun, the Hans can take the bridge before we can cut it. Are you ready?"

Together they rose and as one fired up and across the crevasse and into the group of soldiers around the gun. Several fell, and as Tohkta worked the bolt on his rifle, the gunner began to swing the muzzle. Fire sliced toward them and they fired again and again. Bullets bounded into the rock, into Ibrahim, tore Tohkta's rifle from his grasp and ripped his thigh. But as he fell so did the Chinese gunner, and the two tribesmen left standing shot the next nearest man, too.

Tohkta lurched to his feet. The gun was silent, the crew a

struggling mob of the dead and dying. He lifted Ibrahim's rifle and shot a man who lifted himself from the trail near the gun. The man fell, clutched at the edge of the trail and, as the rock crumbled in his fingers, clutched at the barrel of the machine gun.

A moment later the man was spinning down into the gorge and the gun was falling fast behind him. Tohkta felt like crying out in triumph, but the day had been too expensive in lives and a dozen or more soldiers had poured onto the shelf where the stanchions of the bridge were fastened. Chinese and Tochari defenders alike were firing into each other at near point-blank range.

Then the roar of guns dropped to an occasional shot as tribesmen fled up the trail toward Tohkta. Across the river, at the turn of the last switchback, a slim figure astride a gray horse moved. Chu Shih rode forward. His mount leaped the mound of dead horses and men as if they were a low gate and not sprawled bodies on a narrow trail with a sheer drop on one side.

The soldiers parted as their commander rode amongst them; then, with riflemen in the lead, he started out onto the bridge.

Tohkta boiled with rage. He would never let them cross! He stumbled into a prone position and taking careful aim at Chu Shih's head squeezed the trigger.

The rifle clicked on an empty chamber. He was out of ammunition!

Down on the shelf there was flickering movement. The form of Batai Khan stood and drew the broadsword from the scabbard across his back. The razor-sharp blade flashed as he brought it down on one of the two ropes that held the right side of the bridge. The blade bit and bit again. Then the rope gave way and suddenly the bridge sagged and swung.

Chu Shih turned in his saddle, the horse rearing as the weakened bridge bucked and twisted like a living thing. There was a shot and Batai Khan jerked. More soldiers came running down the trail, firing their rifles. The first of these skidded to a stop, working the bolt of his gun, and Batai Khan's great sword struck, disemboweling the man. Suddenly Han soldiers on all sides were firing. The men on the tilting, swaying bridge, the soldiers on the trail, all fired as the ancient Tochari leader turned, his massive body pierced by a half dozen bullets, and brought his blade down on the other right-hand rope.

The ends of the second tether, not cut through, spun and twisted as they unraveled. There was a frozen moment, then the soldiers ran panic-stricken back toward the rock shelf. For a moment the eyes of the Tochari chieftain and the Chinese officer locked, then Batai Khan raised his sword and bellowed, *"Yol Bolsun!"*

A single shot brought him down. The sword clattering to the rocks beside him. A single shot from an unknown trooper on the bridge . . . a shot that did no good at all, for the primitive rope shredded and the floor of the bridge peeled away, hanging twisted almost a thousand feet over the roaring waters.

Chu Shih's horse fell, sliding, taking four soldiers with it. The officer grabbed for one of the ropes on the high side of the bridge, held for a moment, then tumbled toward the river far below.

Tohkta struggled to stand as two villagers ran past him, axes at the ready. In a moment the villagers reformed their positions along the trail and, with scathing fire, drove the remaining Han soldiers up the switchback trail. Following them down to the bridgehead Tohkta watched as the axmen cut the bridge away. It collapsed with a crash against the far wall of the gorge. On the rock shelf above it lay the body of Batai Khan.

"Yol Bolsun," Tohkta whispered as Kushla came to stand beside him.

"What was that, my love?" she said.

"It means good-bye or good luck . . . May There Be a Road." After a moment Tohkta laughed. For even though Batai Khan had destroyed their bridge he had bought them time. Time to live, to raise another generation in freedom, time to plan . . . if necessary time to escape. This, in its own way, was as much of a road as that once joined by their bridge. He had a vision of a Buddhist's spinning prayer wheel. Even as they had once been connected to their future by the bridge, now they were connected to the future by the lack of it. A season? A year? A decade? Who could tell, but, as the Tochari know, nothing but the mountains lasts forever.

By torchlight, Tohkta Khan gathered his dead and returned to the village with his bride. The future given them by Batai Khan would begin tomorrow, and there was much to do.

BY THE WATERS OF SAN TADEO

T HE DOZEN SHACKS that made up the village of San Esteban huddled, dwarfed and miserable, below the craggy ramparts that walled them away from the world. The lofty circle of mountains, with their ice-choked ravines and thick tangles of beech forest, formed an enclosing wall as impassable as the mountains of the moon. Only in one direction was escape from the village possible . . . through the narrow mouth of the inlet, eight miles from the village.

Julie Marrat had thought of all that many times in the last few weeks, and each time she had come to the same conclusion, and each time that conclusion was just as hopeless. There was but one way of escape . . . by boat.

There were three boats at the inlet, and all of these belonged to Pete Kubelik. One was the schooner that he used for infrequent trips up the coast and to bring in supplies. There were also two fishing boats, not much more than dinghies, far too small in which to brave the sea that lay outside. Yet escape she must, and immediately.

Returning to the bedside, she looked down at the dying man who was her father. Lovable, impractical, and a dreamer with an always restless heart, George Marrat had never been able to remain still. Now, this lonely inlet far south on the coast of Chile had trapped him, and once there he could not leave.

Two things ensured that. One was his own health, which failed rapidly in the cold, dreary world of San Esteban, where the sun rarely shone and the sky was overcast nearly three hundred days of the year. Yet had it been his health alone, Julie could have managed. The other element was Pete Kubelik.

From the moment they drew their ketch up to the jetty and

Julie turned to look into the piglike eyes of the big trader, she had been frightened. Right then she asked her father to leave, knowing that this was not a place they should stay.

He was amazed. "Why, Julie? We've only just come! We can at least look around, can't we?"

"No, Father, please! Let's go find somewhere else."

Her father had turned to face Kubelik, and the big man's brown face wrinkled in a smile. "I'm afraid my daughter doesn't like it here," he confessed.

"Well," Kubelik had replied, "it ain't much of a place for women, that's true, but there's gold here, plenty of it!"

"Gold?" Her heart sank at the eagerness in her father's voice. What would he do if he found it? she wondered. No man ever cared less for money, but in her father's mind the concept of gold was so much more than money. It was the reward that he was searching for, the last reward that would somehow repair the life that luck had deserted. But, ironically, that life without luck was not his . . . it was hers. "There's gold here?"

"Yes, sir!" Kubelik had turned and waved a hand at the long spit of black sand that pointed into the inlet from a nearby island. "We've washed many a good stake out of that beach! Best beach placer I ever saw! Was that why you came here?"

Had there been anxiety in the big man's voice? Julie had looked at him again, and felt such revulsion that she could scarcely stand to be near him.

Plodding along beside her father, Kubelik had dwarfed him with his huge body. His face was round and moonlike under the thick black beard. Wrinkles ran out in a network of tiny lines from the corners of both eyes, eyes that were small and cruel. His hands were dirty, the fingernails black and broken. And then, for the first time, she'd seen the gun. It was in a holster under his sheepskin coat.

Not until later did Julie wonder that none of the others came near them. An Indian woman standing in the door of a driftwood cabin hurriedly stepped back and closed the door when Julie started toward her. Despite the inhospitable gesture, Julie had not been alarmed, taking it for granted that the woman was naturally shy.

By midnight, when they moved into the inner room at Kubelik's station and to bed, they had met only one other man. He was a pasty Austrian named Rudy, and seemed to be Kubelik's shadow. He rarely spoke, but whenever Kubelik and Rudy shared a look, Julie realized there was some silent communication. She saw other people moving among the shacks, but they did not come near the store.

That inner room had been Pete Kubelik's suggestion. She had wanted to return to the boat, hoping that her father could be talked into leaving, but Kubelik laughed at her and waved her objections away with an impatient hand. He would take it as an insult, he said. By all means, they should stay. Entranced by his stories of the coast, her father listened, and they remained. And in the morning, their boat was gone.

She had just gotten out of bed when she saw through the small window the empty pier where the ketch had been left. Fear gripping her heart, she awakened her father. George Marrat's face went pale, and for the first time, he was afraid.

They rushed down to the beach, but the ketch was nowhere to be seen.

Kubelik had come from the house, rubbing his eyes. "What's the matter. Something wrong?"

"Our boat's gone!" Marrat exclaimed. "Lord, man! What will we do? What could have happened to it?"

"Wind, maybe," Kubelik suggested, "or some thief. No use standing here. Come in an' let's fix breakfast. Then we can take one of my boats an' look around."

Yet when her eyes happened to meet those of Kubelik, his had been triumphant.

Her father, despite his interest in the gold, was genuinely worried. He knew the mountains were impassable, that the forests were undergrown with thick moss, laden with moisture, and a man could sink to his waist in trying to struggle through. And by the end of the day, they realized that the boat was gone and they knew they would not find it.

"How about taking us to Puerto Montt?" Marrat had suggested. "You have the schooner, and we can't stay here. I have money in the bank back in Santiago. Take us out, and I'll pay your price."

"All right," Kubelik had said thoughtfully. "But you'll have to wait until I'm ready to go for supplies. A week or so, maybe."

Yet when the week had passed, he said nothing about leaving. Her father had been placer mining on the beach and caught a severe cold. By that time, they had moved to a small shack, refusing to accept more of Kubelik's hospitality.

"I'm sorry, Julie," George said. "When I get well, we'll get out of here and I'll make it up to you." He coughed, the breath rattling deep in his lungs.

"Get some rest," she said. He nodded and relaxed, breathing more easily. She sat there in the dark, a twenty-six-year-old woman who had failed in life, failed in marriage, who had fled back to her father, a ne'erdo-well adventurer, and ended up here, in a narrow fjord at the end of the earth.

Her grandfather had been a Chilean who migrated north with his son to fish the waters of British Columbia and Alaska. Her father had spent much of his life in Canada, and she was born there, schooled there, and had been wed there.

Like many young girls, Julie had thought that marriage would change her life, and indeed it had. But she discovered that the qualities in a man that had appealed to her when she was being courted were not the qualities that made a good partner for life.

Her husband had been a dashing young bohemian who could quote enough Spencer, Marx, or Freud to prove any point. Unfortunately, for all his obsession with the working man, he could not seem to hold a job. What she had mistaken for intensity turned out to be self-obsession, and the wild ways that she once thought were delightfully liberated proved to be simple self-indulgence.

After six months he had disappeared to prowl the bars and jazz clubs of San Francisco by himself, and she fled back to her father in shame. Julie hid herself away from the world on her father's boat, ashamed because she had not been wise enough to choose the right man and hadn't been strong enough to confront that man about their problems.

George Marrat had never questioned her. Although he had made many a poor choice himself, and life had dealt him many a blow, he still met the morning with a smile and fixed his eyes on the horizon. He planned a trip south to show his daughter his homeland, to take her mind off her problems. They would prospect on the southern coast. If they could find a cannery and take on a crew, they would fish the southern waters as he had in Ketchikan and Port Albion.

But now they were here in this dismal settlement. And George Marrat was very sick. Julie put her father to bed and hurried to the store for medicine.

Pete Kubelik shook his head. "Medicine?" he said. "Ain't got much. Aspirin, an' some cold tablets. Anything more I can do, let me know."

He came around the counter and leaned against it. Despite her fear, she forced herself to stand still, but couldn't look him in the eye.

"You know," he said, "we could get along, you an' me. Gets mighty lonesome here, of a winter." In the corner, Rudy stifled a whispering laugh.

"I'm sorry, Mr. Kubelik. I couldn't do that. When Father gets well, we will leave."

"Suppose he doesn't get well?"

Cold fear welled up within her. "Oh, he will," she said firmly. "He often has touches of cold like this. He'll get well, and then we'll leave."

Kubelik grinned at her, his teeth yellow and broken. "Well, maybe," he said. "*If* I decide to take you up the coast. Then again, I may just keep you here, sort of company for me."

"That's ridiculous!" She looked up at him for the first time. "You couldn't get away with anything like that! What about the authorities?"

"The Chileans? The army? The police?" He laughed with genuine amusement. "They don't come here. Know why these folks don't come near you? Because I told 'em to stay away, that's why. Know why they stay here? Because they can't get away, either! They are pilin' up gold for me. Me an' Rudy, here!"

He chuckled. "Why, the government thinks this place is abandoned. Nobody ever comes here, at least," his voice dropped to a whisper, "nobody that goes out again."

Two days later her father died.

He died suddenly, in the night. Only for a moment was he rational, and seemed to realize there was little time left. He called her to him. "Julie . . ." His voice was hoarse. "I . . ." He fumbled for words. "I know what happened to the boat. He . . . Kubelik . . . he towed it away. He hid it over at Rio San Tadeo. One of the others told me, that last day, workin' on the spit."

"It's all right, Dad," she said gently, "we'll manage!"

The long gray miles of cold sea and the towering cliffs that flanked it filled her with horror. In all the world, there could be no more desolate place than this coast north of Magellan. "We'll manage," she whispered, but she knew he was dying.

They buried her father at the foot of a huge rock three hundred yards up the canyon from San Esteban. Several of the villagers were out for the funeral, but had she ever hoped for help from them, she gave up now. They were a thin, woe-begone group, obviously afraid of Kubelik, who towered above them.

There were six men in the village, she discovered, four of them Chileans and two Yahgans, natives from the Beagle Channel area. The four women were all Yahgans but one, an Ona woman from Tierra del Fuego.

After the funeral, she talked with them while Pete Kubelik and Rudy ignored her. They had the only weapons among the group, and aside from the pistol which he always carried, Kubelik possessed two shotguns and a rifle. He had killed a man only a few days before their ketch arrived.

Recalling Kubelik's anxiety over their discovery of the place, she realized that was his greatest fear. Here in his little kingdom, he ruled supreme while they slaved for him and lived in abject fear of his rages. As he controlled the only means of escape as well as the only source of food, tobacco, and liquor, he was firmly in the saddle.

"But what about the boats?" she said to Aleman, one of the villagers. "Couldn't you steal one and get away?"

"Not a chance!" he told her. "His schooner has an auxiliary engine, and he'd have us before we made a dozen miles. Besides, where could we go on the supplies we'd have? We are a long way from the nearest port."

During the afternoon preceding her father's burial, she tried to recall exactly what the chart had pictured. The inlet was in the southeast corner of the Gulf of San Esteban, and the Rio San Tadeo was to the north. Although the chart indicated little of the nature of the country back of the coast, she knew it was rugged mountain and glacier. Of the beech forests, she knew only by hearsay, but they were pictured as dark, fearsome places, well-nigh impenetrable.

It was raining when they finished the funeral service. She started away when the grave had been filled, but Pete Kubelik overtook her. "Get your stuff, whatever you got," he ordered, "an' move over to my place."

It didn't take much to bring her to tears, but she intentionally pushed her sorrow and terror to the forefront. "Oh, not now! Please!" She sobbed hysterically, fell to her knees moaning, "My father . . . my father . . ."

She made the most unappealing spectacle of herself possible. Finally, in disgust, he shrugged it off. "All right, tomorrow, then," Kubelik said, and trudged away.

She was rolling up her father's jacket when she found the knife. Evidently, he had planned to use it himself, yet it was no knife she had ever seen aboard the boat. That meant he had acquired it since coming ashore, either finding it or getting it from one of the others.

The thought filled her with excitement. Perhaps . . . if one of the men had given the knife to her father, she might have a friend out there. How could she know who he was?

Holding the coat so anyone peeking through the window could not see the knife, she examined the blade. It was bright and gleaming, and obviously had not been lying out in the weather.

The knife gave her courage. At least she could kill herself. The thought of killing Kubelik came first, but she dismissed the idea at once. He was too big, too strong, and he wore too many thicknesses of clothing. She would never have strength enough to drive the knife home.

Then she remembered the tobacco. Her father had come ashore prepared to trade, carrying a small sack filled with plugs of tobacco, some large packages of smoking tobacco, and a few cartons of cigarettes. In this place, it was a veritable fortune.

She had seen how avidly the men clutched the tiny packets of tobacco that Kubelik passed out. Maybe that was how her father got the knife.

For a long time she thought, wondering about the mountains and the inlet itself. If she could manage to steal a boat, she might get to the San Tadeo at least, and from there perhaps she could find her father's ketch. She would need neither food nor water to go that far. The thought of the eight miles against the engine of the schooner changed her mind. The river was out of the question.

Julie got up and put out her light, yet scarcely had the cabin become dark when there was a scratching at the window. Going to it, she stood to one side and peered out. In the vague light she could see a figure crouching in the darkness. Gently, she lifted the window.

"Missy? This Cuyu . . . you got tobac' . . . sí?"

Cuyu was one of the Yahgans. She remembered him at the funeral. He had been one of those who carried her father's body to the grave and helped fill it in. She remembered his eyes as she'd turned away, how they had seemed strangely gentle and compassionate.

"Yes! Yes, I have tobacco! Come to the door!"

"No door! He watch. He watch alla time! You speak me here!"

"Cuyu, can you get me away from here? Can you? Please!"

The Yahgan was silent. What sort of man was he? Would he be even worse than Kubelik? She dismissed that idea at once. Nobody could be worse.

"Can you get me to our ketch? My father was told it was anchored over on the San Tadeo!"

"San Tadeo? Sí. The boat, it there." There was sudden eagerness in Cuyu's voice.

She was almost frantic with excitement. "Oh, Cuyu! Take me to it and I'll give you all this tobacco! Yes, and more, too. Can we steal a dinghy?"

"No." The finality of his voice ended that possibility. "Maybe mountain."

His voice was doubtful. "You strong? Walk fast? Climb?"

"Yes, oh yes!" Suddenly he hissed, and then like a shadow, he was gone.

Outside, in front of the cabin, she heard a crunch of boots on gravel. Had Kubelik changed his mind? Was he coming now? Or was he suspicious?

Instantly, she slipped off her shoes and got into bed, hunching the blankets around her. He came to the door, and she heard her latch lift, but the bar was in place. He hesitated, and there was no sound. Fear welled up within her. Suppose he broke down the door? Certainly, it would be little effort for a man of his brute strength. Praying she could make it sound right, she turned in the bed, as though in sleep.

Footsteps crunched around the house, and she felt rather than saw his head at the window. She had been unable to close it in time, and hoped he would believe she'd left it open for the air. He stood listening, and she kept her breathing deep and regular, hoping he would not look beneath the window for tracks. Suddenly, a light flashed on her face. After a minute of examination, he turned and walked away. Julie lay rigid, listening to the retreat of his footsteps on the coarse gravel.

It could have been no more than a minute before she heard the Yahgan again. Instantly, she was at the window. "I take," he whispered, "you bring tobac', sí?"

Swiftly, she dressed. She pulled on her boots and thrust the knife into the capacious pocket of her coat. It took her only a moment to climb through the window. She passed the tobacco to the Yahgan, but he returned it to her. "You keep—for now," he whispered.

Tugging at her sleeve, he moved off and away. Almost before she realized it, they were working their way through the gray trunks of ancient, long dead trees, and then into the timber itself. Her feet tangled in a soft, sinking bed of moss and she almost fell.

Cuyu caught her sleeve again and guided her in the darkness to a deadfall. She perceived his purpose; by walking on the fallen tree, they could keep out of the moss. Yet it was only a short distance, and then they were struggling in the knee-deep moss again. It was heavy with moisture, and before they had gone fifty yards she was soaked from the knees down. Yet Cuyu seemed to have eyes like a cat, for he found one deadfall after another.

How long they struggled and fought against the clinging, wet fingers of the forest she had no idea. Time and again she fell. She scratched her hands and face, but she kept going, fighting with the strength of desperation for every inch of distance. Suddenly, they emerged from the forest.

She was amazed. Before them, white and wide in the night, lay a glacier! Overhead, the clouds had momentarily parted and a few friendly stars shone through, but the Yahgan was looking at neither the stars nor the glacier. He was moving swiftly out over the icy surface, and the measure of his fear was the measure of her own. From time to time he glanced back. Was he expecting pursuit so soon?

Yet they made better progress now. Nor did Cuyu waste time. He led off swiftly and she almost had to run to keep up. That the Yahgan was frightened was obvious.

Leaving the glacier, they went up a steep, rocky trail along an icy black cliff, then down through a ravine. It was growing gray in the east, and despite all their travel, she had the feeling they had gained little ground. From time to time now, Cuyu stopped. He kept staring ahead, then listening.

Something worried him. She was fighting exhaustion now, for they had not only encountered the roughest possible travel, but had kept up a pace far beyond her strength. Yet the Yahgan showed no evidence of tiring and no intention of slowing down. It was plain that he knew that if they were caught, while she might be taken back to the inlet, he would be killed on the spot.

Cuyu turned now, changing his course to proceed more

directly north, but his eyes continued to watch toward his left. Once, through a break in the curtain of trees shrouding the cliff on her left, she thought she saw water.

Was the fact that they must go down to the water what Cuyu feared? Kubelik, guessing their route or seeing their tracks, might use the boat to come around the point and head them off. It would be pitifully easy, and in a matter of an hour he could render useless their night of struggle.

The dim game trail they had been following dipped sharply down into a fantastically rugged gorge. Here the moss was scarce, but the trees were laden with snow, and there was an occasional patch of ice. They went down the steep side, passing themselves from tree trunk to tree trunk to keep from sliding or falling all the way to the bottom.

A brawling stream roared along over stones, and Cuyu dropped on his stomach and drank. Julie followed suit, then got to her feet and looked around.

The gorge curved sharply right before them, and the course of the stream led down toward the north. While the direction was perfect for them and would make travel easier, it must also lead to the inlet she thought she had seen. Now she comprehended the reason for Cuyu's hurry. He hoped to get to the mouth of the river before they could be headed off.

He started again, with only a glance at her, nearly running wherever the path was smooth enough to permit it. At times they had to climb down over great tumbled masses of white boulders, or walk gingerly across slippery rocks, some of them covered with encroaching peat moss from the forest.

They came out of the trees and into the open delta of rocks and sand where the inlet met the mouth of the San Tadeo River. There was no boat in sight, but they ran now, trying to cover the exposed area as quickly as possible. They reached the woods where the river poured forth, a wide course of dark water rushing down from the mountains, and Cuyu paused to let her catch her breath. For a brief moment he grinned at her.

"Almos' to boat . . . you'll see."

Slowly, they started upstream along the watercourse, and soon, through the branches of the trees ahead, she could see the white of the ketch's hull. It was only a matter of minutes to reach the vessel. The trim craft was tied up in a deep backwater out of the main flow of the river. A good anchorage, Julie realized, but a difficult one for her to maneuver out of even with Cuyu's help. The ketch would have to be carefully backed and turned into the river, with most of the backing being into the current.

Without bothering to pull the boat in to shore, she climbed out on a low hanging branch and dropped to the deck. Cuyu followed as she made her way to the pilot house.

"You take us away?" he asked.

She could see that he was more terrified than ever, now that they had reached their destination. Terrified because, unlike the stretches of forest and glacier, this was a place where Kubelik would have to come on any search for them that he might make. She thought of the difficult job of fighting the river's current with a reversed engine, of how the ketch would slip sideways even as it moved back, and feared what roots or rocks lurked beneath the black waters of the San Tadeo. Sometime toward morning there would be a tide, and that would make her job much easier, but high tide was hours away and she was sure they didn't have an hour, let alone hours.

"I can try," she mumbled. The thought of the miles of gray, whitecapped water frightened her. She had spent many months at sea, but never without her father. She took a deep breath and reached out for the switch that activated the pumps. Nothing happened. She tried again.

But the moment she touched the console, she heard it. Off in the distance, but not distant enough, was the low *thot-thot* of an auxiliary engine. It could only belong to Kubelik's schooner. She turned, and through the open hatchway could see a movement through the trees that blocked her view of the river.

"Quick!" she said to Cuyu. "We must get off the boat and hide." But the native was already headed across the deck. He jumped for a branch and pulled himself up. Julie, desperate to know the full extent of her troubles, flipped up the cover and glanced into the electrical console. The battery cable had been removed, and the deck boards were scarred where Kubelik had yanked it up through the narrow channel. He had made sure that no one was going to be taking the ketch out of the river, at least not without winching it out of the backwater and upriver against the current. She dropped the cover and ran.

Back on deck, she saw Cuyu motioning frantically from the bank. She'd started for the branch when a shot rang out.

The Yahgan fled. The schooner was drawing into the backwater, and standing in the bow, a rifle in his hands, was Pete Kubelik!

"Cuyu!" Her cry seemed lost in the space between the trees. *"Look out!"*

She saw the Yahgan glance back, and then he left his feet and dove into the brush and in that instant the rifle barked. Did he stumble? Or was he already falling of his own volition?

The rifle barked again, but she heard no whine of bullet nor was she hit. Cuyu must have still been alive then, and another shot had been sent to finish the job. She heard Kubelik shout, and turned back to the companionway. Dropping down the ladder, she ran for her father's cabin. Just as she unlatched the door she both heard and felt Kubelik's schooner bump up alongside the ketch.

Hanging from leather loops attached to the side of the bunk was George Marrat's old Mannlicher carbine. Julie jerked it free and grabbed up the leather cartridge wallet that hung with it. Footsteps pounded overhead. She had no time to load and barely time to think. Kubelik was coming down the ladder. As she ducked into the companionway she could see the back of his legs as he descended. She slid through the galley door and threw the lock, although that would hold him only an instant.

Scrambling onto the mess table and pushing open the skylight, she tossed the rifle through and started to crawl out herself. Behind and beneath her, the door splintered open. She rolled through the hinged skylight as Kubelik roared, charging across the cabin.

Julie grabbed the carbine and plunged overboard. The icy

water hit her like a fist, a cold, solid hammer in her stomach. Down she went, striking out toward the shore but still sinking. Her clothes, heavy shoes, and seven pounds of rifle carried her to the muddy bottom. Her ears popped and she pushed off, hitting the surface and gulping air. She saw a vague shape to her left and grabbed out, her hand scraping along the side of Kubelik's schooner. Her eyes cleared, and looking past the bow, she saw Kubelik stalking along the rail of the ketch, rifle in hand.

Julie Marrat took a deep breath and sank away from the boat. A couple of strokes and she felt the bottom again, and then the dirt and roots making up the side of the backwater. A submerged branch hit her in the face, and she grabbed at it, pulling herself up and along a fallen log to the shore. She stumbled up and water poured from her clothes in a rush.

There was a whip of air by her body and then the slam of a rifle shot. Pete Kubelik jacked another round into the chamber of his rifle, the spent case bouncing off the deck of the ketch. On the schooner, Rudy came running forward, shotgun in hand. She fell, rather than ran, into a dark space between the trees.

"You come back here!" Kubelik roared. "You come back or I'll kill you!"

Now it was the air that was a freezing fist closing on her lungs. Her sopping clothes clung to her as she slogged, almost knee deep in moss, deeper into the forest. Even as she ran she was sobbing with fear. Soon she slowed, realizing that she was leaving a trail even a blind man could follow, and found a deadfall like Cuyu had used. She worked her way deeper and deeper into the immense stand of beeches, and finally, shivering, collapsed from exhaustion.

Her breath came in shuddering gasps, but as she slowly caught her wind she became aware of the silence. There was no noise of pursuit . . . there was almost no noise at all. For the moment she was safe.

Except the cold would kill her. It was still in the midforties, but her wet clothes would rapidly give her hypothermia, and in the night the temperature would drop another ten or fifteen degrees. She tried to hold herself still and quiet her chattering teeth. There were still no sounds of pursuit. She crawled around behind a fallen log and pulled off some chunks of bark, but they seemed too damp to burn. A long crack in the fallen tree, however, gave her access to the inside of the trunk, hollowed out by heart-rot, and from there she used the knife to scrape out some light, dry, strips of wood.

Using a box of safety matches that she had taken from the shack in San Esteban, she struck match after match with no answering flame; they had become too wet. Finally, she tried holding the match head against the striking area with the ball of her thumb as she rasped it along. The match flared but the pain in her hand made her drop it in the moss, where it went out. Blowing on her burned thumb, she was not surprised to find herself cursing in a manner befitting a sailor or dockhand. Gritting her teeth, she struck another match. There was the smell of burning sulfur, and even as she pulled her thumb away she knew she'd blistered it again; however, she lit her tiny fire and slowly fed the flames. Then she stripped the achingly cold clothes off, wrung them out, and laid them out across the log near the fire.

Shuddering, half frozen, and naked, she huddled by the log and prayed for her clothes to dry. In the dark and silent wood, exposed in every way, Julie was sure that this was when Kubelik would find her. He would follow her tracks, even where she had tried to make it hard for him. He would smell her fire. He would find her and . . .

She turned and, fumbling with the cartridges, loaded the gun. She put a round in the chamber and set the safety. "Damn you," she whispered. "Damn you, if you come here, I'll kill you!"

Then she laughed.

She laughed at the picture of herself, stark naked and freezing in a primitive forest, clutching a rifle and daring a man like Pete Kubelik to come and get her. What made it funny was the thought of her husband, champion of the working class, seeing her now. That her often drunk, ineffective coffeehouse bolshevik could never even imagine this, which made her cough out a hard, mean laugh from lips that were set in a snarl.

how that, sir. They talked of it. But they think he will
...ing, sir."

...ank you, girl. Now you'd best get inside before they
...ou're gone—" His voice broke off sharply as two men
...running through the rain.

...h were roughly dressed, and in a momentary lull in the
..., he saw one of them wore a black patch over his eye. A
...ean man he was, with the face of evil on him.

...o here you are!" His voice sounded shrill in the storm.
...at are you doin' out here on the road, wench?" He
...bed at her shoulder and the girl stepped back.

...stantly, the rider pushed his horse between them. In his
...d was a drawn saber. "Get back there, man! Leave the girl
...e! She came to bring me a message, and it will be none
...our affair!"

..."Who're you?" The man with the patch peered up at him
...m the rain, careful to keep free of the saber point. He
...nked his eyes, then drew back, smiling suddenly, almost
...ering. "Ahhhh, Tom! It's the Yank! It's that American who's
...en about the tavern. He's no bit of trouble for us, let's be
...ck inside."

...Without another word, they turned and hurried back
...rough the rain.

...When they had gone, the rider glanced down at the girl.
...Put your foot in my stirrup, girl, and we'll have you back to
...e inn in no time."

...When she had her foot in his stirrup, he put an arm about
...r waist to steady her. "Say nothing of this now, not to any-
...e. You understand?"

..."Oh, yes sir! I'll not speak, sir!"

...Dropping her to the ground, he then rode arou...
...able. A hard-faced man with a wooden leg ...
...m, peering through the rain. "Oh, it's ...
...e bridle. "Don't you worry, sir. I'll ...
...The American stamped his fe...
...e water, then walked swiftly acros...
...de door of the inn. There he repea...
...pened the portal.

...Wind almost tore the door from his ha...

"Come on, damn you."

From somewhere inside her there came a deep swell of emotion. Some of it was the loss of her father. Some of it was fear of this terrible man. Some of it was anger, finally not with herself, but with her no-good husband.

But most of it was an emotion that had no name, something ancient and primal, the feeling that a tiny animal might have when, after being pursued to the end of its endurance, it turns and bares its teeth. Not only does it have to fight, but something inside it has changed . . . now it *wants* to fight.

———

MORNING FOUND PETE Kubelik painfully awake in his room at the San Esteban trade store. He had clumsily fallen off one of the deadfalls that Julie Marrat had skillfully negotiated in her escape the previous day. Kubelik had sprained his ankle, and now the swelling had become serious and excruciating. He took a swallow from a bottle of vodka he had half finished the night before and limped to the front door of the store. Throwing off the heavy bar, he stepped out into the gray and drizzling dawn.

Today he and Rudy would have to finish up what that damn girl had started. Regardless of the pain that shot through him every time he took a step, regardless of the hangover pounding in his temples, he'd find Julie Marrat, and if he couldn't make her come back with him, he'd kill her. He'd kill her anyway, but there'd be more pleasure for him if he brought her back alive.

He surveyed the long beach and the high cliffs. Time to get moving. He shook his head, trying to clear it, but that movement made his vision blur with pain.

Maybe he'd just kill her.

An invisible club knocked Pete Kubelik's bad leg out from under him. He went face-first into the sand, gasping in shock. He lurched around, trying to sit up even as the crack of the gunshot echoed back from the cliffs. Looking down, he saw blood welling from a hole dead center in his knee. He clawed for the pistol behind his hip.

Down on the beach, less than one hundred yards from

the door of his store, the dark sand moved and shook. Julie Marrat stood up from the place where she had lain, half buried, through the night, the sights of her father's old carbine trained on Kubelik's front door. She worked the bolt on the rifle, and when Rudy came charging out of the building, shotgun in hand, she shot him in the stomach. Then she started forward.

Kubelik half raised the .45, but she spoke before he could bring it to bear.

"Don't! I won't kill you if you throw it away."

He was tempted to try, but the barrel felt heavy, too heavy, and down in his leg the pain was starting to rise like a giant comber. He dropped the gun and began to curse, a long quiet stream of the foulest language Julie had ever heard.

She picked the gun up. "I came back for my battery cable," she said. "You shouldn't have taken it . . . or stolen our boat." She went up to the store and took the bolt from Kubelik's rifle. Then, using a rock, she beat the hammers from the trader's shotguns. The cable she eventually found lying on the deck of the schooner.

She fired up the schooner's auxiliary and threw off the lines. Several of the other inhabitants of the station had come down to the water and were watching her curiously. She called out to them.

"I'll leave this boat in the mouth of the San Tadeo River if you want it." They looked at her as she turned and headed down the inlet and toward the gulf. The last time she looked back, they had walked over to where Pete Kubelik lay in the sand. They had all taken up sticks or rocks, but were not striking him. They were just standing there. Finally, they slipped out of sight as she rounded the headland and started down to the sea.

MEETING AT FALMO

NIGHT, AND THE storm . . . howling e roared over the Lizard and above the Falmouth. Volleys of rain rattled along the cob a scattering of broken teeth.

Shoulders hunched against the wind and ra stared through the darkness toward a bend in the It was January of 1794, and the worst storm of was raging over the Atlantic, screaming above l and lashing Mount's Bay with its fury.

Suddenly, a woman darted from the rocks beside and lifted her hand. Startled, the man drew up sha hand dropping to his greatcoat pocket.

"Oh, sir! Sir!"

He looked down into the white, rain-wet face of a was shabbily dressed, with an old piece of sailcloth as a shield from the rain.

"What are you doing out here, girl?" he demanded get a nasty bit of cold!"

"Sir, beggin' your pardon, but are you Mr. Talleyra

"Talleyrand?" He was puzzled. "No, I'm not Tal and what would a serving wench like you be wanti him?"

"It's up ahead, sir. I'm maid at the Bos'n's Locker, inn, it is. There's a bad lot there, a-plottin' they are, a ainst Mr. Talleyrand."

And you came out here to warn him?"

did, sir. I'd want no man murdered by them, no man, sir."

what makes you think Talleyrand will be h ly yesterday he sailed from England for Am

gasped and went out. He stood stock-still, listening carefully until the lights were glowing again. The inn shutters rattled and, on the hearth, the flames guttered and spat.

The man with the black patch over his eye was hunched over a table with two other men. "I tell you, Tom, they will never pass the Lizard this night!"

"What then?" Tom was a burly man in a shabby cloak.

"Then it's here they will come! Only this morning, Brynie sighted their ship, and fighting a head wind she was! They'll put in here or be blown miles off their course."

"And if they come, we can still earn our guineas."

The American gave them no second glance, walking to a table near the fire and stripping off his rain-wet cloak. He removed his saber and placed it beside the cloak, but within easy grasp.

A compact, well-built man he was, but not large. Obviously a gentleman, but more than that. His was a strong, handsome face, his hair silvering at the temples. With it he wore the air of one born to command, yet it was a face that showed suffering, and was marked by some deep tragedy.

Drawing a book from his pocket, he opened it. He glanced up at the innkeeper. "Sherry," he said, "and if you have it, a bit of bread and cheese."

He glanced at the pages of the book, then at the three men. Slovenly rogues they were, if he had ever seen them. Scum, but a bloody, dangerous sort of scum, and plotting no good to anyone.

"Simple," Tom said then, waving a dirty hand, "they will come ashore, and if they come ashore, it's here they must come. So then, we have them."

"You speak of *them* . . . it is *him* we want."

"Garnet will know him."

"A tall man, he is, a tall man with a limp, a fair bit of nobleman and church."

The American turned a page of his book. The plotters had spoken in low tones, but their voices carried to him. Still, they had said nothing to be noted . . . had he not been warned by the maid.

Talleyrand . . . he knew the name well. A refugee from the

French revolution now living in England, but about to leave for America. His was the reputation of a shrewd diplomat, cool but charming. He had a narrow escape from the guillotine, but evidently had not left all his enemies when he fled from France. These rogues were British if he had ever seen them, the sort of scum that can be had to kill for hire. But Garnet— that name had a French sound.

Obviously, the plotters were correct. No ship could beat past the Lizard on such a night, and if by some chance she did pass, then she could never hope to get beyond Land's End in the face of such a wind.

Tom jerked his head toward the American. His voice lowered, but could still be heard. "Who's that one? What . . . ?"

One of the others whispered a name, and all their faces turned toward him. The American felt shame mingled with anger send hot blood creeping up his neck and face. He turned a page of the book and the print blurred before his eyes. Dimly he heard the words, "Not him. He'll not interfere, not the likes of him."

So they thought him a coward as well, did they? Many things, but never that. He had been no coward at Saratoga, he—

On the hearth, the flames hissed as a drop of water fell down the chimney. The host, seeing his empty glass, crossed the flags to him. "Yes, Salem, if you please," the American said. "It's a foul night and the wine warms a man. They bottle with this, I think, some of the sunshine of Spain."

"That they did, sir. Would you have me leave the bottle?"

"If you will . . ."

Battalions of wind threw their weight against the shutters, then withdrew, rattling them with angry fingers.

So they would never forget? A man made one mistake . . . but it was the worst mistake. The worst of all.

The maid moved about the room, frightened and pale. From time to time she darted a glance at him, but the American continued to read.

Finally, the three arose, drew their cloaks about them and left the tavern. The innkeeper moved to stoke the fire, then placed a heavy chunk on the coals. He threw a glance at the

American, then jerked his head after the departing trio. "A bad lot that, sir. Gallows bait for sure."

"They are staying here?"

"The night only, sir. I'd not have them longer if I had to call the watch from Falmouth."

"A good idea." The American turned a page of his book, then picked up his glass and drained it. "Salem?"

"Sir?"

"There will be some Frenchmen coming along. One will be named Talleyrand. Would you tell him, from a friend, to have a care? To be on his guard?"

"From *them,* sir? There's that in the wind?"

"More than we know, I'm thinking. You'll tell him?"

"Of course, sir. But—"

"As a precaution only. I'll be back."

The maid started to speak, then stopped. Yet she hurried to the door and looked up at him, her eyes frightened. He chucked her gently under the chin. "You worry too much," he said.

He opened the door then, stepped out and drew it behind him. Falmouth was a cluster of roofs several hundred yards away. The Bos'n's Locker stood on the harbor road away from the town. Overhead the sign creaked dismally in the wind.

Drawing his collar tighter, the American bent his head into the wind and turned down the road in the direction of the docks. There was no trusting the men he had seen. It would be like them not to wait for Talleyrand to come to the inn, but to murder him along the coast and throw his body in the sea.

It was not in him to sit idly by while a man was attacked without warning. Or was it in part because he was irritated with inaction?

Rain whipped his face and pounded at him with tiny, angry fingers. He could see the men ahead of him along the road, and when they stopped near some dark buildings along the wharf, he drew back into the shadows himself.

From the darkness nearby a man stepped. "Followin' 'em, are ye? Now Dick'll be proud to know that. He—"

The American stepped quickly from the shadows and

one hand grasped the newcomer by the throat, the other by the shoulder. Fiercely, he slammed the man back against the building, took a twist of the man's collar and let up only when he became afraid unconsciousness would keep the other from understanding his words. "Open your mouth," the very calmness of the American's voice was more frightening than rage would have been, "and I'll have the heart out of you. Get away from here now, and be glad that I haven't opened you up with my saber."

Gagging and pawing at his bruised throat, the man staggered back, then turned and hurried away into the storm. The American watched him for a few minutes, then glanced back to where the others waited in the darkness. Far away down the channel he thought he saw a light, and he moved along the building, well back in the darkness, his saber in his hand.

"Bloody awful night!" It was the man the others had called Dick.

"It is that."

"Any sign of her?"

"I be'ant lookin'. Soon enough when they put down a boat. If she comes, she'll come soon, you can mark that."

"Where then, Dick? Where'll we do't?"

"We've got to see him, first. Garnet will show us the man."

An hour passed on heavy feet. The wind did not abate, but the ship came. Her sails rolled up slowly, and the sailors at the canvas were unseen in the howling dark. They heard the rumble of her anchor going down, and later the chunk of oars, a sound caught only at intervals when the wind hesitated to gather force.

The American shifted his saber and dried his palm on his trousers beneath his greatcoat. Then he clutched the sword again.

He did not hear the boat come alongside, only suddenly there were men walking and he heard the sound of them speaking French. It was a language he knew, and he listened. He learned much of what he knew in Quebec, and this was but little different. But no names were called, and the three men went by, two tall men and one short, stout, and slipping as he walked. At times he ran a few steps to keep up, and puffed when he slowed down.

Dick and his companions fell in behind, and the American followed them. And so they came again to the inn.

By then he was before them. He had run, and gotten around them and into the back door as from the stable. When they entered, he was again at his table, a glass of sherry poured, and engrossed in his book. They entered, and he glanced up.

"You are from the port?" the American asked.

"From the sea." The man who replied was tall, cold of eyes, and walked with a slight limp. The American knew him from description to be Talleyrand. "We are for America," the man said.

"It is my country."

Talleyrand glanced at him with quick interest. "Then you can tell us of your country. We go there as strangers. What can you tell of America? Is it a fair land?"

The American closed his book carefully. "A fair land? Yes, it is. If I were to tell you of it as I think of it, you would think me a poet rather than a soldier. And I do think of it, I think of it always."

The newcomers warmed themselves at the fire and the American went on, speaking to them but to himself also. "You will find it colder there than here, but the houses are strong and tight and warm. There will be less talk of art and more of the frontier, less of books and more of land, but there will be good food, and good drink. You will find it a land of strong men, of full-breasted women, fit to mother a race of kings."

"And this man Washington? Have you met him? We in France have heard much of him."

The American hesitated, glancing at his wineglass. "Washington? Yes, I knew him. He is a great man, a greater man than most of us believed. Though he does not, you might say, have a flair. He is a shrewd, thoughtful, considering man, but he has a temper."

"So I have heard." Talleyrand clasped his hands behind his back. "It needs a great man to retreat when all around him are demanding a victory. He knew the important thing was not to risk his army, to keep his fighting force intact."

The American gestured to the table. "Will you join me, gentlemen? With the wind as it is, you must plan to stay for hours, perhaps for days. You are Monsieur de Talleyrand?"

"I am. And this is Monsieur de Fougier. And our companion, Paul Garnet."

The American looked around at the name. Garnet had a hard face with cold eyes and a tight-lipped mouth. So this was the traitor? He hesitated over that thought.

"You will like my country," he said gently. "It is a fine, strong land. The earth will be frozen now, beneath the snow. The rooftops will be white, and a thousand chimneys will lift their fingers of smoke toward the sky, but soon after you are there, the spring will come. The trees will bud and the fields grow green, and the men will plow the earth and you will hear the heavy wagons along the dirt roads. It is a young land, monsieur, a growing, raw, wonderful land, and . . . and . . ."

Talleyrand smiled slightly. "And it is your country."

"Yes," the American said quietly, "it is my country. It will always be my country, the only one for me. I have only learned that now . . . and now it is too late."

Suddenly, he looked up and saw that Dick was in the doorway. Tom was moving nearer, and Garnet suddenly arose and stepped back.

The American's hand was beneath his coat. "Talleyrand, watch yourself, sir. I have been waiting to warn you. Your life is in danger."

Talleyrand did not move from the table. His eyes flickered over the faces, came to rest on that of Garnet. If he was surprised, he gave no evidence of it. This man, who was for many years to be Europe's master of intrigue, who was to think always of his country and not of its ruler, was never to be surprised.

"You are clumsy, Paul. Had it not been for the storm, we would have gotten away from you."

"It does not matter. There was the storm!"

"But we are warned."

"And unarmed," Garnet replied coolly, triumphant now.

"I am not."

Their eyes turned to the American. He had drawn a pistol from beneath his dress coat. In his right hand he held the hilt of the still-sheathed saber.

There was something in that still, cold, handsome face that sent a shiver of apprehension through Garnet. This man . . . this man would not be afraid to die. He would die hard, and not alone.

De Fougier lurched backward, his face white. The three men faced the assassins. One pale and cowering, one tall and straight and cool, one the mysterious soldier, with a pistol in his hand.

"Well, gentlemen," Talleyrand said coolly, "what is it to be? Are you ready to die, or will you retire quietly?"

Garnet was furious. He glared at the American. "He has but one shot, and there are four of us!"

The American smiled. "One shot, for *you*. And then the saber. I fancy the saber, my man. I was of the cavalry before this."

Dick spoke up angrily. "Belay the gab! It's him you want, ain't it?" He pointed an outstretched finger at Talleyrand. "Then by the . . . !" He lunged, a dagger suddenly gripped in his fist.

The American's pistol exploded and Dick halted in mid-stride, his mouth falling open. At the same instant there was a second explosion and Garnet turned half around, then fell across the corner of the table. The table tipped, crashed on its side, and the wine bottle rolled off, struck the fallen man on the back, then rolled off onto the floor. The American stood with drawn saber. But the two others fled into the storm, the wind slamming closed the door behind them.

The second shot had been fired by Talleyrand, who held a small pistol. There was a flicker of irony in the Frenchman's eyes. "Yes, my American friend, even a diplomat knows that words must occasionally be backed with force." He glanced at the fallen man. "Very likely you've saved my life."

The American bent and retrieved the bottle from the floor. "And we did not break the wine."

Talleyrand glanced at the bodies of the two men. "It would be just as well if we went to some other place. There'll be trouble here soon."

"Monsieur?"

Talleyrand turned to face the American. "Yes?"

"If you will take the advice of one who is gone from his own country—go back to France. If that is not politically possible now, then go back when you can, as soon as you can. Believe me, monsieur, far better than any other, I know there is no country like one's own, and you will not be happy serving another."

"It is good advice, but now we go to America. Could you give me letters of introduction to someone there? It would be a great favor."

The American shook his head regretfully. "I am sorry, that I cannot do. I am perhaps the only American who cannot."

Their eyes held. Talleyrand hesitated. "Then, your name, sir? You can tell me that."

The American stiffened. His face was resigned and cold with pride and tragedy. "My name is Benedict Arnold."

CRASH LANDING

DYEA WAS THE first to speak. "Don't anyone move." His voice was quiet, and its very calm destroyed the moment of rising panic. "The plane seems to be resting insecurely, we must act carefully and with intelligence. I will investigate."

With infinite care, he straightened himself from his seat, glancing briefly at the wreckage of the nose. There was no possibility that pilot or co-pilot were alive. The stewardess was sitting in the aisle, where she had been thrown by the crash. She looked toward him uncertainly.

"Miss Taylor," he said, recalling her name from the tab above her breast pocket, "I was an officer in the Army, and I have some experience with this sort of thing. If all will cooperate, I'm sure we will be all right."

He could see the relief in her eyes, and she nodded quickly. "Sit still," he said, before she could rise. "I'll only be a moment. The plane is resting, I believe, on a mountainside. Its position seems to be precarious."

The crashed commuter plane lay on the mountain, and could be no more than a dozen feet from the crest of the ridge. Balancing his weight, his body leaning against the slant, he eased down the incline to the door in the back of the cabin. Fortunately, it had not jammed. The wind, which had been blowing hard, seemed to have lulled, and he stepped carefully from the door.

Snow swirled around him as he took a few steps back, along the fuselage, and then he looked down into an awful void that dropped away beneath the very tail of the plane. For a long moment he stared, awed by what he could sense rather than see. The slightest gust of wind or concerted movement could start the ship sliding, and in an instant it would fall off into the black void.

Yet, where he stood, the rock was solid, covered only by a thin coating of ice and snow blown by the wind. Moving carefully, he checked the position of the cliff edge and the area nearest the crashed plane. Then he returned to the door.

Dyea stood outside and looked within. Five faces had turned to stare at him. "You must move one at a time, and at my direction. The ship is in an extremely dangerous position. If there is any confusion or hurry, it may start sliding. You, in the right front seat, rise carefully. If you're not sure you can move under your own power, please tell me now."

A voice came from that seat where no face showed. "I cannot move. You must all go first."

"Thank you." Dyea looked at a fat man who clutched a briefcase and was near the door. "You, sir, will begin. Rise carefully and cross to the door. Bring your blanket with you. Be sure the blanket will catch on nothing."

As if hypnotized, the man rose from his seat. Patiently, he gathered the blanket, and with extreme economy of movement, he folded it; then, with the blanket under his arm, he moved to the door. As he stepped to the snow, Dyea pointed. "Walk ten steps forward, then three to the left. There is a rock there that will protect us from the wind."

The man moved away, and Dyea turned to the next person. Only when the five who were capable of moving had been removed from the plane did Dyea look to the hostess. "Miss Taylor, get to your feet," he said, "move carefully and gather all the remaining blankets and pass them to me."

"What about this man?" She indicated the seat from which the voice had come.

"He must wait. All our lives are in danger. Free of the plane, they may still die of cold and exposure. We must think first of the greatest number. Furthermore," he added, "the gentleman's courage has already been demonstrated.

"When you've given me all the blankets and coats, get your first aid kit and as much food as you can. Move very carefully and slowly. The ship is resting upon the very lip of a cliff that looks to be more than six hundred feet high."

As the stewardess began her collecting of blankets, Dyea looked toward the seat back where the remaining occupant sat. "My friend, moving you is going to be extremely dangerous. Do not suggest that we shouldn't attempt it, for we shall. However, I'll move you myself. Miss Taylor will be out of the ship at the time. We may both die. Therefore, think of any message you may want to send to anyone who survives you. Also, if there is any identification, pass it to the stewardess."

"And you?" The voice from the seat was calm, yet seemed tightly held against some pain, or fear. "What of you?"

"There is no one," Dyea said quietly, "I am a man alone."

Steadily, the stewardess made her trips; a dozen blankets, food, then medicine. One of the men appeared out of the darkness and accepted an armful of blankets. "One per person," Dyea said to him, "then a second as far as they go. The same for the coats. Then move this food and the medicine kit into the shelter."

"May I help?" the man asked, nodding toward the plane.

"Thank you, no. The added weight and movement would only increase the risk." He turned toward the stewardess. "Are any others alive?"

She looked into several of the seats, then stopped at one where he saw only a thin hand. "Yes, this girl is alive!"

"Good. We will proceed as planned. Come out."

Miss Taylor tiptoed carefully to the door and stepped out into the snow. Dyea turned to her, and she saw his strong, harshly cut face in the glow of the moon.

"If the plane carries us away," he advised, "you will keep these people huddled together until daylight." He glanced at the luminous dial of his wristwatch. "It is now three o'clock in the morning. It will begin to grow light shortly after six, possibly a little before. When it has become gray, make a stretcher of a couple of coats, load anyone who may not be able to walk, and move eastward along the ridge.

"When you've gone perhaps a quarter of a mile, away from this precipice, angle down the mountain toward the trees. Once there, build a fire and build a shelter. You have matches?"

"Yes." She hesitated. "Good luck."

"Thanks. I'll move the injured man first."

"I'll wait."

"No. Please don't." Dyea's voice was flat. "Now," he lifted his voice to the man in the plane, "your name and address, please? And any message for the stewardess?"

There was a moment of silence. "I am Victor Barclay, of Barclay and Paden, attorneys. My wife and children are living in Brentwood, California." He hesitated. "Only my love to them."

Miss Taylor turned her dark, serious eyes to the big man beside her. "And you, sir?"

"No message," Dyea said.

"Your name?"

"It does not matter."

"But isn't there someone?"

"No."

"I would like to know."

He smiled. She saw it clearly in the moonlight. The dark seriousness of his face changed. "My name is Dyea. Spelled D-Y-E-A. My family pronounced it dee-ah, the accent on the first syllable."

He hunched his shoulders against the cold. "Go now. Stay clear of the plane. I believe the wings are both gone, but some part might be under the snow and might drag you over. The rock will give you shelter."

When the woman was gone, Dyea stepped into the ship. With the decrease of weight, the situation was even more precarious. He walked carefully to the seated man. A blanket was over his legs, but obviously, both were broken. No other injuries were apparent. "All right, Barclay," Dyea said, "I'm going to pick you up. It may hurt like the devil. Despite that, you must hold yourself very still. If you move, you'll overbalance me on this incline and I'll fall. A fall would start the plane sliding."

"Very well. I'm ready."

Dyea's eyes flickered for the first time. He looked down the plane toward the tail, then at the door. He touched his lips with his tongue and, setting his feet carefully, stooped and picked up the injured man. As he straightened, he felt a sickening sensation of movement beneath him. He stood stock-still, holding the lawyer as if he were a child. The movement stopped with a faint grating sound; turning, Dyea took his first step. As he put down his foot with the combined weight of nearly four hundred pounds, he felt the ship shift beneath him. A queer sensation went up his spine, such a feeling as he had known but once before, when ice cracked beneath his feet out on a lake, a half mile from shore.

He took another step. There was no further movement, and he climbed down into the snow and walked over to the dark huddle of figures waiting in the lee of the rock.

Placing the lawyer on a coat spread out for him, Dyea straightened. "I think both thighs are fractured. I did not examine him. Possibly the lower part of the left leg, also. Keep him very warm and set the legs if you can."

Barclay looked up through the sifting flakes. His eyes were large with pain. "Don't go back," he said, "that little girl may not be alive by now."

"She was unconscious," Miss Taylor said.

"It's no matter. I'm going back."

"Don't be a fool, man!" Barclay burst out. "That plane almost went with us. It won't stand any more moving around. You know it and I know it. There's no use losing two lives when the one may go anyway."

Dyea did not reply. He turned, chafing his hands together. Then he walked quietly and stopped beside the plane. He looked around him, feeling the bitter cold for the first time. Then he glanced back to where the survivors were gathered, obscured by the swirling snow. The wind was rising. It would be a bitter night and a miserable tomorrow. Rescue parties might be days in coming but, with luck, the group could survive.

He balked at the door, and the thought that the girl must be dead by now flashed through his mind. Maybe, but probably not. He knew that was his fear of returning to the plane sneaking up on him. He shook his head and chuckled. The sound of it revived him, and he put a hand on each side of the plane door, a foot on the edge.

He stepped inside the plane and moved, gently as possible,

to the girl's seat. As he bent to look at her, she opened her eyes and looked right into his.

"Don't move," he said, "there has been an accident."

She looked at him very carefully, at his eyes, his face, and his hair. In the plane, the moonlight shone through the windows, bright between scudding clouds. "I know," she said. "Who are you?"

"It does not matter. Think of this. Several of the passengers were killed, but six have been removed and are safe. If you and I can get out, we will be safe, too, and we're the last."

Her eyes were wide and gray. They bothered him, somehow. They reminded him of other eyes. "Where are we?"

"On a very high mountain. It is very cold and the wind is blowing hard. We're on the edge of a high cliff. When I pick you up, the plane may slip. It did with the last person I carried, but he was very heavy. So you must hold very still."

"Maybe I can walk. Let me try."

"No. If you stumbled or fell, the shock would start us moving. I must carry you."

"You're very brave."

"No, I'm not. Right now I'm scared. My stomach feels empty and my mouth is dry. I'll bet yours is, too, isn't it?"

"You're risking your life for me."

"You're a romantic child. And believe me, the risk is much less than you might suppose."

He had been on one knee, talking to her. Now he slid an arm beneath her legs and another around her body, under her arms. An arm slid trustfully around his neck and he got carefully to his feet. After Barclay's weight, she seemed very light. He stood still, looking toward the door. It was seven steps, every step an increasing danger.

She looked toward the door, too, then at him. "Isn't it strange? I'm not afraid anymore."

"I wish I could say I wasn't."

He took his first step, placing his foot down carefully, then, shifting his weight, he swung the other leg. Then the right and again the left. Nothing happened. He took a deep breath, looked at the black rectangle of the door, then took another step. As if moved by the added weight, the ship quivered slightly. The movement was only a tremor, but Dyea immediately stepped again, and then again.

Under his feet the plane started to move, and he knew that this time it was going all the way. He lunged at the door and shoved the girl out into the snow. He saw her land, sprawling. The nose of the plane was sliding down while the tail held almost still, the body rotating. Fortunately, it was swinging in an arc opposite from where the girl had fallen. Then the whole plane slid in one section over the edge of the cliff. As it fell free, Dyea, with one agonized, fear-driven snap of his muscles, sprang upward and outward into the blackness and swirling snow.

There was one awful instant when, hands spread high and wide, he seemed to be hanging in space. He hit a steep slope partially covered with snow. He slid, then felt his lower body going over . . . he clutched, grabbing a fingerhold just as he began to fall. His arms gave a frightful jerk but he held himself, swinging in black, swirling snow over a vast, cold emptiness.

The moon emerged from under a cloud, and he started upward. He was no more than four feet below the edge, the cliff before him not as sheer as he'd thought. The brow sloped steeply back, and on the very edge was the girl, peering over at him.

"I'll get help," she said.

"No." He knew his fingers would not retain their hold. "Can you brace yourself against something? Can your heels dig in?"

She glanced around, then nodded. "Then slip out of your coat and lower the end toward me. Hang on tight, but if you feel yourself going, just let go."

His fingers were slipping in their icy crack, already so numb he could scarcely feel them. Snow swirled in his face and the wind whipped at his mouth, stealing his breath away. He gasped, then the coat slapped him in the face. He let go with one hand and swung it around and up, grasping the suede coat. He felt the weight hit her, but she held it. Carefully, he drew himself up, hand over hand. When his feet were in the crack where his fingers had been, he climbed over and lay beside her in the snow.

"I never was an Army officer," he whispered. "I never was anything."

His arm was stretched out and his cuff pulled back. He could see the dial on his watch. It was just eleven minutes past three.

WITH THESE HANDS

H E SAT BOLT upright in his seat, hands clasped in his lap, eyes fixed in an unseeing stare upon the crushed shambles of the forward part of the plane. His mind without focus, fixed in the awful rigidity of shock.

Awareness returned slowly, and with it a consciousness of cold. Not a shivering cold, not even the icy edge of a cutting wind, but the immense and awful cold of a land of ice, of a land beyond the sun. Of frigid, unending miles lying numb and still under the dead hand of the Arctic.

No movement . . . no life. No sound of people, no hum of motors, no ticking of clocks; only silence and the long white miles where the lonely wind prowled and whispered to the snow.

He had survived. He alone had survived. That thought isolated itself in his consciousness and with it came the dread of living again, the dread of the necessity for struggle.

Yet he need not struggle. He could die. He need only sit still until the anesthesia of shock merged without pain into the anesthesia of death. He need only remain still. He need only wait . . . wait and let the cold creep in. Once he moved the icy spell would be broken and then he must move again.

He was alive. He tried to shut away the thought and find some quiet place in his brain where he could stuff his ears and wait for death. But the thought had seeped into consciousness, and with it, consciousness of cold.

It was a cold where nails break sharply off when struck with a hammer; a cold where breath freezes and crackles like miniature firecrackers; a cold that drove needles of ice into his nose and throat . . . there was no anesthesia, no quiet slipping away, this cold would be a flaying, torturing death.

Icy particles rattled against the hull of the plane; a wind

sifted flakes across the hair of the sitting dead. Of them all, he alone had survived. Curtis who had believed so much in luck, Allen who had drilled for oil in the most inhospitable deserts and oceans of the world, of the seven men returning to Prudhoe Bay, he alone had survived.

He slumped in his seat.

That was it. He had moved. To live he must move again, he must act. What could he do? Where could he go? Outside lay the flat sweep of a snow-clad plain and beyond the dark edge of forest, black and sullen under a flat gray sky.

Movement had broken the rigidity of shock. With that break came the realization; there must be no panic, for panic was the little brother of death.

"Sit still," he said aloud, "you've got to think."

If he was to survive it must be by thinking. To think before he moved and then to waste no movement. This power had enabled men to survive. Reason, that ability to profit by experience and not only from their own meager experience, but from the experience of others. That was the secret of man's dominance, of his very survival, for he not only had learned how to control heat, flood, and wind, but how to transmit to future generations the knowledge of harsh experience.

This was an ancient enemy, this cold. Men had survived it, held it away with walls and fire, and if he, Drury Hill, oil company executive and once a citizen of the air-conditioned city of Dallas, Texas, was to survive, it must be by brains, ingenuity, and perhaps through those shared experiences.

He would need matches, he would need fuel. Shelter first, then fire. Fire here was out of the question. There would be spilled gasoline from ruptured tanks. And this plane was his lodestone for rescuers. His only beacon to the outside world. Very well, then, the forest. He had matches and a lighter, recently filled. He would need tools or a tool. He would need a blanket or another heavy coat.

Carefully, he straightened to his feet. He moved to the body of Curtis, avoiding looking at his face. He searched his pockets and found a lighter, more matches, and a nail file. One by one he searched those he could reach, but it was "Farmer" Peterson whom he blessed.

Peterson came from Minnesota and had trapped his way through college. An astute geologist, he was still a country boy at heart. His pockets yielded a waterproof matchbox filled with wooden matches and a large clasp knife of the type carried by sailors, the blade all of five inches long.

In the back of the plane he found several Army blankets and some cans of C rations. Making a bundle of one blanket, he then took along a roll of blueprints for the new tank and distribution complexes to use as tinder to start a fire.

Pausing to think, he remembered that he must not allow himself to perspire, for when activity ceased the perspiration would turn to ice and then his clothing would become a chilling hull in which death could come quickly.

He sorted through the debris where the lockers had broken open, finding a cup and several other useful utensils. He stuffed them into the blanket along with the food and Curtis's coat, and dropped down from the ruins of the plane.

The black battalions of the forest were a dark fringe where sky and snow had a meeting place. With curious reluctance, he stepped away from the plane and, leaving behind his last link with civilization, comfort, and tangible evidence of man, he walked off over the snow.

It was cold . . . his boots crunched on the snow . . . his breath crackled lightly. The all-pervading chill seemed to penetrate the thickest clothing. Yet the movement warmed him and he paused, glancing back. The distance to the plane frightened him, but he turned, and face down from the raw wind, he walked on.

He floundered into the black and white silence of the tree line. This was the ragged fringe of the forest and the growth was not tall . . . white snow, gray and barren sky, the spidery undergrowth and the solemn columns of the trees.

Then he saw, scarcely fifty feet into the trees, a deadfall. This had been a greater tree than most, uprooted and flung down, black earth clinging to the root mass and making a solid wall against the northeast.

Lowering his blanket pack into the hollow where the roots had been, he gathered four thick branches for a foundation, and then with some of the blueprint paper for tinder, he built a small pyre of twigs. The tiny flame leaped up, hissed spitefully at the cold, and then reached warily for the paper. It caught . . . edges of flame crept along the folds, then the flame began to eat hungrily into the tiny stack of fuel. He watched with triumph as the flames increased and twined their hot fingers about the cold pile of twigs.

He had achieved a fire . . . a minor victory won. Man's first companion against the cold and dark, his first step forward from the animal. It was a simple thing, but it was the first thing.

Yet as the flames sank their eager teeth into his small stack of fuel, he realized with quick fear that he could well become the slave of the fire, devoting all of his time to serving it. He must keep his fire small and remain close or all his strength would be required to feed the insatiable flame.

The root mass of the deadfall was more than seven feet of solid wall with a web of extending roots. Taking his time, Hill gathered evergreen boughs for a thick bed against the very base of the protecting wall, which supplied him not only with a windbreak, but with a reflector for his fire. Through the straggling roots, which extended out and down from the root mass, he wove other evergreen boughs, and into the roots overhead he did the same thing. Soon he had a cuplike hollow with an open face toward the fire.

After gathering more fuel, he banked his fire, placed sticks close at hand, then rolled up in his blankets on the bed of spruce boughs. He slept almost at once, awakening from time to time to replenish the flames, warned by the searching fingers of increasing cold.

At daybreak, he awoke in pain. The muscles of his back and neck were a tightly knotted mass. He had been hurt in the crash, and he was just now realizing it. The night in the cold and his odd sleeping position on the ground seemed to have turned his entire body into an assortment of seized and overstretched muscles. He moved and it hurt, but that wasn't the worst part. It was the sense of fragility that scared him, the sense that if he was called upon to use his body, it would fail him.

He moved close to the fire and, slowly, carefully, began to

stretch, trying to loosen his knotted muscles. In two hours he felt slightly better, he made hot, strong black tea, and while the wind moaned among the icy branches overhead he ate one of the boxes of rations, and listened to the cracking and complaining of the trees. Out across the open field, the wind lifted tiny ghosts of snow and floated them eerily along.

Each day he must think . . . he must plan. He must go farther afield for fuel, for later he might become weak and must depend upon that which was close by. He must add to his shelter and he must return to the plane to search for whatever else might be useful. And he must keep the plane clear of snow.

During that first day, he thought little beyond his work. He brought more blankets from the plane. He located two more deadfalls that he could draw upon for fuel. He built a framework of evergreens that could be shifted to whatever angle to protect him from the wind. He added more boughs to his bed.

By now they would know the plane was down . . . a search would have already begun. Drury Hill believed their ship had been off course when it crashed, and with the present overcast, there was small hope of immediate rescue.

That night, he took stock of his situation. With no more exertion than was needed to live, his food supply would last three days. From his experience flying from Fairbanks to Prudhoe and back, he knew three days was simply not enough. In the vast area they must search, he could not gamble on them finding him in less than a week.

He must find other sources of food. He was too far from the coast for seals. There were caribou, but he had no rifle nor had he yet seen their tracks. There were lichens that could be eaten. That was what he had read. Hovering over his fire in the darkness and cold, he strove to remember every iota of information culled from his reading, listening, and living.

On the second morning he awoke in a black depression. The pain was back in full force. He had slept fitfully through the awful cold and now he lay staring into the fire. It was no use. He was a fool to expect rescue. He was one man in all this vast waste. They would never find him. He stared at his grimy hands, felt the stubble on his jaws, and then stiffly, he pushed himself to a sitting position and stoked the fire.

His head ached and his mind was dull . . . was he becoming ill? Had he overworked? It had been twenty years since he had done anything like this . . . twenty good years of living and leisure and seeing all the world held.

This could be a miserable way to die . . . on the other hand, suppose he lived? A fire of optimism blazed up within him . . . it would be something . . . they had said he was past his prime . . . that he should take it easy. He cursed. He made tea and ate several crackers. He must find food.

With a stout stick cleaned of bark, he started out, keeping to crusty patches of snow or ground swept bare by wind. He found, growing on some damp soil, a patch of Idelana lichen and gathered a bundle of it to take along. He searched for berries, having heard that some low-growing bushes held their berries all winter long. His back hurt as he walked but soon he was standing straighter and as he warmed up he felt less and less like a crippled old man.

Twice Arctic hares bounded away over the snow and once he saw a herd of caribou in the distance.

Nothing moved in the forest when he started back. The trees were more scattered. He crossed two streams frozen hard by the subzero cold. The branches of trees creaked in the wind. He cupped a gloved hand over his nose and tried to breathe slowly, his exhalations warming the incoming breath.

Wind picked up the snow . . . he should improvise some snowshoes . . . a gust of wind whined in the trees . . . he glanced at the sky. A storm was blowing up.

Darkness came suddenly and he found himself floundering through soft drifts. Feeling his way back to solid ground, he started on, then caught a whiff of wood smoke and then saw the black blob of his shelter. He started toward it, collecting wood as he went. His fire was almost gone, and he nurtured it carefully back to life.

With some meat from a can and some of the lichen, which he soaked to remove the acid, he made a thick stew. Huddled in his shelter of boughs, Dru Hill of Dallas, Abu Dhabi, and

Caracas . . . all places that were warm and populated . . . added fuel to his fire and slowly ate the stew. He ate, and found it good.

Around him the walls of his shelter became suddenly friendly and secure. The wind caught at his fire and flattened the flame. It would use a lot of fuel tonight. He grinned as he leaned back against the root mass. He had plenty of fuel. Here he was, a lone man in an uncharted wilderness, yet he had created this little bit of civilization, it was a long way from being a building, even a crude one, but it was shelter nonetheless. He thought of the buildings he had ordered built, the oil and gas wells he'd drilled, the tank complexes and pipelines. All had been a natural outgrowth of this same simple need. Shelter and fuel. At one end of the spectrum it demanded a wood fire and a windbreak, at the other cracking plants and parking lots. He saw in himself an extension of the natural order of things. Man against the elements. Man triumphant against the elements. The third night coming and he was still alive. He could win. He could beat this racket. Old Dru Hill wasn't dead yet.

Tomorrow he would make some snares and catch a few Arctic hares or snowshoe rabbits. Maybe he could make a net and trap some birds. He would have meat and there were more lichens. East through the woods, there might be berries. He might even improve his shelter.

At seven in the morning, he heard the throbbing motors of a plane. The sky was heavily overcast but he rushed out, shouting loudly, uselessly. He heard it overhead, heard it pass on . . . at least they were trying. Hope mounted, then died. He considered a dozen unreasonable doubts, worried over fifty objections. They might never return to this locality.

Yet he did not despair, for they would continue to search. He worked through the fourth day at his usual tasks, a man below medium height, inclined to be fat, but he hurt less . . . in some strange way his body seemed to be stronger. To the west he found a vast stretch of tundra broken by only occasional outcroppings of rock and by the stalks of some plant. Intrigued, he dug into the snow and frozen ground and got out the fattish sulfur-yellow roots. They tasted sweet and starchy. He collected enough to fill his pockets.

No more planes came over . . . by nightfall he was dead tired and glad for sleep. On the fifth morning, two snow-shoe rabbits were in his snares . . . on the sixth morning a third rabbit. He had no luck with the larger and more cautious Arctic hares. On that day, he ate nothing but food he had gathered himself, except for tea.

He had avoided the plane except to clean off the snow . . . only once after his first leaving had he entered, but the motionless bodies of his former companions had filled him with gloom. Instead he collected debris from the crash, pounding sheets of aluminum into a crude stove and reflector.

On the seventh morning, his snares were empty and for the first time he failed to add to his supply of food. On the eighth day, they were again empty . . . he struggled to the tundra for more of the yellow roots. Returning, he found a patch of black crowberries and, sitting there in the open, he ate all he could find.

Since that one time he had heard no planes . . . had the search been abandoned? Had it been a searching plane at all?

On the ninth morning, he found a small snowshoe rabbit in a snare and made a rich stew using lichen and the yellow roots. But still he heard no planes. He no longer listened for them nor looked for them. He went on about the business of survival . . . he gathered lichen and roots, he checked his snares . . . the rabbits were more cautious now . . . he added to his supply of fuel.

Returning to the plane, he found his bag, forgotten until now. Back at his fire, defying the cold and the loneliness, he shaved. Almost at once he felt better. The smooth feel of his cheeks under his hand was better than the scraggy beard. He concealed the bag under the trunk of the tree.

His clearing had taken on a lived-in look. The snow was trodden down, there was a huge stack of fuel, the lazy smoke of the fire. There were the skins of the rabbits he had staked out. He added fuel to his fire, including a chunk of birch, and walked away.

Alone on the edge of the tundra, he looked across the flat

white sea of snow . . . what lay beyond? Just a vast space, or perhaps a settlement? A trapper's cabin? He was slogging along over the snow, head down, when he smelled smoke. A lot of smoke . . .

His head came up—then he broke into a clumsy run. From the site of his shelter rose a bright column of flame!

Heart pounding, he lunged across the snow. Twice he fell, plunging headlong, facedown in the snow. He had been almost a mile away . . . he stumbled into the clearing and stopped, blank with despair.

His shelter was gone. His blankets were gone. The other coat was gone. Only charred, useless masses remained. More than half his fuel was gone and the rest still burned.

In a panic, he tore at the pile of fuel, pulling the pieces back, rubbing the fire away in the snow. A spark blowing into the dry, resinous stuff of the shelter must have set it off. A low wind whined among the bare boughs overhead, moaned in the evergreens, stirring the blackened ashes of his fire, rattling the dead fingers of the birch, whispering out over the tundra, a lonely reminder of the cold and the night to come.

Soon it would be dark . . . it would be colder. Wind would come . . . his clothing would turn to ice now for he had perspired freely . . . his strength was burned out from the running and the work . . . he would die . . . he would freeze.

He stared around him . . . what to do? Where to begin again? Begin again? He was a fool to begin again. Begin again . . . ? He laughed hysterically. His little corner of civilization was gone. But what had it been? A pitiful shelter. An almost irreplaceable pile of wood. Some junk that he had used to survive. Before the crash he probably would never have recognized it as a camp, he might have thought it trash collected by the wind. Before the crash he never would have recognized what had burned as being the difference between life and death. He never realized how little it took, never realized how simple the things were . . . as long as they were the right things.

He had to do something. . . .

With his knife he made rawhide strips of the rabbit skins. It was growing dark, the wind was increasing. Another storm was coming. He must contrive something new . . . there was a patch of willows no more than two hundred feet away. He went there, scanned a thick clump a dozen feet around, and then going into the clump he broke off all the central trees, none of them in the center being over two inches in diameter, mostly less. Then he drew the tops of the outer ones down and tied them together with the rawhide strips. When he had several of them with their tops tied at the center, he went out and wove others among them, using some willows but mostly evergreens. As the dark closed in he was making a strong, hivelike shelter with a hole in the top for smoke to escape. A shelter strong because it was made of living trees.

Trampling down the snow, he dug a hole with his knife and built a small fire there. He carried boughs within and scattered them around, then made a bed near the fire. Outside he threw more evergreens on the house, then gathered fuel. One of the deadfalls was close by, and working until long after dark, he carried as much of it to the door as he could, and several armsful inside.

Finally he made a door of woven boughs and pulled it across the entrance. Outside the snow was falling, the wind was blowing with hurricane force. Inside his wigwam of willow and evergreen, its framework rooted in the ground, he was secure.

His blankets were gone and his food was gone . . . including the precious tea . . . but outside the snow fell and packed tighter and thicker about his shelter. Inside it grew warmer. A drop from overhead fell and hissed gently in the flames. Reclining on the boughs, he considered the situation again. This storm would end hope of rescue . . . everything would be shrouded in snow and he doubted if he would have the strength to uncover the plane . . . and for days he would not have the time. He must find food again, set snares, gather more fuel.

If he could only trap a caribou! Sitting up suddenly . . . there was that book about China . . . what had its name been? It had told how they trapped deer in the Altin Tagh . . . a hole about eight to twelve inches in diameter and a couple of feet deep . . . less could do . . . and a ring of sharp sticks, the sharp ends pointing toward the center. When the deer stepped into the hole, the sharp sticks would prevent it being withdrawn. Then he could rush in with his knife . . . he grinned at himself. What preposterous thing would he think of next?

Awakening in the dark, icy cold of morning, he rebuilt his fire and this time the shelter grew quickly warm, testifying to the thick outer covering of snow. He squatted beside the fire, dreading the outer cold but dreading more the cold his leaving would let into his shelter.

He must have food, and unless the snow had buried the snares completely, he might have something. There had been a few more stalks of the yellow root not too far away on the tundra. The idea of the previous night returned. If he could kill a larger animal his food problem would be solved for days on end . . . and if trapped, he might kill it with a sharp stick or his knife. Banking his fire carefully, he went out of the hut, closing the door and covering it with snow.

All was white and still, but with a strange difference. Suddenly, almost with shock, he realized why. The sky was clear!

Now, if ever, a plane might come. But were they still searching? Had they given up? Then he remembered . . . the crashed plane was shrouded in snow and would be invisible from the sky!

He started toward it, then stopped. The chance of rescue was a wild gamble and he needed food. In this country, one's strength need wane only a little for the cold to kill. Weakness and exhaustion were fatal. Turning, he walked toward the snares. Two were buried and useless . . . the third had been tripped and the rabbit had escaped. He reset them and went through the woods to the tundra and found two stalks of the yellow-rooted plant. The roots were pitifully small.

Circling back, he stopped suddenly. In the snow before him were the tracks of a herd of caribou. The tracks were fresh and the herd must have passed within a few minutes! He was following them when suddenly he heard the roar of a plane!

Wheeling around, he ran from under the trees and stared up at the sky . . . it was there, big and silver and beautiful! It was low enough to see him. But it was also low enough to be quickly out of sight. He sprang into the air, shouting hoarsely. It disappeared off over the trees to the north. Rushing toward his shelter, he could only think that the crashed plane had been covered with snow. He went past the shelter and finally got to the plane. He had no more than reached it when he heard the ship returning.

It was coming too fast . . . he could never make it. Desperately, he began trying to uncover some part, the silver of a wing, to the sunlight. But the snow was heavy and he was too late, the plane soared off to the south and its sound died rapidly away.

Glumly, he started to turn back and then went to work and cleaned the snow from the one undamaged wing and the fuselage. It was a slow, heavy task and noon had come and gone before he completed it. He was physically exhausted and ravenously hungry.

A plane had come, crossed over the area and gone. He must, he told himself, appreciate the significance of that. It meant his last chance for rescue was gone. They would not cover the same ground twice. As he prepared his meal, he considered that, using the two yellow roots and his prize . . . an Arctic hare found in a snare set that very morning.

All right then. No rescue. If he was to survive until spring and then walk out, he must do it on his own. Dru Hill was surprised to find that he did not view the situation with alarm. He could survive . . . he had proved that . . . and if he could trap a caribou, he would have a good supply of meat. He could trap two if he could trap one. He could dry or smoke the meat and so build supplies for spring. He could make a pair of snowshoes and, now that hope of rescue was abandoned, he could afford to go further afield for food, not needing to remain near the crashed ship.

He took a deep breath and thought of the miles of wilderness that surrounded him. He didn't have much but the woods could provide, they had shown him that. He no longer thought of this Arctic forest with fear. It was beautiful, the trees comforting, the vast expanse of tundra a wonder and a challenge. His hearing had become supernaturally acute, his sense of smell delicate. He could survive.

This was something he never could have imagined two weeks ago. A man needed lights, an automobile, the complex comforts of the modern world. He, in his chosen profession, had provided the electricity, the gasoline, and the plastics to provide those comforts.

He grinned to himself. Farther afield there might be better hunting grounds, berries, perhaps more game. He thought of something else . . . of the change in himself. Here he was, calmly and with confidence considering surviving the entire winter where a few days before he had doubted his ability to survive a few hours. But he was right. His doubts were gone, and justly so. This place was warm and could be made warmer. He could take some metal from the plane for heads for a spear and for arrows. He could . . . he heard voices.

He pushed aside the door and thrust his head out. Three men, two of them in Canadian Air Force uniforms, and the third was Bud Robinson, were slogging down the path.

He stood there and they stared at him, and then Robinson said, "By the Lord Harry! It's Dru Hill!"

Robinson looked around curiously. "We never dreamed anyone would be alive, but when we flew over this morning, Gene thought he saw a black spot on the snow. Only it was not on the snow, but where the snow had melted off the trees over your fire, here."

"We flew clear back to the post," Gene explained, "but it kept nagging me. There shouldn't be anything black after all that snow falling, so we took a chance and came back. It's lucky for you that we did."

Hours later the plane dropped down onto the runway of an airfield surrounded by warehouses and industrial buildings. Nearby a pipeline ran toward the distant sea. Dru Hill was hustled across the field and into a waiting ambulance. He insisted on sitting in front with the driver and at the hospital they gave him a clean bill of health, something he had not doubted.

They left him alone finally, the reporters, and doctors, company representatives, and police, in a brand-new motel room near the airfield. The walls and roof seemed strangely close. He paced the odd green carpeting far into the night. To

Dru Hill the room smelled of cleansers and cigarettes and wallpaper glue. It was uncomfortably warm. He opened the window, letting in the cold night air and a small shard or two of ice. Beyond the parking lot was a line of scraggly pines obscuring a set of trash bins and the highway. The sound of engines and tires on the asphalt filled his ears. The air outside smelled like gasoline. Gasoline and garbage.

But then the wind blew and after a moment it carried away those smells, replacing them momentarily with the smell of the great Alaska beyond. Beyond the suburbs, the trailers, the gravel pits, and oil wells. He remembered how, as the plane lifted itself from the snow, he had looked back. The trees at the edge of the forest were only a dark line. The place where he had built his hut, staked his furs, and piled the wood for his fire could no longer be seen.

But he knew it was there.

THE DIAMOND OF JERU

THE PENAN PEOPLE of Borneo say that the forest and the earth will provide for you if only you will let them. I hadn't exactly found that to be true, but what did I know? I was an American, stopping briefly in their land and ignorant of their ways.

———

I WAS DOWN TO my last few coins when John and Helen Lacklan arrived in Marudi. I'd come down from Saigon to make my fortune but luck had not been with me. For over a year I'd been living like a beachcomber who had accidentally found his way inland. There was a longing in me to make my way back home but no money to do it with. I'd told myself it was better to stay where I was and wait for an opportunity. Around Sarawak, in those days, a white man could go a long way just on confidence and the color of his skin.

My luck paid off in this way: a friend in the government office offered to send me some tourists, Mr. and Mrs. John Lacklan. He had set me up, time and again, with minor engineering and construction jobs and was responsible for my having been able to keep body and soul together over the last few months. The Lacklans were an American couple, in from Singapore. They were recently married and, most importantly, they were looking for a diamond.

Now they find diamonds around Bandak, around Kusan, and near Matapura, to name only a few places. They also find some rare colors in the Sarawak River. Most so-called "fancy" stones are found in Borneo, for diamonds come in a variety of colors, including black. But after looking over the possibilities they had come up the Baram River to Marudi or

Claudtown, as some called it, and Vandover was going to send them to me.

It was late in the day and the wind picked up slightly, coming in over the river to where we sat on his porch near the old fort. "I told him about you." Vandover poured cold beer into my glass. "He wants to go up the Baram. You want enough money to get you home and . . ." He eyed me mischievously. "I suspect that you wouldn't mind having one more go at the river yourself. All the better if Mr. Lacklan is paying."

We toasted my good fortune and I let the beer slide back down my throat. Cold beer had been a rare and precious luxury in my world for too long. If everything worked out I would soon be done with Borneo and on my way back . . . back to the land of cold beer.

———

IT WAS DARK by the time I got home. I navigated my way across the room to the bed. Without lighting a lamp I undressed and lay back under the mosquito netting. Above my head fireflies cruised lazy circles against the ceiling, flickering, on . . . off . . . on . . .

Money to go home. A buck or two to help get my feet back under me at the worst. At the best . . . ?

I, too, had come to Borneo hunting diamonds. If you were lucky you washed them out of a river just like panning for gold. I had found a fortune of them, in a pool just below a dried-up waterfall. I had spent a month in the bush digging them from the river, but ultimately, the river had taken them back.

Eager to return with my treasure and careless, I'd put my canoe into a rapid at the wrong angle and almost lost my life. As it was I lost the boat, the diamonds, and most of my kit. A family of Iban pulled me from the water and took care of me until I was on my feet again. I was seven weeks getting back, nursing broken ribs and a persistent fever.

What money I had left had slowly trickled away; paid out to Raj, my houseboy, and for food, drink, and quinine. I've heard it said that, in the tropics, you rented your life from the devil malaria and quinine was the collector. After my disaster on the Baram the disease had become a most demanding landlord.

But now I would have another chance. We would go upstream of the pool where I found my diamonds, closer to the source, the find would be better this time and I'd have Lacklan's fee even if we didn't locate a single stone. With the good feeling of money in my pockets I drifted off to sleep.

MY PLACE WAS a deserted bungalow that I'd adopted and repaired. When Lacklan and his wife appeared, I was seated on the verandah idly reading from Norman Douglas's *South Wind.*

They turned in the path, and I got to my feet and walked to the screen door. "Come in," I called out, "it isn't often I have visitors."

As they came up on the porch, I noticed that Helen's eyes went at once to the book I had been reading. She glanced up quickly, and smiled.

"It's rather wonderful, isn't it?"

She was tall and lean, with fine thin limbs and dark blue eyes that shone in the shadow of her wide-brimmed straw hat. She had a face like that of a model from one of those fashion ads but with more character, faint friendly lines around the corners of her eyes and mouth, no makeup. Her nose was large but perfectly shaped and her jaw betrayed strength, a strength that also was apparent in her body, beautifully formed but built for a lifetime of swimming and skiing. Her skin, where it disappeared under the fabric of her sundress, looked like it was taking on a healthy shade of copper from the equatorial sun.

She had commented on my book. . . . "It's an old friend," I said, smiling.

Lacklan looked from one to the other of us, irritated. "You're Kardec?" he demanded. "I'm John Lacklan." He was tall and slightly stooped. A thin blue vein pulsed in one of his temples as he peered at me from behind glasses with round, nearly black lenses. Vandover had told me he was an administrator at one of the big government labs back in the States. Atom bombs or something.

Lacklan pushed ahead, up the stairs. "I understand you're the authority on diamonds?" The way he said "authority" indicated that he doubted it.

"Well"—I hesitated because I was well aware of all that I didn't know—"maybe. Will you sit down? We'll have a drink."

Raj was already at my elbow. He was a Sea Dyak, not over sixteen, but his mind was as quick and intelligent as anyone I've ever encountered.

"Scotch," Helen said, "with soda . . . about half."

Raj nodded and glanced at Lacklan, who waved a careless hand. "The same," he said.

When Raj returned with our drinks, Helen sat there sipping hers and watching me. From time to time, she glanced at her husband, and although she said nothing, I had an idea that she missed nothing.

"You've been up the Baram, above Long Sali?" he asked.

"Yes." I saw no reason for explaining just how far I had gone. Marudi was a rough sixty miles from the mouth and Long Sali was a village a hundred fifteen miles farther up-river.

"Are there diamonds up there? Gemstones?"

"There are," I agreed, "but they are scattered and hard to find. Most of the stones are alluvial and are washed out of creeks back up the river. Nobody has ever located their source."

"But you know where diamonds can be found, and you can take us to them. We're not wasting our time?"

In this part of the world I had become used to the cultures of Chinese and Malay, Muslim and British, all of these groups had a sense of politeness or patience bred into them. In comparison the directness and force of Lacklan's questions was like an attack.

"You are not wasting your time," I assured him. "I've found diamonds. I can't promise, but with luck, I can find more. Whether they are bort or gem quality will be anyone's guess."

"You speak the language?" he asked.

"I speak marketplace Malay," I said, "and a scattering of Iban. Also," I added dryly, "I know that country."

"Good! Can you take us there?"

"Us?" I asked cautiously. "Your wife, too?"

"She will go where I go."

"It's our project, Mr. Kardec," Helen Lacklan said. She stretched out a long, firm hand to show me the ring on her finger. An empty setting stared up at me like a blind eye. "John gave me this ring five years ago. We're going to find the stone together."

It was a wonderful, romantic notion but far easier said than done.

"You know your business best," I said carefully, "but that's no country for a woman. It's jungle, it's miserably hot, and there are natives up there who have never seen a white man, let alone a white woman. Some of them can't be trusted."

I was thinking of one nefarious old codger in particular.

"We'll be armed." His manner was brusque and I could see his mind was made up. I suddenly had a vision that both amused me and made me very nervous: John Lacklan as Henry Stanley blasting his way through the forests of central Africa. His chin was thrust out in a way that told me he was primed for an argument . . . I knew to never come between a man and his weapons, especially when he's a client. I turned to her.

"I don't want to offend you, Mrs. Lacklan, but it is very rough country, bad enough for men alone, and with a woman along . . ." I could see I was going to have to give her a better argument. "There will be snakes and leeches. I'm not trying to scare you, it's just a fact. We'll be on the water and in the water all day, every day, and with the humidity we'll never get dry, not until we get back. We'll be eating mostly fish we catch ourselves and rice. There is the risk of infection from any cut or scrape and an infection while you're upriver can kill you."

She was quiet for a moment. "I believe I'll be all right," she said. "I grew up in Louisiana, so the heat and humidity . . . well, they are only a little bit worse here." She laughed and her teeth were white and perfect. "Really, Mr. Kardec, I'm quite strong."

"I can see that," I said, and then wished I'd said nothing at all.

Lacklan's head snapped up and for a moment he glared at me. This man was deeply jealous, though Helen didn't seem the kind of person who would give him reason. Of course, that very fact made her all the more attractive.

She caught his reaction to me and quickly said, "Perhaps it would be better if I stayed here, John. Mr. Kardec is right. I might make trouble for you."

"Nonsense!" he replied irritably. "I want you to go."

His eyes narrowed as they turned back to me and burned as they looked into mine. I couldn't tell if he was disturbed about my appreciation of his wife or because I'd made her consider not going upriver with him or, and I only thought of this later, because I'd made her consider staying in Marudi where she would be on her own while we were gone.

"We will both go, Mr. Kardec. Now what will it cost me and when can we leave?"

I explained what they would need in the way of clothing and camping gear. Warned them against wearing shorts, no reason to make life easy for the mosquitoes and leeches. And then told them my price.

"I get a thousand, American. The canoes, Raj, and four Iban crewmen will run you six-fifty. Kits, food, first-aid and mining supplies, maybe another three to three-fifty. Depends on whose palm I have to grease."

"Is that the best you can do?" he objected. "You're taking more than half for yourself!"

"Look, Mr. Lacklan, I've been where you need to go. I've found diamonds . . . lots of diamonds. I lost them all but I know where they were. If it was easy, or cheap, I'd be back there working that streambed right now instead of trying to make a deal with you."

I could see something behind his glasses. A calculation taking place, like in one of the computers he probably used at work, punch cards feeding in data, tubes glowing with orange light. "All right," he said. "But how are we going to split up our take? After all, I'm paying for this expedition. I should get a piece of whatever you dig out."

I guess I recoiled a bit. Anyway, Helen looked at me in concern and Lacklan leaned back in his chair smugly. I hadn't really given it much thought. I'd figured that I'd take them there and they'd work the river in one area and I'd find somewhere else. I could see that this might lead to problems, especially once he realized that he could enlist the boat crews in the digging and panning.

"We'll split what we find, fifty-fifty," I said. "With the best stone to be for Mrs. Lacklan's ring." He was still gazing at me, one eyebrow arched above the round steel rim of his dark glasses. I gave in a little more. "I'll give Raj and the boat crews a bonus from my share."

Helen Lacklan turned to him. "That's fair, darling, don't you think?"

"Yes, I suppose it is."

We settled on a date, ten days from then, to leave. They went to the door and Helen hesitated there. "Thank you," she said graciously. "I enjoyed the drink."

They walked away toward the town.

It's maybe only once in a lifetime that a man sees such a woman, and I confess I looked after them with envy for him. It made my throat dry out and my blood throb in my pulses just to look at her, and it was that as much as anything else that made me worry about taking the job. A man needed all his attention on such a trip as this . . . and no man could remain other than completely aware of such a woman when she was near him.

Nothing moves fast in the tropics, yet despite that I had lined up the boats, boatmen, and equipment within a week. Raj was instrumental in bringing everything together as always. Even when I had no money he stuck with me. "You make better job, boss," he'd say when I pushed him to look for work elsewhere. "We don't work much but we make lots money!" I'm not sure that I'd have liked the irregular pay if I had been in his place. But Raj seemed to come alive when trying to figure out something he'd never done before and the jobs we got were always a challenge of one kind or another.

Around Marudi I caught sight of John and Helen once or twice, it wasn't a big place. He was not one to take his attention from whatever he was doing to nod or say hello but once or twice I got a smile from her. Then for several days in a row I didn't see either of them.

The day before we were supposed to leave I spotted the Lacklans coming up the path from town. And something— their postures, the way they walked?—told me the plan had gone wrong.

"Kardec?" There was a bluster in his manner that seemed ready to challenge any response that I might have. "We've made other arrangements. I'll pay whatever expenses you've incurred so far." Helen did not meet my eyes.

"Other arrangements?" The answer was evasive. "You've decided not to go?"

"We'll be going, but with someone else. How much do I owe you?"

Frankly, it made me angry. The deal had been all set, and now . . . I stated my price and he paid me. Helen merely stood there saying nothing, yet it seemed she was showing a resentment or anger that I had not seen before.

"Mind telling me how you're going?"

"Not at all. But it doesn't really matter, does it?"

His very arrogance and coolness angered me, and also to have all my excellent planning go for nothing. "It matters a great deal," I told him. "There's one other man that would take you upriver who is trustworthy, a native named Inghai, and he's down with a broken leg. If you go back in there with another native, you're a fool!"

"You're calling me a fool?" He turned on me sharply, his eyes ugly. For a minute I thought he was going to swing on me and I'd have welcomed it. I'd have liked nothing so much as to help him lose a few teeth.

Then I had an awful premonition. Jeru was up to his old tricks again. "Look," I asked, "is it a native? Did he show you a diamond? A big stone? Something about twenty carats?"

They were surprised, both of them. "And what if he did?"

"You tried to buy it and he wouldn't sell. Am I right?"

"So what?"

"If I am right, then this was the same fellow who guided two parties up the Baram before, one group from Kuching, one came over from Sibu. None of them ever came back."

"You're implying that he had them killed? For what reasons? For the diamonds they found?"

"Diamonds mean nothing to him. I believe he used the one stone he has to lure them upriver so he could murder them for their possessions."

"Nonsense!"

"He was an old man, wasn't he? With a deep scar on his cheek?"

Their expressions cleared. "No." Lacklan was triumphant. "He was a youngster. No older than your houseboy."

So they had switched, that was all. The trick was the same. The stone was the same. And they were not the first to do it. It had been done by the Piutes in Colorado, eighty or ninety years ago, with gold nuggets for bait.

"Have it your own way, Lacklan. It wouldn't matter if you were going alone, but you're taking your wife along."

His face flamed and his eyes grew ugly. "My wife is my own concern," he said, "and none of your affair."

"You're right, of course, only I'd do a lot of thinking before I'd let bullheadedness risk my wife's life. Risk your own all you like."

"Nonsense!" Lacklan scoffed. "You're just trying to scare us to keep our business."

So they walked away and I could see Helen talking with him as they went up the road toward town. Whatever she said, I heard him answer angrily.

———

WHAT THE LACKLANS were getting into had a certain smell to it. It was the smell of an old reprobate named Jeru who was hidden out upriver with a small band of renegades. Jeru was reputedly the last of the oldtime Sea Dyak pirates and the story was that he had fled upriver from the Brook militia and was living like a tribal chief with a group of followers who had been outcasts from their own longhouses.

No one really knew if this was true but it was known that Jeru had appeared in the cities along the coast and lured people, usually foreigners, into the backcountry. And once they disappeared they never returned.

It had been years since the last time this had happened and the story had been spreading that Jeru might be dead . . . nonetheless, it had me worried.

———

THAT NIGHT THERE were four of us there on the verandah of the resident officer's bungalow. Van apologized for the deal with the Lacklans falling through. "There's no accounting for people, I suppose."

I didn't mention John Lacklan's hair-trigger jealousy and the fact that I might have helped arouse it.

"I've got another possibility for you though," he said. "There's a canal job. It cuts through from one of the creeks about a mile above town. Hasn't been used in years but Frears wants it open again. I told him you could do it, bossing a native crew. It'll pay almost what Lacklan would but it will take longer. We'll get you home yet."

"Van," I said, "I'm worried. Their story sounded so familiar. Remember Carter? That was two years before my time, but he came down from Hong Kong on a vacation. He met some native on the coast who had a big diamond and wouldn't sell it. The native agreed to show him where there were more. He went upriver and was never heard of again.

"A few months later, the same thing happened to Trondly at Kuching. There was also that story about the two who went up-country from Sibu and Igan, and another from Bintulu."

"That was old Jeru. Word has it he's dead."

"Maybe. But this sounds like the same come-on. And it sounds like the same diamond. Huge thing, high quality, native won't sell but he will take them to where he found it. If it's not Jeru then it could be someone else playing the same game. If a native finds a gemstone and sells it, he spends the little he got, and that's the end of it. This way that stone represents a permanent income. Rifles, ammo, blankets, trinkets, food, clothing, tools, and trade goods . . . and every few months a new supply."

"Fantastic idea." Vandover rubbed his long jaw. "It sounds like that old blighter of a Jeru, or his ghost. Maybe he figured he was getting too well known to keep doing it himself."

"It could be," Fairchild agreed. "You'd better call Kuching on it. Sounds to me like a police matter."

My scotch tasted good, and the furniture on the verandah was comfortable. Turning the glass in my fingers, I looked over at Fairchild. "Using your outboard? It is a police matter but I don't think it can wait. That fathead can fry in his own juice for all I care, but I'd not like to see Helen Lacklan trapped because of him."

"Use it," Fairchild assented. "If Rector wasn't due in to-morrow I'd go with you."

———

By DAYLIGHT THE native huts and banana and rubber plantations were behind us. Only Raj accompanied me. Although a Sea Dyak of the coast, his mother was Penan, one of the forest people. His uncles had occasionally taken him off on long migrations following the wild sego harvest and he spoke a number of the inland dialects. He knew of old Jeru as well and liked none of what he'd heard. From a *blotto,* the hollowed-out tree trunk that is the native boat, he learned from three natives that the boy and his two white clients were six hours ahead of us.

Raj sat up in the bow of the canoe, on the other side of my quickly loaded supplies. The strong brown stream was muddy and there were occasional logs, but this outboard was a good one and we were making better time than Lacklan would be making. I did not attempt to overtake them because I neither wanted them to think me butting in nor did I want their guide to know I was following.

I was carrying a Mauser big-game rifle, a beautiful weapon. It gave me a comforting feeling to have the gun there as I watched the boat push its way up the Baram. The river trended slightly to the south-southeast and then took a sharp bend east, flowing down from among a lot of eight-thousand-foot peaks. Mostly jungle, yet there were places where stretches of tableland waved with grass. This was wild country, rarely visited, and there were small herds of wild pigs and a good many buffalo.

We avoided villages as the necessary social activity that would accompany our stopping would slow us down considerably. I made camp on a small island cut off from shore by a few yards of rushing water. We slung our hammocks, draped mosquito netting over them, and slid into our dry clothes to sleep.

AS WE PRESSED on the river narrowed and grew increasingly swift. We were well into the Kapuas Mountains, the rugged chain that is the spine of Borneo and terminates in the thirteen-thousand-foot dome of Kinabalu. The air was clear and the heat less oppressive at the increased altitude. At times we pushed through patches of water flowers miles long and so thick it looked like we could have gotten out of the boat and walked.

I put on a bit more speed for the motor would soon be useless in the rocks and shallower rapids and I wanted to be able to catch up when necessary. We ascended cascades, the easier ones with the outboard howling at full throttle, the more difficult by shoving and hauling the boat through torrents of water streaming between the rocks and over low falls.

I wondered how the Lacklans were making out; I couldn't really imagine John Lacklan in chest-deep water pushing a canoe ahead of him. And though she might be willing to try, I couldn't imagine him allowing Helen to do such a menial job. How they were negotiating the river was a question that worried me because if neither of the Lacklans were doing the physical work, then there had to be more natives helping out besides just the one guide. The crew of the *blotto* had not mentioned the number in the crew and I'd heard no mention of an outboard like mine . . . that meant oarsmen and probably two boats to split the weight of both the men and supplies into manageable amounts. So that meant four to eight natives, I hesitated to guess at their tribe and if they were from Jeru's group, that was probably a moot point.

"Raj," I called forward, "how many boats do you think they have?" We were stopped in a shallow sandy part of the stream at the top of a rocky cascade. I was bailing the water from the canoe and Raj was carefully wiping off our equipment. We were both soaking wet.

"Two, boss."

"And how many men on paddles, four?"

"Six. Two paddle in each boat, one rests."

I looked up at him narrowly. "How the hell do you know that?"

"I can see them!" He grinned at me and pointed . . .

In the distance, through some trees and across the river, two boats were turning into the shore. I sloshed around for a better look. It was midafternoon and it looked like they were going to camp. There were two big dugouts each with four people in them and as I watched the men in the bows jumped out and dragged the hollowed-out logs up onto the shore. In one boat was a slender figure in a wide straw hat, that must be Helen, and in the other sat John Lacklan, wearing a cork sun helmet. For an instant his glasses flashed in the sun as he rose from the boat.

"We'd better pull out here and camp ourselves. I don't want to be seen."

We hauled the boat to shore, built a smoky fire to keep the sand flies away, and as Raj began to make camp I took my field glasses and crept along the bank to a spot across the river from the Lacklan camp. I slid in behind a decomposing log covered in plates of bracket fungus and focused my binoculars on the beach across the river.

Two of the tattooed natives were cooking a pot of what had to be rice and another had walked upstream and dropped a line into the water, patiently waiting for a fish to strike. The three others had vanished into the forest. Lacklan was sitting on the sand jotting notes in a book or journal and Helen was tying up their hammocks. I put down the glasses and glanced around. My spot was back within the tree line and relatively dry, even so it wouldn't be long before the leeches got at me.

The air over the river was thick with brightly colored butter-flies, some as big as my hand. They fluttered in and out of patches of sunlight like continuously falling leaves. I squinted through the lenses again. Lacklan looked comfortable on his small crescent of beach. The fisherman and one of the cooks looked to be in their mid-thirties, hard capable men, though small. Each had a *parang* at his side and near the kit of one of the natives that I assumed had gone into the jungle was an old single-barreled shotgun, its stock held together with copper wire.

The fisherman looked up suddenly and the two other members of the boat crews came wandering back into camp. With them was a slight younger man whose posture was somehow more assertive than the older men, tough as they might be. This would be the boy I'd been told about. He wore a button-down shirt that was missing most of its buttons and was tucked into an old pair of dungarees. The clothes were castoffs from someone down in the settlements but he wore them with a certain flair. Unlike the others, he did not have the traditionally pierced ears. Over his eyes he had on a set of sunglasses, the type that aviators tended to wear. The returning men sat close around the rice pot and the fisherman returned to his chore.

I was getting set to pull back into the trees and make my way back to our camp when I saw Helen walk away from the spit of beach across the river. She had obviously been waiting for the other men to come back, because as soon as they sat down she walked over to the place where Lacklan was sitting and spoke to him, then she picked up a small pack and walked away.

She headed downriver and in a moment was out of sight, lost in a tangle of vines and tree trunks. I slid back a ways, then moved through the forest on my side of the river, trying to catch up. If she went too far I was afraid she'd see our camp. Unless the two of them ran into trouble I was not of a mind to try explaining what I was doing there to a para-noid little tyrant like John Lacklan. I moved downstream as quickly as I could without being seen. Noise wasn't a problem here because the river would drown out anything short of a gunshot.

I dodged back toward the water and crouched down. I couldn't see anything. Then, I noticed some movement on the bank upstream of where I had been looking. It was a piece of fabric moving in the breeze. The khaki blouse that Helen Lacklan had been wearing hung from a branch near a calm backwater. Now, what . . . ?

Alarmed, I almost stood up. Then there was a bursting spray of silver as Helen's head appeared above the surface and shook the water from her hair. She swam for the bank and I would like to say that I was gentleman enough to avert my eyes when she climbed out but that in all honesty would not be true.

She fumbled with a pile of gray fabric on the sand that I now realized was the pants that she had been wearing, and then splashed back into the water with a bar of soap in her hand and began to wash.

The idea of a bath reminded me that I might not get one myself until I got back to Marudi, unless I could share Helen Lacklan's soap. An entertaining but not very realistic thought. Before I was tempted to watch when Helen climbed out again and got dressed, I slipped away from the riverbank and made my way back to camp.

―――――

THE NEXT DAY, travel was harder. We had to creep our way slowly upriver, cautiously coming around every bend, always alert for the chance that John Lacklan's canoes had stopped or that there would be a stretch of river long enough for them to look back and see us trailing them. To make matters worse, although they were heavily loaded, there was an extra man to switch off paddling in each of their boats and in the rougher spots all of them, including John and Helen, helped out. We had the outboard but I was afraid to start the damned thing because of the noise. It had enabled us to catch up but now we merely had its weight to contend with.

Mountains loomed up around us and the way was narrower. Somewhere, hidden in these peaks, I had heard there were huge caves. We were nearing the place where I had originally found my diamonds, a long day or two and we'd be there.

That gave me an idea. What would happen if I dropped into the Lacklan camp some afternoon and let them know my old diamond placer was nearby? John would almost certainly object but I wondered if he wouldn't be tempted to take a day or two out to see what might be found there. With luck I could derail the whole plan, if there was a plan at all. I leaned forward to speak to Raj. "Jeru's camp, does anyone know where it is?"

"No, boss. Very far upriver." He paused for a moment. "If I was Jeru I would not be on river. Policemans, they do not like to get out of the boat. They do not like jungle because their rifles are no good."

He was right, the limited light, limited range, and plentiful cover in the forest did reduce the effectiveness of firearms considerably.

"I have heard on the coast that the pirate Jeru went to a longhouse where all mans dead of sickness. He took longhouse for those who follow him. They are all very bad. They take heads, even now they take heads."

If Borneo is famous for one thing it is its native headhunters. As romantically gruesome as the practice is, it had been dramatically curtailed in recent years, at least along the coast. In the interior, the severed heads of tribal enemies are still kept for their magical power, and a freshly taken head has the most power.

The sun was just touching the rim of the mountains when Lacklan's boats tucked into the shore and Raj and I stopped paddling and let the current carry us back downstream about half a mile before finding a place to camp.

As was becoming my habit I took my field glasses and started upriver, out of camp. At the last moment Raj's voice stopped me for a moment.

"Boss?" I turned to where he was standing by the fire. "If there no trouble, we hunt for diamonds, okay?"

"Sure, Raj," I said. "We're up here, might as well." He was right. I'd given up the canal job to come after the Lacklans;

we were using up the supplies I'd bought for them and nothing lucrative awaited us back in Marudi. On the day after tomorrow I would drop in on my favorite tourists and find out if I could get them away from their guides. Then we'd see if we could dig some diamonds. I didn't want to return from this fool's errand with nothing. On top of it all I had a sixteen-year-old Dyak kid who thought I was just enough off my rocker that he had to remind me occasionally to keep my eyes on the target.

THE RIVER WAS wide here, and though I was farther away than the first time I had spied on the Lacklans, the water was slow enough that I could hear some of what was going on in their camp. There was a clank of pots as one of the older men laid out his cooking supplies, the hard bark of an ax as someone back in the forest chopped wood.

Helen Lacklan sat in a patch of sunlight reading a book. From its bright red cover and small size I recognized it as a popular guidebook on Indonesia and Malaysia. John Lacklan sat in the boat cleaning his gun. It looked from this distance to be a bolt-action Winchester; with an ebony cap on the forestock I figured that it was one of the fancier models. From its long barrel and scope and the fact that the Lacklans came from New Mexico I assumed that it was his prized gun for deer or bighorn sheep . . . whichever, it wasn't the best weapon for the jungle. This was a place where speed and maneuverability counted most. As I watched he carefully depressed the stop and slid the bolt back into the rifle, then pressed five long cartridges back into its magazine. For the first time I was glad he was armed.

He tucked his cleaning supplies into a small pack and then stalked over to a mound of supplies and set the rifle down. He paused and made a comment to Helen but she barely looked up. He stood there, tension building up in him, for a moment, but then broke off and went to the other end of the camp. I realized that I was witnessing an argument or the aftermath of one.

Over the wash of the river, slow and quiet at this point, I

heard a man's voice raised in anger. Then John Lacklan was standing over Helen yelling and gesticulating wildly. His thin face was turning a dark red under the fresh burn he'd been getting, and although I couldn't understand the words, his voice was hoarse. Suddenly, Helen threw her book at him and leaped to her feet. The red-covered guidebook bounced off of his shoulder and he backed up a step. She advanced toward him and it almost looked like she was daring him to hit her. They paused and he backed away. In some way, she had called his bluff.

I squirmed back into the shadows of the forest. At the last minute as I headed back to my camp I noticed the flamboyantly dressed Iban boy and two of the men from the boat crew standing in the tree shadows across from me. The older crewmen had averted their gazes with expressions of shock and embarrassment on their faces; such outbursts of emotion as they had just witnessed were not considered at all acceptable in Malaya, but the boy studied them carefully and with a knowing smirk from behind his dark glasses.

———

I LAY IN MY hammock that night wondering what would happen tomorrow afternoon when I faced them again. It was going to be awkward and I was going to have to act like there was never any problem between us. I didn't know if they would accept the story I was going to make up about deciding to use their supplies to look for diamonds, but it probably made more sense than what I was actually up to.

Had I really followed them hoping for the worst so that I could step in and rescue Helen Lacklan and make her husband look the fool that I took him to be? And if that was true how much of a fool was he? He had chosen another guide to keep his wife and I apart. I had thought the idea amusing at the time, then I'd thought it dangerous. I had had one short opportunity to appreciate Helen Lacklan and I doubted if she had given much thought, if any, to me. But here I was, following them through the bush and rapidly developing a case that would do a sophomore proud on a married woman I hardly knew. Paranoid he might be but I was beginning to guess few people called John Lacklan stupid.

Well, I would follow along for one more day, until we reached my old diamond placer, then I would do my best to divert them from whatever this Iban boy had planned. If they didn't want to follow me I would leave them to their destiny.

For better or for worse, I thought, I was back upriver. Even though it had cost me all the supplies that Lacklan had paid for, supplies that I might have sold, and losing the canal-cleaning job. I realized I'd better make the best of it. This was what I'd wanted all along: another chance at the diamonds. I drifted off to sleep as a soft rain began tapping at the shelter half strung over my mosquito net. Somehow I'd gotten what I'd wanted all along.

———

A HIGH-PITCHED CRACK OF thunder brought me awake just before dawn. I lay listening, waiting for the echoes to roll back from the mountains or down the river canyon. Through some trick of the rain or the forest vegetation the echo didn't come. I thought about returning home with the money from a diamond find in my pocket . . . I thought about returning home with enough to explain my having disappeared into the Far East for almost two years.

An hour later when the gibbon monkeys began to noisily greet the sun, Raj rolled out of his hammock and made up some breakfast. We didn't take long to get packed. I walked up the riverbank, the water running slightly higher because of last night's rain, just far enough to see if the Lacklans had left camp yet. Their boats were gone so we pushed out into the stream and dug our paddles in against the current.

Around us the forest released great plumes of steam as the sun's heat cut into the trees. Trunks, some two hundred feet tall, leaned out over the water leaving only the narrowest slot of sky overhead. In the jungle itself one rarely could see more than sixty yards without the view being blocked by the growth. Even the tops of the trees were obscured by a much lower canopy with only the massive trunks hinting at the true size of the forest giants.

We pushed past the Lacklans' campsite from the night before. They must have had an early start because their fire was cold, not even a thin line of smoke rising from behind the piled-up rocks they had used as a hearth. The shadows between the boles of the trees behind their camp were black as night, the few penetrating rays of the morning sun overshooting this area to glance off the emerald leaves of the higher forest.

Suddenly I stopped paddling. The canoe lost momentum and Raj looked around quickly.

"Boss? What's wrong?"

Hidden under the trees, deep within the shadows but not quite deep enough to keep the morning light from revealing it, was the stern of a *blotto*.

"Turn in!" I commanded, and we made for the shore.

Leaving Raj to haul our boat out of the water I grabbed up my gun and splashed up onto the rocky beach. I hit the darkness of the forest and froze, letting my eyes adjust.

The two dugouts rested in narrow lanes between the trees, back along the shore were drag marks from where they had been pulled out of the water and across the mud flat to the jungle. Everything, supplies, mining equipment, camping gear, everything but the paddles were gone!

Could they have headed away from the river to a legitimate place to placer for diamonds? Had they hidden the canoes or just pulled them away from the rising waters of the river? I walked back out to their campsite.

The fire was dead and there was no sign it had been doused with water. They had not had breakfast.

Then I saw it. Shining brightly in a patch of sunlight; the answer to my questions . . . the worst answer to my questions. A long thin cylinder of brass. I picked it up and turned it over. It was stamped .30-06. The empty cartridge casing smelled powerfully of gunpowder even in this dampness. It had not been thunder I had heard just before dawn. It had been John Lacklan's rifle!

I HAD TRACKED ANIMALS while hunting in Arizona and Nevada but following a trail in the jungles of Borneo was a different experience altogether. Luckily, the Lacklans and their captors had left camp after the rain stopped and they were not trying to hide their trail. The fact that there were ten of them heavily laden with the goods from the canoes helped also.

Raj and I were burdened only with water, light packs, our *parangs*—Raj's being more along the lines of a traditional headhunting sword, thus larger than mine—and my rifle.

They left occasional slip marks in the mud, breaks or machete cuts on protruding branches and vines. The trail was not hard to follow. But another problem soon became apparent.

Away from the river we found ourselves climbing a tall ridge cut by many small streams. The trail then followed the top of the ridge as it switchbacked along between the Baram River on one side and a deeply cut canyon on the other. Visibility was so limited and the landscape so broken that although I could easily follow the trail or backtrack my own path I had no idea which direction was north, south, east, or west. I could barely tell which way was up- or downriver unless I could see the water close up and by now we were hundreds of feet above the banks. To make matters worse it was dark, dark as deep twilight, and the humidity had increased tremendously. I was overheated, slick with sweat, and making far too much noise as I pushed along the trail.

Raj was doing better than I and it wasn't only because of his youth. Although he had lived his life in Marudi he often went with his uncles to the forest and had some of the natural ease of the jungle peoples. He seemed to be able to instinctively place his feet in the most solid spots whether we were climbing over rocks covered with wet moss or skirting a deep bog of leaf mold. I dropped our pace to the point where I could follow him more exactly, and in relative silence, we pressed on.

By noon we seemed no closer to our quarry and I was down to the last of my canteen. We stopped by a brook that cascaded down the dim mountainside and had some dried pork while I boiled water on a tiny gas stove I had bought for the Lacklans. I didn't always purify my water when I was in the bush but this would be a disastrous time to get sick so we waited while the stove hissed and the pot finally boiled. Raj harvested a vine growing nearby and after pounding it with a rock he made a paste that we rubbed on our legs. *"Kulit elang,"* he said. "Will help a couple hours, leeches don't like." We pressed on.

———

THE DIM LIGHT under the tree canopy was fading and the black cicadas had started their rasping, throbbing chorus when we reached what seemed to be our destination. We were on another river, much smaller than the Baram, and tucked back in the trees at the edge of a gravel bank was a decrepit longhouse. Dugouts were pulled up on the bank and all around the main dwelling stretched a wasteland of squalor such as I had only seen in the native villages that had become ghettos because of their closeness to the large coastal cities.

The last of the sunlight was striking the overgrown slopes of the nearby mountains and the river valley was in shadow but I could barely make out overgrown fields and collapsed farm huts behind the ring of trash that had been ejected over the years from the longhouse. In most cases a Dyak long-house is a fascinating structure; built up, off the ground and out of the floodplains on stilts, sometimes as much as twenty feet high, the interior of the building is twenty feet from floor to ceiling and often over one hundred feet long. Its roof and sides are made of a kind of native thatch or sheathed in tin, where available. Although surrounded by farming huts and storehouses it is the communal dwelling for the entire village.

This longhouse was one of the smaller ones and obviously very old. One corner was drooping dangerously on poorly repaired stilts and in this and other areas the verandah had all but given way. Across the distance I could hear harsh laughter and a slight strain of *sapeh* music on the wind, lights could be seen coming on through the doors and breaks in the walls.

Raj edged closer, he seemed jumpy, his fingers toyed with the hilt of his *parang*.

"You were right, boss." He whispered, although we were a good half mile away. "This is the longhouse of *Tuan* Jeru."

I was surprised by his use of the term *"Tuan,"* which indicates respect, and by his nervous whisper. I had seen Raj stand calmly by and thrust the same *parang* he was now nervously tapping deep into the side of a boar that attacked one of our workmen on a construction job. He had then pivoted like a matador and finished the enormous animal off when it turned to attack him instead. He had been barely fifteen at the time.

"Are you afraid of going in there? Tell me why?" I wasn't feeling too good about it myself but I figured I better know as much as possible.

Raj's chin came up and the dying light in the sky glinted in his eyes. "I am not afraid of any man!" he stated flatly. "But it is said that *Tuan* Jeru is a *bali saleng,* a black ghost, that he has killed many mans and taken their blood to bless the buildings of the English and Dutch and now for the oil companies."

"Do you believe that?" I demanded. "You've worked with me on many buildings. Have you ever seen a foreigner take the time to make a sacrifice of blood or anything else?"

"No . . ."

I wasn't sure that this was really the right argument to use and I actually had a fair amount of respect for the beliefs of Raj and his people, but if he went in there scared, witch doctor or not, Jeru would take advantage of the situation.

"How many do you think are down there?"

"If the stories are true, twenty mans, maybe ten womans, maybe more."

"What else do the stories say?" I asked.

"The mans of *Tuan* Jeru are *sakit hati;* they are killers and rapists from the oil camps and towns on the coast. No village would have them. They are collectors of blood and they take heads to make magic."

"Do you want to stay here, guard our backs?" I gave him a chance to get out with honor.

"I will go with you, boss," the boy said.

"Good. Now, what do you think is going on down there?"

"I think they have big *arak* party. Everyone get very drunk. They have all new trade goods, shotgun shell, fancy rifle. I think we wait."

"What about the Lacklans? Will they be all right?"

Raj paused, he wanted to tell me what he thought I wanted to hear but he knew I would press him for the truth. "I don't know, boss," he said. "I think maybe they cut off man's head. The woman, I don't know . . . These people, they not Iban, not Kayan, not Kelabit," he named off the three major tribal groups, "they something different now . . . outlaws, you know. I bet they get drunk like Iban though, you'll see."

I hoped so, because outlaws or not I was betting that just like a normal village they had plenty of dogs and roosters. The typical longhouse celebration in Sarawak was a roaring drunk and I hoped that was what they were building up to because otherwise we weren't going to get in there without raising an alarm.

I wanted to be ready when the moment came, so we moved in closer, carefully waded through the rushing waters of the stream, and circled away downwind of the skeletal silhouette of the longhouse. We settled down just inside the secondary tree line and waited to see what would happen. The noise from inside was getting louder and I was sure that Raj had been right about them working themselves up to an all-night drunk. I just wasn't sure what was going to happen to John and Helen . . . or when.

They might be dead already and I couldn't wait much longer without trying to find out. I decided to split the difference; wait another hour but if I heard a commotion I'd go in with the rifle and hope for the best. If there were twenty men in the longhouse, at least five would have the cheap single-shot shotguns that were common in the backcountry of Borneo. Someone in there had possession of Lacklan's deer rifle and certainly there would be a full complement of spears, blowpipes, and machetes. My only hope was to get in and get as many of them covered as possible before anyone thought to grab a weapon. It wasn't much of a plan; get in fast, get out fast, and put my confidence in the local *arak's* potency.

Now, in my experience, *arak* has the punch of the best (or worst, depending on your expectations) moonshine. It seemed to have the chemical properties of torpedo fuel or the infamous "Indian whiskey" that was made in the old days in Oklahoma. One shot would make you stagger, a couple more would make you stupid. Imbibing further could leave one blind or even dead. Waiting for a level of intoxication that would give me an edge was a risky business.

About a half hour later two men staggered out on the verandah and hung over the railing. They alternated between what sounded like telling jokes and laughing hysterically with being violently ill. After three or four rounds of this odd combination of social interaction they parted, one going back into the light and noise of the longhouse, the other slumped, snoring, against the railing. The sound of the crowd inside had taken on a harsher tone and I figured I'd better move in before something bad happened . . . if it hadn't already.

Touching Raj on the shoulder I slipped past him and made my way down toward the river. We crept in past the outer circle of trash and one of my worst fears came suddenly true.

Three dogs rushed us out of the darkness under the longhouse. Barking and snarling they rushed through the moonlight like dark missiles, low to the ground . . . missiles with pale flashing teeth.

I took a swipe at the first with my rifle butt and connected heavily. It backed off yelping. Raj moved quickly, snatching up the smallest of them by grabbing a fist of flesh on either side of the dog's neck just below the ears. He spun in a tight circle with the frantic beast snapping in his outstretched arms and let go, hurling the dog far out into the river. I clubbed with my rifle again, and drawing his *parang,* Raj swatted an animal with the flat of the blade. The two remaining dogs backed up, growling but no longer willing to attack. I was just beginning to curse our luck and wonder if we should either hide or charge the ladder to the longhouse when a door above us slammed open and a man staggered out onto the verandah and called out into the night in what sounded like Iban.

Instantly Raj answered in an angry adult tone I'd never heard him use before. The man above us muttered something and then whistled sharply and called out some kind of command. We stood frozen in the darkness as he wandered back inside and closed the door.

Raj heaved a sigh of relief and I turned to peer into the darkness where he was standing. "What, in the name of God, was that all about?" I demanded.

He laughed, a giddy, semihysterical cackle. "I told him to call off his damn dogs!"

WE WERE A moment getting our wind back, then we worked our way under the longhouse and edged toward the back where, because of the slope of the gravel, the stilts were not so long. The ground beneath the building stank from garbage and worse. Above us feet tramped rhythmically on the ancient plank floor and shrill voices cried out. Toward the back the floor was low over our heads and then I was boosting Raj onto the verandah, and swinging up myself. Moving carefully on the weathered boards we eased up to a crack in the wall and peered in.

The light was probably dim, but with our pupils dilated by hours in the darkness it was blinding. Raj backed up for a moment and I blinked and squinted. In the center of a seated group a dancer leaped and whirled, his moves theatrically depicting . . . something, I couldn't tell what. There were men and women in the room, but fewer women than I had thought. Bottles, mostly old beer and wine, were lying about. Some were obviously empty, others still in use. I knew from past experience that they no longer held beer or wine; they had been filled and refilled time and again with *arak*.

The dancer disappeared from view and another took his place. He was a thin old man but he moved with an energy that, while not youthful, was surprisingly vigorous. He whirled and stomped, spinning a parang over his head with a glittering flash of steel. I suddenly saw that the dark area that I had noticed on one side of his face was not a shadow or a tattoo but a deep and twisted mass of scar tissue. He mimed climbing onto something higher than himself, something that moved unsteadily. He fought, he carried something away. He was raiding a ship or a boat . . . this must be Jeru! Not only was he here, still alive after all these years, but he was telling his story in a dance.

I bent to Raj's ear. "Is that him?"

The boy nodded; his body alive with fear and excitement.

"You watch our backs," I told him. I didn't want him working up a scare by watching this man that he believed to be a witch and I didn't want both of us to be night blind.

When I turned back to the crack Jeru was hacking his way through the forest and then something . . . he mimed men marching and everyone laughed. He was showing them he'd been chased by soldiers, paddled up a river, cut off men's heads with his *parang*. He stepped out of sight for a moment and came back with a long Japanese military rifle. He shook it in the air and then after handing it to someone, mimed cutting off what I surmised to be the Japanese soldier's head. He pointed to the roof with a harsh cry and, crouching, I could see a cluster of dark spheres hanging from the rafters. Severed heads. No doubt the unfortunate Jap was one of them.

The story continued with Jeru finding something in a stream. He held the imaginary something up to the light, turning it this way and that. He reached for his neck and pulled a leather strap off, over his head. In a setting or basket of leather there gleamed a stone.

This was it. The huge diamond that he had used for many years to lure men upriver, never to return. A diamond of fabulous size and quality, so the story went; from where I was all I could tell was that it was large and wrapped in braided strings of leather. It glowed rather than flashed, for this was a raw stone with none of the facets of a cut one, but there was a white fire hiding deep within it.

The old man took on a posture of humility, he moved stiffly, portraying a sense of age that obviously was not his natural state. Again, he got a laugh. He was showing the stone to someone, offering it, walking away as if disinterested, then leading them on. He took an old stove-in pith helmet from the place it hung on the wall and wore it for a moment as he paddled an imaginary boat. Then he was himself again and, beating his companion to the ground, he drew his *parang* and cut off the man's head.

The audience was silent now and a sense of tension penetrated the wall and clutched at my heart. Even Raj, eyes turned to the night, could feel it and he moved closer to me, his hand on his knife.

————

JOHN LACKLAN STAGGERED into view, pushed along by the rough shoves of the boy who had been his guide. His hands were tied, his clothing torn, his body scratched and bruised. How badly he had been treated I didn't know; the trip through the jungle might have left him in the condition that he was in. I admired him in that moment, though, for he held his head high, in his eyes was the hollow look of fear but he didn't beg, or cry, or even tremble. He was keeping himself together although I thought I could tell that it was a near thing.

Without looking away I ran a shell into the chamber of my rifle and set the safety. I wasn't at all sure about my original plan of barging in and spiriting them away; there were easily as many shotguns in the room as I had expected plus the Japanese rifle and the boy carried Lacklan's Winchester over his shoulder. Not only were there more guns than I would have liked but several were cradled in the hands of Jeru's outlaws, held casually but ready for use.

The boy stepped in behind Lacklan and kicked the back of his left knee, knocking him to a kneeling position. Lacklan started to get back up but the boy unlimbered the rifle and poked him hard in the kidney with the muzzle. John Lacklan gave a choking cough of pain and collapsed back to the floor. Old Jeru whirled his parang and then tested the edge against his thumb.

"Find me a door!" I whispered to Raj. "Damn quick!"

Now there was a commotion somewhere in the room. "Get off me!" I heard Helen call out. Then she lurched into view, a portly Iban trying to drag her down by one arm. She shook him off; he was surprised, I think, by that same physicality that had caught my attention. She was bigger than he was and lithely powerful.

"Stop it! You stop this!" she yelled at them. Raj was back tugging at my sleeve but the boy, sunglasses pushed up on his forehead, stepped in quickly and pressed the rifle barrel against Helen's throat . . . even if John Lacklan got his head cut off I wasn't going in there if it risked Helen's getting killed.

The boy yelled at her in Iban, then in English. "Sit, missy. You sit or I kill you." He jabbed at her with the gun barrel. "Everybody die, you don't sit down."

She didn't even move.

"You can't kill him. Take our things, our money. You can't kill him!" she cried.

"We're Americans, damn it. Let us go or you'll regret this." John's voice wavered.

In my travels around the world I've noticed that identifying yourself as an American never helps, it just makes the locals get violent or want more money.

The boy shrugged, "We kill Englang, Dutch . . . America, who cares." He suddenly spoke in his own tongue for a moment and everyone laughed. Old Jeru the hardest.

"You don't want John's head." Helen spoke in a manner that let me know she wanted all to hear. "I know that Dyak tribesmen only take the heads of powerful enemies, of warriors. The head of a strong man is magic but a weak man . . . a weak man is nothing. My husband is not a warrior, he's not even a strong man. Did he walk here? No. You had to carry him over the last hill . . ."

"Be quiet, Helen!" John hissed. "Don't make this any worse than it is."

But she ignored him. "He's a scholar. What are you going to say? There are the heads of the Japanese soldiers, we fought their machine guns with knives but we won. There is the head of the man who read books, aren't we brave!"

The boy turned to Jeru and they spoke quietly for a moment. Others in the crowd seemed a bit nervous. The bottles started being passed around again but with them there started a low mutter of conversation.

Jeru spoke and the boy turned to Helen with a smirk. He spoke in Iban to the crowd and there was scattered laughter but it sounded forced. He said to her, "We cut off head; see what happens. No magic, we throw out!"

"No!" she cried and started to say something else but John bellowed at her.

"Helen, shut up! Just shut up!" He was almost crying in fear or frustration. He lurched to his feet and the boy smashed the butt of the rifle into the pit of his stomach. I was ready to move and Raj was even tugging me toward the door when Helen threw herself on the boy. Jeru knocked her to the floor but John charged him. With his hands tied all he could have done would have been to knock Jeru down but the old man deftly rapped John Lacklan on the head with the butt of his *parang* and Lacklan went to the floor, out cold.

Jeru hawked and spat. Then with a further growl of disgust he dragged Lacklan into a corner and dropped him. He motioned to the boy and the young man led the quietly sobbing Helen to the same spot, then they both stepped forward to the seated group and took up *arak* bottles.

I got the feeling that there had been a reprieve of sorts and I'd better make the best of it. Pulling myself away from the scene beyond the crack in the wall I let my eyes readjust to the darkness. When my vision started to come back I motioned Raj ahead of me. "Let's get on the ground, we've got to get to work."

We dropped down under the longhouse and I made my way back to the spot where the broken floor sagged toward the mud. This whole corner of the building was ready to collapse and I figured that it would be unlikely that anyone would be using it for anything. I shrugged out of my pack and dug out my mountaineer stove. I pumped up the pressure and fired it. Using the light from the flame I found a place where several broken logs and a piece of the *attap* thatch wall all lay together. I wedged the stove into the broken wood just under the thatch and let the plume of fire bite into the thatch.

I grabbed Raj and led him back to the spot where we had climbed onto the longhouse verandah.

"You stay here. When I come back I'm going to be coming fast, if anyone needs help getting off the porch you help. If you run into any of Jeru's people . . ."

"I know what to do, boss." He tapped the hilt of his *parang*.

"Right. If I'm not with you, go straight up the hill and follow the crest east, okay?"

I pulled myself up onto the aging boards again, and careful to walk along a crosspiece so as to make less noise, I slid up to the wall and took a fast glance through the crack. Heavily tattooed bodies moved back and forth, momentarily obscuring my vision. Nothing much was going on but more people were up and around. Well, that couldn't be helped.

I moved along the wall to the door that Raj had found. I breathed deep and waited for the fire to catch. Suddenly there was an excited burst of Iban from inside the building, the sound of running feet and a breaking bottle. It was only then that I smelled smoke. There was a rush of feet and a door in the front of the place crashed open. I couldn't see what was happening but I figured someone was going for water. I didn't move until I heard the crash of the floor giving way.

———

I HIT THE DOOR and came into the big room with the Mauser up, sling around my left arm. The long room was filled with smoke and the back, where I had started the fire, was listing. Flames were beginning to take the roof. An older man stood right in front of me with a bottle in his hand, he seemed to be standing back, bemused, while the main crowd moved toward the blaze. I dropped the rifle from my shoulder and clipped him on the side of the head as I went past.

A woman tore by me and in the confusion didn't even notice that I was there. Someone seemed to have fallen through the burning floor and that was fine with me. I dropped beside the Lacklans pulling my knife.

Lacklan twisted around in panic and kicked at me with both feet as I reached for his arms. Helen got it first.

"John, stop! It's help."

I grabbed one of the kicking feet and cut off the ropes that bound them, when they had tied his feet I didn't know. She extended her hands to me and I quickly swiped the blade between them catching the bindings by luck. Then there was the roar of an explosion and a scattering of bird shot tore into my boot and ankle like a swarm of angry bees. I dropped the knife and turned, bringing the rifle up.

A short, tattooed native struggled to reload his crude shotgun. Others stood behind him frozen, but they were all looking at me. Suddenly one of the men in back came up with the Japanese rifle, I didn't even know I had him in my sights until I squeezed the trigger.

The concussion in the long room was even louder than the shotgun. The rifleman went down and all hell broke loose. Men and women scattered, two shotguns belched fire in the light of the roaring flames, throwing huge plumes of white smoke. I wasn't hit but burning paper and powder smoldered in my clothes. I put three shots into the crowd as fast as I could work the bolt and then I was pushing Lacklan toward the door and praying that Helen was following. In my last look the room was an inferno of flame, burning thatch falling from the ceiling. Around the cluster of heads hanging from the rafters wasps swarmed in panic, driven from their nests in the empty eyes and mouths by the heat and smoke.

We crashed out into the fire-streaked night. Lacklan stumbled and a man dropped a bucket of water and came at me with a knife. I deflected it with my rifle barrel and kicked him hard on the hip. He fell and I gave him another in the face. The gun was empty and I had no time to reload.

I pulled Helen past me, pointed to the end of the verandah, and yelled, "Go! Find Raj!"

I turned, knowing that to run at that moment would be the end of me. Three men rushed forward in the shifting light and I went to meet them. I clubbed and punched and kicked and bit. One cut me across the back. Then I was on the wooden floor slamming my knee into his midsection. My rifle flopped uselessly, its sling still entwined with my arm.

There was a flare of light and an explosion of wood. One of my attackers threw himself off of me and there was Jeru, standing over me holding a pistol so ancient it must have come to Sarawak with the first white rajah. I twisted sharply, Jeru fired again, missing. He struggled to cock the enormous relic, twisting the cylinder by hand. I scrambled sideways, put a knee into someone's stomach; suddenly I was fighting with one of the men who attacked me again. We struggled, turned, and then hit the railing of the verandah. With a splintering crash at least twenty feet of it let go and we were falling.

In midair I pushed away from the man I was fighting, hit the ground, and rolled. My rifle, still bound to my arm by a twist of the sling, rapped me on the back of the head. My vision went gray but I heard Jeru's gun bellow and the hard bite of black powder hit my nostrils. He was leaning over the railing peering into the darkness, the torn side of his face a dark knot of rage. I grabbed my rifle and ran underneath the burning longhouse.

Flames licked along the floor above me. The structure groaned as walls twisted and buckled. In back, the corner where I had started the fire was dark. Someone had managed to put out the flames, a futile gesture for the fire had spread to the rest of the building.

I made it to the darkness and looked back. The dim forms of Jeru's men began to appear in the firelight. Some ran off toward the river, probably for more water, but four or five of them started forward under the building, coming after me.

I'd had just about enough. I snapped four fresh cartridges into the magazine of the Mauser and dropped a fifth into the chamber. I backed up farther into the darkness and brought the rifle up. I took aim at the first man, then shifted to one of the pilings beside him. I fired and splinters flew. They dropped to the ground but then came on, worming their way forward through the debris under the longhouse. The first had a shotgun and the second man carried a long blowpipe with a spear blade bound to one end. I squinted, fired, and the heavy bullet took the blowpipe man along the top of the shoulder as I had intended, then burned the back of his calf. He screamed, and I ran, blindly, uphill into the jungle.

I NEARLY TOOK A header into some kind of hole, leaves whipped my face, and I slowed down. I cursed myself for not killing both of the men I'd shot at under the longhouse. I had a total of nine bullets left, three in the gun and six jingling in my pocket, I couldn't afford to waste them.

I had to find Raj and the Lacklans. If they hadn't made it out I'd have to go back . . . I wasn't looking forward to suicide.

I cut left along the hillside, heading in the direction they would have taken if they had gone straight up the hill. I stopped to catch my breath and found I couldn't keep my knees from shaking. I squatted down, sucking air, and felt the prickles of adrenaline recede from my limbs. I had shot a man. Several actually, but one of them I had killed for sure. Unbidden, a phrase that my father had used came to mind, "If you fool around with a bandwagon, you're liable to get hit with a horn." It wasn't as amusing as it had been but I was realizing that it didn't only apply to me getting into this situation, it applied to those poor chaps I'd shot, too.

Those men down there had lived as traditional Iban and Kayan or whatever. Some, perhaps many, had traveled to the cities and oil fields to try a different kind of life. But somewhere, something had gone wrong. Instead of staying on to collect their paychecks, instead of returning home to farm and fish, they had come here. In a country that was virtually without violent crime they joined with a man who made a living robbing tourists and diamond hunters. A man who was continuing to take heads not of his enemies in war, a practice, if not what I would call civilized, then at least honored by Iban tradition, but of people he had lured into a trap.

Helen had thought quickly back there. She'd confronted that old witch doctor with his own hypocrisy, given other circumstances it might have been funny. It was something else, too, though. Some of those men in there had believed in what she'd said. There was magic in the head of a brave enemy. To take a man's head was, in a strange way, actually an honor. If you had a vision of yourself as a warrior you didn't kill tourists. Helen might have planted a seed of doubt in a few of the men down there. Either old Jeru might have fewer followers come morning or they'd all be coming after me, the more honorable enemy.

I started up the hill again, going slowly in order to make as little noise as possible. In the dark phosphorescent mushrooms glowed dimly. The sounds of insects and animals filled the night, covering the noises that I made but also covering the sounds of anyone who might be following me. It felt like hours since Raj and I had the fight with the dogs but I could still occasionally see the moon through gaps in the trees; I didn't know what time it was but it had been headed down as we approached the longhouse. Higher and higher I climbed, pulling myself along using the trunks of the smaller trees and rocks and handfuls of undergrowth. I was exhausted, my legs were shot, and my arms and lower legs were covered with leeches.

Finally I reached the bare crest of the ridge and looked out across a vast panorama, dimly lit by the setting moon. I turned east and started climbing again.

When the landscape was left in blackness, when the last of the silver light had faded from the sky, I rested. I carefully cleaned the leeches off by feel. One leg was puckered with bird shot but most of it had not penetrated my boot. I stopped myself from touching it. I knew Borneo, it was going to get infected and the less I scared myself the better. I got up and pressed on and it was only a few hundred yards farther when I heard voices ahead.

It was Raj and the Lacklans, and they had collapsed at the foot of a rock outcropping, half dead from exhaustion. "Raj?" I called out; I didn't want him taking a swipe at me in the dark.

"Boss?"

"Yeah. Hold on, I'll be over there in a minute." I picked my way across the rocks toward them.

It was a subdued reunion. We were all dead tired from running and climbing over a thousand feet of mountain. I'm not sure that Helen and John had realized what was going on yet. They were just happy to be away from Jeru's longhouse and all in one piece.

Not long after I got my breath back, I began to notice that it was cold. Now, there's not too many places on the island of Borneo where you could say that but we were well over eight thousand feet and we were all dressed for the heat. To make things worse we were worn-out and the clouds were beginning to pile up against the mountain range, I could feel the moisture on my cheek and lips and when I looked up the stars were dimmer. Raj's teeth were chattering and the Lacklans were huddled together strangely; though Helen was curled up close to him, John was positioned almost as if he was trying to pretend she wasn't there. Well, whatever they were going through was their problem. I was worried about the cold.

"Let's get up," I told them. "We're going to go on a bit farther."

They looked at me uncomprehendingly, but Raj stumbled to his feet and picked up our packs; he had brought mine along from the longhouse somehow.

"Mr. Kardec?" Helen was sitting up. "I don't know if my husband can . . . he hurt his leg before we got to that village."

"Let me see it," I said. "We have to go on. We need some shelter or at least a fire and some food."

Lacklan pulled away from me as I squatted down beside him. "I can make it. I don't need help." Then he said, "I don't need your help."

———

WE HELD TO THE RIDGE and we kept climbing. I needed someplace to camp and this was probably not the place to find it but the slopes on either side of us were too steep to negotiate in the dark, especially given our condition. I was beat, every muscle hurt, and my body begged to stop moving. John had turned his ankle and could walk only with difficulty but he and Helen were managing the altitude the best; after all, they lived near Santa Fe, over a mile above sea level. Raj was cold and something else was bothering him but he wasn't ready to talk about it. He helped John Lacklan along and kept his mouth shut.

Something was going on between John and Helen; she had

tried to help him at first but he was having none of that. Finally, she gave up and he was on his own for a while but then, because he was stumbling badly, Raj offered to help and he'd accepted. Helen came up to me in the dark; she took my hand and pressed the haft of my knife into it. I returned it to its sheath.

"Thank you," she said. After that she walked with me more and more, and while I liked that in some ways, it disturbed me, too.

During a pause to rest I got Raj aside and questioned him on what went on before I joined them. "Nothing," he said. "They just act like they having big fight but they don't fight, they don't talk."

"Did they ask what we were doing here?"

He laughed softly. "Oh, yes. I tell them that you come to save them from the *bali saleng*."

For a Dyak, a people who tend to tell you only what you want to hear, Raj is sometimes too straightforward.

We came to the rocky upthrust of another peak, its blackness vaguely defined in the starlight, but there was shelter here, a bowl of rocks and, within it, the black mouth of a cave. From the sounds in the jungle below I could tell it was still a couple of hours until dawn. Huddled just inside the entrance we rested and I emptied my rucksack onto a rock. I used some peroxide on my leg and poured some across the cut in my back, then got up. With the empty bag I headed back into the night.

"Mr. Kardec, where are you going?" Helen's voice spoke out of the darkness.

"To find some fuel, I'll have to go down into the forest a ways."

"Are we still in danger?"

"I don't know. Come morning I expect they'll be after us."

"And they'll find us, too," Lacklan mumbled softly.

"But will they come up here?" she asked. "I read that many of the tribes feel that there are spirits in the mountains, especially the peaks, and will never go there."

I had heard the same. The natives were very aware of the *Toh,* the spirits of the forest and mountains. An area that was rarely visited was often considered to have dangerous *Toh* and was therefore avoided. It was Sarawak's version of our own self-fulfilling fear of the unknown. The high mountains were reputed to be the home of powerful *Toh*.

I didn't reply as I thought about it. I hoped she was right.

"So, maybe this place is safe. At least that's what I read." She was looking for some reassurance but she didn't get it from her husband.

"You and that confounded guidebook," he snapped. "We don't know that will work!"

"Well if that confounded guidebook is where she learned about headhunting, it probably saved your life." I said I'd had enough of Lacklan's attitude and he wasn't a potential client anymore. "Jeru wasn't even going to sharpen his *parang*."

"I'm glad you enjoyed that at my expense. I'll have you know that the weapons I've made could blow this miserable island off the map."

I was amazed. He was fuming because she had told that bunch of renegades he wasn't a warrior. He was an egomaniac and a fool. Or maybe just a brilliant man who was so small inside that he had become lost in the forest.

"Mr. Lacklan," I told him. "I don't know if you're suicidal or exactly what your problem is but I look at life this way— an adventure is something you return home to tell about. If you don't make it back, it's just an exotic funeral. Be happy Helen did what she did. I am. If she hadn't I might have died because I was stupid enough to try and help you."

"And why did you come after us? Because you are the good Samaritan? Or because you are after my wife?"

"John!" Helen flinched and I could see that he'd aimed that barb more at her than me.

"I don't know," I said, "but this late in the game I'd be a fool to try to figure it out." I grabbed up the knapsack and headed out into the darkness. I started down the slope and Raj came scrambling after me. I hadn't planned on his coming but was just as happy; I knew he would be very uncomfortable if the Lacklans decided to continue the fight.

The purple light of predawn was just coming to the sky as

we made our way along the mountainside about one hundred feet above the forest. I was headed toward an area below us that I had glimpsed from the ridge; it was lighter in color and I was sure it was a rock slide. Where it had hit the trees we might find some downed wood.

Sure enough, it was a slide. A huge lip of rock had flaked off and gone crashing down into the jungle. Underneath the scar were the dark mouths of several caves, probably connected to the cave above where the Lacklans waited. Thirty feet into the tree line we found all the wood we wanted, picking out the dry pieces was easy for little of it was damp. I figured that we were so high that we were above most of the rain that soaked the lower elevations, either that or we were just lucky.

We gathered as much wood as we could fit in our packs and turned to go back up the mountain. For an instant Raj froze and so did I. Between ourselves and the brightening sky was a moving, flickering black cloud. There were bursts of darkness against the sky, a sound like water rushing up a shallow sandy beach; wings, thousands and thousands of wings. The dawning sky was darkened with bats. A thin cloud rising over the jungle, they coalesced into a dense riot of swooping, dodging confusion directly over us. Their wings cupping the thin air they streamed toward the mountainside. Under the scar of the fallen brow of rock, they flew, pouring into the cave mouths just above us.

Then from above us I heard a thin scream. Raj and I looked at each other, then I grabbed up my rifle and took off up the hill. The gun and the wood and the previous twenty-four hours of clambering up and down hillsides slowed me down. However, we made it to the top without having to ditch our loads and I eased around the rocks, rifle at the ready.

The Lacklans were well out of the circle of rocks and away from the cave, crouched behind the rocks and harried-looking. I almost laughed but couldn't summon the energy; a miniature tornado of bats fluttered and turned around the tunnel entrance, the last stragglers of the mass from below using the back door.

I'd had enough alarms for one day. Leaving Raj to start a fire in a small pocket in the rocks I went back into the cave and refilled my pack with its supplies. I ducked and shook my head as the last of the bats flew past but I got my rope, stove fuel, first-aid kit, and most importantly the little food I'd been able to bring along.

We warmed ourselves silently around the fire; the Lacklans didn't seem to feel like talking and I didn't feel comfortable conversing with them either. I shared our dried pork and heated two cans of condensed soup over the fire. It wasn't much and it wasn't very good but it was all I had and we needed anything we could get. When we were done I put out the fire. I hated to do it as we were all chilled but the sun was coming up and our smoke might have been visible. In the treetops below us the gibbons began their whooping cries, staking out their territory for the day.

"We're going to have to keep going," I said. "We're not safe until we're back on the river and we won't be safe even then." I looked in their eyes and was afraid of what I saw.

John, with his leg barely capable of bearing his weight, was nearly finished. Helen would go on without complaining but she couldn't go farther without rest. Raj could do what was necessary, he'd shut his mind down and go at it like a Chinese coolie, he'd survive if he could, regardless of the suffering. I hoped I could do the same but I wasn't sure.

"We'll be okay," I said, standing up. I looked out across the high ridge and the forest and clouds that swept away in both directions and I realized we weren't going to make it.

All we needed was rest. All we needed was to move slowly and accommodate John's injury. All we needed was time and I saw then that we were out of time.

Off down the backbone of the mountains, three miles away but plainly visible as the sunlight poured across a low shoal of clouds to the east, was a group of men. They were coming up the ridge toward us and there was an easy dozen of them . . . more men than I had bullets, more men than I cared to engage even with my pockets full of ammunition.

"Raj!" I called. "I think we've got trouble." Instantly he

was beside me, John and Helen not far behind. I pointed. "Is that Jeru?"

"Yeah, boss."

"What are we going to do?" This question was from Helen but there was no panic in her voice. She stood there, dirty, clothing torn, having had no sleep, and little rest . . . it was an honest question, she was ready to get started.

"I hold them off as long as possible. You get out of sight; retreat into the cave. Take my rope, I believe there's a way out down below."

"You believe?" John was belligerent.

I shrugged. "With any luck they'll be satisfied with me and they won't know where you've gone."

"You'll be killed!" Helen grabbed my arm and turned me toward her. Her eyes searched mine, for what I didn't know; it was one of those moments when men and women have different things in mind.

"I might be. With luck I can kill enough of them that they decide I'm not worth it."

John shifted on his bad leg. "How much ammunition have you got?"

"Nine rounds."

"She's right, you'll be killed."

"You got a better idea?"

Nobody said anything. The men on the distant ridge were getting closer.

I turned. "Let's start by getting out of sight." I ripped open my pack and pulled out the bottle of stove fuel. Going to where we'd had our fire I picked up a fair-sized branch and blew on the white coals at one end. Ash flew away on my breath and deep in the darker cracks flickers of red glowed. I poured a bit of the fuel on the branch right up near the sparks and I blew again. In a minute I had a flaming torch.

The cave angled down, turned, and then dropped off abruptly, a black shaft corkscrewing downward. It would be a nasty climb but that in itself might save us. Bats skittered nervously on the ceiling, they didn't like the smoke from my torch.

"Raj," I called. "Get me my rope." He wasn't behind me,

only the distant forms of the Lacklans peering in from the entrance. "Raj?"

I cursed and tossed my torch down the shaft. It fell, bounced, flared, and went out. In the darkness I could see reflected daylight deep in the shaft. Well, the lower cave *was* a way out, that was something in our favor. We could run, or they could. It wouldn't be much of a lead, but it would hold off the inevitable an hour, three? It would hold off the inevitable for them, not me. I headed back out of the cave. "Damn it, Raj, where's my rope?"

When I got to the entrance he was holding it in his hands but that was all. He looked at me strangely.

"Come on!" I insisted. We had to get him and the Lacklans started or this would all be for nothing.

"I stay with you, boss."

"This is no time for loyalty or bravery or whatever it is, Raj. If you don't go with them they'll never find the boats. Get going!"

He shuffled forward, hesitated . . . he was scared! Scared of the cave.

I moved over to him and spoke softly, "What's wrong?"

"I go. But this not good. You think *Toh* big joke. I hope you right."

Suddenly I had an inkling of an idea. Maybe we could get out of this, all of us. If it worked it was going to take brains, and luck, and courage. But I'm better at courage when I think I've got a chance.

"Raj, if you're worried about the spirits, what about them?" I pointed out at the ridge. Jeru and his men were out of sight, negotiating a low spot, but I doubted we had more than half an hour. "Is Jeru afraid of *Toh*?"

He frowned. "Maybe . . ." Then he looked up at me, squinting. "His mans, they afraid, I think. Jeru he make *obat,* a spell, he say he *bali saleng*. He say what he does okay, but all mans still afraid."

"Good," I said. "Come with me." I snatched the coil of rope out of his hand and I ran to get my stove fuel.

"What's going on?" John Lacklan grabbed at me but I avoided him.

"I've got an idea!" I said and tossed him my rifle. "If they get within five hundred yards shoot once, I'll be back."

"Tell me what you're up to, damn it!"

I didn't tell him, I was already headed down the slope toward the mouth of the lower caves. I hoped he would show good judgment because as soon as I was over the edge I could no longer see the oncoming men.

———

RAJ AND I put our backs into it. We pulled three big partly rotten logs up the hill to the caves, both of us straining like a team of oxen on the rope. We laid a fire just inside where the tunnels converged and got it burning, then tossed every branch we could find up into a pile alongside it. We worked, getting everything into position and doing a fair job of it until I heard the boom of the Mauser.

I tossed the fuel bottle to Raj and took off running. "Don't do anything until you hear me whistle," I yelled back. I hit the mountainside and scrambled, arms and legs tearing at the earth and rock. I must have had my second wind but my muscles felt strange and hollow, it was not a good feeling.

I paused just under the lip to get a lungful of air then, hugging the ground, my leg throbbing, I slipped over the top. John was down inside the pocket of rocks where we'd had our fire and Helen was right behind him.

"What's happened?" I whispered.

"They're close. I shot and they went to ground."

"Okay. Give me the rifle. Stay clear of the cave mouth but if anything happens to me get back in the cave and stay there no matter what happens."

"What are you going to do?"

"Put on a show," I said and taking a deep breath, I stepped out.

———

"TUAN JERU! COME out and face me!" I stood there, the Mauser slung diagonally across my back. I would have rather left it with Lacklan but if they hadn't seen it on me they would have suspected an ambush. As it was I'd be lucky not to get a bullet or a blowgun dart.

After a moment there was a motion in the brush and the slight form of Jeru appeared with the boy in the aviator glasses at his side. They started for me across the last few feet of the rocky ridge. Jeru wore a wood-sheathed *parang* on one hip and the ancient pistol on the other.

The boy carried Lacklan's rifle. They stopped a short distance away.

"You speak poorly," sneered Jeru, commenting on my fragmentary Malay.

"I speak this language no better than I have to," I said loudly, my main audience was Jeru's followers, "but I speak the language of the spirits well. My *obat* is as good as yours in this place. Go away from here. Go and leave us to ourselves. The gods of this mountain do not want you!" I pinched my fingers together, placed them between my lower lip and upper teeth, and whistled as loud as I could.

The boy took a step back and shook his head in shock. He brought up the long rifle but I didn't move. I tried to calmly stare him down . . . I was sure I was going to die.

Then there came a sound from the cave like a sudden rush of wind. In the boy's glasses I saw reflected a momentary flash of orange flame in the tunnel mouth. Raj, on my signal, had poured the entire bottle of stove fuel on the fire.

With a rush like a great wave crashing on a reef the bats vomited from the cave. They came piping and flapping blindly into the morning sunlight driven by the smoky fire that Raj was now stoking with all the wood he could find. With the lower entrances to the tunnels blocked by smoke and flame they sought the upper opening in numbers that were terrifying to behold. They were a great disoriented black cloud that shot from the hole in the mountaintop as if from a high pressure hose. They fluttered and dove and poured into the sky above our heads.

Jeru crouched in surprise and I stepped in and before the boy could pull the rifle's trigger I slapped the barrel aside and kicked him in the groin. He went down, leaving me with the gun, and I saw two of Jeru's men racing away down the ridge, their tattooed backs glistening with the sweat of exertion and fear.

I turned to the old man and with a whining growl he drew his *parang*. He cut at me with such speed that I barely could move in time, shoving the rifle sideways into the blade. There was a ringing of steel and Lacklan's gun was torn from my grasp, falling to the rocks at my feet. Jeru reversed and I leaped back, the blade slicing air near my belly. He was fast; for an old man he was awfully fast.

I got my knife out and took a cut at him but he thrust along my arm, his blade leaving a trace of fire and a line of blood . . . he was better at this than I was. Better by a long shot.

He stabbed and cut. We fought back and forth there on that high ridge with a clear sweep of forest below us on one side and the white glare of the clouds beneath us on the other. And then he cut me, the knife grazing my chest, the blade momentarily catching on the Mauser's leather strap, and it was all over. His blade snagged and I caught his arm and was behind him in one movement. It was my fight then and for him it was hopeless. As good as he was with a knife, he was an old man. I was stronger than he was and I was heavier, too. I broke his arm but there was no give in him so I clipped him on the jaw, a punch that would have put away a much bigger man, and I'm not proud to say that I broke that, too.

He was unconscious. I was down, the world spinning around me, my chest bloody, my arm bloody, too bloody. The boy scrambled away, sobbing. There was the sound of gunfire. Helen was standing over me working the bolt on John's fancy rifle. Brass flew, bright against the sky. Men fled downhill, disappearing into the trees.

They broke open the first-aid kit, poured something in my wounds that hurt more than the knife had. Raj was getting me on my feet and my head was clearing; I had never really been out, just gray for a while, like I'd held my breath too long.

We were at the edge of the slope when I remembered. I pulled away from Raj's hands and went back. Jeru moaned when I turned him on his back. He looked at me, eyes no longer full of anger but neither was there fear. He waited for me to do whatever I had to do. It took only a moment.

"Thank you, *Tuan* Jeru," I told him. "Go to a village where no one knows you, live your days as an old man should. Cross my path again and I'll take *your* head and hang it on my porch."

I left him there, bats circling above, and I staggered off after the others. We went down past the cave where the fire still burned but was now low and dying. Then we were in the jungle and soon it was darker and hotter.

———

IT WAS TWO days back to the boats. Two days of struggle and pain. John Lacklan and I setting our pitiful pace. His leg was swollen and my cuts and the places where the buckshot hit me had become infected. As much as I disliked the man he had a certain kind of toughness. It was the toughness of the littlest kid on the team or perhaps the brainy child that nobody liked . . . but he wasn't going to let that leg stop us. I had to make myself keep pace with him.

The boats were intact. In this I was surprised for I was sure that even if we got to the river without another fight I thought they would have stolen or destroyed the boats. I guess with their burned longhouse, several dead, and wounded leader they had enough to deal with. Raj took us downriver in the bigger dugout with Fairchild's motor jury-rigged to the stern. On the trip downriver I got sicker and they tell me when I arrived in Marudi I was unconscious and running a high fever. For the second time in two years I had returned from upriver barely alive. But this time I had the difference.

———

I LAY IN BED and got better. Vandover came down and brought the doctor. He shot me with penicillin, cleaned my wounds and dusted them with sulfa, then they sat on the verandah and drank the last of my scotch. I stared at the peeling paint on the ceiling.

She came to visit me an hour before the mail boat left for Singapore. The room was closed and dark but sunlight blazed through every crack in the shutters. She was dressed in a white traveling outfit and as she stood in the doorway she was a vague figure beyond the patched mosquito netting. I sat up.

"Mr. Kardec?" She came into the room, taking off a large pair of dark glasses. "I just came to thank you. You saved our lives." I could see that the wedding ring, with its empty socket, was missing from her finger.

I wanted to make some kind of smart comment but I didn't really know what it would be. "How's your husband?" I asked.

"He's got a bad sprain. All that walking we did made it worse. We're leaving today . . ." She stopped for a moment, holding on to some kind of feeling, I couldn't tell what.

"He won't talk to me," she said. "It's like I did something unforgivable back there but I don't see that I really had a choice."

"I think he's trying too hard to be a strong man." I thought this was right, it felt right. "Something inside of him is desperate. He's barely holding on to something but I don't know what it is. He'd of rather died back there than be saved by you."

"John was so brilliant. You should have seen him when we met. They all listened when he spoke, Dr. Teller, even General LeMay."

"This is a different world, Helen. You knew that, I could see it. Sometimes when there is nothing between you and nature you find out things you wish you didn't know . . . sometimes when you look at yourself you are smaller in the scheme of things than you thought you were." I shifted, sitting up a little farther, leaning back against the headboard. "There's been a time or two when I found myself in the middle of a dark forest praying for God to save me. You have to accept your fear and survive. It's not about your image of yourself, it's just about getting back in one piece."

"I guess so," she said.

We were both silent for a moment. Then she straightened up, all business.

"We should pay you, at least what we were going to for guiding us. We owe you that, and more."

I carefully moved the mosquito net aside and swung my feet to the floor. The cut under my bandages pulled tightly and it burned, but it was a healing pain.

"I don't want any money," and then before I could take it back, I said, "I did it for you. I don't want to lose that."

She crossed the room and bending down, she kissed me. For just a moment she held my face in her hand. "What will you do?" she asked. "How will you ever get home?"

I didn't really wonder how she knew this, I expect Vandover or Fairchild must have told her . . . it didn't matter. I sat straighter, trying to feel the strength in my body. It was there, not much, but coming back. I opened the nightstand drawer.

"Never underrate a man who has lived as I have, Helen. Just as a man who has lived as I have would never underrate a woman like you." I grinned. "I'm not proud and I do what it takes to survive." I held out my hand and opened it to show her. It was ironic, when I had gone into the forest for personal gain I had returned with nothing, but when I had gone intending to help others somehow I had been rewarded.

On my palm lay, in a setting of woven leather, the thong broken from when I had torn it from his neck . . . *the diamond of Jeru!*

DEATH, WESTBOUND

IT WAS NEARLY dark when the westbound freight pulled out of the yards, and two 'boes, hurrying from behind a long line of empties, scrambled into one of the open doors of a boxcar about halfway between the caboose and the locomotive.

There were two more men in the car when they crawled in after their bundles. One of these was sitting at one side of the door where he could see without being seen, a precaution against any shack that might drift along or be standing beside the track. Joe had had experience with shacks, and much worse, with railroad dicks, he knew their kind. Sometimes the shacks were pretty good guys, but a railroad dick is always a louse.

The other occupant of the car lay in the shadow apparently sleeping.

The newcomers, two hard-faced young fellows carrying bundles, looked around.

Joe's curiosity got the better of him. "Westbound, fellas?"

"Yeah—you?"

"Uhuh. L.A., if we can make it."

"We?"

"Yeah, me an' the kid over there."

"Chee, I never even see 'em. S'matter, 's he asleep?"

"Naw, he's sick I guess, we been on this train t'ree nights now, an' he's been sick all the while. I don't know what's the matter. He coughs a lot, maybe he's a lunger."

"Chee, that's kinda tough, ain't it? Sick as a goddam drag when the bulls is all gettin' tough."

"The Santy Fe is the toughest line of 'em all, 'member hearin' 'bout Yermo Red?"

"Aw hell, Yermo was on the U.P. I made it thru there once

on the bum with a coupla Polacks, he was plenty tough, that guy."

"Naw, he just t'ought he was tough, them guys is mostly yellow when there is a showdown."

Joe walked over to look at the kid. The boy's face was damp with perspiration and he looked bad. One of the others, a flat-nosed young fellow with heavy shoulders, walked over.

"Cheesus, he looks bad, don't he? 'At kid should aughta have a doctor!"

"Yeah."

The other young fellow walked over. "S'matter, Heavy? Is he bad off?" Then seeing the kid's face, he murmured: "Gawah!"

All three returned to a spot near the door. A heavy silence had descended upon the group. Joe rolled a cigarette and complied in silence to the others' dumb request for the makin's.

Heavy looked glumly out at the night. "Cheesus, that's a helluva place to get sick in! Wonder if he'll croak?"

The slight youngster with the pale face who answered to the name of Slim, grunted: "Naw, he'll pul t'ru, a guy that has to live like this is too tough to die like anybody else."

Heavy looked at Joe and with a jerk of his head toward the kid: "Known him long?"

"Two weeks I guess. He had a coupla bucks and split 'em with me when I was bad off. He's a good kid. We been hunting jobs ever since, but this depression finished the work, seems like they ain't nothing left to do anymore."

"Wait'll we get a new president, what's Hoover care for us laborin' stiffs?"

Slim snorted derisively: "The next one won't be a bit better. One way or the other we get it in the neck!"

Heavy moved into a corner of the car and carefully arranging a roll of newspapers to form a place to lie, he lay down and drew his coat over his head to sleep. A few minutes later his snores gave ample proof of his success.

Slim jerked his head toward the sleeper: "Will he bother the kid, d'ye think?"

Joe shook his head: "Naw, the kid's out of his head, I guess

he's about all in. When this train stops I'll try and find somebody to give him some dope or somethin'."

They lapsed into silence broken only by the steady pound
and rattle of the swiftly moving freight train and the snores
of the sleeper. At intervals the kid would move and talk in-
distinctly for a minute or so and then once more fall into silence. Outside the car the night was quite moonlit and they
could see the fields flickering by in monotonous rotation.
The countless cracks in the old car made it cold and dismal.
Slim dosed off against the door, knees drawn up to his chin.
Joe sat silent watching the fields outside and thinking.

It had been over a year since he had worked more than a
few hours at a time, over a year of living in boxcars, cheap
flophouses and any dump he could find to crawl into. But
after all, what had it been before? Just a round of jobs, a few
months and then a long drunk, or maybe a short one, if he
got himelf rolled in some bawdy house. The kid here, he'd
been the only pal he'd ever had that played square, an'
now he was sicker'n hell. Life didn't mean much to a guy
when he was just a workin' stiff. Sure, he'd boozed a lot, but
what th' hell? Didn't he have a right to have a little fun? Well,
maybe it wasn't fun, but at least a guy wasn't thinkin' about
the next shift or how much ore he had to get out. Joe dozed
off, but came to with a start as a red light flashed by and the
freight began to slow for a station.

Slim and Heavy both woke up with the awareness that a
hobo acquires when travelling.

"What kind of a burg is this we're comin' into, Joe? Looks
like a damned jerk-water!"

"Yeah—I know the place. Just a water tank and a general
store. Better keep outa sight, from now on, there's a bad bull
in this next town if I remember right!"

The long drag slowly pulled to a bumping, groaning stop,
and Slim, watching his chance when the shack was at the
other end, dropped off.

Up ahead they could hear the shouts of the train crew
as they worked about the engine, and once a shack went by,
his lantern bobbing along beside the train. He just casually

flashed it into the door as he passed, and as all three were out of sight, they were passed unnoticed.

A whistle up forward, more groaning and bumping and jarring, and the train slowly gathered momentum.

Heavy's forehead wrinkled anxiously: "Wonder what's become o' Slim? He should've made it by now!"

And a minute later, as the train gathered speed in the shadow of several oil tanks, he did make it, swinging into the car with a dark object in his hand.

"Whatcha got Slim?" Heavy leaned forward curiously.

"Aw, pull in your neck, Hefty, I just grabbed the kid a cuppa java an' a orange at that lunch counter!"

"But Cheesus, Slim, you only had a nickel!"

"Sure, I got the guy to gimme a cuppa java for the nickel and I swiped the orange when the lunch-counter girl wasn't lookin'. If he wants his cup back he'll have to pick it up in the next town!"

Joe rolled the kid over on his back and slowly raised him to a sitting position: "Here, kid, it's a cuppa coffee, try an' get it down, it'll do you good."

The kid tried to drink, but ended in a coughing spell that left flecks of blood on his lips. Joe laid him back on the floor and returned to the others near the door.

Slim looked helplessly at the orange: "Cheesus, guess he couldn't tackle this, he seems pretty far gone." He raised his hand as if to throw the orange away and then on second thought shoved it into his coat pocket.

Once more the train bumped along, the moon had gone down now and the night was black outside the door. Heavy was once more asleep, and Slim, chin resting on his knees, was dozing off. Joe still sat looking out into the night, his face grimy from cinders and dust, his beard graying in spots. At last he too dozed off into a half-sleep.

The freight was slowing for the next town when a swiftly bobbing flashlight awakened them. Joe was the first to comprehend.

"Cheesus, guys, we're sunk, it's that railroad dick!"

Heavy cursed and jumped for the door to swing out when a harsh voice broke in: "Alright, Bo, stay where y'are or I'll shoot yer guts out! Come on, you, all of ya! Get 'em up in the air!"

"Alright, pile out on the ground an' less look you guys over. Keep 'em up, now!" The railroad dick's voice was harsh and his face ugly in the half-light. His companion, a weasel-faced fellow, glided up and started frisking them with the question: "Got anythin' on ya bigger'n a forty-five?"

Slim spoke agrievedly: "Aw why don't you guys leave us alone? We're just huntin' a place to work. What would we be doin' packin' rods!"

The big fellow stepped forward beligerently: "Shut up, Bum, I'll do the talkin' an' you'll answer when yer spoken to, get me?"

Slim said nothing. The weasel-faced man pulled their personal effects from their pockets smirking over the few odds and ends a man carries about. A couple of jackknives, a piece of soiled string, a dirty handkerchief or two, a pocketbook containing a pair of poll tax receipts, a card for a hod-carriers union two years old, a few letters. The weasel-faced man read the letters with an occasional glance at Slim's angry face. Finally from one of them he extracted a picture of a girl which he held out for the big man to see with an insulting remark.

Slim's eyes swiftly calculated the distance, he jumped and struck viciously, his fist striking the weasel-face on the point of the chin, knocking him flat, the big man sidestepped and struck with the gun barrel felling Slim to the ground. Then stepping toward Heavy and Joe he snapped: "Got tough, did he? Well, suppose you guys try it, I killed a couple of guys fer tryin' to get tough with me!"

Joe's tired voice spoke slowly: "Uh-uh, I heard 'bout that, both of 'em unarmed. You said they got tough, some people said they had thirty bucks on 'em."

"What was that?" The big man whirled toward Joe. "What d'you say?"

"Me? I didn't say nothin', just clearin' my throat."

"Well, ya better be careful, get me? Or I'll slam you like I did him!" He waved his hand toward Slim's fallen figure.

He called to Weasel-face: "Look in that damned car, maybe they left some junk in there worth lookin' over!"

"Okay, Boss!"

Weasel-face scrambled into the car. Then: "Hey, Boss, here's another bum in here sleepin'!"

"D'hell there is! Well, roll the bastard out an' less look him over."

Voice from the car: "Come on, you, crawl outa that! Hey, what's the matter? Get up or I'll boot the hell outa ya!"

A moment later, Weasel-face dragged the kid to the door and dumped him out to the ground.

"Here he is, Boss, playin' sleepy on us!"

The Boss walked up determinedly and kicked the kid forcibly in the ribs, Joe's shout halted him, a frown on his face.

"Hey, Skipper, watch yerself, the kid's sick, he's got the consumption or somethin'!"

"He won't play sick with me; I'll boot his head off: get up, d'ye hear?" He grabbed the kid by the shoulder and jerked him to his feet where the kid hung in a slump. For a moment the Boss gazed into his face, his own growing white: "God! The son-of-a-bitch is dead!" He dropped the kid and turned around.

In the moment of detachment following his discovery, unable to help the kid, the remaining two, supporting the now conscious Slim, had slipped off into the surrounding darkness leaving the two dicks behind, and the crumpled form of the kid lying beside the freight, which slowly moving was once more westbound.

OLD DOC YAK

HE WAS A man without humor. He seemed somehow aloof, invulnerable. Even his walk was pompous and majestic. He strode with the step of kings and spoke with the voice of an oracle, entirely unaware that his whole being was faintly ludicrous, that those about him were always suspended between laughter and amazed respect.

Someone began calling him Old Doc Yak for no apparent reason, and the name stayed with him. He was a large man, rather portly, wearing a constantly grave expression and given to a pompous manner of speech. His most simple remark was uttered with a sense of earthshaking import, and a listener invariably held his breath in sheer suspense as he began to speak, only to suffer that sense of frustration one feels when an expected explosion fails to materialize.

His conversation was a garden of the baroque in which biological and geological terms flowered in the most unexpected places. Jim commented once that someone must have thrown a dictionary at him and he got all the words but none of the definitions. We listened in amused astonishment as he would stand, head slightly tilted to one side, an open palm aslant his rather generous stomach, which he would pat affectionately as though in amused approbation of his remarks.

Those were harsh, bitter days. The waterfronts were alive with seamen, all hunting ships. One theme predominated in all our conversations, in all our thoughts, perhaps even in the very pulsing of our blood—how to get by.

No normal brain housed in a warm and sheltered body could possibly conceive of the devious and doubtful schemes contrived to keep soul and body together. Hunger sharpens the wits and renders less effective the moral creeds and codes by which we guide our law-abiding lives. Some of us who were there could even think of the philosophical ramifications of our lives and of our actions. The narrow line that divides the average young man or woman from stealing, begging, or prostitution, is one that has little to do with religion or ethics but only such simple animal necessities as food and shelter. We had been talking of that when Old Doc Yak ventured his one remark.

"I think," he said, pausing portentously, "that any man who will beg, who will so demean himself as to ask for food upon the streets, will stoop to any abomination no matter how low."

He arose, and with a finality that permitted of no reply, turned his back and walked away. It was one of the few coherent statements I ever heard him make, and I watched his broad back, stiff with self-righteousness, as he walked away. I watched, as suddenly speechless as the others.

There was probably not a man present who had not at some time panhandled on the streets. They were a rough, free-handed lot, men who gave willingly when they had it and did not hesitate to ask when in need. All were men who worked, who performed the rough, hard, dangerous work of the world, yet they were men without words, and no reply came to their lips to answer that broad back or the bitter finality of that remark. In their hearts they felt him wrong, for they were sincere men, if not eloquent.

Often after that I saw him on the streets. Always stiff and straight, he never unbent so far as to speak, never appeared even to notice my passing. He paid his way with a careful hand and lived remote from our lonely, uncomfortable world. From meal to meal we had no idea as to the origin of the next, and our nights were spent wherever there was shelter from the wind. Off on the horizon of our hopelessness there was always that miracle—a ship—and endlessly we made the rounds in search of work. Shipping proceeded slowly, and men struggled for the few occasional jobs alongshore. Coming and going on my own quest, I saw men around me drawn fine by hunger, saw their necks become gaunt, their clothing more shabby. It was a bitter struggle to survive in a man-made jungle.

The weeks drew on, and one by one we saw the barriers we had built against hunger slowly fall away. By that time there were few who had not walked the streets looking for the price of a cup of coffee, but even the ready generosity of a seaport town had been strained, and shipping seemed to have fallen off.

One morning a man walked into the Seaman's Institute and fainted away. We had seen him around for days, a quiet young man who seemed to know no one, to have no contacts, too proud to ask for food and too backward to find other means. And then he walked in that morning and crumpled up on the floor like an empty sack.

It was a long moment before any of us moved. We stood staring down at him, and each of us was seeing the specter of his own hunger.

Then Parnatti was arrested. He had been hungry before, and we had heard him say, "I'm going to eat. If I can make it honest, I'll make it, but I'm going to eat regardless." We understood his feelings, although the sentiments were not ours. Contrary to opinion, it is rarely the poor who steal. People do not steal for the necessities but for the embellishments, but when the time came, Parnatti stole a car from a parking lot and sold it. We saw the item in the paper without comfort and then turned almost without hope to the list of incoming ships. Any one of them might need a man; any one of them might save us from tomorrow.

Old Doc Yak seemed unchanged. He came and went as always, as always his phrases bowed beneath a weight of words. I think, vaguely, we all resented him. He was so obviously not a man of the sea, so obviously not one of us. I believe he had been a steward, but stewards were rarely popular in the old days on the merchant ships. Belly robbers, they called them.

Glancing over the paper one afternoon, searching for a ship that might need men, I looked up accidentally just in time to see Old Doc Yak passing a hand over his face. The hand trembled.

For the first time I really saw him. Many times in the past few days we had passed each other on the street, each on his way to survival. Often we had sat in the main room at the Institute, but I had paid little attention. Now, suddenly, I was aware of the change. His vest hung a little slack, and the lines in his face were deeper. For the moment even his pompous manner had vanished. He looked old and tired.

In the ugly jungle of the waterfront the brawl for existence left little time for thinking of anything except the immediate and ever-present need for shelter and food for the body. Old Doc Yak had been nothing more than another bit of waterfront jetsam discarded from the whirl of living into the lazy maelstrom of those alongshore. Now, again, as on that other night, he became an individual, and probably for the first time I saw the man as he was and as he must have seen himself.

Tipped back against the wall, feeling the tightness of my leather jacket across my shoulders, I rubbed the stubble on my unshaved chin and wondered about him. I guess each of us has an illusion about himself. Somewhere inside of himself he has a picture of himself he believes is true. I guess it was that way with Doc. Aloof from those of us who lived around him, he existed in a world of his own creation, a world in which he had importance, a world in which he was somebody. Now, backed into a corner by economic necessity, he was a little puzzled and a little helpless.

Some of us had rented a shack. For six dollars a month we had shelter from the wind and rain, a little chipped crockery, a stove, and a bed. There was a cot in the corner where I slept, and somebody had rustled an old mattress that was stretched out on the deck—floor, I should say. For a dime or perhaps three nickels, if he was good for them, a man could share the bed with three or four others. For a nickel a man got an armful of old newspapers with which he could roll up on the floor. And with the money gathered in such a way we paid another month's rent.

It wasn't much, but it was a corner away from the wind, a place of warmth, and a retreat from the stares of the police and the more favored. Such a place was needed, and never did men return home with more thankfulness than we returned to that shack on its muddy hillside. Men came and went in the remaining weeks of our stay, the strange, drifting motley of the waterfront, men good, bad, and indifferent. Men were there who knew the ports and rivers of a hundred countries, men who knew every sidetrack from Hoboken to Seattle. And then one night Old Doc Yak walked up the path to the door.

There was rain that night, a cold, miserable rain, and a wind that blew it against our thin walls. It was just after ten when the knock came at the door, and when Copper opened it, Old Doc walked in. For a moment his small blue eyes blinked against the light, and then he looked about, a slow distaste growing on his face. There was a sailor's neatness about the place, but it was crude and not at all attractive.

He looked tired, and some of his own neatness was lacking. He might have been fifty-five, but he looked older then, yet his eyes were still remote, unseeing of us, who were the dregs. He looked around again, and we saw his hesitation, sensed the defeat that must have brought him, at last, to this place. But our shack was warm.

"I would like," he said ponderously, "a place to sleep."

"Sure," I said, getting up from the rickety chair I'd tipped against the wall. "There's room in the double bed for one more. It'll cost you a dime."

"You mean," he asked abruptly, and he actually looked at me, "that I must share a bed?"

"Sorry. This isn't the Biltmore. You'll have to share with Copper and Red."

He was on the verge of leaving when a blast of wind and blown rain struck the side of the house, sliding around under the eaves and whining like a wet saw. For an instant he seemed to be weighing the night, the rain and the cold against the warmth of the shack. Then he opened his oldfashioned purse and lifted a dime from its depths.

I say "lifted," and so it seemed. Physical effort was needed to get that dime into my hand, and his fingers released it reluctantly. It was obviously the last of his carefully hoarded supply. Then he walked heavily into the other room and lay down on the bed. It was the first time I had ever seen him lie down, and all his poise seemed suddenly to evaporate, his stiffnecked righteousness seemed to wilt, and all his ponderous posturing with words became empty and pitiful. Lying on the bed with the rain pounding on the roof, he was only an old man, strangely alone.

Sitting in the next room with fire crackling in the stove and the rattling of rain on the windows, I thought about him. Youth and good jobs were behind him, and he was facing a question to which all the ostentatious vacuity of his words gave no reply. The colossal edifice he had built with high-sounding words, the barriers he had attempted to erect between himself and his doubt of himself were crumbling. I put another stick in the stove, watched the fire lick the dampness from its face, and listened to rain beating against the walls and the labored breathing of the man on the bed.

In the washroom of the Seaman's Institute weeks before we had watched him shave. It had been a ritual lacking only incense. The glittering articles from his shaving kit, these had been blocks in the walls of his self-esteem. The careful lathering of his florid cheeks, the application of shaving lotion, these things had been steps in a ritual that never varied. We who were disciples of Gillette and dull blades watched him with something approaching reverence and went away to marvel.

Knowing what must have happened in the intervening weeks, I could see him going to the pawnshop with first one and then another of his prized possessions, removing bit by bit the material things, those glittering silver pieces that shored up his self-vision. Each time his purse would be replenished for a day or two, and as each article passed over the counter into that great maw from which nothing ever returns, I could see some particle of his dignity slipping away. He was a capitalist without capital, a conqueror without conquests, a vocabulary without expression. In the stove the fire crackled; on the wide bed the old man muttered, stirring in his sleep. It was very late.

He did not come again. Several times the following night I walked to the door, almost hoping to see his broad bulk as it labored up the hill. Even Copper looked uneasily out of the window, and Slim took a later walk than usual. We were a group that was closely knit, and though he had not belonged, he had for one brief night been one of us, and when he did not return, we were uneasy.

It was after twelve before Slim turned in. It had been another wet night, and he was tired. He stopped by my chair where I sat reading a magazine.

"Listen," he said, flushing a little, "if he comes, Old Doc, I mean, I'll pay if he ain't got the dime. He ain't such a bad guy."

"Sure," I said. "Okay."

He didn't come. The wind whined and snarled around the corners of the house, and we heard the tires of a car whine on the wet pavement below. It is a terrible thing to see a man's belief in himself crumble, for when one loses faith in one's own illusion, there is nothing left. Even Slim understood that. It was almost daybreak before I fell asleep.

Several nights drifted by. There was food to get, and the rent was coming due. We were counting each dime, for we had not yet made the six dollars. There was still a gap, a breach in our wall that we might not fill. And outside was the night, the rain, and the cold.

The *Richfield,* a Standard tanker, was due in. I had a shipmate aboard her, and when she came up the channel, I was waiting on the dock. They might need an A.B.

They didn't.

It was a couple of hours later when I climbed the hill toward the shack. I didn't often go that way, but this time it was closer, and I was worried. The night before I'd left the money for the rent in a thick white cup on the cupboard shelf. And right then murder could be done for five bucks. Accidentally I glanced in the window. Then I stopped.

Old Doc Yak was standing by the cupboard, holding the white cup in his hand. As I watched, he dipped his fingers in and drew out some of our carefully gleaned nickels, dimes, and quarters. Then he stood there letting those shining metal disks trickle through his thick fingers and back into the cup. Then he dipped his fingers again, and I stood there, holding my breath.

A step or two and I could have stopped him, but I stood

there, gripped by his indecision, half guessing what was happening inside him. Here was money. Here, for a little while, was food, a room, a day or two of comfort. I do not think he considered the painstaking effort to acquire those few coins or the silent, bedraggled men who had trooped up the muddy trail to add a dime or fifteen cents to the total of our next month's rent. What hunger had driven him back, I knew. What helplessness and humiliation waited in the streets below, I also knew.

Slowly, one by one, the coins dribbled back into the cup, the cup was returned to the shelf, and Old Doc Yak turned and walked from the door. For one moment he paused, his face strangely gray and old, staring out across the bleak, rain-washed roofs toward the gray waters of the channel and Terminal Island just beyond.

Then he walked away, and I waited until he was out of sight before I went inside, and I, who had seen so much of weariness and defeat, hesitated before I took down the cup. It was all there, and suddenly I was a little sorry that it was.

Once more I saw him. One dark, misty night I came up from the lumber docks, collar turned up, cap pulled low, picking my way through the shadows and over the railroad ties, stumbling along rails lighted only by the feeble red and green of switch lights. Reaching the street, I scrambled up the low bank and saw him standing in the light of a street lamp.

He was alone, guarded from friendship as always by his icy impenetrability but somehow strangely pathetic with his sagging shoulders and graying hair. I started to speak, but he turned up his coat collar and walked away down a dark street.

IT'S YOUR MOVE

OLD MAN WHITE was a checker player. He was a longshoreman, too, but he only made his living at that. Checker playing was his life. I never saw anybody take the game like he took it. Hour after hour, when there was nobody for him to play with, he'd sit at a table in the Seaman's Institute and study the board and practice his moves. He knew every possible layout there could be. There was this little book he carried, and he would arrange the checkers on the board, and then move through each game with an eye for every detail and chance. If anybody ever knew the checkerboard, it was him.

He wasn't a big man, but he was keen-eyed, and had a temper like nobody I ever saw. Most of the time he ignored people. Everybody but other checker players. I mean guys that could give him a game. They were few enough, and with the exception of Oriental Slim and MacCready, nobody had ever beat him. They were the best around at the time, but the most they could do with the old man was about one out of ten. But they gave him a game and that was all he wanted. He scarcely noticed anybody else, and you couldn't get a civil word out of him. As a rule he never opened his face unless it was to talk the game with somebody who knew it.

Then Sleeth came along. He came down from Frisco and began hanging around the Institute talking with the guys who were on the beach. He was a slim, dark fellow with a sallow complexion, quick, black eyes, and he might have been anywhere from thirty to forty-five.

He was a longshoreman, too. That is, he was then. Up in Frisco he had been a deckhand on a tugboat, like me. Before that he had been a lot of things, here and there. Somewhere he had developed a mind for figures, or maybe he had been born with it. You could give him any problem in addition, subtraction, or anything else, and you'd get the answer just like that, right out of his head. At poker he could beat anybody and was one of the best pool shots I ever saw.

We were sitting by the fireplace in the Institute one night when he came in and joined us. A few minutes later, Old Man White showed up wearing his old pea jacket as always.

"Where's MacCready?" he said.

"He's gone up to L.A., Mr. White," the clerk said. "He won't be back for several days."

"Is that other fellow around? That big fellow with the pockmarked face?"

"Slim? No, he's not. He shipped out this morning for Gray's Harbor. I heard he had some trouble with the police."

Trouble was right. Slim was slick with the cards, and he got himself in a game with a couple of Greeks. One of the Greeks was a pretty good cheat himself, but Oriental Slim was better and cashing in from the Greek's roll. One word led to another, and the Greek went for a rod. Well, Oriental Slim was the fastest thing with a chiv I ever saw. He cut that Greek, then he took out.

Old Man White turned away, growling something into his mustache. He was a testy old guy, and when he got sore that mustache looked like a porcupine's back.

"What's the matter with that guy?" Sleeth said. "He acts like he was sore about something?"

"It's checkers," I said. "That's Old Man White, the best checker player around here. Mac and Slim are the only two who can even make it interesting, and they're gone. He's sour for a week when he misses a game."

"Hell, I'll play with him!"

"He won't even listen to you. He won't play nobody unless they got some stuff."

"We'll see. Maybe I can give him a game."

Sleeth got up and walked over. The old man had his book out and was arranging his men on the board. He never used regular checkers himself. He used bottle tops, and always carried them in his pocket.

"How about a game?" Sleeth says.

Old Man White growled something under his breath about not wanting to teach anybody; he didn't even look up. He gets the checkers set up, and pretty soon he starts to move. It seems these guys that play checkers have several different openings they favor, each one of them named. Anyway, when the old man starts to move, Sleeth watches him.

"The Old Fourteenth, huh? You like that? I like the Laird and Lady best."

Old Man White stops in the middle of a move and looks up, frowning. "You play checkers?" he said.

"Sure, I just asked you for a game!"

"Sit down, sit down. I'll play you three games."

Well, it was pitiful. I'm telling you it was slaughter. If the old man hadn't been so proud, everything might have been different, but checkers was his life, his religion; and Sleeth beat him.

It wasn't so much that he beat him; it was the way he beat him. It was like playing with a child. Sleeth beat him five times running, and the old man was fit to be tied. And the madder he got, the worse he played.

Dick said afterward that if Sleeth hadn't talked so much, the old man might have had a chance. You see, Old Man White took plenty of time to study each move, sometimes ten minutes or more. Sleeth just sat there gabbing with us, sitting sideways in the chair, and never looking at the board except to move. He'd talk, talk about women, ships, ports, liquor, fighters, everything. Then, the old man would move and Sleeth would turn, glance at the board, and slide a piece. It seemed like when he looked at the board, he saw all the moves that had been made, and all that could be made. He never seemed to think; he never seemed to pause; he just moved.

Well, it rattled the old man. He was sort of shoved off balance by it. All the time, Sleeth was talking, and sometimes when he moved, it would be right in the middle of a sentence. Half the time, he scarcely looked at the board.

Then, there was a crowd around. Old Man White being beat was enough to draw a crowd, and the gang all liked Sleeth. He was a good guy. Easy with his dough, always having a laugh on somebody or with somebody, and just naturally a right guy. But I felt sorry for the old man. It meant so much to him, and he'd been king bee around the docks so long, and treating everybody with contempt if they weren't good at checkers. If he had even been able to make it tough for Sleeth, it would have been different, but he couldn't even give him a game. His memory for moves seemed to desert him, and the madder he got and the harder he tried, the more hopeless it was.

It went on for days. It got so Sleeth didn't want to play him. He'd avoid him purposely, because the old man was so stirred up about it. Once Old Man White jumped up in the middle of a game and hurled the board clear across the room. Then he stalked out, mad as a wet hen, but just about as helpless as an Armenian peddler with both arms busted.

Then he'd come back. He'd always come back and insist Sleeth play him some more. He followed Sleeth around town, cornering him to play, each time sure he could beat him, but he never could.

We should have seen it coming, for the old man got to acting queer. Checkers was an obsession with him. Now he sometimes wouldn't come around for days, and when he did, he didn't seem anxious to play anymore. Once he played with Oriental Slim, who was back in town, but Slim beat him, too.

That was the finishing touch. It might have been the one game out of ten that Slim usually won, but it hit the old man where he lived. I guess maybe he figured he couldn't play anymore. Without even a word, he got up and went out.

A couple of mornings later, I got a call from Brennan to help load a freighter bound out for the Far East. I'd quit my job on the tug, sick of always going out but never getting any place, and had been longshoring a little and waiting for a ship to China. This looked like a chance to see if they'd be hiring; so I went over to the ship at Terminal Island, and reported to Brennan.

The first person I saw was Sleeth. He was working on the same job. While we were talking, another ferry came over and Old Man White got off. He was running a steam winch for the crew that day, and I saw him glance at Sleeth. It made me nervous to think of those two guys on the same job. In a dangerous business like longshoring—that is, a business where a guy can get smashed up so easy—it looked like trouble.

It was after four in the afternoon before anything happened. We had finished loading the lower hold through No. 4 hatch, and were putting the strong-backs in place so we could cover the 'tween decks hatchway. I was on deck waiting until they got those braces in place before I went down to lay the decking over them. I didn't want to be crawling down a ladder with one of those big steel beams swinging in the hatchway around me. Old Man White was a good hand at a winch, but too many things can happen. We were almost through for the day as we weren't to load the upper hold 'til morning.

A good winch-driver doesn't need signals from the hatch-tender to know where his load is. It may be out of sight down below the main deck, but he can tell by the feel of it and the position of the boom about where it is. But sometimes on those old winches, the steam wouldn't come on even, and once in a while there would be a surge of power that would make them do unaccountable things without a good hand driving. Now Old Man White was a good hand. Nevertheless, I stopped by the hatch coaming and watched.

It happened so quick that there wasn't anything anyone could have done. Things like that always happen quick, and if you move, it is usually by instinct. Maybe the luckiest break Sleeth ever got was he was light on his feet.

The strong-back was out over the hatch, and Old Man White was easing it down carefully. When it settled toward the 'tween decks hatchway, Sleeth caught one end and Hansen the other. It was necessary for a man to stand at each end and guide the strong-back into the notch where it had to fit to support the floor of the upper hold. Right behind Sleeth was a big steel upright, and as Old Man White began to lower away, I got nervous. It always made me nervous to think that a wrong move by the winch-driver, or a wrong signal from the hatch-tender spotting for him, and the man with that post at his back was due to get hurt.

Sleeth caught the end of the strong-back in both hands and it settled gradually, with the old winch puffing along easy-like. Just then I happened to glance up, and something made me notice Old Man White's face.

He was as white as death, and I could see the muscles at the corner of his jaw set hard. Then, all of a sudden, that strong-back lunged toward Sleeth.

It all happened so quick, you could scarcely catch a breath. Sleeth must have remembered Old Man White was on that winch, or maybe it was one of those queer hunches. As for me, I know that in the split second when that strong-back lunged toward him, the thought flashed through my mind, "Sleeth. It's your move!"

And he did move, almost like in the checker games. It was as if he had a map of the whole situation in his mind. One moment he was doing one thing and the next . . .

He leaped sideways and the end of that big steel strong-back hit that stanchion with a crash that you could have heard in Sarawak; then the butt swung around and came within an eyelash of knocking Hansen into the hold, and I just stood there with my eyes on that stanchion thinking how Sleeth would have been mashed into jelly if he hadn't moved like Nijinsky.

The hatch-tender was yelling his head off, and slowly Old Man White took up the tension on the strong-back and swung her into place again. If it had been me, I'd never have touched that thing again, but Sleeth was there, and the strong-back settled into place as pretty as you could wish. Only then could I see that Sleeth's face was white and his hand was shaking.

When he came on deck, he was cool as could be. Old Man White was sitting behind that winch all heaped up like a sack of old clothes. Sleeth looked at him then, grinned a little, and said, sort of offhand, "You nearly had the move on me that time, Mr. White!"

AND PROUDLY DIE

W E WERE ALL misfits, more or less; just so much waste material thrown out casually at one of the side doors of the world. We hadn't much to brag about, but we did plenty of it, one time or another. Probably some of us had something on the ball, like Jim, for instance, who just lacked some little touch in his makeup, and that started him off down the odd streets. We weren't much to look at, although the cops used to come down now and again to give us the once-over. As a rule they just left us alone, because we didn't matter. If one of us was killed, they just figured it was a break for the community, or something. And probably they were right.

Maybe Snipe was one of us after all, but he didn't seem to fit in anywhere. He was one of those guys who just don't belong. He couldn't even find a place with us, and we had about hit rock bottom. Maybe in the end he did find a place, but if he did, it wasn't the place he wanted.

He had sort of drifted in, like all the rest. A little, scrawny guy with a thin face and a long nose that stuck out over the place where his chin should have been. His chin had slipped back against his neck like it was ashamed of itself, and he had those watery blue eyes that seemed sort of anxious and helpless, as though he was always afraid somebody was going to take a punch at him.

I don't know why he stayed, or why we let him stay. Probably he was so much of a blank cartridge nobody cared. We were a pretty tight little bunch, otherwise, and we had to be. It was a matter of survival. It was the waterfront, and times were hard. Getting by was about all a guy could do, and we did it and got along because each of us had his own line and we worked well together. Snipe didn't belong, but he seemed to like being around, and we didn't notice him very much. Whenever Sharkey and Jim would get to talking, he'd sit up and listen, but for that matter, we all did. He seemed to think Sharkey was about the last word in brains, and probably he was.

Snipe was afraid to die. Not that there's anything funny about that, only he worried about it. It was like death had a fascination for him. He was scared of it, but he couldn't stay away. And death along the waterfront is never nice. You know what I mean. A sling breaks, maybe, and a half-dozen bales of cotton come down on a guy, or maybe his foot slips when he's up on the mast, and down he comes to light on a steel deck. Or maybe a boom falls, or the swing of a strong-back mashes him. But no matter how it happens, it's never pretty. And Snipe was scared of it. He told me once he'd always been afraid to die.

Once, I'd been down along the docks looking for a live wire to hit up for the price of coffee, when I saw a crowd on the end of the wharf. Guys on the bum are all rubbernecks, so I hurried along to see what was doing. When I got closer, I could see they were fishing a stiff out of the water. You know what I mean—a dead guy.

Well, I've seen some sights in my life, and death is never pretty along the waterfront, like I've said, but this was the worst. The stiff had been in the water about two weeks. I was turning away when I spotted Snipe. He was staring at the body like he couldn't take his eyes off it, and he was already green around the gills. For a minute I thought he was going to pull a faint right there on the dock.

He saw me then. We walked away together and sat down on a lumber pile. Snipe rolled a smoke from a dirty-looking sack of Bull Durham, and I tossed little sticks off the dock, watching them float lazily on the calm, dark water.

Across the channel one of the Luckenbach boats was loading cargo for her eastern trip, and the stack of a G.P. tanker showed over the top of a warehouse on Terminal. It was one of those still, warm afternoons with a haze of heat and smoke hanging over Long Beach. Another tanker was coming slowly upstream, and I sat there watching it, remembering how I'd burned my knees painting the white S on the stack of a tanker like it. I sat there watching, kind of sleepy-like, and wishing I was coming in with a payoff due instead of kicking my heels in the sun wishing for two bits. But all the time, way down deep, I was thinking of Snipe.

I felt in my pockets hoping for a dime I'd overlooked, but I'd shook myself down a dozen times already. Out of the corner of my eye I could see Snipe staring out over the channel, that limp-looking fag hanging from his lip, and his damp, straw-colored hair plastered against his narrow skull. His fingers were too long, and the nails always dirty. I felt disgusted with him and wondered what he wanted to live for. Maybe he wondered, too.

"That stiff sure looked awful, didn't it?" he says.

"None of them look so good t' me."

"I'd hate to look like that. Seawater is nasty stuff. I never did like it."

I grunted. A shore boat was heading for the Fifth Street landing, and I watched it as the wake trailed out in a widening V, like the events that follow the birth of a man. Then we could hear the slap of water under the dock.

"I'd sure hate to die like that. If a guy could die like a hero now, it wouldn't be so bad. I wonder what Sharkey meant the other night when he said when it was no longer possible to live proudly, a man could always die proudly?"

"What the hell difference does it make how you die? A corpse is a corpse, no matter how it got that way. That stuff about a life after death is all hooey. Like Sharkey said, it was an invention of the weak to put a damper on the strong. The little fellow thinks that if the big guy is worried about the hereafter, he'll play it fair in this one, see? A dead man don't mean anything, no more than a rotten potato. He just was something, that's all!"

"But what became of the life that was in him? Where does that go?"

"Where does the flame go when the fire goes out? It's just gone. Now, forget it, and let's find the gang. I'm fed up, talking about stiffs."

We started for the shack. A few clouds had rolled up, and

it was starting to drizzle. Out on the channel the ripples had changed to little waves with ruffles of white riding the crests. There was a tang in the air that smelled like a blow. I looked off toward the sea and was glad I was ashore. It wasn't going to be any fun out there tonight. Snipe hurried along beside me, his breath wheezing a little.

"I'm a good swimmer," he said, reaching for a confidence I could tell he didn't have. "Well, a pretty good swimmer."

Where did a runt like him ever get that hero idea? From Sharkey, I guess. Probably nobody ever treated him decent before. Looking at him, I wondered why it was some guys draw such tough hands. There was Sharkey, as regular a guy as ever walked, a big, fine-looking fellow with brains and nerve, and then here was Snipe, with nothing. Sharkey had a royal flush, and Snipe was holding nothing but deuces and treys in a game that was too big for him.

His frayed collar was about two sizes too large, and his Adam's apple just grazed it every time he swallowed. He didn't have a thing, that guy. He was bucking a stacked deck, and the worst of it was, he knew it.

You see a lot of these guys along the waterfronts. The misfits and the also-rans, the guys who knew too much and those who knew too little. Everything loose in the world seems to drift toward the sea and usually winds up on the beach somewhere. It's a sort of natural law, I guess. And here was Snipe. It wouldn't have been so tough if he'd been the dumb type that thought he was a pretty swell guy. But Snipe wasn't fooled. Way down inside he had a feeling for something better than he was, and every time he moved he knew it was him, Snipe, that was moving.

You could see him seeing himself. It gave you kind of a shock, sometimes. I had never quite got it until then, but I guess Sharkey had from the first. You could see that Snipe knew he was Snipe, just something dropped off the merry-go-round of life that didn't matter.

Instead of going on with me, he turned at the corner and walked off up the street, his old cap pulled down over his face, his funny, long shoes squidging on the sloppy walk.

It was warm and cheery inside the shack. Sharkey had had

the guys rustle up some old papers and nail them over the walls as insulation. When you couldn't do anything else, you could read the latest news of three months back or look at pictures of Mae West or Myrna Loy, depending if you liked them slim or well upholstered. Most of them looked at Mae West.

The big stove had its belly all red from the heat, and Tony was tipped back in a chair reading the sports. Deek was playing sol at the table, and Jim was standing by in the kitchen watching Red throw a mulligan together. Sharkey had his nose in a book as usual, something about the theory of the leisure class. I had to grin when he showed it to me. We sure were a leisure class, although there wasn't one of us liked it.

It was nice sitting there. The heat made a fellow kind of drowsy, and the smell of mulligan and coffee was something to write home about. I sat there remembering Snipe walking off up the street through that first spatter of rain, and how the wind whipped his worn old coat.

He was afraid of everything, that guy. Afraid of death, afraid of cops, scared of ship's officers, and of life, too, I guess. At that, he was luckier than some, for he had a flop. It would be cold and wet on the streets tonight, and there would be men sleeping in boxcars and lumber piles, and other guys walking the streets, wishing they had lumber piles and boxcars to sleep in. But we were lucky, with a shack like this, and we only kept it by working together. In that kind of a life, you got to stick together. It's the only answer.

Windy Slim was still out on the stem. He never came in early on bad nights, it being easier to pick up a little change when the weather is wet and miserable. Copper was out somewhere, too, and that was unusual, him liking the rain no better than a cat. The drizzle had changed now to a regular downpour, and the wind was blowing a gale.

We all knew what it would be like at sea, with the wind howling through the rigging like a lost banshee and the decks awash with black, glassy water. Sometimes the shack sagged with the weight of the wind, and once Sharkey looked up and glanced apprehensively at the stove.

Then, during a momentary lull, the door jerked open and

Slim stomped in, accompanied by a haze of wind and rain that made the lamp spit and almost go out. He shook himself and began pulling off his coat.

"God have pity on the poor sailors on such a night as this!" Jim said, grinning.

"Say—" Slim stopped pulling off his wet clothes and looked at Sharkey. "Brophy and Stallings picked up Copper tonight!"

"The devil they did!" Sharkey put down his book. "What happened?"

"Copper, he bums four bits from some lug down on the docks where he used to work an' goes to the Greek's for some chow. He has a hole in his pocket but forgets it. After he eats he finds his money is gone. The Greek hollers for a bull, an' Brophy comes running, Cap Stallings with him.

"Snipe, he was with Copper when he raised the four bits, but when the bull asks him did Copper have any money, the little rat is so scared he says he don't know nothing about it. He always was scared of a cop. So they took Copper an' throwed him in the can."

"The yellow rat!" Tony said. "An' after all the feeds Copper staked him to!"

"Why have him here, anyway?" Red said. "He just hangs around. He ain't any good for anything!"

Me, I sat there and didn't say anything. There wasn't anything you could say. Outside the wind gathered and hurled a heavy shoulder against the house, the lamp sputtered and gulped, and everybody was quiet. Everybody was thinking what I was thinking, I guess, that Snipe would have to go, but there wasn't any place for him to go. I tried to read again, but I couldn't see anything but that spatter of falling rain and Snipe walking away up the street. Red was right, he wasn't any good for anything, not even himself.

The door opened then, and Snipe came in. It was all in his face, all the bitter defeat and failure of him. That was the worst of it. He knew just what he'd done, knew just what it would mean to that tough, lonely bunch of men who didn't have any friends but themselves and so had to be good friends to each other. He knew it all, knew just how low he must have sunk, and only felt a little lower himself.

Sharkey didn't say anything, and the rest of us just sat there. Then Sharkey took a match out of his pocket and handed it to Snipe. Everybody knew what that meant. In the old days on the bum, when the crowd didn't like a fellow, they gave him a match as a hint to go build his own fire.

Sharkey picked up the poker then and began to poke at the fire. Out in the kitchen everything was quiet. Snipe stood there, looking down at Sharkey's shoulders, his face white and queer. Then he turned and went out. The sound of the closing door was loud in the room.

The next morning Sharkey and a couple of us drifted down to the big crap game under the P.E. trestle. Everybody was talking about the storm and the ferry to Terminal Island being rammed and sunk during the night. About a dozen lives lost, somebody said.

"Say, Sharkey," Honolulu said, looking up from the dice. "One of your crowd was on that ferry. That little guy they called Snipe. I saw him boarding her at the landing."

"Yeah?"

"Yeah."

Sharkey looked down at the dice and said nothing. Slim was getting the dice hot and had won a couple of bucks. The lookout got interested, and when all at once somebody hollers "Bull," there were the cops coming up through the lumberyard.

Two or three of our boys were in the inner circle, and when the yell came, everybody grabbed at the cash. Then we all scattered out, running across the stinking tideflat east of the trestle. I got a fistful of money myself, and there was a lot left behind. I glanced back once, and the cops were picking it up.

The tide wasn't out yet, and in some places the water was almost knee deep, but it was the only way, and we took it running. I got all wet and muddy but had to laugh, thinking what a funny sight we must have made, about twenty of us splashing through that water as fast as we could pick 'em up and put 'em down.

I was some little time getting back to the shack, and when

I did get there, Sharkey was sitting on the steps talking to Windy and Jim. They looked mighty serious, and when I came up, they motioned me to come along and then started back for the trestle.

Thinking maybe they were going back after the money, I told them about the cops getting it, but Slim merely shrugged and said nothing. He had a slug of chewing in his jaw and looked serious as hell.

Finally we got to the mud flat, and though it was still wet, Sharkey started picking his way across. We hadn't gone far before I could see something ahead, partly buried in the gray mud. It looked like an old sack, or a bundle of dirty clothes. When we got closer I could see it was a body— probably washed in by the tide.

It sort of looked as if the man had been walking in and, when the mud on his feet got too heavy, just laid down. Even before Sharkey stooped to turn his head over, I could see it was Snipe. He had on that old cap of his, and I couldn't have missed it in a million.

He looked pretty small and pitiful, lying there in the mud mingled with the debris left by an outgoing tide. Once in a while even yet, I think of how he looked, lying there on that stinking mud flat under a low, clouded sky, with a background of lumberyard and trestle. There was mud on the side of his face, and a spot on his nose. His long fingers were relaxed and helpless, but somehow there wasn't a thing about him that looked out of place. We stood there looking at him a minute, and none of us said anything, but I was thinking: "Well, you were afraid of it, and here it is— now what?"

We left him there and said nothing to anybody. Later, Red saw them down there picking him up but didn't go near, so we never knew what the coroner thought of it, if anything. I often wonder what happened when that ferry went down. She was hit hard and must have sunk like a rock, with probably fifty or sixty people aboard. It was Snipe's big chance to be a hero, him being such a good swimmer. But there he was.

As I said to Sharkey, it was a hell of a place to be found dead.

SURVIVAL

TEX WORDEN SHOVED his way through the crowd in the Slave Market and pushed his book under the wicket.

The clerk looked up, taking in his blistered face and swollen hands. "What'll you have, buddy? You want to register?"

"Naw, I'm here to play a piano solo, what d'you think?"

"Wise guy, eh?"

Tex's eyes were cold. "Sure, and what about it?"

"You guys all get too smart when you get ashore. I'm used to you guys, but one of these days I'm going to come out from behind here and kick hell out of one of you!"

"Why not now?" Worden said mildly. "You don't see me out there running down the street, do you? You just come out from behind that counter, and I'll lay you in the scuppers."

At a signal from the man behind the wicket a big man pushed his way through the crowd and tapped Tex Worden on the shoulder. "All right, buddy, take it easy. You take it easy, or you get the boot."

"Yeah?"

"Yeah!"

Tex grinned insultingly and turned his back, waiting for the return of his book. The clerk opened it grudgingly, then looked up, startled.

"You were on the *Raratonga*!"

"So what?"

"We heard only one of the crew was saved!"

"Who the hell do you think I am? Napoleon? And that saved business, that's the bunk. That's pure malarkey. I saved myself. Now come on, get that book fixed. I want to get out of here."

The plainclothes man was interested. "No kiddin', are you Tex Worden?"

"I am."

"Hell, man, that must have been some wreck. The papers say that if it wasn't for you none of them would have gotten back. Dorgan was on that boat, too!"

"Dorgan?" Tex turned to face him. "You know Dorgan?"

"*Knew* him? I should say I did! A tough man, too. One of the toughest."

Worden just looked at him. "How tough a man is often depends on where he is and what he's doing." He was looking past the plainclothes man, searching for a familiar face. In all this gathering of merchant seamen hunting work, he saw no one.

Times were hard. There were over seven hundred seamen on the beach, and San Pedro had become a hungry town. Jobs were scarce, and a man had to wait his turn. And he didn't have eating money. Everything he had had gone down with the *Raratonga.* He had money coming to him, but how long it would be before he saw any of it was a question.

Near the door he glimpsed a slight, bucktoothed seaman in a blue pea jacket whose face looked familiar. He edged through the crowd to him. "Hi, Jack, how's about staking a guy to some chow?"

"Hey? Don't I know you? Tex, isn't it?"

"That's right. Tex Worden. You were on the *West Ivis* when I was."

"Come on, there's a greasy spoon right down the street." When they were outside, he said, "I don't want to get far from the shipping office. My number's due to come up soon."

"How long's it been?"

"Three months. Well, almost that. Times are rough, Tex." He looked at Worden. "What happened to you?"

"I was on the *Raratonga.*"

The sailor shook his head in awe. "*Jee-sus!* You were the only one who came back!"

"Some passengers made it. Not many, but some."

"How's it feel to be a hero? And with Hazel Ryan yet. And

Price! The actress and the millionaire! You brought them back alive."

"Me an' Frank Buck. If this is how it feels to be a hero, you can have it. I'm broke. There's a hearing today, and maybe I can hit up the commissioner for a few bucks."

The other seaman thrust out a hand. "I'm Conrad, Shorty Conrad. Paid off a ship from the east coast of South America, and I lied to you. It didn't take me three months because I've got a pal back there. I'll say a word for you, and maybe you can get a quick ship-out."

They ordered coffee and hamburger steaks. "This is a tough town, man. No way to get out of this dump unless you can take a pierhead jump or get lucky. If you know a ship's officer who'll ask for you, you got a better chance."

"I don't know nobody out here. I been shipping off the East Coast."

A burly Greek came along behind the counter. He stared hard at them. "You boys got money? I hate to ask, but we get stiffed a lot."

"I got it." Shorty showed him a handful of silver dollars. "Anyway, this is Tex Worden. He was on the *Raratonga*."

"You got to be kiddin'."

The Greek eyed him with respect. "That where you got blistered?" he motioned toward Worden's hands. "What happened to them?"

"Knittin'," Tex said. "Them needles get awful heavy after a while."

He was tired, very, very tired. The reaction was beginning to set in now. He was so tired he felt he'd fall off the stool if he wasn't careful, and he didn't even have the price of a bed. If he hit the sack now, he'd probably pass out for a week. His shoulders ached, and his hands were sore. They hurt when he used them, and they hurt just as much when he didn't.

"It was a nasty blow, Shorty. You never saw wind like that."

"She went down quick, eh? I heard it was like fifteen minutes."

"Maybe. It was real quick. Starb'rd half door give way, and the water poured in; then a bulkhead give way, and the rush of water put the fires out. No power, no pumps—it was a madhouse."

They were silent, sipping their coffee and eating the greasy steaks. Finally Shorty asked, "How long were you out there?"

"Fifteen days, just a few miles off the equator. It rained once—just in time."

Faces of men he knew drifted by the door. He knew some of them but could not recall their names. They were faces he'd seen from Hong Kong to Hoboken, from Limehouse to Malay Street in Singapore or Grant Road in Bombay, Gomar Street in Suez, or the old American Bar on Lime Street in Liverpool. He'd started life as a cowboy but now he'd been at sea for fifteen years.

It was a rough crowd out there on Beacon Street, but if he did not know them all, he knew their kind. There were pimps and prostitutes, seamen, fishermen, longshoremen, and bums, but they were all people, and they were all alive, and they were all walking on solid ground.

There were gobs there from the battle wagons off Long Beach and girls who followed the fleet. There was an occasional drunk looking for a live wire who might spring for another bottle, and he liked it.

"Maybe I'll save my money," he said aloud, "buy myself a chicken ranch. I'd like to own a chicken ranch near Modesto."

"Where's Modesto?"

"I don't know. Somewhere north of here. I just like the sound of it."

Tex Worden looked down at his hands. Under the bandages they were swollen with angry red cracks where the blisters had been and some almost raw flesh that had just begun to heal. In the mirror he saw a face like a horror mask, for tough as his hide was, the sun had baked it to an angry red that he could not touch to shave. He looked frightening and felt worse. If only he could get some sleep!

He did not want to think of those bitter, brutal days when he rowed the boat, hour after hour, day after day, rowing with a sullen resignation, all sense of time forgotten, even all sense of motion. There had been no wind for days, just a dead calm, the only movement being the ripples in the wake of the lifeboat.

He got up suddenly. "I almost forgot. I got to stop by the commissioner's office. They want to ask me some questions. Sort of a preliminary inquiry, I guess."

Shorty stole a quick look at him. "Tex—you be careful. Be real careful. These aren't seamen. They don't know what it's like out there. They can't even imagine."

"I'll be all right."

"Be careful, I tell you. I read something about it in the papers. If you ain't careful they'll crucify you."

———

THERE WERE SEVERAL men in business suits in the office when they entered. They all looked at Tex, but the commissioner was the only one who spoke. "Thank you, son. That was a good job you did out there."

"It was my job," Tex said. "I done what I was paid for."

The commissioner dropped into a swivel chair behind his desk. "Now, Worden, I expect you're tired. We will not keep you any longer than we must, but naturally we must arrive at some conclusions as to what took place out there and what caused the disaster. If there is anything you can tell us, we'd be glad to hear it."

Shorty stole a glance at the big man with the red face. A company man, here to protect their interests. He knew the type.

"There's not much to tell, sir. I had come off watch about a half hour before it all happened, and when I went below, everything seemed neat and shipshape. When the ship struck, I was sitting on my bunk in the fo'c'sle taking off my shoes.

"The jolt threw me off the bench, an' Stu fell off his bunk on top of me. He jumped up an' said, 'What the hell happened?' and I said I didn't know, but it felt like we hit something. He said, 'It's clear enough outside, and we're way out to sea. Must be a derelict!' I was pulling on my shoes, and so was he, an' we ran up on deck.

"There was a lot of running around, and we started forward, looking for the mate. Before we'd made no more than a half-dozen steps, the signal came for boat stations, and I went up on the boat deck. Last I saw of Stu he was trying to break open a jammed door, and I could hear people behind it.

"We must have hit pretty hard because she was starting to settle fast, going down by the head with a heavy list to starb'rd. I was mighty scared because I remembered that starb'rd half door, and—"

"What about the half door, Worden? What was wrong with it?"

"Nothing at all, commissioner," the company man interrupted. "The company inspector—"

"Just a minute, Mr. Winstead." The commissioner spoke sharply. "Who is conducting this inquiry?"

"Well, I—"

"Proceed with your story, Worden."

"The half door was badly sprung, sir. Somebody said the ship had been bumped a while back, and I guess they paid no mind to repairs. Anyway, it wasn't no bother unless they was loaded too heavy, and—"

"What do you mean, Worden? Was the ship overloaded?"

Winstead scowled at Worden, his lips drawing to a thin, angry line.

"Well, sir, I guess I ain't got no call to speak, but—"

"You just tell what happened at the time of the wreck, Worden. That will be sufficient!" Winstead said, interrupting.

"Mr. Winstead! I will thank you not to interrupt this man's story again. I am conducting this inquiry, and regardless of the worth of what Worden may have to say, he is the sole remaining member of the crew. As a seafaring man of many years' experience, he understands ships, and he was there when it happened. I intend to hear all—let me repeat, all—he has to say. We certainly are not going to arrive at any conclusions by concealing anything. If your vessel was in proper condition, you have nothing to worry about, but I must say your attitude gives rise to suspicion." He paused, glancing up at the reporters who were writing hurriedly. "Now, Worden, if you please. Continue your story."

"Well, sir, I was standing by number three hatch waiting for the last loads to swing aboard so's I could batten down the hatch, an' I heard Mr. Jorgenson—he was the mate—say to Mr. Winstead here that he didn't like it at all. He said loading so heavy with that bad door was asking for trouble, and he went on to mention that bad bulkhead amidships.

"I don't know much about it, sir, except what he said and the talk in the fo'c's'le about the bulkhead between hatches three and four. One of the men who'd been chipping rust down there said you didn't dare chip very hard or you'd drive your hammer right through, it was that thin. When I was ashore clearing the gangway, I saw she was loaded down below the Plimsoll marks."

"Weren't you worried, Worden? I should think that knowing the conditions you would have been."

"No, sir. Generally speaking, men working aboard ship don't worry too much. I've been going to sea quite a while now, and it's always the other ships that sink, never the one a fellow's on. At least that's the way it is until something happens. We don't think about it much, and if she sinks, then she sinks, and that's all there is to it."

"I see."

"Yes, sir. There was trouble with that half door before we were three days out. Me an' a couple of others were called to help Chips caulk that half door. You know—it's a door in the ship's side through which cargo is loaded. Not all ships have 'em. That door had been rammed some time or another, and it didn't fit right. In good weather or when she carried a normal load it was all right.

"But three days out we had a spot of bad weather; some of that cargo shifted a mite, and she began to make water, so we had to recaulk that door.

"To get back to that night, sir. When I got to my boat station, I saw one of the officers down on the deck with his head all stove in. I don't know whether he got hit with something or whether it was done by the bunch of passengers who were fighting over the boat. Ever'body was yellin' an' clawin', so

I waded in an' socked a few of them and got them straightened out.

"I told them they'd damn well better do what they were told because I was the only one who knew how to get that lifeboat into the water. After that they quieted down some. A couple of them ran off aft, hunting another boat, but I got busy with the lifeboat cover.

"All of a sudden it was still, so quiet it scared you. The wind still blowing and big waves all around but ghostly still. You could hear a body speak just like I'm speakin' now. It was like everything quieted down to let us die in peace. I could tell by the feel of her that we hadn't long. She was settlin' down, and she had an ugly, heavy feel to her.

"Mister, that was a tryin' time. All those people who'd been yellin' an' fightin' stood there lookin' at me, and one little fellow in a gray suit—he had a tie on, an' everything. He was Jewish, I think. He asked me what he could do, and I told him to get to the other end of the boat, to loose the falls and lower away when I did.

"I got the boat cover off, and we got the boat into the water, and the ship was down so far and canted over—a bad list to her—that it was no problem gettin' those few folks into the lifeboat.

"I took a quick look around. The boat 'longside was already in the water, and there were two A.B.s with it, Fulton an' Jaworski, it was. They had maybe thirty people in that boat, and I saw one of the stewards there, too. There was nobody else in sight, but I could hear some yelling forward.

"Just then she gave a sort of shudder, and I jumped into the boat and told the Jew to cast off. He had trouble because she was rising and falling on the water, but a woman helped him. I didn't know who she was then, but later I found out it was that actress, Hazel Ryan.

"We shoved off, and I got oars into the water, and we started looking for others. When we got out a ways, I could see Sparks—one of them, anyway, in the radio shack.

"Then the ship gave a kind of lunge and went down by the head. She just dipped down and then slid right away, going into the water on her beam ends with all the port-side boats just danglin' there, useless, as they couldn't be got into the water. At the last minute, as she went under, I saw a man with an ax running from boat to boat cutting the falls. He was hoping they'd come up floating, and two or three of them did.

"All of a sudden I see a man in the water. He was a pleasant-looking man with gray hair, and he was swimming. He looked so calm I almost laughed. 'Cold, isn't it?' he says, and then he just turns and swims away, cool as you please. You'd have thought the beach wasn't fifty feet away.

"It's things like that fairly take your wind, sir, and there I was, trying to pull the lifeboat away from the ship and hopin' for the best.

"I turned my head once and looked back. Mostly I was trying to guide the boat through wreckage that was already afloat. When I looked back—this was just before she went under—I glimpsed somebody standin' on the bridge, one arm through the pilot-house window to hang on, and he was lighting his pipe with his free hand.

"It just didn't seem like it could be happening. There I was just minutes before, a-comin' off watch, all set for a little shuteye, and now here I was in a lifeboat, and the ship was goin' down.

"There must have been nearly a hundred people in the water and not a whisper out of any of them. Like they was all in shock or somethin' of the kind. Once a guy did yell to somebody else. Then something exploded under water— maybe the boilers busted. I wouldn't know. Anyway, when it was over, a lot of those folks who'd been in the water were gone. I fetched the bow of my boat around and rowed toward something white floating in the water. It was a woman, and I got her into the boat."

"Was that Hazel Ryan?" a reporter asked.

"No, it was Lila, a stewardess. Then I held the boat steady whilst another man climbed in. He pointed out three people clingin' to a barrel. I started for them.

"The sea was rough, and folks would disappear behind a wave, and sometimes when you looked, they weren't there anymore. Those people were havin' a time of it, tryin' to hang to that barrel, so I got to them first, and folks helped them aboard. The Ryan woman was one of them.

"I'll give her this. First moment she could speak, she asked if there was anything she could do, and I said just to set quiet and try to get warm. If I needed help, I'd ask for it.

"It was funny how black everything was, yet you could see pretty well for all of that. You'd see a white face against the black water, and by the time you got there, it was gone.

"One time I just saw an arm. Woman's, I think it was. She was right alongside the boat, and I let go an oar an' grabbed for her, but her arm slipped right through my fingers, and she was gone.

"Some of those we'd picked up were in panic and some in shock. That little Jewish fellow with the necktie and all, he didn't know a thing about the sea, but he was cool enough. We moved people around, got the boat trimmed, and I got her bow turned to meet the sea and started to try to ride her out."

"What about the radio?"

"We didn't think about that for long. At least I didn't. There hadn't been much time, and the chances were slim that any message got off. It all happened too fast.

"Sparks was in there, and he was sending. I am sure of that, but he hadn't any orders, and most shipmasters don't want any Mayday or SOS goin' out unless they say. If he sent it, he sent it on his own because the old man never made the bridge."

"The man you saw lighting his pipe?"

"Jorgenson, I think. He was watch officer, but they were changing watch, so I don't know. He wasn't heavy enough for the old man.

"Anyway, I'd no time to think of them. The sea was making up, and I was havin' the devil's own time with that boat. She'd have handled a lot easier if we'd had a few more people aboard.

"Lila, she was hurting. Seemed like she was all stove up inside, and the shock was wearing off. She was feeling pain, turning and twisting like, and the Ryan woman was trying to help. She and that little Jew, they worked over her, covering her with coats, trying to tuck them under so she'd ride easier. The rest just sat and stared."

"No other boats got off?"

"I don't know—except that boat with Fulton and Jaworski. They were good men, and they'd do what could be done. The ship had taken a bad list, so I don't think many of the boats on the topside could be launched at all."

"How was the weather?"

"Gettin' worse, sir. There was nobody to spell me on the oars because nobody knew anything about handling a boat in a heavy sea. I shipped the oars and got hold of the tiller, which made it a mite easier.

"Lila had passed out; spray was whipping over the boat. I was hanging to that tiller, scared ever' time a big one came over that it would be the last of us. There was no way to play. You just had to live from one sea to the next."

"How long did the storm last?"

"About two days. I don't rightly remember because I was so tired everything was hazy. When the sea calmed down enough, I let Schwartz have the tiller. I'd been gripping it so hard and so long I could hardly let go."

"You were at the tiller forty-eight hours without relief?"

"Yes, sir. Maybe a bit more. But after that she began to settle down, and the sun came out."

"The boat was provisioned according to regulations?"

"Yes, sir. We'd some trouble about water later but not much."

"How about the crew and the officers? Were they efficient in your opinion?"

"Sure. Yes, they were okay. I've been going to sea quite a spell, and I never have seen any seaman or officer shirk his job. It ain't bravery nor lack of it, just that he knows his job and has been trained for it.

"Sometimes you hear about the crew rushing the boats or being inefficient. I don't believe it ever happens. They're trained for the job, and it is familiar to them. They know what they are to do, and they do it.

"Passengers are different. All of a sudden everything is dif-

ferent. There's turmoil an' confusion; there's folks runnin' back
and forth, and the passengers don't know what's going on.

"Sometimes one of them will grab a crewman and yell
something at him, and the crewman will pull loose and go
about his business. The passenger gets mad and thinks
they've been deserted by the crew when chances are that seaman had something to do. Maybe his boat station was elsewhere. Maybe he'd been sent with a message for the engineer
on watch below.

"Maybe those crewmen you hear about rushing the boats
are just getting there to get the boat cover off and clear the
falls. This wasn't my first wreck, and I've yet to see a crewman who didn't stand by."

"How long before she sank?"

"Fifteen minutes, give or take a few. It surely wasn't more,
though. It might have been no more than five. We'd made
quite a bit of water before the cargo shifted and she heeled
over. With that half door underwater—well, I figure that door
gave way and she just filled up and sank."

"Mr. Commissioner?" Winstead asked. "I'd like permis-
sion to ask this man a few questions. There are a few matters
I'd like to clear up."

"Go ahead."

"Now, my man, if you'd be so kind. How many were in the
boat when you got away from the scene of the wreck?"

"Eight."

"Yet when you were picked up by the *Maloaha* there were
but three?"

"Yes."

"How do you account for that?"

"Lila—she was the stewardess—she died. Like I said,
she'd been hurt inside. She was a mighty good woman, and
I hated to see her go. Clarkson—he went kind of screwy.
Maybe he didn't have all his buttons to start with. Anyway,
he got kind of wild and kept staring at a big shark who was
following us. One night he grabbed up a boat hook and tried
to get that shark. It was silly. That shark was just swimmin'
along in hopes. No use to bother him. Well, he took a stab at
that shark and fell over the side.

"Handel, he just sat an' stared. Never made no word for anybody, just stared. He must've sat that way for eight or nine days. We all sort of lost track of time, but he wouldn't take water, wouldn't eat a biscuit. He just sat there, hands hanging down between his knees.

"I'd rigged a sort of mast from a drifting stick and part of a boat cover. The mast this boat should have carried was missing. Anyway, the little sail I rigged gave us some rest, and it helped. Late one day we were moving along at a pretty fair rate for us when I saw a squall coming. She swept down on us so quick that I gave the tiller to Schwartz and stumbled forward to get that sail down before we swamped. With the wind a-screaming and big seas rolling up, I'd almost reached the sail when this Handel went completely off his course. He jumped up and grabbed me, laughing and singing, trying to dance with me or something.

"Struggling to get free, I fell full length in the boat, scrambled up and pulled that sail down, and when I looked around, Handel was gone."

"Gone?" Winstead said.

"You mean—over the side?" the commissioner asked.

"That's right. Nearest thing I could figure out was that when I fell, he fell, too. Only when I fell into the bottom, he toppled over the side.

"Rain and blown spray was whipping the sea, and we couldn't see him. No chance to turn her about. We'd have gone under had we tried.

"For the next ten hours we went through hell, just one squall after another, and all of us had to bail like crazy just to keep us afloat."

"So," Winstead said, "you killed a passenger?"

"I never said that. I don't know what happened. Whatever it was, it was pure accident. I'd nothing against the man. He was daffy, but until that moment he'd been harmless. I figure he didn't mean no harm then, only I had to get free of him to save the boat."

"At least, that is your story?"

"Mister, with a ragin' squall down on us there was no time

to coddle nobody. I didn't have a straitjacket nor any way to get him into one. It was save the boat or we'd all drown."

"Yet even with your small sail up, you might have lasted, might you not?"

Worden considered the matter, then he shrugged. "No way to tell. I was the only seaman aboard, and it was my judgment the sail come down. I'd taken it down."

"All right. We will let that rest for the moment. That accounts for three. Now what became of the other two?"

"The Jew—Schwartz, he come to me in the night a few days later. We were lyin' in a dead calm, and most of our water was gone. Sky was clear, not a cloud in sight, and we'd a blazin' hot day ahead. He told me he was goin' over the side, and he wanted me to know because he didn't want me to think he was a quitter.

"Hell, that little kike had more guts than the whole outfit. I told him nothing doing. Told him I needed him, which was no lie. It was a comfort just to have him there because what he didn't know he could understand when I told him. He wouldn't accept the fact that I needed him.

"It even came to the point where I suggested I toss a coin with him to see who went over. He wouldn't listen to that, and we both knew I was talkin' nonsense. I was the only seaman. The only one who could handle a boat. It was my job to bring that boat back with as many people as possible. I ain't goin' for any of that hero stuff. That's all baloney. Sure, I wanted to live as much as any man, but I had a job to do. It was what I signed on to do. At least when I signed on, it was to do a seaman's job. I ain't done nothing I wouldn't do again."

"I see. And what became of the other man?"

"He was a big guy, and he was tough. He tried to take charge of the boat. There's a lot happens in an open boat like that when everybody is close to shovin' off for the last time. People just ain't thinkin' the way they should. This big guy, he had more stamina than the rest of them. Most of them tried to take a hand in rowin' the boat.

"We'd no wind, you see, and I was hopin' we could get out of the calm into the wind again, but he wouldn't do anything.

He just sat. He said I was crazy, that I was goin' the wrong way. He said I drank water at night when they were all asleep. Twice when I passed water forward for somebody else, he drank it.

"Then one night I woke up with him pourin' the last of our water down his damn throat. The Ryan woman, she was tuggin' at his arm to try to stop him, but hell, it was too late.

"It was her callin' to me that woke me up, and I went at him. He emptied the cask and threw it over the side. I tried to stop him, and we had it out, right there. He was some bigger than me and strong, but there was no guts to him. I smashed him up some and put him between the oars. I told him to row, that he'd live as long as he rowed. First we had to circle around and pick up the cask."

"An empty cask?" Winstead asked incredulously. "What in God's world did you do that for?"

"Mister, it's only in the movies where some guy on the desert an' dyin' of thirst throws away a canteen because it's empty. Shows how little some of those screenwriters know. Supposin' he finds water next day? How's he goin' to carry it?

"You throw away an empty canteen in the desert an' you're committin' suicide. Same thing out there. We might get a rain squall, and if we did, we'd need something to hold water. So we circled and picked up that cask."

"And what happened to Dorgan?"

Tex Worden's face was bleak. "He quit rowin' twenty-four hours before we got picked up."

Winstead turned to the commissioner. "Sir, this man has admitted to killing one passenger; perhaps he killed two or three. As to his motives—I think they will appear somewhat different under cross-examination.

"I have evidence as to this man's character. He is known along the waterfronts as a tough. He frequents houses of ill fame. He gets into drunken brawls. He has been arrested several times for fighting. His statements here today have cast blame upon the company. I intend to produce evidence that this man is not only a scoundrel but an admitted murderer!"

Tex sat up slowly.

"Yes, I've been arrested for fighting. Sometimes when I

come ashore after a long cruise I have a few too many, and sometimes I fight, but it's always with my own kind. After a trip on one of those louse-bound scows of yours, a man has to get drunk. But I'm a seaman. I do my job. There's never a man I've worked with will deny that. I'm sorry you weren't in that boat with us so you could have seen how it was.

"You learn a lot about people in a lifeboat. Me, I never claimed to be any psalm singer. Maybe the way I live isn't your way, but when the time comes for the men to step out, I'll be there. I'll be doin' my job.

"It's easy to sit around on your fat behinds and say what you'd have done or what should have been done. You weren't there.

"Nobody knows what he'd do until he's in the spot. I was the only guy in that boat knew a tiller from a thwart. It was me bring that boat through or nobody. I'd rather lose two than lose them all. I wasn't doin' it because it was swell of me or because they'd call me a hero. I was bringin' them in because it was my job.

"Handel now. He wasn't responsible. Somethin' happened to him that he never expected. He could have lived his life through a nice, respected man, but all of a sudden it isn't the same anymore. There's nobody to tell to do something or to even ask. He's caught in a place he can't see his way out of. He'd never had just to endure, and there was nothing in him to rise to the surface and make him stand up. It sort of affected his mind.

"Hazel Ryan? She has moxie. When I told her it was her turn to row, she never hesitated, and I had to make her quit. She wasn't all that strong, but she was game. A boatload like her an' I could have slept halfway back.

"Dorgan was a bad apple. The whole boat was on edge because of him. He'd been used to authority and was a born bully. He was used to takin' what he wanted an' lettin' others cry about it. I told him what he had to do, and he did it after we had our little set-to."

"Who did you think you were, Worden? God? With the power of life and death?"

"Listen, mister"—Worden leaned forward—"when I'm

the only seaman in the boat, when we have damn' little water, an' we're miles off the steamer lanes, when there's heat, stillness, thirst, an' we're sittin' in the middle of a livin' hell, you can just bet I'm Mister God as far as that boat's concerned.

"The company wasn't there to help. You weren't there to help, nor was the commissioner. Sure, the little fat guy prayed, an' Clarkson prayed. Me, I rowed the boat."

He lifted his hands, still swollen and terribly lacerated where the blisters had broken to cracks in the raw flesh. "Forty hours," he said, "there at the end I rowed for forty hours, tryin' to get back where we might be picked up. We made it.

"We made it," he repeated, "but there was a lot who didn't."

The commissioner rose, and Winstead gathered his papers, his features set and hard. He threw one quick, measuring glance at Worden.

"That will be all, gentlemen," the commissioner said. "Worden, you will remain in port until this is straightened out. You are still at the same address?"

"Yes, sir. At the Seaman's Institute."

Shorty glanced nervously out the window, then at Winstead. Tex turned away from the desk, a tall, loose figure in a suit that no longer fit. Winstead left, saying nothing, but as Worden joined Shorty, the commissioner joined them.

"Worden?"

"Yes, sir?"

"As man to man, and I was once a seaman myself, Mr. Winstead has a lot of influence. He will have the best attorney money can hire, and to a jury off the shore things do not look the same as in a drifting lifeboat.

"The *Lichenfield* docked a few minutes ago, and she will sail after refueling. I happen to know they want two A.B.s. This is unofficial, of course. The master of the vessel happens to be a friend of mine."

They shook hands briefly.

There was a faint mist falling when they got outside. Tex turned up his coat collar. Shorty glanced toward Terminal Island. "You got an outfit? Some dungarees an' stuff?"

"I'd left a sea bag at the Institute." He touched the blue shirt. "This was in it. I can draw some gear from the slop chest."

"They got your tail in a crack, Tex. What's next, the *Lichenfield*?"

"Well," he said shortly, "I don't make my living in no courtroom."

SHOW ME THE WAY TO GO HOME

I T WAS THE night the orchestra played "Show Me the Way to Go Home," the night the fleet sailed for Panama. The slow drizzle of rain had stopped, and there was nothing but the play of searchlights across the clouds, the mutter of the motors from the shore boats, and the spatter of grease where the man was frying hamburgers on the Fifth Street landing. I was standing there with a couple of Greek fishermen and a taxi driver, watching the gobs say good-bye to their wives and sweethearts.

There was something about the smell of rain, the sailors saying goodbye, and the creak of rigging that sort of got to you. I'd been on the beach for a month then.

A girl came down to the landing and leaned on the rail watching the shore boats. One of the gobs waved at her, and she waved back, but didn't smile. You could see that they didn't know each other; it was just one of those things.

She was alone. Every other girl was with somebody, but not her. She was wearing a neat, tailored suit that was a little worn, but she had nice legs and large, expressive eyes. When the last of the shore boats was leaving she was still standing there. Maybe it wasn't my move, but I was lonely, and when you're on the beach you don't meet many girls. So I walked over and leaned on the rail beside her.

"Saying good-bye to your boyfriend?" I asked, though I knew she wasn't.

"I said good-bye to him a long time ago."

"He didn't come back?"

"Do they ever?"

"Sometimes they want to and can't. Sometimes things don't break right."

"I wonder."

"And sometimes they do come back and things aren't like they were, and sometimes they don't come back because they are afraid they won't be the same, and they don't want to spoil what they remember."

"Then why go?"

"Somebody has to. Men have always gone to sea, and girls have waited for them."

"I'm not waiting for anybody."

"Sure you are. We all are. From the very beginning we wait for somebody, watch for them long before we know who they are. Sometimes we find the one we wait for, sometimes we don't. Sometimes the one we wait for comes along and we don't know it until too late. Sometimes they ask too much and we are afraid to take a chance, and they slip away."

"I wouldn't wait for anyone. Especially him. I wouldn't want him now."

"Of course not. If you saw him now, you'd wonder why you ever wanted him. You aren't waiting for him, though—you're waiting for what he represented. You knew a sailor once. Girls should never know men who have the sea in their blood."

"They always go away."

"Sure, and that's the way it should be. All the sorrow and tragedy in life come from trying to make things last too long."

"You're a cynic."

"All sentimentalists are cynics, and all Americans are sentimentalists. It's the Stephen Foster influence. Or too many showings of 'Over the Hill to the Poorhouse' and 'East Lynne.' But I like it that way."

"Do people really talk like this?"

"Only when they need coffee. Or maybe the first time a girl and a man meet. Or maybe this talk is a result of the saying good-bye influence. It's the same thing that makes women cry at the weddings of perfect strangers."

"You're a funny person." She turned to look at me.

"I boast of it. But how about that coffee? We shouldn't

stand here much longer. People who lean on railings over water at night are either in love or contemplating suicide."

We started up the street. This was the sort of thing that made life interesting—meeting people. Especially attractive blondes at midnight.

Over the coffee she looked at me. "A girl who falls in love with a sailor is crazy."

"Not at all. A sailor always goes away, and then she doesn't have time to be disillusioned. Years later she can make her husband's life miserable telling him what a wonderful man so-and-so was. The chances are he was a fourteen-carat sap. Only he left before the new wore off."

"Is that what you do?"

"Very rarely. I know all the rules for handling women. The trouble is that at the psychological moment I forget to use them. It's depressing."

"It's getting late. I'm going to have to go home."

"Not alone, I hope."

She looked at me again, very coolly. "You don't think I'm the sort of girl you can just pick up, do you?"

"Of course not," I chuckled. "But I wished on a star out there. You know that old gag."

She laughed. "I think you're a fool."

"That cinches it. Women always fall in love with fools."

"You think it is so easy to fall in love as that?"

"It must be. Some people fall in love with no visible reason, either material, moral, or maternal. Anyway, why should it be so complicated?"

"Were you ever in love?"

"I think so. I'm not exactly sure. She was a wonderful cook, and if the way to a man's heart is through his stomach, this was a case of love at first bite."

"Do you ever take anything seriously?"

"I'm taking you seriously. But why not have a little fun with it? There's only one thing wrong with life: people don't love enough, they don't laugh enough—and they are too damned conventional. Even their love affairs are supposed to run true to form. But this is spontaneous. You walk down where the sailors are saying good-bye to their sweethearts because you said good-bye to one once. It has been raining a little, and there is a sort of melancholy tenderness in the air. You are remembering the past, not because of him, because his face and personality have faded, but because of the romance of saying good-bye, the smell of strange odors from foreign ports, the thoughts the ocean always brings to people—romance, color, distance. A sort of vague sadness that is almost a happiness. And then, accompanied by the sound of distant music and the perfume of frying onions, I come into your life!"

She laughed again. "That sounds like a line."

"It is. Don't you see? When you went down to the landing tonight you were looking for me. You didn't know who I was, but you wanted something, someone. Well, here I am. The nice part of it is, I was looking for you."

"You make it sound very nice."

"Why not? A man who couldn't make it sound nice while looking at you would be too dull to live. Now finish your coffee and we'll go home."

"Now listen, I . . ."

"I know. Don't say it. But I'll just take you to the door, kiss you very nicely, and close it."

THERE HAD BEEN another shower, and the streets were damp. A fog was rolling from the ocean, the silent mist creeping in around the corners of the buildings, encircling the ships to the peaks of their masts. It was a lonely, silent world where the streetlights floated in ghostly radiance.

"You were wondering why men went to sea. Can't you imagine entering a strange, Far Eastern port on such a night as this? The lights of an unknown city—strange odors, mysterious sounds, the accents of a strange tongue? It's the charm of the strange and the different, of something new. Yet there's the feeling around you of something very old. Maybe that's why men go to sea."

"Maybe it is, but I'd never fall in love with another sailor."

"I don't blame you."

We had reached the door. She put her key in the lock, and

we stepped in. It was very late, and very quiet. I took her in my arms, kissed her goodnight, and closed the door.

"I thought you said you were going to say goodnight, and then go?" she protested.

"I said I was going to kiss you good night, and then close the door. I didn't say on which side of it I'd be."

"Well . . ."

The hell of it was my ship was sailing in the morning.

THICKER THAN BLOOD

E HAD IT coming if ever a man did, and I could have killed him then and nobody the wiser. If he had been man enough, we could have gone off on the dock and slugged it out, and everything would have been settled either way the cat jumped. There's nothing like a sock on the chin to sort of clean things up. It saves hard feelings and time wasted in argument. But Duggs was the chief mate, who wasn't man enough to whip me and knew it.

Bilge water, they say, is thicker than blood, and once men have been shipmates, no matter how much they hate each other's guts, they stand together against the world. That's the way it is supposed to be, but it certainly wasn't going to be that way with Duggs and me. I decided that in a hurry.

From the hour I shipped on that freighter, Duggs made it tough for me, but it wasn't only me but the whole crew. You don't mind so much if a really tough guy makes you like it, but when a two-by-twice scenery bum like Duggs rubs it in to you just because he has the authority, it just naturally hurts.

If we'd gone off on the dock where it was man to man, I'd have lowered the boom on his chin and left him for the gulls to pick over. But we were aboard ship, and if you sock an officer aboard ship, it's your neck.

Sometimes I think he laid awake nights figuring ways to be nasty, but maybe he didn't have to go to that much effort. I suspect it just came naturally. He made it rough for all of us but particularly me. Not that I didn't have my chances to cool him off. I had three of them. The first was at sea, the second in Port Swettenham, and the third—well, you'll hear about that.

Every dirty job he could find fell to Tony or me, and he

could think of more ways to be unpleasant without trying than you could if you worked at it. Unless you have been at sea, you can't realize how infernally miserable it can become. There are a thousand little, insignificant things that can be done to make it miserable. Always something, and it doesn't have to be anything big. Often it is the little things that get under your skin, and the longer it lasts, the worse it gets.

Of course, the food was bad, but that was the steward's fault. Curry and rice and fried potatoes for three straight weeks. That was bad enough, but Duggs kept finding work for us to do after we were off watch. Emergencies, he called them, and you can't refuse duty in an emergency. There were men aboard that ship who would have killed Duggs for a Straits dollar. Me, I'm an easygoing guy, but it was getting to me.

One morning at four o'clock I was coming off watch. It was blowing like the bull of Barney, and a heavy sea running. Duggs had just come on watch, and he calls to me to go aft with him and lend a hand. The log line was fouled. Back we went, and the old tub was rolling her scuppers under, with seas breaking over her that left you gasping like a fish out of water, they were that cold.

We reeled in the log line, hand over hand, the wind tearing at our clothes, the deck awash. He did help some, I'll give him that, but it was me who did the heavy hauling, and it was me who cleared the little propeller on the patent log of seaweed and rope yarns.

Right there was the perfect opportunity. Nobody would have been surprised if we'd both been washed over the side, so it would have been no trick to have dumped him over the rail and washed my hands of him. Duggs had on sea boots and oilskins, and he would have gone down quick.

I finished the job, tearing skin from my hands and getting salt into the raw wounds, the ship plunging like a crazy bronco in a wild and tormented sea. Then, in the moment when I could have got him and got him good, he leaned over and shouted to be heard above the wind, "There! I'm sure glad *I* managed to get that done!"

And I was so mad I forgot to kill him.

The next time was in Port Swettenham. Duggs knew I had a girl in Singapore, but instead of letting me go ashore, he put me on anchor watch. All night long I stood by the rail or walked the deck, looking at the far-off lights of town and cussing the day I shipped on a barge with a louse-bound, scupper-jumping, bilge-swilling rat for mate. And my girl was ashore expecting me—at least, I hoped she was.

We sailed from Singapore, called at Baliwan and Penang, and finally we crawled up the river to Port Swettenham.

It was hot and muggy. Keeping cool was almost impossible, and I had only two changes of clothes for working. One of them I managed to keep clean to wear off watch; the other was stiff with paint and tar. When time allowed I'd wash the one set and switch. The mate deliberately waited one day until I'd changed into clean clothes, and then he called me.

We were taking on some liquid rubber, and down in the empty fuel-oil tank in the forepeak was a spot of water about as big as a pie plate. He told me to climb down fifteen feet of steel ladder covered with oil slime and sop up that water. Aside from being a complete mess before I'd reached the bottom, there was almost an even chance I'd slip and break a leg.

Forward we went together, then down in the forepeak, and stopped by the manhole that let one into the tank. He held up his flashlight, pointing out that dime's worth of water. I had a steel scraper in my hand, and when he leaned over that manhole, I thought what a sweet setup that was.

I could just bend that scraper over his head, drop him into the tank, put the hatch cover on, then go on deck and give them the high sign to start pumping rubber. There'd be a fuss when the mate turned up missing, but they'd never find him until they emptied the tank, and if I knew the old man, I knew he'd never pump the rubber out of that tank for a dozen mates. And just then Chips stuck his head down the hatch and yelled for Duggs.

Time passed, and we tied up in Brooklyn. I drew my pay and walked down the gangway to the dock. Then I turned and looked back.

From beginning to end that voyage had been plain, un-adulterated hell, yet I hated to leave. When a guy lives on a ship that long, it begins to feel like home no matter how rough it is, and I had no other.

Six months I'd sailed on that packet, good weather and bad. Around the world we'd gone and in and out of some of the tiniest, dirtiest ports in the Far East. I'd helped to paint her from jack staff to rudder and stood four hours out of every twenty-four at her wheel across three oceans and a half-dozen seas. She was a scummy old barge, but as I stood there looking back, I had to cuss just to keep from feeling bad. Then I walked away.

After that there were other ships and other ports, some good and some bad, but I never forgot Duggs and swore the first time I found him ashore, I'd beat the hell out of him. Every time I'd see that company flag, and they had thirty-odd ships, I'd go hunting for Duggs. I knew that someday I'd find him.

One day in Portland I was walking along with a couple of guys, and I glimpsed that house flag over the top of a ware-house at the dock. Thinks I, now's my chance to get that mug; this will be him.

Sure enough, when I walked down the dock, there he was, giving the last orders before casting off and standing right at the foot of the gangway ready to board. It was now or never. I walked up, all set to cop a Sunday on his chin, and I say, "Remember me?"

He sized me up. "Why, sure! You're Duke, aren't you?" There'd been a time they called me that—among other things.

"That's me. And you—!"

"Well, well!" He was grinning all over. "What do you know about that? We were just talking about you the other day, and we were wondering what had become of you!

"Remember Jones? He's skipper on the *Iron Queen* now, and Edwards—he was third, you'll remember, he's with the *Bull Line*. They're all scattered now, but that was a good crew, and we came through a lot together. I'll never forget the night you hit that Swede in the Dato Kramat Gardens in Penang! Man, what a wallop that was! I'll bet he's out yet!

"Well," he says then, "I wish we could talk longer. It's like old times to see somebody from the old ship, and we came through, didn't we? We came through some of the roughest weather I ever did see, but we made it! And they say bilge water is thicker than blood. Well, so long, Duke, and good luck!"

Then Duggs stuck out his mitt, and I'll be damned if I didn't shake hands with him!

THE ADMIRAL

AFTER I FINISHED painting the hatch-combing, I walked back aft to the well deck where Tony and Dick were standing by the rail looking down into the Whangpoo. The sampan was there again, and the younger woman was sculling it in closer to the ship's side. When she stopped, the old woman fastened a net on the end of a long stick and held it up to the rail, and Tony put some bread and meat into it.

Every day they came alongside at about the same time, and we were always glad to see them, for we were lonely men. The young woman was standing in the stern as always, and when she smiled, there was something pleasant and agreeable about it that made us feel better. The old woman gave the kids some of the bread and meat, and we stood watching them.

Probably they didn't get meat very often, and bread must have been strange to them, but they ate it very seriously. They were our family, and they seemed to have adopted us just as we adopted them when they first came alongside at Wayside Pier. They had come to ask for "bamboo," which seemed to mean any kind of lumber or wood, and for "chow-chow," which was food, of course. The greatest prize was "soapo," but although most of the Chinese who live like that sell the soap or trade it, our family evidently used it—or some of it.

That was one reason we liked them, one reason they had become our family, because they were clean. They wore the faded blue that all the Chinese of that period seemed to wear, but theirs was always newly washed. We had thrown sticks of dunnage to them or other scrap lumber and some that wasn't scrap, but then the mate came by and made us stop.

There were five of them, the two women and three young ones, living in a sampan. Tony had never seen the like, nor had I, but it was old stuff to Dick, who had been out to the Far East before.

He told us lots of the Chinese lived that way, and some never got ashore from birth to death. There is no room for them on China's crowded soil, so in the seemingly ramshackle boats they grow up, rear families, and die without knowing any other home. There will be a fishnet on the roof of the shelter of matting, and on poles beyond the roof the family wash waves in the wind. Sometimes the younger children have buoys fastened to their backs so they will float if they fall over the side.

Two of the children in our family were girls. I have no idea how old they were. Youngsters, anyway. We never saw them any closer than from our rail to the sampan. They were queer little people, images of their mother and the old woman but more serious. Sometimes we'd watch them play by the hour when not working, and they would never smile or laugh. But it was the Admiral who was our favorite. We just called him that because we didn't know his name. He was very short and very serious. Probably he was five years old, but he might have been older or younger. He was a round-faced little tyke, and he regarded us very seriously and maybe a little wistfully, for we were big men, and our ship was high above the water.

We used to give them things. I remember when Tony came back from a spree and brought some chocolate with him. When he was painting over the side on a staging, he dropped it to the Admiral, who was very puzzled. Finally he tasted it and seemed satisfied. After that he tasted everything we dropped to him.

Tony had a red silk handkerchief he thought the world of, but one day he gave it to the Admiral. After that, whenever we saw the Admiral, he was wearing it around his head. But he was still very serious and maybe a little prouder.

Sometimes it used to scare me when I thought of them out there on the Whangpoo in the midst of all that shipping.

Partly it was because the Chinese had a bad habit: they would wait till a ship was close by and then cut across her bows real sharp. Dick said they believed they could cut off evil spirits that were following them.

There were wooden eyes painted white with black pupils on either side of the bow of each sampan or junk. They were supposed to watch for rocks or evil spirits. Those eyes used to give me the willies, always staring that way, seeming to bulge in some kind of dumb wonder. I'd wake up at night remembering those eyes and wondering where the Admiral was.

But it got Tony more than me. Tony was a hard guy. He was said to have killed a cop in Baltimore and shipped out to get away. I always thought the old man knew, but he never said anything, and neither did the rest of us. It just wasn't any of our business, and we knew none of the circumstances. Something to do with payoffs, we understood.

Tony took to our family as if they were his own flesh and blood. I never saw a guy get so warmed up over anything. He was a tough wop, and he'd always been a hard case and probably never had anybody he could do for. That's what a guy misses when he's rambling around—not somebody to do something for him but somebody to think of, to work for.

One day when we were working over the side on a staging, the sampan came under us, and Tony turned to wave at the Admiral. "Lookit, Duke," he says to me, "ain't he the cute little devil? That red silk handkerchief sure sets him off."

It was funny, you know? Tony'd been a hard drinker, but after our family showed up, he began to leave it alone. After he gave that red silk handkerchief to the Admiral, he just quit drinking entirely, and when the rest of us went ashore, he'd stay aboard, lying in his bunk, making something for the Admiral.

Tony could carve. You'd have to see it to believe how good he was. Of course, in the old days of sail, men aboard ship carved or created all sorts of things, working from wood, ivory, or whatever came to hand. Tony began to carve out a model of our own ship, a tramp freighter from Wilmington.

That was the night we left for Hong Kong and just a few hours after the accident.

We had been painting under the stern, hanging there on a plank staging, and it was a shaky business. The stern is always the worst place to paint because the stage is swinging loose underneath, and there isn't a thing to lay hold of but the ropes at either end.

Worse still, a fellow can't see where the ropes are made fast to the rail on the poop deck, and those coolies are the worst guys in the world for untying every rope they see knotted. One time at Taku Bar I got dropped into the harbor that way. But this time it was no trouble like that. It was worse.

We were painting almost overhead when we heard somebody scream. Both of us turned so quickly we had to grab the ropes at either end to keep from falling, and when we got straightened around, we saw the Admiral in the water.

Our family had been coming toward our ship when somehow the Admiral had slipped and fallen over the side, and now there he was, buoyed up by the bladder fastened to his shoulders, the red handkerchief still on his head. Probably that had happened a dozen times before, but this time a big Dollar liner was coming upstream, and she was right abeam of us when the Admiral fell. And in a minute more he'd be sucked down into those whirling propeller blades.

Then the plank jerked from under my feet, and I fastened to that rope with both hands, and I felt my heart jump with sudden fear. For a minute or so I had no idea what had happened, and by the time I could pull myself up and get my feet on the staging again, Tony was halfway to the Admiral and swimming like I'd seen nobody swim before.

It was nip and tuck, and you can believe it when I say I didn't draw a breath until Tony grabbed the Admiral just as the big liner's stern hove up, the water churning furiously as she was riding high in the water. Tony's head went down, and both he and the Admiral disappeared in the swirl of water that swept out in a wake behind the big liner.

There was a moment there when they were lost in the swirl

of water behind the steamer, and then we saw them, and Tony was swimming toward the sampan towing the Admiral, who had both hands on Tony's shoulder.

That night when we slipped down the Whangpoo for Hong Kong, Tony started work on his boat. For we were coming back. We had discharged our cargo and were heading south to pick up more, and by the time we returned, there would be cargo in Shanghai for us.

You'd never guess how much that boat meant to us. All the time we were gone, we thought about our family, and each of us picked up some little thing in Hong Kong or Kowloon to take back to them. But it was the carving of the boat that occupied most of our time. Not that we helped because we didn't. It was Tony's job, and he guarded it jealously, and none of us could have done it half so well.

We watched him carve the amidships house and shape the ventilators, and we craned our necks and watched when he fastened a piece of wire in place as the forestay. When one of us would go on watch, the mate would ask how the boat was coming. Everybody on the ship from the old man to the black cook from Georgia knew about the ship Tony was carving, and everyone was interested.

Once the chief mate stopped by the fo'c'sle to examine it and offer a suggestion, and the second mate got to telling me about the time his little boy ran his red fire engine into the preacher's foot. Time went by so fast it seemed no time at all till we were steaming back up the Whangpoo again to anchor at Wayside Pier. We were watching for our family long before they could have seen us.

The next morning the boat was finished, and Chips took it down to the paint locker and gave it a coat of paint and varnish, exactly like our own ship; the colors were the same and everything. There wasn't much of a hold, but we had stuffed it with candy. Then we watched for the sampan.

Dick was up on the crosstree of the mainmast when he saw it, and he came down so fast it was a crying wonder he didn't break a leg. When he hit the deck, he sprinted for the rail. In a few minutes we were all standing there, only nobody was saying anything.

It was the sampan. Only it was bottom up now and all stove in. There wasn't any mistaking it, for we'd have known that particular sampan anywhere even if it hadn't been for the red silk handkerchief. It was there now, a little flag, fluttering gallantly from the wreckage.

SHANGHAI,
NOT WITHOUT GESTURES

S HE CAME IN from the street and stood watching the
auction, a slender girl with great dark eyes and a clear,
creamy complexion. It was raining outside on Kiangse Road,
and her shoes were wet. From time to time she shifted uncomfortably and glanced about. Once her eyes met mine,
and I smiled, but she looked quickly away, watching the auction.

There was always an auction somewhere, it seemed. One
day it might be on Range Road or somewhere along the
Route Frelupt, tomorrow in Kelmscott Garden. Household
effects, usually, for people were always coming or going. The
worlds of international business, diplomacy, and the armed
services are unstable, and there is much shifting about, from
station to station, often without much warning.

I knew none of these people, being an outsider in Shanghai and contented to be so, for a writer, even when a partici-
pant, must also be the observer. As yet I was not a writer, only
someone wishing to be and endlessly working toward that
end.

There were beautiful things to be seen, Soochow curtains,
brass-topped tea tables, intricately carved chests of drawers,
even sometimes swords or scimitars with jeweled hilts or the
handmade guns of long ago. I used to imagine stories about
them and wonder what sort of people had owned them before. It wasn't much of a pastime, but they were dark days,
and it was all I could afford.

The girl interested me more. Reading or thinking stories is
all right, but living them is better. This girl had obviously not
come to buy. She had come to get in out of the rain, to find a
place to sit down. Probably it was cold in her rooms.

Rooms? No—more likely just one room, a small place with a few simple things. Some worn slippers, a Japanese silk kimono, and on the old-fashioned dresser would be a picture—a man, of course. He would be an army or naval officer, grave and attractive.

By the way she seemed to be moving her toes inside her shoes and bit her lower lip from time to time, I knew she was tired of walking and her feet were sore.

When I tried to move closer to her, she noticed it and got up to go. I was persistent. There was a story here that I knew well. I had often lived it. When she stepped into the rain, I was beside her.

"Wet, isn't it?" I said, hoping to hear her voice, but she hurried on, turning her face away and ignoring me.

"Please," I said, "I'm not being fresh. I'm just lonely. Weren't you ever lonely?"

She started to walk slower and glanced at me. Her eyes were dark and even larger than I had thought. She smiled a little, and she had a lovely mouth. "Yes," she said, "I am often lonely."

"Would you like some coffee?" I suggested. "Or tea? What does one drink in Shanghai?"

"Almost everything," she said, and laughed a little. She seemed surprised at the laugh and looked so self-conscious I knew she was hungry. Once you have been very hungry you know the signs in someone else. It makes you feel very different. "But I would like some coffee," she admitted.

We found a little place several blocks away run by a retired French army officer and his wife. We sat down and looked across the table at each other. Her dark suit was a little shabby but neat, and she was obviously tired. I have become sensitive to such things.

There was the slightest bit of an accent in her voice that intrigued me, but I could not place it. I have heard many accents, but I was younger then, and that was the other Shanghai before the guns of Nippon blasted Chapei into smoking ruins and destroyed the fine tempo of life.

"You are new here?" she asked. "You don't belong here?"

"I have just come," I said, "but I belong nowhere."

"Then you must be at home. Nobody belongs in Shanghai. Everyone is either just going or just arriving."

"You?" I suggested.

She shrugged a shoulder. "I am like you. I belong nowhere. Perhaps Shanghai more than anywhere else because it is a city of passersby. Not even the Chinese belong here because this city was started for Europeans. It was only a mud flat then."

She moved her feet under the table, and I heard them squish. She had been walking a long time, and her feet were soaked.

"I'm part Russian, but I was born in Nanking. My grandfather left Russia at the time of the Revolution, and for a time they lived in Siberia. There was an order for his arrest, and he escaped over the border with his wife and children. She was French. He met her in Paris when he was a military attaché there.

"I am told he had a little money, but he could never seem to find a place, and the money disappeared. My father was an interpreter in Peking and then in Nanking."

She sipped her coffee, and we ordered sandwiches. This time there was money enough, and for once I had more in prospect. "He knew nothing about the Revolution or the tsar's government and cared less. Everyone talked politics in Peking—all the Russians did, at least. So he came to Nanking where I was born."

"An interesting man. I thought only grand dukes left Russia. What did he do then?"

"My grandfather died and left him whatever there was. For a time we lived very well, and my father drank."

The sandwiches came, and it was several minutes before she touched one, then a small bite only, which she took a long time chewing. I knew the signs, for when one is hungry, it is the taste one wants. In the movies, when they portray a hungry man, he is always gulping down his food, which is entirely false. It is not at all that way, for when one has been truly hungry for some time, the stomach has shrunk, and one can eat but a little at a time. Only in the days after that first meal can one truly eat, and then there is never enough.

"What did he drink?" I asked.

"Fine old Madeira at first. And port. He would sit in the cafes and talk of Tolstoi and Pushkin or of Balzac. He was a great admirer of Balzac. Father had always wished to become a writer, but he only talked of it. He could never seem to sit down and do it."

"There are thousands like him. If one wishes to be a writer, one shouldn't talk about it, one should do it."

"Then he could not afford such wines. He drank vodka then, and finally samshu or Hanskin."

The decline and fall of a refined palate. "And then he died?"

She nodded, but I had known that it had to be. For a man to sink from fine old Madeira to Hanskin—after that there is nothing to do but die.

Our coffee was finished. I looked into the cup, made a mental calculation, and decided against ordering another. "Shall we go?" I suggested.

The rain had resolved itself into a fine mist, and streetlights were glowing through the fog that was coming in off the river. It would be this way all night. She hesitated, glanced quickly at me, and held out her hand. "I'd better go."

I took her hand. "Why not come with me? It's going to be an unpleasant night." Her eyes met mine, and she looked quickly away. "Why not?" I said. "It isn't all that much of a place, but it's warm."

"All right," she said.

We walked rapidly. It was not going to be a nasty night; it was already one. A taxi skidded around a corner throwing a shower of spray that only just missed us. A rickshaw passed, going the other way, its curtains drawn. I was glad when we reached the door.

For myself it did not matter. Sometimes I walked for hours in the rain, but she was not dressed warm, and the rain was cold and miserable. The Shanghai streets were not a place to be at night and alone.

My place was warm. My boy was gone. I called him my "number-only" boy. I told him when he took the job he couldn't be the "number-one" boy because there would not be a number two, three, or four.

It was not just a room but a small apartment, pleasant in a way. Drifting men have a way of fixing up almost any place they stop to make it comfortable. Seamen often fix things up like any old maid might do and for much the same reason.

Yet the apartment was not mine. I'd been given the use of it by a Britisher who was up-country now. His name was Haig, and he came and went a good deal with no visible means of support, and I was told that he often stayed up-country months at a time. He had been an officer in one of the Scottish regiments, I believe. I had a suspicion that he was still involved in some kind of duty, although he had many weird Asiatic connections.

Some of the books were mine, and it pleased me when she went to the books immediately. It always makes a sucker out of a man who truly loves books to see someone taking a genuine interest in them.

Later, when she came out of the shower wearing my robe, her eyes were very bright. I hadn't realized she was so pretty. We sat by the fire, watching the coals.

"Lose your job?" I asked finally.

"Two weeks ago, and it came at a bad time. My rent was up last week, and there is always a demand for lodgings here. This morning they said not to come back unless I could pay."

"That's tough. What's your line?"

"I've done a lot of things. A secretary, usually. I can handle five languages very well and two others a little. I worked for Moran and Company in Tientsin, and then here for a transport firm, but lately there has been so little business, and the owner has been gambling. I don't know what I'm going to do."

Outside was China. Outside was Shanghai, the old Shanghai when it was an international city. Outside were the millions, of all nationalities. French, English, Japanese, Dutch, German, Sikh, Portuguese, Hebrew, Greek, Malay, and of course, Chinese. Outside was the Whangpoo, a dark river flowing out of China, out of old China and into the new, then down to the sea. Outside rivers of men flowed along the dark streets, men buying and selling, men fighting and gambling, men bargaining and selling, loving and dying. Millions of men, women, and children, opening countless doors, going into lives of which I knew nothing, eating the food of many countries, speaking in tongues I had never heard, praying to many gods.

Listening to her as she spoke of China, I remembered the shuffle of feet in the noontime streets. There was nothing I could do. It was bad for a man to be broke but so much worse for a woman. Especially for such a girl as this.

Perhaps I was a fool, but I, too, had been hungry. Soon there would be a ship, and I would go to Bombay or Liverpool or New York, while she—

"You wouldn't have come had there been any other place to go, would you?"

"No."

A lock of her dark hair had fallen against my robe. It looked good there. So black against the soft white of her throat.

"But I am grateful. What could I have done?"

Well, what? I had a feeling I was going to make a fool of myself. Americans are a sentimental lot, and every cynic is a sentimentalist under the skin. I knew enough about women to be skeptical but had been hungry enough to be human.

A wind moaned about the eaves, and rain dashed against the window.

"Listen," I said, "this isn't quite the sporting thing, is it? To have you come here because there was nowhere else to go and because I bought you a cup of coffee? Or maybe because of breakfast in the morning? I don't like the sound of it.

"Well, hell, I'm going to sleep on the sofa, and you can have the other room."

After the door closed, I stood looking at it. If she hadn't been so damned lovely it would have been easier to be gallant. Probably right now she was thinking what a sap I was. Well, she wouldn't be the only one.

I had a feeling I was going to be sorry for this in the morning.

THE MAN
WHO STOLE SHAKESPEARE

W HEN I HAD been in Shanghai but a few days, I
rented an apartment in a narrow street off Avenue
Edward VII where the rent was surprisingly low. The door at
the foot of the stairs opened on the street beside a mon-
eychanger's stall, an inconspicuous place that one might pass
a dozen times a day and never notice.

At night I would go down into the streets and wander about
or sit by my window and watch people going about their
varied business. From my corner windows I could watch a
street intersection and an alleyway, and there were many
curious things to see, and for one who finds his fellow man
interesting, there was much to learn.

Late one afternoon when a drizzle of despondent rain had
blown in from the sea, I decided to go out for coffee. Before
reaching my destination, it began to pour, so I stepped into a
bookstore for shelter.

This store dealt in secondhand books published in several
languages and was a jumble of stacks, piles, and racks filled
with books one never saw elsewhere and was unlikely to see
again. I was hitch reading from Sterne when I saw him.

He was a small man and faded. His face had the scholarly
expression that seems to come from familiarity with books,
and he handled them tenderly. One could see at a glance that
here was a man who knew a good book when he saw one,
with a feeling for attractive format as well as content.

Yet when I glanced up, he was slipping a book into his
pocket. Quickly, with almost a sense of personal guilt, I
looked toward the clerk, but he was watching the rain. The
theft had passed unobserved.

Now there is a sort of sympathy among those who love

books, an understanding that knows no bounds of race, creed, or financial rating. If a man steals a necktie, he is a thief of the worst stripe. If he steals a car, nothing is too bad for him. But a man who steals a book is something else— unless it is my book.

My first thought when he slipped the book into his pocket was to wonder what book he wanted badly enough to steal. Not that there are only a few books worth stealing, for there are many. Yet I was curious. What, at the moment, had captured his interest? This small, gentle-seeming man with the frayed shirt collar and the worn topcoat?

When he left, I walked over to the place where the book had been and tried to recall what it might have been, for I had only just checked that shelf myself. Then I remembered.

It had been a slim, one-play-to-the-volume edition of Shakespeare. He had also examined Hakluyt's *Voyages,* or at least one volume of the set, Huysmans's *Against the Grain,* and Burton's *Anatomy of Melancholy.*

This was definitely a man I wished to know. Also, I was curious. Which play had he stolen? Was it the play itself he wished to read? Or was it for some particular passage in the play? Or to complete a set?

Turning quickly, I went to the door, and barely in time. My man was just disappearing in the direction of Thibet Road, and I started after him, hurrying.

At that, I almost missed him. He was just rounding a corner a block away, so he had been running, too. Was it the rain or a feeling of guilt?

The rain had faded into a drizzle once more. My man kept on, walking rapidly, but fortunately for me, he was both older than I, and his legs were not as long.

Whether he saw me, I do not know, but he led me a lively chase. It seemed scarcely possible for a man to go up and down so many streets, and he obviously knew Shanghai better than I. Yet suddenly he turned into an alley and dodged down a basement stairway. Following him, I got my foot in the door before he could close it.

He was frightened, and I could understand why. In those wilder years they found several thousand bodies on the street every year, and he perhaps had visions of adding his own to the list. Being slightly over six feet and broad in the shoulder, I must have looked dangerous in that dark passageway. Possibly he had visions of being found in the cold light of dawn with a slit throat, for such things were a common occurrence in Shanghai.

"Here!" he protested. "You can't do this!" That I was doing it must have been obvious. "I'll call an officer!"

"And have to explain that volume of Shakespeare in your pocket?" I suggested.

That took the wind out of him, and he backed into the room, a neat enough place, sparsely furnished except for the books. The walls were lined with them.

"Now see here," I said, "you've nothing to worry about. I don't intend to report you, and I'm not going to rob you. I'm simply interested in books and in the books people want enough to steal."

"You're not from the bookstore?"

"Nothing of the kind. I saw you slip the book into your pocket, and although I did not approve, I was curious as to what you had stolen and why." I held out my hand. "May I see?"

He shook his head, then stood back and watched me, finally taking off his coat. He handed me the book from his pocket, which was a copy of *Henry IV*, bound in gray cloth with a thin gold line around the edges. The book was almost new and felt good to the hands. I turned the pages, reading a line or two. "You've a lot of books," I said, glancing at the shelves. "May I look?"

He nodded, then stepped back and sat down. He certainly was not at ease, and I didn't blame him.

The first book I saw was Wells's *Outline of History*. "Everybody has that one," I commented.

"Yes," he said hesitantly.

Ibsen was there, and Strindberg, Chekhov, and Tolstoi. A couple of volumes by Thomas Hardy were wedged alongside three by Dostoevsky. There were books by Voltaire, Cervantes, Carlyle, Goldoni, Byron, Verlaine, Baudelaire, Cabell, and Hume.

The next book stopped me short, and I had to look again to make sure the bookshelf wasn't kidding. It was a quaint, old-fashioned, long-out-of-date *Home Medical Advisor* by some Dr. Felix Peabody, published by some long-extinct publisher whose state of mind must have been curious, indeed.

"Where in the world did you get this?" I asked. "It seems out of place stuck in between Hegel and Hudson."

He smiled oddly, his eyes flickering to mine and then away. He looked nervous, and since then I have often wondered what he must have been thinking and what went through his mind at that moment.

Scanning the shelves to take stock of what his interests were, I came upon another queer one. It was between Laurence Sterne's *Sentimental Journey* and George Gissing's *Private Papers of Henry Ryecroft*. It was *Elsie's Girlhood*.

After that I had to sit down. This man was definitely some kind of a nut. I glanced at him, and he squirmed a little. Evidently he had seen my surprise at the placement of some of the books or the fact that he had them at all.

"You must read a lot," I suggested. "You've a lot of good books here."

"Yes," he said; then he leaned forward, suddenly eager to talk. "It's nice to have them. I just like to own them, to take them in my hands and turn them over and to know that so much that these men felt, saw, thought, and understood is here. It is almost like knowing the men themselves."

"It might be better," I said. "Some of these men were pretty miserable in themselves, but their work is magnificent."

He started to rise, then sat down again suddenly as though he expected me to order him to stay where he was.

"Do you read a lot?" he asked.

"All the time," I said. "Maybe even too much. At least when I have books or access to them."

"My eyes"—he passed a hand over them—"I'm having trouble with my glasses. I wonder if you'd read to me sometime? That is," he added hastily, "if you have the time."

"That's the one thing I've plenty of," I said. "At least until I catch a ship. Sure I'll read to you."

As a matter of fact, he had books here to which I'd heard

all my life but had found no chance to read. "If you want, I'll read some right now."

It was raining outside, and I was blocks from my small apartment. He made coffee, and I read to him, starting with *The Return of the Native* for no reason other than that I'd not read it and it was close at hand. Then I read a bit from *Tales of Mean Streets* and some from Locke's *Essay Concerning Human Understanding.*

Nearly every day after that I went to see Mr. Meacham. How he made his living, I never knew. He had some connection, I believe, with one of the old trading companies, for he seemed very familiar with the interior of China and with people there.

The oddity of it appealed to some irony in my sense of humor. A few weeks before I'd been coiling wet lines on the forecastle head of a tramp steamer, and now here I was, reading to this quaint old gentleman in his ill-fitting suit.

He possessed an insatiable curiosity about the lives of the authors and questioned me about them by the hour. That puzzled me, for a reader just naturally acquires some such knowledge just by reading the bookjackets, and in the natural course of events a man can learn a good deal about the personal lives of authors. However, he seemed to know nothing about them and was avid for detail.

There was much about him that disturbed me. He was so obviously alone, seemingly cut off from everything. He wasn't bold enough to make friends, and there seemed to be no reason why anybody should take the trouble to know him. He talked very little, and I never did know where he had come from or how he happened to be in such a place as Shanghai, for he was a contradiction to everything one thinks of when one considers Shanghai. You could imagine him in Pittsburgh, St. Louis, or London, in Glasgow or Peoria, but never in such a place as this.

One day when I came in, I said, "Well, you name it. What shall I read today?"

He hesitated, flushed, then took a book from the shelf and handed it to me. It was *Elsie's Girlhood,* a book of advice to a young girl about to become a woman.

For a minute I thought he was kidding, and then I was sure it couldn't be anything else. "Not today," I said. "I'll try Leacock."

When I remembered it afterward, I remembered he had not seemed to be kidding. He had been perfectly serious and obviously embarrassed when I put him off so abruptly. He hesitated, then put the book away, and when I returned the next day, the book was no longer on the shelf. It had disappeared.

It was that day that I guessed his secret. I was reading at the time, and it just hit me all of a sudden. It left me completely flabbergasted, and for a moment I stared at the printed page from which I was reading, my mouth open for words that would not come.

Yes, I told myself, that had to be it. There was no other solution. All the pieces suddenly fell into place, the books scattered together without plan or style, with here and there books that seemed so totally out of place and unrelated.

That night I read later than ever before.

Then I got a job. Dou Yu-seng offered to keep the rent paid on my apartment (I always suspected he owned the building) while I took care of a little job up the river. I knew but little about him but enough to know of affiliations with various war lords and at least one secret society. However, what I was to do was legitimate.

Yet when I left, I kept thinking of old Mr. Meacham. He would be alone again, with nobody to read to him.

Alone? Remembering those walls lined with books, I knew he would never actually be alone. They were books bought here and there, books given him by people moving away, books taken from junk heaps, but each one of them represented a life, somebody's dream, somebody's hope or idea, and all were there where he could touch them, feel them, know their presence.

No, he would not be alone, for he would remember Ivan Karamazov, who did not want millions but an answer to his questions. He would remember those others who would people his memories and walk through the shadows of his rooms: *Jean Valjean, Julien Sorel, Mr. John Oakhurst,* gambler, and, of course, the little man who was *the friend of Napoleon.*

He knew line after line from the plays and sonnets of Shakespeare and a lot of Keats, Kipling, Li Po, and *Kasidah.* He would never really be alone now.

He never guessed that I knew, and probably for years he had hidden his secret, ashamed to let anyone know that he, who was nearly seventy and who so loved knowledge, had never learned to read.

THE DANCING KATE

I T WAS A strip of grayish-yellow sand caught in the gaunt
fingers of the reef like an upturned belly except here and
there where the reef had been longest above the sea. Much
of the reef was drying, and elsewhere the broken teeth of
the coral formed ugly ridges flanked by a few black, half-
submerged boulders.

At one end of the bar the stark white ribs of an old ship
thrust themselves from the sand, and nearby lay the rusting
hulk of an iron freighter. It had been there more than sixty
years.

For eighteen miles in a northeast and southwest direction
the reef lay across the face of the Coral Sea. At its widest,
no more than three miles but narrowing to less than a mile.
A strip of jagged coral and white water lost in the remote
emptiness of the Pacific. The long dun swells of the sea ham-
mered against the outer rocks, and overhead the towering
vastness of the sky became a shell of copper with the afternoon sun.

At the near end of the bar, protected from the breaking
seas in all but a hurricane, a hollow of rock formed a natural
cistern. In the bottom were a few scant inches of doubtful
water. Beside it, he squatted in torn dungarees and battered
sneakers.

"Three days," he estimated, staring into the cistern, eyes
squinting against the surrounding glare. "Three days if I'm
careful, and after that I'm washed up."

After that—thirst. The white, awful glare of the tropical
sun, a parched throat, baking flesh, a few days or hours of
delirium, and then a long time of lying wide-eyed to the sky
before the gulls and the crabs finished the remains.

He had no doubt as to where he was. The chart had been

given him in Port Darwin and was worn along the creases, but there was no crease where this reef lay, hence no doubt of his position. He was sitting on a lonely reef, avoided by shipping, right in the middle of nowhere. His position was approximately 10°45' S, 155°51' E.

The nearest land was eighty-two miles off and it might as well be eighty-two thousand.

It started with the gold. The schooner on which he had been second mate had dropped anchor in Bugoiya Harbor, but it was not fit anchorage, so they could remain only a matter of hours. He was on the small wharf superintending the loading of some cargo when a boy approached him.

He was a slender native boy with very large, beautiful eyes. When the boy was near him, he spoke, not looking at him. "Man say you come. Speak nobody."

"Come? Come where?"

"You come. I show you."

"I'm busy, boy. I don't want a girl now."

"No girl. Man die soon. He say *please,* you come?"

Dugan looked at his watch. They were loading the last cargo now, but they would not sail for at least an hour.

"How far is it?"

"Ten minutes—you see."

A man was dying? But why come to him? Still, in these islands odd things were always happening, and he was a curious man.

The captain was coming along the wharf, and he walked over to him. "Cap? Something's come up. This boy wants to take me to some man who is dying. Says not to say anything, and he's only ten minutes away."

Douglas glanced at the boy, then at his watch. "All right, but we've less than an hour. If we leave before you get back, we'll be several days at Woodlark or Murua or whatever they call it. There's a man in a village who is a friend of mine. Just ask for Sam. He will sail you over there."

"No need for that. I'll be right back."

Douglas glanced at him, a faint humor showing. "Dugan, I've been in these islands for fifty years. A man never knows—never."

Misima, although only about twenty miles long and four or five miles wide, was densely wooded, and the mountains lifted from a thousand to three thousand feet, and as the south side was very steep, most of the villages were along the northern shore.

The boy had walked off and was standing near a palm tree idly tossing stones into the lagoon. Taking off his cap, he walked away from the wharf, wiping the sweat from his brow. He walked back from the shore and then turned and strolled toward the shade, pausing occasionally. The boy had disappeared under the trees.

At the edge of the trees Dugan sat down, leaning his back against one. After a moment a stone landed near his foot, and he glimpsed the boy behind a tree about thirty yards off. Dugan got up, stretched, and hands in his pockets, strolled along in the shade, getting deeper and deeper until he saw the boy standing in a little-used path.

They walked along for half a mile. Dugan glanced at his watch. He would have to hurry.

Suddenly the boy ducked into the brush, holding a branch aside for him. About thirty yards away he saw a small shanty with a thin column of smoke lifting it. The boy ran ahead, leading the way.

There was a young woman there who, from her looks, was probably the boy's mother. Inside, an old man lay on an army cot. His eyes were sunken into his head, and his cheeks were gaunt. He clutched Dugan's hand. His fingers were thin and clawlike. "You must help me. You are with Douglas?"

"I am."

"Good! He is honest. Everybody knows that of him. I need your help." He paused for a minute, his breathing hoarse and labored. "I have a granddaughter. She is in Sydney." He put his hand on a coarse brown sack under his cot. "She must have this."

"What is it?"

"It is gold. There are men here who will steal it when I die. It must go to my granddaughter. You take it to her, and you keep half. You will do this?"

Sydney? He was not going to Sydney; still, one could sell

it and send the money to Sydney. He pressed a paper into his hand. "Her name and address. Get it to her—somehow. You can do it. You will do it."

"Look," he protested, "I am not going to Sydney. When I leave Douglas, I'm going to Singapore and catch a ship for home—or going on to India."

"You must! They will steal it. They have tried, and they are waiting. If they think you have it, they will rob you. I know them."

"Well." He hesitated. He had to be getting back. Douglas's appointment at Woodlark was important to him. He would wait for no man in such a case, least of all for me, who had been with him only a few weeks, the man thought. "All right, give me the gold. I've little time."

The woman dragged the sack from under the cot, and he stooped to lift it. It was much heavier than it appeared. The old man smiled. "Gold is always heavy, my friend. Too heavy for many men to bear."

Dugan straightened and took the offered hand; then he walked out of the shack, carrying the gold.

It *was* heavy. Once aboard the schooner it would be no problem. He glanced at his watch and swore. He was already too late, and the tide—

When he reached the small harbor, it was too late. The schooner was gone!

He stood, staring. Immediately he was apprehensive. He was left on an island with about two dozen white people of whom he knew nothing and some fifteen hundred natives of whom he knew less. Moreover, there was always a drifting population, off the vessels of one kind or another that haunt Indonesian seas.

Woodlark was eighty miles away. He knew that much depended on the schooner being there in time to complete a deal for cargo that otherwise would go to another vessel. He had been left behind. He was alone.

A stocky bearded man approached. He wore dirty khakis, a watch cap, and the khaki coat hung loose. Did he have a gun? Dugan would have bet that he had.

From descriptions he was sure he knew the man.

"Looks like they've gone off and left you," he commented, glancing at the sack.

"They'll be back."

"Douglas? Don't bet on it. He calls in here about once every six months. Sometimes it's a whole year."

"It's different this time," he lied. "He's spending about three months in the Louisiades and Solomons. He expects to be calling in here three or four times, so I'll just settle down and wait."

"We could make a deal," the man said. "I could sail you to the Solomons." He jerked his head. "I've got a good boat, and I often take the trip. Come along."

"Why? When he's coming back here?"

Deliberately he turned his back and walked away. Zimmerman—this would be Zimmerman.

At the trade store they told him where he could find Sam, and he found him, a wiry little man with sad blue eyes and thin hair. He shook his head. "I have to live here."

"Douglas said—"

"I can imagine. I like Douglas. He's one of the best men in the islands, but he doesn't live here. I do. If you get out of here, you'll do it on your own. I can tell you something else. Nobody will take the chance. You make a deal with them, or you wait until Douglas comes back."

Twice he saw the boy, and he was watching him. He lingered near the trees where he'd been when he first followed him, so he started back. He'd have to see the old man, and packing that gold was getting to be a nuisance.

When he got back to the shack, the woman was at the door, mashing something in a wooden dish. "He's dying," she said. "He hasn't talked since you left."

"Who is it?" The voice was very weak.

He went inside and told the old man he would have to leave his gold.

The schooner was gone, and he had no way to get to Woodlark and overtake her.

"Take my boat," he said.

His eyes closed, and nothing Dugan said brought any response. And Dugan tried. He wanted to get away, but he wanted no more of his gold. From Sam's manner he knew Zimmerman was trouble, very serious trouble.

The woman was standing there. "He is dying," she said.

"He has a boat?"

She pointed and he walked through the trees to the shore. It was there, tied up to a small dock. It wasn't much of a boat, and they'd make a fit pair, for he wasn't much of a small-boat sailor. His seamanship had been picked up on freighters and one tanker, and his time in sail was limited to a few weeks where somebody else was giving orders. He'd done one job of single handing with a small boat and been shot with luck. On one of the most dangerous seas he had experienced nothing but flying-fish weather all the way. Still, it was only eighty miles to Woodlark, and if the weather remained unchanged, he'd be all right. If—

The boy was there. "Three of them," he said, "three mans—very bad mans." And then he added, "They come tonight, I think."

So how much of a choice did he have? He left at dark or before dark, or he stayed and took a chance on being murdered or killing somebody. Anyway, the sea was quiet, only a little breeze running, and eighty miles was nothing.

The best way to cope with trouble was to avoid it, to stay away from where trouble was apt to be.

The only thing between where he was and Woodlark were the Alcesters. He had sailed by them before and would know them when he saw them.

He glanced down at the boy. "I'll leave the boat on Woodlark."

The boy shrugged. "Wherever."

He had shoved off at sundown with a good breeze blowing, and even with his caution he made good time, or what was good time for him. He had the Alcesters abeam before daybreak, but there was a boat behind him that was coming on fast. His silhouette was low, so he lowered the sail a little to provide even less and gradually eased the helm over and slid in behind one of the Alcesters.

It was nearing daylight, but suddenly it began to grow darker, and the wind began blowing in little puffs, and there was a brief spatter of rain. He was running before the wind when the storm came, and from that time on it was sheer panic. On the second or third day—he could not remember which—he piled up on the reef, a big wave carrying the boat over into the lagoon, ripping the hull open somewhere en route.

When daylight came again, the storm was blowing itself out; the boat was gone but for a length of broken mast and a piece of the forward section that contained a spare sail, some line, and some odds and ends of canned goods. And the gold.

He had saved the gold.

Dawn was a sickly thing on that first morning, with the northern sun remote behind gray clouds. He made his way along the reef, avoiding the lacerating edges of the coral until he reached the bar.

The old freighter, one mast still standing and a gaping hole in her hull, was high and dry on the sandbar. A flock of gulls rose screaming into the air as he approached, and he walked over the soft sand into the hole.

The deck above him was solid and strong. Far down there was a hatch, its cover stove in, which allowed a little light at the forward end. Here all was secure. Sand had washed in, making a hard-packed floor. Dugan put down a tin of biscuits and the few cans he had brought along and went back outside.

It was just one hundred and fifty steps to the water of the lagoon and the hollow in the reef where rain had collected in the natural cistern. The hollow in the reef was just three feet deep and about the size of a washtub. It was half full, and the water, although fresh, was warm.

For the moment he had food, shelter, and water.

Gathering driftwood, of which there was a good bit, he built a shade over the cistern that would prevent a too rapid evaporation but could be removed when it rained.

There would be fish, shellfish, and crabs. For a time there might be eggs, and the first thing he must do would be to cover the reef, as much of it as he could reach, and see what he could find that was useful. Then he must get a fragment of that torn canvas and make a pennant to fly from the mast of the wrecked ship.

The work kept him busy. Scrambling over the reef, careful not to slip into a hole or break an ankle on the rough, often slippery rock, he gathered driftwood. Slowly the several piles grew.

At night he sat beside his fire in the hulk and ate fish and a biscuit.

After a while he lost all awareness of the sea. It was there, all around him, and it was empty. Occasionally, when his eyes strayed that way, he saw distant smoke. He rarely looked at the sack of gold.

For the first time he deliberately faced his situation. From his pocket he took the worn chart, but he did not need it to face the fact. The reef was a lonely, isolated spot in the Coral Sea, in an area where ships came but rarely. Aside from the sandbar itself there was only the ruffled water and a few black stumps of coral rising above it.

This was no place for a man. It was a place for the wind and the gulls, yet there was a little water, there was a little food, and while a man lived, there was always a chance. It was then that he looked up and saw the schooner.

It was tacking, taking a course that would bring it closer to the reef. He shouted and waved a hand, and somebody waved back. He turned and walked toward the wreck.

When the dinghy came in close to pick him up, he waded out and lifted his bag of gold into the boat. Then he climbed in. There were two men in the dinghy, and they stared at him. "My—my water—it was about gone. You came just in time."

The men stared at the sack, then at him. The place where the sack rested against the thwart had dented the sack. Only sand or flour or something of the kind would make such an impression. And the sack had been heavy. He couldn't say it was shells or clothing. They'd know he lied.

Yet it was not until he came alongside the schooner that he realized how much trouble he had bought for himself. He glanced at the schooner's name and felt a chill.

The *Dancing Kate*.

Bloody Jack Randall's schooner. Of course, he was never

called Bloody Jack to his face, but behind his back they knew him by that name. He had killed a man in a saloon brawl at Port Moresby. There'd been a man shot in Kalgoorlie, but insufficient evidence released Randall. He was reported to have broken jail in New Caledonia after killing a guard.

After he was aboard, it was Randall's mate, a lean, wiry man with haggard features, who kicked the sack. "Hey? What you got in there? It looks mighty heavy."

"Gold."

It was a sullen, heavy day with thick clouds overhead and a small sea running. Kahler's eyes went to the sack again. "Gold?" He was incredulous.

"Yes." He slid his knife into his hand, point toward them, cutting edge uppermost. "This weighs about a pound. I measured the weight by this, and it is more than they thought."

"They?"

"A man in Misima asked me to deliver it to his granddaughter in Sydney."

"What kind of a damned fool would do that?" Kahler asked.

"A man who knew who he could trust." He glanced at Randall. "Where you bound?"

Randall hesitated. "East," he said finally. "We been scouting around."

"How about Woodlark? I'll pay my passage."

"All right." Randall walked forward and gave the change of course to the Bugi seaman. There were four of the Bugis, some of the best sailors among the islands; there was Randall himself, Kahler, and the big man who rowed the boat. That would be Sanguo Pete, a half-caste.

Taking his sack, he walked forward and sat down with his back against the foremast.

Kahler came forward. "We'll have chow pretty quick. One of those Bugis is a first-rate cook." He glanced down at him. "How'd you survive on that reef? You must be tough."

"I get along."

"By this time they probably figure you're dead," Kahler said.

THE DANCING KATE / 223

"Maybe."

He knew what they were thinking. If something happened to him now, no one would know any better. Well, he promised himself, nothing was going to happen. He was going to meet Douglas at Woodlark.

When they went below to eat, he let them go first. He paused for a moment near one of the Bugi seamen. His Indonesian was just marketplace talk, but he could manage. He indicated the sack. "It is a trust," he said, "from a dying man. He has a granddaughter who needs this." He gestured toward the reef. "The sea was kind," he said.

"You are favored," the Bugi replied.

"If there is trouble—?"

"We are men of the sea. The troubles of white men are the troubles of white men."

He went below. There was a plate of food at the empty place. Randall had not begun to eat. Coolly, before Randall could object, he switched plates with him.

"What's the matter?" Randall demanded. "Don't you trust me?"

"I trust nobody," he said. "Nobody, Mr. Randall."

"You know me?"

"I know you. Douglas told me about you."

They exchanged glances. "Douglas? What do you know about him?"

"I'm his second mate. I'm joining him at Woodlark. Then we'll arrange to get this"—he kicked the sack—"to that girl in Sydney."

"Why bother?" Kahler said. "A man could have himself a time with that much gold."

"And it will buy that girl an education."

"Hell! She'll get along—somehow."

The food was good, and when supper was over, he took his gold and went on deck. Randall was a very tough, dangerous man. So were the others, and it was three to one. He could have used Douglas or Hildebrand. Or Charlie—most of all, Charlie.

The sails hung slack, and the moon was out. There was a Bugi at the wheel, another on lookout in the bow. These were tricky, dangerous waters, much of them unsurveyed. He settled himself against the mainmast for a night of watching.

The storm that had wrecked his boat had blown him east, far off his course. It could be no less than a hundred miles to Misima and probably a good bit more.

The hours dragged. A light breeze had come up, and the vessel was moving along at a good clip. The moon climbed to the zenith, then slid down toward the ocean again. He dozed. The warmth of the night, the easy motion of the schooner, the food in his stomach, helped to make him sleepy. But he stayed awake. They, of course, could sleep by turns.

At one time or another there had been a good bit of talk about Randall, Sanguo Pete, and Kahler. They had a hand in more than one bit of doubtful activity. He was half asleep when they suddenly closed in on him. At one moment he had been thinking of what he'd heard about them, and he must have dozed off, for they closed in quickly and silently. Some faint sound of bare feet on the deck must have warned him even as they reached for him.

He saw the gleam of starlight on steel, and he ripped up with his own knife. The man pulled back sharply, and his blade sliced open a shirt, and the tip of his knife drew a red line from navel to chin, nicking the chin hard as the man drew back.

Then he was on his feet. Somebody struck at him with a marlin spike, and he parried the blow with his blade and lunged. The knife went in; he felt his knuckles come up hard against warm flesh, and he withdrew the knife as he dodged a blow at his head.

The light was bad, for them as well as for him, and one might have been more successful than three; as it was, they got in each other's way in the darkness. The man he had stabbed had gone to the deck, and in trying to crawl away, tripped up another.

He had his gun but dared not reach for it. It meant shifting the knife, and even a moment off guard would be all they would need.

One feinted a rush. The man on the deck was on his feet, and they were spreading out. Suddenly they closed in. The half-light was confusing, and as he moved to get closer to one man, he heard another coming in from behind. He tried to make a quick half turn, but a belaying pin caught him alongside the skull. Only a glancing blow, but it dazed him, and he fell against the rail. He took a cut at the nearest man, missed but ripped into another. How seriously, he did not know. Then another blow caught him, and he felt himself falling.

He hit the water and went down. When he came up, the boat was swinging. The Bugi at the wheel was swinging the bow around. As the hull went away from him, the bow came to him, and there were the stays. He grabbed hold and pulled himself up to the bowsprit.

For a moment he hung there, gasping for breath. He could see them peering over the rail.

"Did you get him, Cap?"

"Get him? You damned right I did! He's a goner." He turned then. "You cut bad, Pete?"

"I'm bleedin'. I got to get the blood stopped."

"He got me, too," Kahler said. "You sure we got him?"

Randall waved at the dark water. "You don't see him, do you? We got him, all right."

After a moment they went below, and the tall yellow seaman at the wheel glanced at the foremast against the sky, lined it up with his star. His expression did not change when he saw Dugan come over the bow and crouch low.

There was no sound but the rustle of bow wash, the creak of rigging, and a murmur of voices aft. He moved aft, exchanging one glance with the Bugi, and when he was close enough, he said, "Thanks." Not knowing if the man understood, he repeated, *"Terima kasi."*

He knew the Bugi had deliberately put the rigging below the bowsprit in his way. The wonder was that even with the distraction of the fighting Randall had not noticed it.

His gun was still in the side pocket of his pants, and he took it out, struggling a bit to do so, as the dungarees were a tight fit. He put the gun in his hip pocket where it was easier of access. He did not want to use a gun, and neither did they.

Bullet scars were not easy to disguise and hard to explain when found on rails or deck houses.

Sanguo Pete loomed in the companionway and stood blinking at the change from light to darkness. There was a gash on his cheekbone that had been taped shut, and there was a large mouse over one eye. He hitched up his dungarees and started forward, a gun strapped to his hips. He had taken but two steps when he saw Dugan crouched close to the rail.

Pete broke his paralysis and yelled, then grabbed for his gun. It was too late to think about the future questions. As Pete's hand closed on the butt, Dugan shot him.

Randall loomed in the companionway, but all he saw was the wink of fire from Dugan's gun. He fell forward, half on deck.

Pete lay in the scuppers, his big body rolling slightly with the schooner.

The Bugi looked at Dugan and said, "No good mans."

"No good," Dugan agreed.

One by one he tilted them over the side and gave them to the sea.

"My ship is waiting at Woodlark Island," Dugan said.

The Bugi glanced at him. "Is Cap'n Douglas ship. I know." Suddenly he smiled. "I have two brother on your ship—long time now."

"Two brothers? Well, I'll be damned!"

Kahler was lying on the bunk when he went below. His body had been bandaged, but he had lost blood.

"We're going to Woodlark," Dugan said. "If you behave yourself, you might make it."

Kahler closed his eyes, and Dugan lay down on the other bunk and looked up at the deck overhead. The day after tomorrow—

It would be good to be back aboard, lying in his own bunk. He remembered the brief note in the Pilot Book for the area.

This coral reef, discovered in 1825, lies about 82 miles east-northeast of Rossel Island. The reef is 18 miles in length, in a northeast and southwest direction. The greatest breadth is 3 miles, but in some places it is not more than a mile wide. At the northeastern end of the reef there are some rocks 6 feet high. No anchorage is available off the reef.

Wreck. The wreck of a large iron vessel above water lies (1880) on the middle of the southeastern side of the reef.

If they wanted to know any more, they could just ask him. He'd tell them.

OFF THE MANGROVE COAST

THERE WERE FOUR of us there, at the back end of creation, four of the devil's own, and a hard lot by any man's count. We'd come together the way men will when on the beach, the idea cropping up out of an idle conversation. We'd nothing better to do; all of us being fools or worse, so we borrowed a boat off the Nine Islands and headed out to sea.

DID YOU EVER cross the South China Sea in a forty-foot boat during the typhoon season? No picnic certainly, nor any job for a churchgoing son; more for the likes of us, who mattered to no one, and in a stolen boat, at that.

Now, all of us were used to playing it alone. We'd worked aboard ship and other places, sharing our labors with other men, but the truth was, each was biding his own thoughts, and watching the others.

There was Limey Johnson, from Liverpool, and Smoke Bassett from Port-au-Prince, and there was Long Jack from Sydney, and there was me, the youngest of the lot, at loose ends and wandering in a strange land.

Wandering always. Twenty-two years old, I was, with five years of riding freights, working in mines or lumber camps, and prizefighting in small clubs in towns that I never saw by daylight.

I'd had my share of the smell of coal smoke and cinders in the rain, the roar of a freight and the driving run-and-catch of a speeding train in the night, and then the sun coming up over the desert or going down over the sea, and the islands looming up and the taste of salt spray on my lips and the sound of bow wash about the hull. There had been nights in the wheelhouse with only the glow from the compass and out there beyond the bow the black, glassy sea rolling its waves up from the long sweep of the Pacific . . . or the Atlantic.

In those years I'd been wandering from restlessness but also from poverty. However, I had no poverty of experience and in that I was satisfied.

It was Limey Johnson who told us the story of the freighter sinking off the mangrove coast; a ship with fifty thousand dollars in the captain's safe and nobody who knew it was there anymore . . . nobody but him.

Fifty thousand dollars . . . and we were broke. Fifty thousand lying in a bare ten fathoms, easy for the taking. Fifty thousand split four ways. A nice stake, and a nice bit of money for the girls and the bars in Singapore or Shanghai . . . or maybe Paris.

Twelve thousand five hundred dollars a piece . . . if we all made it. And that was a point to be thought upon, for if only two should live . . . twenty-five thousand dollars . . . and who can say what can or cannot happen in the wash of a weedy sea off the mangrove coast? Who can say what is the destiny of any man? Who could say how much some of us were thinking of lending a hand to fate?

Macao was behind us and the long roll of the sea began, and we had a fair wind and a good run away from land before the sun broke upon the waves. Oh, it was gamble enough, but the Portuguese are an easygoing people. They would be slow in starting the search; there were many who might steal a boat in Macao . . . and logically, they would look toward China first. For who, they would ask themselves, would be fools enough to dare the South China Sea in such a boat; to dare the South China Sea in the season of the winds?

She took to the sea, that ketch, like a baby to a mother's breast, like a Liverpool Irishman to a bottle. She took to the sea and we headed south and away, with a bearing toward the east. The wind held with us, for the devil takes care of his own, and when again the sun went down we had left miles behind and were far along on our way. In the night, the wind held fair and true and when another day came, we were run-

ning under a high overcast and there was a heavy feel to the
sea.

As the day drew on, the waves turned green with white
beards blowing and the sky turned black with clouds. The
wind tore at our sheets in gusts and we shortened sail and
battened down and prepared to ride her out. Never before
had I known such wind or known the world could breed
such seas. Hour by hour, we fought it out, our poles bare and
a sea anchor over, and though none of us were praying men,
pray we did.

We shipped water and we bailed and we swore and we
worked and, somehow, when the storm blew itself out, we were
still afloat and somewhat farther along. Yes, farther, for we saw
a dark blur on the horizon and when we topped a wave, we
saw an island, a brush-covered bit of sand forgotten here in
the middle of nothing.

We slid in through the reefs, conning her by voice and
hand, taking it easy because of the bared teeth of coral so
close beneath our keel. Lincoln Island, it was, scarcely more
than a mile of heaped-up sand and brush, fringed and bordered by reefs. We'd a hope there was water, and we found it
near a stunted palm, a brackish pool, but badly needed.

From there, it was down through the Dangerous Ground,
a thousand-odd miles of navigator's nightmare, a wicked
tangle of reefs and sandy cays, of islands with tiny tufts of
palms, millions of seabirds and fish of all kinds . . . and the
bottom torn out of you if you slacked off for even a minute.
But we took that way because it was fastest and because
there was small chance we'd be seen.

Fools? We were that, but sometimes now when the fire is
bright on the hearth and there's rain against the windows and
the roof, sometimes I think back and find myself tasting the
wind again and getting the good old roll of the sea under me.
In my mind's eye, I can see the water breaking on the coral,
and see Limey sitting forward, conning us through, and hear
Smoke Bassett, the mulatto from Haiti, singing a song of his
island in that deep, grand, melancholy bass of his.

Yes, it was long ago, but what else have we but memories?
For all life is divided into two parts: anticipation and mem-

ory, and if we remember richly, we must have lived richly. Only sometimes I think of them, and wonder what would have happened if the story had been different if another hand than mine had written the ending?

Fools . . . we were all of that, but a tough, ruddy lot of fools, and it was strange the way we worked as a team; the way we handled the boat and shared our grub and water and no whimper from any man.

There was Limey, who was medium height and heavy but massively boned, and Long Jack, who was six-three and cadaverous, and the powerful, lazy-talking Smoke, the strongest man of the lot. And me, whom they jokingly called "The Scholar" because I'd stowed a half-dozen books in my sea bag, and because I read from them, sometimes at night when we lay on deck and watched the canvas stretch its dark belly to the wind. Smoke would whet his razor-sharp knife and sing "Shenandoah," "Rio Grande," or "High Barbaree." And we would watch him cautiously and wonder what he had planned for that knife. And wonder what we had planned for each other.

———

THEN ONE MORNING we got the smell of the Borneo coast in our nostrils, and felt the close, hot, sticky heat of it coming up from below the horizon. We saw the mangrove coast out beyond the white snarl of foam along the reefs, then we put our helm over and turned east again, crawling along the coast of Darvel Bay.

The heat of the jungle reached out to us across the water and there was the primeval something that comes from the jungle, the ancient evil that crawls up from the fetid rottenness of it, and gets into the mind and into the blood.

We saw a few native craft, but we kept them wide abeam wanting to talk with no one, for our plans were big within us. We got out our stolen diving rig and went to work, checking it over. Johnson was a diver and I'd been down, so it was to be turn and turn about for us . . . for it might take a bit of time to locate the wreck, and then to get into the cabin once we'd found it.

We came up along the mangrove coast with the setting sun, and slid through a narrow passage into the quiet of a lagoon where we dropped our hook and swung to, looking at the long wall of jungle that fronted the shore for miles.

Have you seen a mangrove coast? Have you come fresh from the sea to a sundown anchorage in a wild and lonely place with the line of the shore lost among twisting, tangling tentacle roots, strangling the earth, reaching out to the very water and concealing under its solid ceiling of green those dark and dismal passages into which a boat might make its way?

Huge columnar roots, other roots springing from them, and from these, still more roots, and roots descending from branches and under them, black water, silent, unmoving. This we could see, and beyond it, shutting off the mangrove coast from the interior, a long, low cliff of upraised coral.

Night then . . . a moon hung low beyond a corner of the coral cliff . . . lazy water lapping about the hull . . . the mutter of breakers on the reef . . . the cry of a night bird, and then the low, rich tones of Smoke Bassett, singing.

So we had arrived, four men of the devil's own choosing, men from the world's waterfronts, and below us, somewhere in the dark water, was a submerged freighter with fifty thousand dollars in her strongbox.

Four men . . . Limey Johnson—short, powerful, tough. Tattooed on his hands the words, one to a hand, *Hold—Fast.* A scar across the bridge of his nose, the tip of an ear missing . . . greasy, unwashed dungarees . . . and stories of the Blue Funnel boats. What, I wondered, had become of the captain of the sunken ship, and the others who must have known about that money? Limey Johnson had offered no explanation, and we were not inquisitive men.

And Long Jack, sprawled on the deck looking up at the stars? Of what was he thinking? Tomorrow? Fifty thousand dollars, and how much he would get of it? Or was he thinking of the spending of it? He was a thin, haggard man with a slow smile that never reached beyond his lips. Competent, untiring . . . there was a rumor about Macao that he had killed a man aboard a Darwin pearl fisher . . . he was a man who grew red, but not tan, with a thin, scrawny neck like a buzzard, as taciturn as Johnson was talkative. Staring skyward from his pale gray eyes . . . at what? Into what personal future? Into what shadowed past?

Smoke Bassett, powerful tan muscles, skin stretched taut to contain their slumbering, restless strength. A man with magnificent eyes, quick of hand and foot . . . a dangerous man.

And the last of them, myself. Tall and lean and quiet, with wide shoulders, and not as interested in the money. Oh, yes, I wanted my share, and would fight to have it, but there was more than the money; there was getting the money; there was the long roll of the ketch coming down the China Sea; there was the mangrove coast, the night and the stars . . . there were the boat sounds, the water sounds . . . a bird's wing against the wind . . . the distant sounds of the forest . . . these things that no man can buy; these things that get into the blood; these things that build the memories of tomorrow; the hours to look back upon.

I wanted these more than money. For there is a time for adventure when the body is young and the mind alert and all the world seems there for one's hands to use, to hold, to take. And this was my new world, this ancient world of the Indies, these lands where long ago the Arab seamen came, and where the Polynesians may have passed, and where old civilizations slumber in the jungles; awaiting the explorations of men. Where rivers plunge down massive, unrecorded falls, where the lazy sea creeps under the mangroves, working its liquid fingers into the abysmal darkness where no man goes or wants to go.

What is any man but the total of what he has seen? The sum of what he has done? The strange foods, the women whose bodies have merged with his, the smells, the tastes, the longings, the dreams, the haunted nights? The Trenches in Shanghai, Blood Alley, Grant Road in Bombay, and Malay Street in Singapore . . . the worst of it, and the best . . . the temples and towers built by lost, dead hands, the nights at sea, the splendor of a storm, the dancing of dust devils on the desert. These are a man . . . and the solid thrill of a blow landed, the faint smell of opium, rubber, sandalwood, and spice, the stink of copra . . . the taste of blood from a split lip.

Oh, yes, I had come for things other than money but that evening, for the first time, no man gave another good night.

Tomorrow there would be, with luck, fifty thousand dollars in this boat . . . and how many ways to split it?

No need to worry until the box was aboard, or on the line, being hoisted. After that, it was every man for himself. Or was I mistaken? Would we remain friends still? Would we sail our boat into Amurang or Jesselton and leave it there and scatter to the winds with our money in our pockets?

That was the best way, but with such men, in such a place, with that amount of money . . . one lives because one remains cautious . . . and fools die young.

———

AT THE FIRST streaks of dawn, I was out of my blankets and had them rolled. While Smoke prepared breakfast, we got the diving outfit up to the side. We were eating when the question came.

"I'll go," I said, and grinned at them. "I'll go down and see how it looks."

They looked at me, and I glanced up from my plate and said, "How about it, Smoke? Tend my lines?"

He turned to me, a queer light flicking through his dark, handsome eyes, and then he nodded.

A line had been drawn . . .

A line of faith and a line of doubt . . . of the three, I had chosen Smoke Bassett, had put in him my trust, for when a man is on the bottom, his life lies in the hands of the man who tends his lines. A mistaken signal, or a signal ignored, and the diver can die.

I had given my life to Smoke Bassett, and who could know what that would mean?

———

JOHNSON WAS TAKING soundings, for in these waters, chart figures were not to be trusted. Many of the shores have been but imperfectly surveyed, if at all, and there is constant change to be expected from volcanic action, the growth of coral, or the waves themselves.

When we anchored outside the reef, I got into the diving dress. Limey lent me a hand, saying to me, "Nine or ten fathoms along the reef, but she drops sharp off to fifty fathoms not far out."

Careful . . . we'd have to be careful, for the enemies of a diver are rarely the shark or the octopus, but rather the deadline and constant danger of a squeeze or a blowup. The air within the suit is adjusted to the depth of the water and its pressure, but a sudden fall into deeper water can crush a man, jamming his entire body into his copper helmet. Such sudden pressure is called a squeeze.

A blowup is usually caused by a jammed valve, blowing a man's suit to almost balloon size and propelling him suddenly to the surface where he lies helpless until rescued. While death only occasionally results from a blowup, a diver may be crippled for life by the dreaded "bends," caused by the sudden change in pressure, and the resulting formation of nitrogen bubbles in the bloodstream.

When the helmet was screwed on, Limey clapped me on the top and I swung a leg over to the rope ladder. Smoke Bassett worked the pump with one arm while he played out the hose and rope. Up—down. *Chug-chug.* A two-stroke motion like a railroad hand car. It didn't take much energy but each stroke was a pulse of oxygen . . . like a breath, or the beating of your heart. The big mulatto grinned at me as he worked the handle.

Clumsy, in the heavy shoes and weighted belt, I climbed down and felt the cool press of water rise around me. Up my body . . . past my faceplate.

It was a slow, easy descent . . . down . . . down . . . and on the bottom at sixty feet.

In the dark water, down where the slow weeds wave in the unstirring sea . . . no sound but the *chug-chug-chug* of the pump, the pump that brings the living air . . . down in a green, gray, strange world . . . cowrie shells . . . a big conch . . . the amazing wall of the reef, jagged, broken, all edges and spires . . . a stone fish, all points and poison.

Leaning forward against the weight of the water, I moved like some ungainly monster of the deep, slowly along the bottom. Slowly . . . through the weeds, upon an open sand field beneath the sea . . . slowly, I walked on.

A dark shadow above me and I turned slowly . . . a shark . . . unbelievably huge . . . and seemingly uninterested . . . but could you tell? Could one ever know?

Smell . . . I'd heard old divers say that sharks acted upon smell . . . and the canvas and rubber and copper gave off no smell, but a cut, a drop of blood in the water, and the sharks would attack.

Chug-chug-chug . . . I walked on, turning slowly from time to time to look around me. And the shark moved above me, huge, black, ominous . . . dark holes in the reef where might lurk . . . anything. And then I saw . . . something.

A blackness, a vast deep, opening off to my right, away from the reef. I looked toward it, and drew back. Fifty fathoms at some places, but then deeper, much deeper. Fifty fathoms . . . three hundred feet.

A signal . . . time for me to go up. Turning, I walked slowly back and looked for the shark, but he had gone. I had failed to hold his interest . . . and I could only hope that nothing in my personality would induce him to return.

When the helmet was off, I told them. "Probably the other way. But when you go down, Limey, keep an eye open for that shark. I don't trust the beggar."

On THE THIRD day, we found the hulk of the freighter. At the time, I was below, half asleep in my bunk. Bassett was in the galley cooking, and only Long Jack was on deck, handling the lines for Limey. Dozing, I heard him bump against the vessel's side and I listened, but there was nothing more, only a sort of scraping, a sound I could not place, as if something were being dragged along the hull.

When I heard the weighted boots on the deck, I rolled over and sat up, kicking my feet into my slippers. Johnson was seated on the rail and his helmet was off and Long Jack was talking to him. When they heard my feet on the deck, they turned. "Found it!" Limey was grinning his broken-toothed smile. "She's hanging right on the lip of the deep. She's settin' up fairly straight. You shouldn't have much trouble gettin' the box."

THERE WAS A full moon that night, wide and white; a moon that came up over the jungle, and standing by the rail, I looked out over the lagoon and watched the phosphorescent combers roll up and crash against the outer reef. When I had been standing there a long time, Smoke Bassett walked over.

"Where's Limey?"

"Fishin'," he said, "with a light."

"Tomorrow," I said, "we'll pick it up."

"Anson Road would look mighty good now. Anson Road, in Singapore . . . an' High Street. You know that, Scholar?"

"It'll look better with money in your pocket."

"Look good to me just anyway." Smoke rolled a cigarette. "Money ain't so important."

We watched the moon and listened to the breakers on the reef. "You be careful down there," Smoke Bassett told me suddenly. "Mighty careful." He struck a match and lit his cigarette, as he always did, one-handed.

Lazily, I listened to the sea talking to the reef and then listened to the surf and to the jungle beyond the line of mangroves. A bird shrieked, an unhappy, uncanny sound.

"Them two got they heads together," Smoke Bassett said. "You be careful."

Long Jack . . . a queer, silent man around whom one never felt quite comfortable. A taciturn man with a wiry strength that could be dangerous. Only once had we had words and that had been back in Macao when we first met. He had been arrogant, as if he felt he could push me around. "Don't start that with me," I told him.

His eyes were snaky, cold, there were strange little lights in them, and contempt. He just looked at me. I didn't want trouble so I told him, "You could make an awful fool of yourself, Jack," I said.

He got up. "Right now," he said, and stood there looking at me, and I know he expected me to take water.

So, I got up, for this was an old story, and I knew by the way he stood that he knew little about fistfighting, and then a fat man, sitting in a dirty singlet and a blue dungaree coat, said, "You *are* a fool. I seen the kid fight in Shanghai, in the ring. He'll kill you."

Long Jack from Sydney hesitated and it was plain he no longer wanted to fight. He still stood there, but I'd seen the signs before and knew the moment was past. He'd had me pegged for a kid who either couldn't or wouldn't go through.

That was all, but Long Jack had not forgotten, I was sure of that. There had been no further word, nor had we talked much on the trip down the China Sea except what was necessary. But it had been pleasant enough.

The next morning when I got into the suit, Limey came up to put on the copper helmet. There was a look in his eyes I didn't like. "When you get it out of the desk," he said, "just tie her on the line and give us a signal."

But there was something about the way he said it that was wrong. As I started into the water, he leaned over suddenly and stroked his hand down my side. I thought he wanted something and turned my faceplate toward him, but he just stood there so I started down into the water.

When I was on the deck of the freighter, I started along toward the superstructure and then saw something floating by my face. I stepped back to look and saw it was a gutted fish. An instant, I stood there staring, and then a dark shadow swung above me and I turned, stumbled, and fell just as the same huge shark of a few days before whipped by, jaws agape.

On my feet, I stumbled toward the companionway, and half fell through the opening just as the shark twisted around and came back for another try.

And then I knew why Limey Johnson had been fishing, and what he had rubbed on my arm as I went into the water. He had rubbed the blood and guts of the fish on my suit and then had dumped it into the water after me to attract the shark.

Sheltered by the companionway, I rubbed a hand at my sleeve as far around as I could reach, trying to rub off some of the blood.

Forcing myself to composure, I waited, thinking out the situation.

Within the cabin to the right, I had already noticed the door of the desk compartment that held the cash box stood open to the water. That meant the money was already on our boat; it meant that the bumping I'd heard along the side had been the box as it was hoisted aboard. And letting me go down again, rubbing the blood and corruption on my sleeve had been a deliberate attempt at murder.

Chug-chug-chug . . . monotonously, reassuringly, the steady sound of the pump reached me. Smoke was still on the job, and I was still safe, yet how long could I remain so under the circumstances?

If they had attempted to kill me they would certainly attempt to kill Smoke, and he could not properly defend himself, even strong as he was, while he had to keep at least one hand on the pump. Outside, the shark circled, just beyond the door frame.

Working my way back into the passage, I fumbled in the cabin, looking for some sort of weapon. There was a fire ax on the bulkhead outside, but it was much too clumsy for use against so agile a foe, even if I could strike hard enough underwater. There was nothing . . . suddenly I saw on the wall, crossed with an African spear of some sort, a whaler's harpoon!

Getting it down, I started back for the door, carefully freeing my lines from any obstructions.

Chug . . . chug . . . chug . . .

The pump slowed, almost stopped, then picked up slowly again, and then something floated in the water, falling slowly, turning over as I watched, something that looked like an autumn leaf, drifting slowly down, only much larger.

Something with mouth agape, eyes wide, blood trailing a darkening streamer in the green water . . . it was Long Jack, who had seen the last of Sydney . . . Long Jack, floating slowly down, his belly slashed and an arm cut across the biceps by a razor-edged knife.

An instant I saw him, and then there was a gigantic swirl in the water, the shark turning, doubling back over, and hurling himself at the body with unbelievable ferocity. It was my only chance; I stepped out of the door and signaled to go up.

There was no response, only the *chug-chug-chug* of the pump. Closing my valve only a little, I started to rise, but desperately as I tried, I could not turn myself to watch the shark. Expecting at any moment that he would see me and attack, I drifted slowly up.

Suddenly the ladder hung just above me although the hull was still a dark shadow. I caught the lower step and pulled myself slowly up until I could get my clumsy feet on the step. Climbing carefully, waiting from moment to moment, I got to the surface and climbed out.

Hands fumbled at the helmet. I heard the wrench, and then the helmet was lifted off.

Smoke Bassett had a nasty wound over the eye where he had been struck by something, and where blood stained his face it had been wiped and smeared. Limey Johnson was standing a dozen feet away, only now he was drawing back, away from us.

He looked at the harpoon in my hands and I saw him wet his lips, but I said nothing at all. Bassett was helping me out of the helmet, and I dared not take my eyes from Johnson.

His face was working strangely, a grotesque mask of yellowish-white wherein the eyes seemed unbelievably large. He reached back and took up a long boat hook. There was a driftwood club at my feet, and this must have been what had struck Bassett. They must have rushed him at first, or Long Jack had tried to get close, and had come too close.

When I dropped the weight belt and kicked off the boots, Smoke was scarcely able to stand. And I could see the blow that had hit him had almost wrecked the side of his face and skull. "You all right? You all right, Scholar?" His voice was slurred.

"I'm all right. Take it easy. I'll handle it now."

Limey Johnson faced me with his new weapon, and slowly

his courage was returning. Smoke Bassett he had feared, and Smoke was nearly helpless. It was Limey and me now; one of us was almost through.

Overhead the sun was blazing . . . the fetid smell of the mangroves and the swamp was wafted to the ketch from over the calm beauty of the lagoon. The sea was down, and the surf rustled along the reef, chuckling and sucking in the holes and murmuring in the deep caverns.

Sweat trickled into my eyes and I stood there, facing Limey Johnson across that narrow deck. Short, heavy, powerful . . . a man who had sent me down to the foulest kind of death, a man who must kill now if he would live.

I reached behind me to the rail and took up the harpoon. It was razor sharp.

His hook was longer . . . he outreached me by several feet. I had to get close . . . close.

In my bare feet, I moved out away from Smoke, and Limey began to move warily, watching for his chance, that ugly hook poised to tear at me. To throw the harpoon was to risk my only weapon, and risk it in his hands, for I could not be sure of my accuracy. I had to keep it, and thrust. I had to get close. The diving dress was some protection but it was clumsy and I would be slow.

There was no sound . . . the hot sun, the blue sky, the heavy green of the mangroves, the sucking of water among the holes of the coral . . . the slight sound of our breathing and the rustle and slap of our feet on the deck.

He struck with incredible swiftness. The boat hook darted and jerked back. The hook was behind my neck, and only the nearness of the pole and my boxer's training saved me. I jerked my head aside and felt the thin sharpness of the point as it whipped past my neck, but before I could spring close enough to thrust, he stepped back and bracing himself, he thrust at me. The curve of the hook hit my shoulder and pushed me off balance. I fell back against the bulwark, caught myself, and he lunged to get closer. Three times he whipped the hook and jerked at me. Once I almost caught the pole, but he was too quick.

I tried to maneuver . . . then realized I had to get outside of the hook's curve . . . to move to my left, then try for a thrust either over or under the pole. In the narrow space between the low deckhouse and the rail there was little room to maneuver.

I moved left, the hook started to turn, and I lunged suddenly and stabbed. The point just caught him . . . the side of his singlet above the belt started to redden. His face looked drawn, I moved again, parried a lunge with the hook, and thrust again, too short. But I knew how to fight him now . . . and he knew, too.

He tried, and I parried again, then thrust. The harpoon point just touched him again, and it drew blood. He stepped back, then crossed the deck and thrust at me under the yard, his longer reach had more advantage now, with the deckhouse between us, and he was working his way back toward the stern. It was an instant before I saw what he was trying to do. He was getting in position to kill Bassett, unconscious against the bulwark beside the pump.

To kill . . . and to get the knife.

I lunged at him then, batting the hook aside, feeling it rip the suit and my leg as I dove across the mahogany roof of the deckhouse. I thrust at him with the harpoon. His face twisted with fear, he sprang back, stepped on some spilled fish guts staining the deck. He threw up his arms, lost hold of the boat hook, and fell backward, arms flailing for balance. He hit the bulwark and his feet flew up and he went over, taking my harpoon with him . . . a foot of it stuck out his back . . . and there was an angry swirl in the water, a dark boiling . . . and after a while, the harpoon floated to the surface, and lay there, moving slightly with the wash of the sea.

———

THERE'S A PLACE on the Sigalong River, close by the Trusan waters, a place where the nipa palms make shade and rustle their long leaves in the slightest touch of wind. Under the palms, within sound of the water, I buried Smoke Bassett on a Sunday afternoon . . . two long days he lasted, and a wonder at that, for the side of his head was curiously crushed.

How the man had remained at the pump might be called a mystery . . . but I knew.

For he was a loyal man; I had trusted him with my lines, and there can be no greater trust. So when he was gone, I buried him there and covered over the grave with coral rock and made a marker for it and then I went down to the dinghy and pushed off for the ketch.

———

SOMETIMES NOW, WHEN there is rain upon the roof and when the fire crackles on the hearth, sometimes I will remember: the bow wash about the hull, the rustling of the nipa palms, the calm waters of a shallow lagoon. I will remember all that happened, the money I found, the men that died, and the friend I had . . . off the mangrove coast.

GLORIOUS! GLORIOUS!

T HE FOUR MEN crouched together in the narrow shadow of the parapet. The sun was setting slowly behind a curtain of greasy cloud, and the air, as always at twilight, was very clear and still. A hundred and fifty yards away was the dirty gray earth where the Riffs were hidden. The declining sun threw long fingers of queer, brassy light across the rise of the hill behind them.

On their left the trench was blown away by artillery fire; here and there a foot or a shoulder showed above the dirt thrown up by explosions. They had marched, eaten, and fought beside those men, dead now.

"Better keep your head away from that opening, kid, or you'll get it blown away."

Dugan pulled his head back, and almost on the instant a spout of sand leaped from the sandbag and splattered over his face.

Slim smiled wryly, and the Biscayan looked up from the knife he was sharpening. He was always sharpening his knife and kept it with a razor edge. Short, thick-bodied, he had a square-jawed, pock-marked face and small eyes. Dugan was glad they were fighting on the same side.

"You got anything to eat?" Slim asked suddenly, looking over at Dugan.

"Nothing. I ate my last biscuit before that last attack," he said. "I could have eaten forty."

"You?" Slim looked at the Irishman.

Jerry shrugged. "I ate mine so long ago I've forgotten."

He was bandaging his foot with a soiled piece of his shirt. A bullet had clipped the butt of his heel the day before, making a nasty wound.

Somewhere down the broken line of trenches there was a

brief volley followed by several spaced rifle shots, then another brief spatter of firing.

Slim was wiping the dust from his rifle, testing the action. Then he reloaded, taking his time. "They're tough," he said, "real tough."

"I figured they'd be A-rabs or black," Jerry said, "and they ain't either one."

"North Africa was never black," Dugan said. "Nearly all the country north of the Niger is Berber country, and Berbers are white. These Riffs—there's as many redheaded ones as in Scotland."

"I was in Carthage once," Slim said. "It's all busted up—ruins."

"They were Semitic," Dugan said. "Phoenicians originally."

"How you know so much about it?" Slim asked.

"There was a book somebody left in the barracks all about this country and the Sahara."

"You can have it," Jerry said. "This country, I mean."

"Book belonged to that colonel—the fat one." Dugan moved a small stone, settled himself more comfortably. "He let it lay one time, and somebody swiped it."

"Hey!" Jerry sat up suddenly. He held the bandage tight to survey the job he was doing, then continued with it. "That reminds me. I know where there's some wine."

Slim turned his long neck. "Some *what*?"

He looked gaunt and gloomy in his dirty, ill-fitting uniform. One shoulder was stained with blood, and the threads had begun to ravel around a bullet hole. He had been hit nine times since the fighting began, but mostly they were scratches. He'd lost one shoe, and the foot was wrapped in canvas. It was a swell war.

Jerry continued to wrap his foot, and nobody said anything. Dugan watched him, thinking of the wine. Then he looked across at the neat row of men lying side by side near the far parapet. As he looked, a bullet struck one of them, and the body jerked stiffly. It did not matter. They were all dead.

"Over there in the cellar," Jerry said. He nodded his head

to indicate a squat gray stone building on the peak of a coni-
cal hill about a quarter of a mile off. "The colonel found a
cellar the monks had. He brought his own wine with him and
a lot of canned meat and cheese. He stored it in that cellar—
just like in an icebox. I helped pack some of it in not over two
weeks ago. He kept me on patrol duty three days extra just
for breaking a bottle. He brought in a lot of grub, too."

The Biscayan glanced up, mumbling something in Spanish. He pulled a hair from his head and tested the edge of the
blade, showing his teeth when the hair cut neatly.

"What's he say?"

"He says it may still be there." Jerry shifted his rifle and
glanced speculatively at the low hill. "Shall we have a look?"

"They'd blow our heads off before we could get there,"
Slim protested, "night or no night."

"Look," Jerry said, "we're liable to get it, anyway. This is
going to be like Anual, where they wiped them all out. Look
how long we've been here and no relief. I think they've written us off."

"It's been seventy-five days," Dugan agreed.

"Look what happened at Chentafa. The officer in command saw they'd had it and set fire to the post; then he died
with his men."

"That's more than these will do."

"Hell," Jerry said, "I think they're already dead. I haven't
seen an officer in a week. Only that corporal."

"They pick them off first. Those Moors can shoot." Slim
looked at Dugan. "How'd you get into this outfit, anyway?"

"My ship was in Barcelona. I came ashore and was shang-
haied. I mean an army patrol just gathered in a lot of us, and
when I said I was an American citizen, they just paid no attention."

"Did you get any training?"

"A week. That was it. They asked me if I'd ever fired a gun,
and like a damned fool I told them I had. Hell, I grew up with
a gun. I was twelve years old before I found out it wasn't part
of me. So here I am."

"They wanted men, and they didn't care where or how
they got them. Me, I've no excuse," Slim said. "I joined the

Spanish Foreign Legion on my own. I was broke, hungry, and in a different country. It looked like an easy way out."

Far off to the left there was an outburst of firing, then silence.

"What happened to the colonel? The fat one who had all that wine brought in?"

"Killed himself. Look, they tell me there's a general for every twenty-five men in this army. This colonel had connections. They told him spend a month over there and we'll promote you to general, so he came, and then we got pinned down, and he couldn't get out. From Tetuan to Chaouen there's a whole line of posts like this one here at Seriya. There's no way to get supplies, no way to communicate."

The talk died away. It was very hot even though the sun was setting.

A big Russian came up and joined them. He looked like a big schoolboy with his close-cropped yellow hair and his pink cheeks. "They come," he said.

There was a crackle of shots, and the four climbed to their feet. Dugan lurched from weariness, caught himself, and faced about. The Russian was already firing.

A long line of Moors was coming down the opposite slope, their advance covered by a barrage of machine-gun fire from the trenches farther up the hill. Here and there a captured field gun boomed. Dugan broke open a box of cartridges and laid them out on a sandbag close at hand. Slowly and methodically, making each shot count, he began to fire.

The Biscayan was muttering curses and firing rapidly. He did not like long-range fighting. Jerry leaned against the sandbags, resting his forehead on one. Dugan could see a trickle of sweat cutting a trail through the dust.

Somewhere down the parapet one of their own machine guns opened up, the gray and white line before them melted like wax, and the attack broke. Slim grounded his rifle butt and leaned against the sandbags, fumbling for a cigarette. His narrow, cadaverous features looked yellow in the pale light. He looked around at Dugan. "How d'you like it, kid? Had enough?"

Dugan shrugged and reloaded his rifle, then stuffed his

pockets with cartridges. The powder smoke made his head ache, or maybe it was hunger and the sound of guns. His cheek was swollen from the rifle stock, and his gums were sore and swollen. All of them were indescribably dirty. For seventy-five days they had held the outpost against a steady, unrelenting, consistent, energy-draining attack that seemed to take no thought of men lost. Their food was gone; only a little of the brackish water remained, and there would be no relief.

"They've written us off," Slim said. "We're dead." He was hollow eyed and sagging, yet he was still a fighting man. He looked at Jerry. "How about that wine?"

"Let's go get it. There's a machine gun there, too, and enough ammo to fight the battle of the Marne."

"Does the sergeant major know?"

"He did." Jerry indicated the line of dead bodies. "He's over there."

"Who's in command?" Dugan asked.

"Maybe nobody. The lieutenant was killed several days ago, shot from behind. He was a fool to hit that Turk. He slugged one guy too many."

The sun was gone, and darkness was falling over the low hills. There was no movement in the trenches across the way. The Russian stood up, then sat down abruptly, his throat shot away. He started to rise again, then just sat back down and slowly rolled over.

Slim picked him up as though he were a child and carried him to the line of bodies, placing him gently on the ground. Then he unbuckled his cartridge pouches and hung them around his own waist. Dugan looked through an opening in the sandbagged parapet at the broad shoulders of shadow along the slope. A dead Moor hung head down over the barbed wire about fifty feet away, and a slight breeze made his burnoose swell.

When it was dark, the corporal came along the trench. He looked old. His thin, haggard face was expressionless. He said what they all knew.

"There won't be any relief. I think everything behind us is

wiped out, too. We wouldn't stand a chance in trying to get away. They're out there waiting, hoping we try it.

"There'll be at least one night attack, but with daybreak they'll come. There's thirty-eight of us left. Fire as long as you can, and when they get through the wire, it's every man for himself."

He looked around vacantly, then started back up the line. His shoes were broken, and one leg was bandaged. He looked tired. He stopped suddenly, looking back. "If any of you have the guts to try it, go ahead." He looked from Jerry to Slim, then at Dugan. "We're through."

Slim walked over to the dead officer and took his automatic, then the cartridges for it. He took some money, too, then dropped it into the sand. Having a second thought, he picked it up.

"If a man could get away," he said, looking over at Dugan, "this would pay a boatman. Gibraltar—that would be the place."

Dugan sat down, his back to the parapet. He glanced along the trench. Far down he could see movement.

Thirty-eight left! There had been 374 when they occupied the post. He tilted his head back and looked at the stars. They had looked the same way at home. How long ago was that?

Jerry got up. He glanced at Slim, and the Texan shrugged. "Let's go," he said. And they went.

Jerry pointed. "We'll go down that shallow place, and there's a ditch. Follow that to the right and it takes you right up to the building. If we get into that ditch, we've got it made."

There was no moon, but the stars were bright. The rear parapet had been partly knocked down by the explosion of a shell. They went over fast, Jerry first, then Dugan. Flat on their faces, they wormed across the dark ground, moving fast but silently. The ground was still hot. In the darkness his hand touched something warm. It was a gun, an automatic. He thought of Slim and felt suddenly sick; then he remembered the sergeant who had been killed out here a few days before. He took the gun but turned at right angles. The Biscayan was close behind him, his knife in his teeth, his rifle lying across his forearms.

Dugan heard a slight movement and looked up suddenly into the eyes of a Moor. For a split second they both stared, and then Dugan jerked his rifle forward, and the muzzle struck the Moor right below the eye. The Moor rolled back and then came up, very fast, with a knife. Dugan kicked him on the kneecap, then hit him with the butt and followed with the barrel. He went down, but another loomed up.

There was a scream as the Biscayan ripped one up, and then Slim broke into the fight with an automatic. Then there was a roar of shots from all along the parapet. It was the expected night attack, sooner than believed and almost successful.

Dugan came up running, saw a Moor loom up before him, and shot without lifting the rifle above his belt line. The Moor spun out of the way and fell, and Dugan fell into the ditch just one jump ahead of the Biscayan. Then Slim and Jerry joined them. Jerry was carrying three rifles and a bandoleer of cartridges.

They went along the ditch at a stumbling run. Dugan slipped once and almost fell, but when he straightened up, the stone house was looming above them. Jerry led them to the trap door at the end of the ditch.

The room was empty except for a desk and a couple of chairs. One chair was tipped on its side, and there were papers scattered about. The room had a musty smell, as the door and windows were heavily shuttered and barred. Both openings could be covered by rifles from the trenches below, and as the position was not a good one, the Moors had not taken it.

Jerry dragged the heavy desk aside and struck a match to find the iron ring concealed in a crack. With a heave he opened the cellar. In the flare of the match Dugan saw that Jerry's scalp was deeply lacerated and dried blood matted his hair on one side.

Slim slid into the hole and a moment later was handing up bottles. Then he sent up a magnum of champagne, and the Biscayan came up with some canned fruit and cheese.

"This guy had a taste for knickknacks," Slim said. "There's everything down here that you could get into a can."

"He took three hot ones right through the belly on the first day," Jerry said. "He was scared and crying like a baby. I don't believe he'd ever done a day's duty in his life."

Dugan took a bottle of Château Margaux and a can of the cheese. The wine tasted good. After a bit he crawled into a corner, made a pillow of some cartridge pouches, and went to sleep. When he awakened, light was filtering into the room from around the shutters. Jerry was sitting wide legged near the cellar door, and he was drunk. Slim was at the desk.

"Kid," Slim said, "come here."

He had a map laid out. "See? If you get the chance, take the ditch to here, then down along that dry creek. It's not far to the coast, and most of those boat guys will give you a lift for money. You got any money?"

"About twenty bucks. I've been hiding it in case."

"Here." Slim took the money he'd taken from the dead officer. "You take this."

"What about you?"

"I ain't goin' to make it, kid. I got a hunch. If I do, we'll go together. If you board that boat, they may take your rifle, but you keep your sidearm, you hear? Keep it hidden. You may need it before you get across."

He turned to look at Dugan. "How old are you, kid?"

"Twenty-two," Dugan said, and he lied. He was just past sixteen.

"You look younger. Anyway, go through their pockets, whoever's dead. They won't mind, and you'll need whatever there is.

"Don't go near the army or a big town. Head for the seacoast and stay out of sight. Anybody you meet out here will try to stop you. Don't let it happen. You get away—you hear?"

Jerry lifted the bottle in a toast. "Tomorrow we die!" he said.

"Today, you mean," Slim said.

The Biscayan came up from the cellar with a machine gun. It was brand-spanking-new. He went down again and came up with several belts of ammo, then a box of them. He set the machine gun up at a shuttered window and fed a belt into it.

Dugan looked at the automatic he had picked up. It was in good shape. He found another in the cellar and several spare clips. He loaded them.

Scattered shooting broke into a steady roar. A shell exploded not too far away.

Slim had found two Spanish versions of the Colt pistols and loaded them. He strapped them on, pleased. "You know what I'm going to do? I'm going to get good and drunk, and then I'm going to open that door and show them how we do it down in Texas!"

He emptied half a bottle of the wine and looked at Dugan. "You ever been in Texas, kid?"

"I worked on a ranch there—in the Panhandle."

"I grew up on a ranch," Slim said. "Rode for a couple of outfits in New Mexico before I started out to see the world. I knew this would happen sometime. Just never figured it would be here, in a place like this."

He picked up the bottle of wine and looked at it. "What I need is some tequila. This here is a she-male's drink! Or some bourbon an' branch water."

Dugan took his rifle and walked to the window. He helped the Biscayan move the machine gun to a more advantageous position, a little closer, a little more to the left. He checked his rifle again and loaded two more and stood them close by. From a crack in the shutters he studied the route he might get a chance to take. It must be done before the whole country was overrun by the Moors.

Suddenly Jerry moved, the dried blood still caked in his stubble of beard. He crawled on hands and knees to the edge of the trapdoor from the ditch. Then he stopped, breathing hoarsely, waiting.

Dugan had heard nothing above the occasional rattle of distant rifle fire as the Riffs began to mop up. Suddenly the trapdoor began to lift, very cautiously, then with more confidence. When it had lifted about a foot, a big Riff thrust his head up and stared into the room. All the occupants were out of his immediate range, and he lifted his head higher, peering into the semidarkness. In that instant Jerry swung the empty magnum. The solid *bop* of the blow was loud in the room, and the man vanished, the door falling into place. Jerry jerked it open, slammed it back, and leaped down into the hole. There was a brief scuffle, and then Jerry came back through the trapdoor, carrying a new rifle and a bandoleer.

Now the crescendo of firing had lifted to a loud and continuous roar, and Slim started to sing. In the tight stone room his voice boomed loudly.

> Glorious! Glorious!
> One keg o' beer for the four of us!
> Glory be to heaven that there isn't
> Ten or 'leven,
> For the four of us can drink it all alone!

The Biscayan took down the bar and threw the shutters wide. Below them and away across the tawny hill the Riffian trench was suddenly vomiting up a long line of men. From behind the parapet before them a scattering fire threw a pitiful challenge at the charging line.

Dugan wiped the sweat from his eyebrows and leaned against the edge of the window. He was sagging with incredible exhaustion, and his body stank from the unwashed weeks, the sweat and the dirt. He lifted the rifle and held it against his swollen cheek and began to fire.

Behind him Jerry and Slim were singing "Casey Jones." Dugan looked down at the Biscayan, a solid chunk of man who lived to fight. Hunched behind the machine gun, he waited, watching the line as an angler watches a big fish approaching the hook.

Suddenly the firing stopped, waiting for a killing volley at close quarters.

Dugan had stopped, too. One man, a tall Moor on a fine-looking horse, had ridden out on a point a good six hundred yards away, watching the attack. He stood in his stirrups, lifting a hand to shout a command, unheard at the distance. For what seemed a long minute Dugan held his aim, then squeezed off the shot, and the man stood tall in his stirrups, then fell from the saddle to the dust and lay there. Then the Biscayan opened fire.

Dugan looked down at him, aware for the first time that the Biscayan was drunk. The gray line melted before him, and the Biscayan lifted the bottle for another drink.

The unexpected fire from the stone house, cutting a wide swath in their ranks, paralyzed the attack. Then a bunch of the Riffs broke away from the main attack and started toward the stone house. Jerry was up, firing slowly, methodically. Suddenly the machine gun swung, fired three short bursts, and the bunch of attackers melted away. From behind the parapet came a wavering cheer. Dugan winced at the few voices. So many were gone!

Dugan squinted his eyes against the sun, remembering the line of silent men beside the parapet and the big Russian with the schoolboy pink in his cheeks.

The Biscayan lifted his bottle to drink, and it shattered in his hand, spilling wine over him. With a lurid burst of Spanish he dropped the neck of the bottle and reached for another. And he had never been a drinking man.

Slim sat on the floor, muttering. "I'm goin' to get damn good an' drunk an' go out there and show 'em how we do it down in Texas."

He started to rise and sat down hard, a long red furrow along his jaw. He swore in a dull, monotonous voice.

Dugan saw the line of Moors sweep forward and across the parapet. There was scattered shooting, some rising dust, then silence. He blinked, feeling a lump in his throat. He had known few of them, for they had been together too short a time. Only weeks had passed since he lay in his bunk aboard ship, feeling the gentle roll as it steamed west from Port Said.

The sunlight was bright and clear. Outside, except for the scattered bodies of the slain, all was quiet and peaceful under the morning sun. Dugan looked across the valley, thinking of what he would do. There was little time. Perhaps time had already run out.

The afternoon was waning before they attacked again.

This time they were careful, taking advantage of the slight roll of the hill to get closer. The last hundred yards was in the open, and they seemed unaware of the ditch, which would be hidden from them until they were almost fallen into it.

Dugan's face was swollen and sore from the kick of the rifle. He was hot and tired, and he switched rifles again.

A single shot sounded, lonely against the hills, and something gasped beside him. He turned to see Jerry fall across the sill. Before he could pull him back, three more bullets chugged into his body.

"Kid," Slim said, "you better go. It's time."

He took the bar down from the door and looked down the sunlit hill. A knot of Moors was coming toward him, good men, fighting men, dangerous men. Slim stepped out with a pistol in each hand and started down toward them.

He was drunk. Magnificently, roaring drunk, and he had a pistol in either hand. "I'm a-goin' to show them how we do it down in Texas!" He opened fire, then his body jerked, and he went to his knees.

Dugan snapped a quick shot at a Moor running up with a rifle ready to fire, and then Slim got up. He had lost one gun, but he started to fire from waist level. His whole left side was bloody.

Dugan turned to yell at the Biscayan, but the man was slumped across his machine gun. He had been shot between the eyes.

Dugan pushed him away from the gun and swung it toward the front of the house. In the distance, against the pale-blue sky, above the heat waves dancing, a vulture swung in slow circles against the sky. Slim was down, all sprawled out, and the enemy was closing in.

He pointed the gun toward them and opened up, singing in a hoarse, toneless voice.

> Glorious! Glorious!
> One keg o' beer for the four of us!
> Glory be to heaven that there isn't
> Ten or 'leven,
> For the four of us can drink it all alone!

His belt went empty, and the hill was bare of all but the bodies. He got up and closed the heavy plank door.

He caught up a bandoleer and another pistol. Then he dropped through the trapdoor.

All was still. He stepped over the dead Moor and went out into the shadowed stillness of the ditch.

And then he began to run.

BY THE RUINS OF
"EL WALARIEH"

FROM THE HILLSIDE above the ruins of El Walarieh one could watch the surf breaking along the shore, and although the grass was sparse, thin goats grazed among the occasional clumps of brushwood high on the hill behind me. It was a strange and lonely coast, not without its own wild beauty.

Three times I had been there before the boy approached. He was a thin boy with large, beautiful eyes and smooth brown skin. He squatted beside me, his shins brown and dirty, looking curiously toward the sea, where I was looking.

"You sit here often?"

"Yes, very often."

"You look at something?"

"I look at the sea. I look at the sea and the shore, sometimes at the clouds." I shifted my position a little. "It is very beautiful."

"Beautiful?" He was astonished. "The sea is beautiful?" He looked again to be sure that I was not mildly insane.

"I like the sea, and I like to look at those ruins and to wonder who lived there, and what their lives were like."

He glanced at the ancient, time-blackened ruins. "They are no good, even for goats. The roofs have fallen in. Why do you look at the sea and not at the goats? I think the goats are more beautiful than the sea. Look at them!"

I turned my head to please him. There were at least fifty, and they browsed or slept upon the hillside above me. They were white against the green of the hill. Yes, there was beauty there, too. He seemed pleased that I agreed with him.

"They are not my goats," he explained, "but someday I shall own goats. Perhaps as many as these. Then you will see beauty. They shall be like white clouds upon the green sky of the hillside."

He studied the camera that lay on the grass near my feet. "You have a machine," he said. "What is it for?"

"To make pictures. I want to get pictures of the sea and the ruins."

"Of the goats, too?"

To please him, I agreed. "Yes, also of the goats."

The idea seemed to satisfy him, yet he was obviously puzzled, too. There was something he did not understand. He broached the idea to me, as one gentleman to another. "You take pictures of the sea and the ruins . . . also of the goats. Why do you take these?"

"To look at them. To catch their beauty."

"But why a picture?" He was still puzzled. "They are here! You can see them without a picture. The sea is here, the sky, the ruins . . . the goats, too. They are always here."

"Yes, but I shall not always be here. I shall go away, and I want them to remember, to look at many times."

"You need the machine for that? I can remember. I can remember all of the goats. Each one of them." He paused, thinking about it. "Ah! The machine then is your memory. It is very strange to remember with a machine."

Neither of us spoke for a few minutes. "I think you have machines for many things. I would not like that."

The following day I was back on the hillside. It had not been my plan to come again, yet somehow the conversation left me unsatisfied. I had the feeling that somehow I'd been bested. I wanted the goatherd to understand.

When he saw me sitting there, he came down the hillside. He saluted me gravely, then sat down. I handed him a cigarette, and he accepted it gravely. "You have a woman?" he asked.

"No."

"What, no woman? It is good for a man to have a woman."

"No doubt." He was, I thought, all of thirteen. "You have a woman?" I asked the question gravely.

He accepted it in the same manner. "No. I am young for a woman. And they are much trouble. I prefer the goats."

"They are no trouble?"

He shrugged. "Goats are goats."

The comment seemed to explain much. He smoked in silence, and I waited for him to speak again. "If I had a woman, I would beat her. Women are good when beaten often, but they are not so productive as goats."

It was a question I did not wish to debate. He seemed to have all the advantage in the argument. He undoubtedly knew goats, and spoke of women with profound wisdom. I knew neither goats nor women.

"If you like the hillside," he said at last, "why do you not stay? The picture will be no good. It will be the sea and the ruins only at one time, and they are not always the same. They change," he added.

"My home is elsewhere. I must go back."

"Then why do you leave? Is it not good there? I think you are very restless." He looked at me. "Have you goats at home?"

"No." I was ashamed to admit it, feeling that the confession would lower me in his esteem. "I have no goats."

"A camel?" He was giving me every chance.

"No," I confessed reluctantly, "no camel." Inspiration hit me suddenly. "I have horses. Two of them."

He considered that. "It is good to have a horse, but a horse is like a woman. It is unproductive. If you have a horse or a woman, you must also have goats."

"If one has a woman," I ventured, "one must have many goats."

He nodded. I had but stated a fact.

WHERE THERE'S FIGHTING

T HE FOUR MEN were sprawled in a cuplike depression at the top of the pass. From where the machine gun was planted it had a clear field of fire for over four hundred yards. Beyond that the road was visible only at intervals. By a careful watch of those intervals an enemy could be seen long before he was within range.

A low parapet of loose rock had been thrown up along the lip of the depression, leaving an aperture for the .30-caliber gun. Two of the men were also armed with rifles.

It was very still. The slow warmth of the morning sun soaked into their bones and ate the frost away, leaving them lethargic and pleased. The low rumble as of thunder in the far-off hills were the bombs over Serbia, miles away.

"Think they'll ever come?" Benton asked curiously.

"They'll come," Ryan said.

"We can't stop them."

"No."

"How about some coffee? Is there any left?"

Ryan nodded. "It'll be ready soon. The part that's coffee is done, the part that's chicory is almost done, and the part that's plain bean is doing."

Benton looked at the two who were sleeping in the sun. They were mere boys. "Shall we wake them?"

"Pretty soon. They worry too much. Especially Pommy. He's afraid of being afraid."

"Sackworth doesn't. He thinks we're bloody heroes. Do you?"

"I'd feel heroic as blazes if I had a shave," Ryan said. "Funny, how you like being shaved. It sets a man up somehow."

Pommy turned over and opened his eyes. "I say, Bent? Shall I spell you a bit? You've been there hours!"

Benton looked at him, liking his fresh, clean-cut look.

"I could use some coffee. I feel like I was growing to this rock."

The young Englishman had risen to his feet.

"There's something coming down there. A man, I think."

"Couldn't be one of our men. We didn't have any over there. He's stopped—looking back."

"He's coming on again now," Sackworth said after a moment. He had joined them at the first sign of trouble. "Shall I try a shot?"

"Wait. Might be a Greek."

The sun climbed higher, and the moving figure came slowly toward them. He seemed to move at an almost creeping pace. At times, out of sight of the pass, they thought he would never show up again.

"He's carrying something," Pommy said. "Too heavy for a rifle, but I saw the sun flash on it back there a way."

The man came into sight around the last bend. He was big, but he walked very slowly, limping a little. He was wearing faded khaki trousers and a torn shirt. Over one shoulder were several belts of ammunition.

"He hasn't carried that very far," Ryan said. "He's got over a hundred pounds there."

Benton picked up one of the rifles and stepped to the parapet, but before he could lift the gun or speak, the man looked up. Benton thought he had never seen a face so haggard with weariness. It was an utter and complete weariness that seemed to come from within. The man's face was covered with a stubble of black beard. His face was wide at the cheekbones, and the nose was broken. His head was wrapped in a bloody bandage above which coarse black hair was visible.

"Any room up there?" he asked.

"Who are you?" Benton demanded.

Without replying, the big man started up the steep path. Once he slipped, skinning his knee against a sharp rock. Puzzled, they waited. When he stood beside them, they were shocked at his appearance. His face, under the deep brown of sun and wind, was drawn and pale, his nose peeling from sunburn. The rags of what must have once been a uniform were mud stained and sweat discolored.

"What difference does it make?" he asked mildly, humorously. "I'm here now."

He lowered the machine gun and slid the belts to the ground. When he straightened, they could see he was a half inch taller than Benton, who was a tall man, and at least thirty pounds heavier. Through his shirt bulging muscles showed, and there was blood clogging the hair on his chest.

"My name's Horne," he added. "Mike Horne. I've been fighting with Koska's guerrillas in Albania."

Benton stared, uncertain. "Albania? That's a long way from here."

"Not so far if you know the mountains." He looked at the pot on the fire. "How's for some coffee?"

Silently Ryan filled a cup. Digging in his haversack, Horne produced some Greek bread and a thick chunk of sausage. He brushed the sand from the sausage gravely. "Want some? I salvaged this from a bombed house back yonder. Might be some shell fragments in it."

"You pack that gun over the mountains?" Ryan asked.

Horne nodded, his mouth full. "Part of the way. It was surrounded by dead Greeks when I found it. Four Italians found it the same time. We had trouble."

"Did you—kill them all?" Pommy asked.

Horne looked at him. "No, kid. I asked them to tea an' then put sand in their bearings."

Pommy's face got red; then he grinned.

"Got any ammo for a .50?" Horne looked up at Benton. "I got mighty little left."

"They put down four boxes by mistake," Benton said.

Ryan was interested. "Koska's guerrillas? I heard of them. Are they as tough as you hear?"

"Tougher. Koska's an Albanian gypsy. Sneaked into Valona alone a few nights ago an' got himself three dagos. With a knife."

Sackworth studied Horne as if he were some kind of insect. "You call that bravery? That's like animals. One can at least fight like a gentleman!"

Horne winked at Ryan. "Sure, kid. But this ain't a gentleman's fight. This is war. Nothing sporting about it, just a case of dog eat dog, an' you better have big teeth."

"Why are you here?" Sackworth demanded.

Horne shrugged. "Why am I any place? Think I'm a fifth columnist or something?" He stared regretfully into the empty cup. "Well, I'm not. I ran a gun in the Chaco a few years ago; then they started to fight in China, so I went there. I was in the Spanish scrap with the Loyalists.

"Hung around in England long enough to learn something about that parachute business. Now that's a man's job. When you get down in an enemy country, you're on your own. I was with the bunch that hopped off from Libya and parachuted down in southern Italy to cut off that aqueduct and supply line to the Sicily naval base. Flock of 'spiggoties' spotted me, but I got down to the water and hiked out in a fishing boat. Now I'm here."

He looked up at Benton, wiping the back of his hand across his mouth. "From Kalgoorlie, I bet. You got the look. I prospected out of there once. I worked for pearls out of Darwin, too. I'm an original swag man, friend."

"What's a swag man?" Pommy asked.

Horne looked at him, smiling. Two of his front teeth at the side were missing.

"It's a bum, sonny. Just a bum. A guy who packs a tucker bag around looking for whatever turns up."

Horne pulled the gun over into his lap, carefully wiping the oil buffer clean. Then he oiled the moving parts of the gun with a little can he took from his hip pocket and slowly assembled it. He handled the gun like a lover, fitting the parts together smoothly and testing it carefully for head space when it was ready for firing.

"That a German shirt you have on?" Sackworth asked. His eyes were level, and he had his rifle across his knees, pointed at Horne.

"Sure," Horne said mildly. "I needed a shirt, so I took it out of a dead German's outfit."

"Looting," Sackworth said with scorn. There was distaste and dislike in his gaze.

"Why not?" Horne looked up at Sackworth, amused. "You're a good kid, so don't start throwing your weight around. This sportsmanship stuff, the old school tie, an' whatnot—that's okay where it belongs. You Britishers who play war like a game are living in the past. There's nothing sporting about this. It's like waterfronts or jungles. You survive any way you can."

Sackworth did not move the rifle. "I don't like him," he said to Benton. "I don't trust him."

"Forget it!" Benton snapped. "The man's all right, and Lord knows we need fighting men!"

"Sure," Horne added quietly. "It's just you an' me are different kind of animals, kid. You're probably Eton and then Sandhurst. Me, I came up the hard way. A tough road kid in the States, then an able seaman, took a whirl at the fight game, and wound up in Chaco.

"I like to fight. I also like to live. I been in a lot of fights, and mostly I fought pretty good, an' I'm still alive. The Jerries use whatever tactics they need. What you need, kid, in war is not a lot of cut an' dried rules but a good imagination, the ability to use what you've got to the best advantage no matter where you are, and a lot of the old moxie.

"You'll make a good fighter. You got the moxie. All you need is a little kicking around."

"I wish we knew where the Jerries were," Ryan said. "This waiting gets me."

"You'll see them pretty quick," Horne said. "There's about a battalion in the first group, and there's only one tank."

Benton lowered his cup, astonished. "You mean you've actually seen them? They are coming?"

Horne nodded. "The main body isn't far behind the first bunch."

"Why didn't you say so?" Sackworth demanded. His face was flushed and angry. "We could have warned the troops behind us."

"Yeah?" Horne did not look up from wiping the dust from

the cartridges. "Well, we couldn't. You see," he added, looking up, "they broke through Monastir Pass two days ago. Your men back there know more about it than we do. This is just a supporting column to polish off any leftovers like us."

"Then—we're cut off?" Pommy asked.

Horne nodded. "You have been for two days. How long you been here?"

"Just three days," Benton said. He studied Horne thoughtfully. "What are you? A Yank?"

Horne shrugged. "I guess so. When I joined up in Spain, they took my citizenship away. It was against the law to fight fascism then. If it was wrong then, it's wrong now. But me, I feel just the same. I'll fight them in China, in Spain, in Africa, or anywhere else.

"In Spain when everything was busting up, I heard about this guy Koska. One of his men was with us, so when he went back, I trailed along."

"They're coming," Sackworth said. "I can see the tank."

"All right," Benton said. He finished his coffee.

"Did you fight any Germans in Spain?" Pommy asked.

"Yeah." Mike Horne brushed invisible dust from the gun and fed a belt of cartridges into it. "Most of them aren't much better than the Italians. They fight better—the younger ones try harder—but all they know how to do is die."

"It's something to know that," Sackworth said.

"Nuts. Anybody can die. Everybody does. And dead soldiers never won any battles. The good soldier is the one who keeps himself alive and fighting. This bravery stuff—that's for milksops. For pantywaists. All of us are scared, but we fight just the same."

"The tank's getting closer," Sackworth said. He was plainly worried and showed it.

"I got the .50," Horne said. He settled himself comfortably into the sand and moved his gun on the swivel. "Let it get closer. Don't fire until they are close up to us. I'll take the tank. You take the first truck with the other gun, I'll take the second, an' so on. Get the drivers if you can."

They were silent. The rumble of the tank and heavy clank

of the tread drew nearer. Behind them rolled the trucks, the men sitting in tight groups. They apparently expected no trouble.

"I'd have expected them to send a patrol," Benton said, low voiced.

"They did," Horne replied.

They looked at him, startled. His eyes were on the gray-green column. He had sighted the fifty at the gun aperture on the tank.

"All right," he said suddenly.

His gun broke into a hoarse chatter, slamming steel-jacketed bullets at the tank. Then its muzzle lifted suddenly and swept the second truck. Soldiers were shouting and yelling, spilling from trucks like madmen, but the two first trucks were smashed into carriers of death before the men could move. The Germans farther back had found their enemy, and steel-jacketed bullets smashed into the parapet. Pommy felt something like a hot whiplash along his jaw.

They were above the column and out of reach of the tank. Mike Horne stood up suddenly and depressed the gun muzzle. The tank was just below. The gun chattered, and the tank slewed around sideways and drove full tilt into the rock wall as though to climb it.

Horne dropped back. "The older ones have a soft spot on top," he said.

The men of the broken column ran for shelter. Some of them tried to rush the steep path, but the fire blasted them back to the road, dead or dying. Others, trying to escape the angry bursts from the two guns, tried to scramble up the walls of the pass but were mowed down relentlessly.

It had been a complete and shocking surprise. The broken column became a rout. Horne stopped the .50 and wiped his brow with the back of his hand. He winked at Ryan.

"Nice going, kid. That's one tank that won't bother your pals."

Ryan peered around the rocks. The pass was empty of life. The wrecked tank was jammed against the rock wall, and one of the trucks had plunged off the precipice into the ra-vine. Another was twisted across the road.

A man was trying to get out of the first truck. He made it and tumbled to the road. His coat was stained with blood, and he was making whimpering sounds and trying to crawl. His face and head were bloody.

"Next time it'll be tough," Horne said. "They know now. They'll come in small bunches, scattered out, running for shelter behind the trucks."

Rifle fire began to sweep over the cup. They were low behind the parapet and out of sight. It was a searching, careful fire—expert fire.

Benton was quiet. He looked over at Horne. Officially in charge, he had yielded his command to Horne's superior knowledge.

"What d'you think?" he asked.

"We'll stop them," Horne said. "We'll stop them this time, maybe next time. After that—"

Horne grinned at Pommy. "First time under fire?"

"Yes."

"Take it easy. You're doing all right. Make every shot count. One cinch is worth five maybes."

Pommy crowded his body down into the gravel and rested his rifle in a niche in the rocks. He looked at Mike Horne and could see a thin trickle of fresh blood coming from under his bandage. The wound had opened again.

Was it deep, he wondered, or just a scratch? He looked at the lines about Horne's mouth and decided it was deep. Horne's sleeve was torn, and he had a dragon tattooed on his forearm.

They came with a rush. Rounding the bend, they broke into a scattered line; behind them, machine guns and rifles opened a hot fire to cover the advance.

They waited, and just before the men could reach the trucks, swept them with a steel scythe of bullets that mowed them down in a row. One man tumbled off the brink and fell into the ravine; then another fell, caught his fingers on the lip, and tumbled head over heels into the ravine as the edge gave way.

"How many got there?" Horne asked.

"A dozen, I think," Ryan said. "We got about thirty."

"Fair enough." Horne looked at Sackworth. The young Englishman was still resentful. He didn't like Horne. "Doing all right?" Horne asked.

"Of course." Sackworth was contemptuous, but his face was drawn and gray.

"Ryan," Horne said, "you and Pommy leave the main attack to the machine guns. Watch the men behind the trucks. Pick them off as they try to move closer. You take the right, Pommy."

The German with the bloody face had fallen flat. Now he was getting to his knees again.

Then, suddenly, three men made a concerted rush. Ryan and Pommy fired instantly, and Ryan's man dropped.

"I missed!" Pommy said. "Blast it, I missed!"

There was another rush, and both machine guns broke into a clattering roar. The gray line melted away, but more kept coming. Men rounded the bend and split to the right and left. Despite the heavy fire a few of them were getting through. Pommy and Ryan were firing continuously and methodically now.

Suddenly a man broke from under the nearest truck and came on in a plunging rush. Both Ryan and Pommy fired, and the man went down, but before they could fire again, he lunged to his feet and dove into the hollow below the cliff on which their pit rested.

"He can't do anything there," Sackworth said. "He—"

A hurtling object shot upward from below, hit the slope below the guns, rolled a few feet, and then burst with an earth-shaking concussion.

Horne looked up from where he had ducked his head. Nobody was hit.

"He's got grenades. Watch it. There'll be another in a minute."

Ryan fired, and a man dropped his rifle and started back toward the trucks. He walked quite calmly while they stared. Then he fell flat and didn't get up.

Twice more grenades hit the slope, but the man was too

close below the cliff. They didn't quite reach the cup thrown from such an awkward angle. "If one of those makes it—" Benton looked sour.

Pommy was shooting steadily now. There was another rush, and Benton opened up with the machine gun. Suddenly another grenade came up from below, traveling an arching course. It hit the slope, too short. It rolled free and fell. There was a terrific explosion.

"Tough," Ryan said. "He made a good try."

"Yeah," Horne said. "So have we."

Hours passed. The machine guns rattled steadily now. Only at long intervals was there a lull. The sun had swung over and was setting behind the mountain.

Horne straightened, his powerful body heavy with fatigue. He looked over at Ryan and grinned. Ryan's face was swollen from the kick of the rifle. Benton picked up a canteen and tried to drink, but there was no water.

"What now?" Pommy said.

Horne shrugged. "We take it on the lam."

"What?" Sackworth demanded. "What does that mean?"

"We beat it," Mike Horne said. "We get out while the getting is good."

"What?" Sackworth was incredulous. "You mean—run? Leave our post?"

"That's just what I mean," Horne said patiently. "We delayed this bunch long enough. We got ours from them, but now it doesn't matter anymore. The Jerries are behind us now. We delayed them for a while. All around through these hills guys are delaying them just for a while. We've done all we could here. Now we scram. We fight somewhere else."

"Go if you want to," Sackworth said stubbornly. "I'm staying."

Suddenly there was a terrific concussion, then another and another.

"What the deuce?" Benton exclaimed. "They got a mortar. They—"

The next shell hit right where he was sitting. It went off with an earsplitting roar and a burst of flame. Pommy went down, hugged the earth with an awful fear. Something tore at his clothes; then sand and gravel showered over him. There was another concussion and another.

Somebody had caught him by the foot. "Come on, kid. Let's go."

They broke into a stumbling run down the slope back of the nest, then over the next ridge and down the ravine beyond. Even then they ran on, using every bit of cover. Once Pommy started to slow, but Horne nudged him with the rifle barrel.

"Keep it up," he panted. "We got to run."

They slid into a deeper ravine and found their way to a stream. They walked then, slipping and sliding in the gathering darkness. Once a patrol saw them, and shots rattled around, but they kept going.

Then it was night, and clouds covered the moon and the stars. Wearily, sodden with exhaustion, they plodded on. Once, on the bank of a little stream, they paused for a drink. Then Horne opened the old haversack again and brought out the remnants of the sausage and bread. He broke each in half, and shared them with Pommy.

"But—"

Pommy's voice caught in his throat. "Gone?" he said then.

Horne nodded in the darkness. "Yeah. Lucky it wasn't all of us."

"But what now?" Pommy asked. "You said they were behind us."

"Sure," Horne agreed. "But we're just two men. We'll travel at night, keep to the hills. Maybe they'll make a stand at Thermopylae. If not there, they might try to defend the Isthmus of Corinth. Maybe we can join them there."

"But if they don't? If we can't?"

"Then Africa, Pommy, or Syria or Suez or Russia or England. They'll always be fighting them somewhere, an' that's where I want to be. It won't stop. The Germans win here, they win there, but they got to keep on fighting. They win battles, but none of them are decisive. None of them mean an end.

"Ever fight a guy, kid, who won't quit? You keep kicking

him, and he keeps coming back for more, keeps trying. You knock him down, but he won't stay down? It's hell, that's what it is. He won't quit, so you can't.

"But they'll be fighting them somewhere, and that's where I want to be."

"Yeah," Pommy said. "Me, too."

THE CROSS AND THE CANDLE

WHEN IN PARIS, I went often to a little hotel in a narrow street off the Avenue de la Grande Armee. Two doors opened into the building; one into a dark hallway and then by a winding stair to the chambers above, the other to the café, a tiny bistro patronized by the guests and a few people of the vicinity.

It was in no way different from a hundred other such places. The rooms were chill and dank in the morning (there was little heat in Paris, even the girls in the Folies Bergère were dancing in goose pimples), the furnishings had that added Parisian touch of full-length mirrors running alongside the bed for the obvious and interesting purpose of enabling one, and one's companion, to observe themselves and their activities.

Madame was a Breton, and as my own family were of Breton extraction, I liked listening to her tales of Roscoff, Morlaix, and the villages along the coast. She was a veritable treasure of ancient beliefs and customs, quaint habits and interesting lore. There was scarcely a place from Saint-Malo to the Bay of Douarnenez of which she didn't have a story to tell.

Often when I came to the café, there would be a man seated in the corner opposite the end of the bar. Somewhat below medium height, the thick column of his neck spread out into massive shoulders and a powerful chest. His arms were heavy with muscle and the brown hands that rested on the table before him were thick and strong.

Altogether, I have seen few men who gave such an impression of sheer animal strength and vitality. He moved in leisurely fashion, rarely smiled, and during my first visits had little to say.

In some bygone brawl, his nose had been broken and a deep scar began over his left eye and ran to a point beneath a left ear of which half the lobe was gone. You looked at his wide face, the mahogany skin, and polished over the broad cheekbones and you told yourself, "This man is dangerous!" Yet often there was also a glint of hard, tough humor in his eyes.

He sat in his corner, his watchful eyes missing nothing. After a time or two, I came to the impression that he was spinning a web, like some exotic form of spider, but what manner of fly he sought to catch, I could not guess.

Madame told me he was a *marin,* a sailor, and had lived for a time in Madagascar.

One afternoon when I came to the café, he was sitting in his corner alone. The place was empty, dim, and cold. Hat on the table beside him, he sat over an empty glass.

He got up when I came in and moved behind the bar. I ordered vin blanc and suggested he join me. He filled the two glasses without comment, then lifted his glass. *"À votre santé!"* he said. We touched glasses and drank.

"Cold, today," he said suddenly.

The English startled me. In the two months past, I had spoken to him perhaps a dozen times, and he replied always in French.

"You speak English then?"

He grinned at me, a tough, friendly grin touched by a sort of wry cynicism. "I'm an American," he said, "or I was."

"The devil you say!" Americans are of all kinds, but somehow . . . still, he could have been anything.

"Born in Idaho," he said, refilling our glasses. When I started to pay, he shook his head and brought money from his own pocket and placed it under an ashtray for Madame to put in the register when she returned. "They call me Tomas here. My old man was an Irish miner, but my mother was Basque."

"I took it for granted you were French."

"Most of them do. My mother spoke French and Spanish. Picked them up around home from her parents, as I did from her. After I went to sea, I stopped in Madagascar four years, and then went to Mauritius and Indochina."

"You were here during the war?"

"Part of the time. When it started, I was in Tananarive; but I returned here, got away from the *Boche,* and fought with the maquis for a while. Then I came back to Paris."

He looked up at me and the slate-gray eyes were flat and ugly. "My girl was dead."

"Bombs?"

"No. A Vichy rat."

He would say nothing more on the subject and our talk drifted to a strange and little known people who live in and atop a mountain in Madagascar, and their peculiar customs. I, too, had followed the sea for a time so there was much good talk of the ways of ships and men.

Tomas was without education in the accepted sense, yet he had observed well and missed little. He had read widely. His knowledge of primitive peoples would have fascinated an anthropologist and he had appreciation and understanding for their beliefs.

After talking with him, I came more often to the café, for we found much in common. His cynical toughness appealed to me, and we had an understanding growing from mutual experiences and interests. Yet as our acquaintance grew, I came to realize that he was a different man when we talked together alone than when others were in the room. Then his manner changed. He became increasingly watchful, talked less and only in French.

The man was watching for someone or something. Observing without seeming to, I became aware the center of his interests were those who came most often to the café. And of these, there were four that held his attention most.

Mombello was a slender Italian of middle years who worked in a market. Picard was a chemist, and Leon Matsys owned a small iron foundry on the edge of Paris and a produce business near The Halles. Matsys was a heavy man who had done well, had educated himself, and was inclined to tell everyone so. Jean Mignet, a sleek, catlike man, was supported by his wife, an actress of sorts. He was pleasant enough to know, but I suspected him of being a thief.

Few women came to the café. Usually the girls who came to the hotel entered by the other door and went to the chambers above, and after a period of time, returned through the same door. To us, they existed merely as light footsteps in the dark hall and on the stairs.

Madame herself, a friendly, practical Breton woman, was usually around and occasionally one of the daughters Mombello would come in search of their father.

The oldest was eighteen and very pretty, but businesslike without interest in the men of the café. The younger girl was thin, woefully thin from lack of proper food, but a beautiful child with large, magnificent dark eyes, dark wavy hair, and lips like the petals of a flower.

Someone among these must be the center of interest, yet I could not find that his interest remained long with any one of the four men. For their part, they seemed to accept him as one of themselves. Only one, I think, was conscious of being watched. That one was Jean Mignet.

On another of those dismal afternoons, we sat alone in the café and talked. (It always seemed that I came there only when the outside was bleak and unhappy, for on the sunny days, I liked being along the boulevards or in St. Germaine.) The subject again arose of strange superstitions and unique customs.

There was a Swede on one of my ships who would never use salt when there was a Greek at the table; an idea no more ridiculous than the fear some people have of eating fish and drinking milk in the same meal.

Tomas nodded. "I've known of many such ideas," he said, "and in some of the old families you will find customs that have been passed along from generation to generation in great secrecy for hundreds of years.

"I know of one"—he hesitated, describing circles on the dark tabletop with the wet bottom of his glass—"that is, a religious custom followed so far as I know by only one family."

He looked up at me. "You must never speak of this around

here," he said, and he spoke so sharply and with so much feeling, I assured him I'd never speak of it anywhere, if he so wished.

"In the family of my girl," he said, "there is an ancient custom that goes back to the Crusades. Her ancestor was a soldier with Saint Louis at Saint-Jean d'Acre. No doubt you know more of that than I do. Anyway, when his brother was killed in the fighting, there was no shrine or church nearby, so he thrust his dagger into a log. As you know, the hilts of daggers and swords were at that time almost always in the form of a cross, and he used it so in this case, burning a candle before the dagger.

"It became the custom of a religious and fighting family, and hence whenever there is a death, this same dagger is taken from its wrappings of silk and with the point thrust into wood, a candle for the dead is burned before it.

"Marie told me of this custom after her mother's death when I came hurriedly into her room and surprised her with the candle burning. For some forgotten reason, a tradition of secrecy had grown around the custom, and no one outside the family ever knew of it.

"That night in the darkened room, we watched the candle slowly burn away before that ancient dagger, a unique dagger where on crosspiece or guard was carved the body of Christ upon the cross and the blade was engraved with the figure of a snake, the snake signifying the powers of evil fallen before God.

"I never saw the dagger again while she lived. It was put away among her things, locked carefully in an iron chest, never to be brought out again until, as she said, she herself died, or her brother. Then, she looked at me, and said, 'Or you, Tomas, for you are of my family now.'"

He looked at me, and underneath the scarred brows, there were tears in his eyes.

"She must have been a fine girl," I said, for he was deeply moved.

"She was the only thing in my life! Only a madman, a mad American, would return to France after the war broke out. But I loved her.

"Look at me. I'm not the kind of man many women could love. I'm too rough, too brutal! I'm a seaman, that is all, and never asked to be more. A good man at sea or in a fight, but I have no words with which to say nice things to a woman, and she was a beautiful girl with an education."

Tomas took out his wallet and removed a worn photograph. When I looked at it, I was frankly astonished. The girl was not merely a pretty girl, she was all he had said, and more. She *was* beautiful.

Furthermore, there was something in her eyes and face that let you know that here was a girl who had character, maybe one who knew what loyalty was.

"She is lovely," I said sincerely. "I never saw anyone more beautiful!"

He was pleased, and he looked at me with his face suddenly lighter. "She was magical!" he said. "The best thing in my life. I came first to her house with her brother, who had been my shipmate on a voyage from Saigon. She was a child then, and I thought of her as nothing else.

"So, when next I came to the house, I brought her a present from Liverpool, and then others from Barcelona and Algiers. Simple things, and inexpensive, the sort of things a sailor may find in almost any port, but they had romance, I suppose, a color.

"I gave them simply because I was a lonely man, and this family had taken me as one of them, and because the giving of things is good for a lonely heart.

"One day, she was twelve then, I think, she had gone to a theater in the Boulevard de Clichy with her brother, and when they came out, she saw me with a girl, a girl from a café in the Pigalle. She was very angry and for days she would not speak to me.

"Her brother teased her, and said, 'Look! Marie thinks already she is a woman! She is jealous for you, Tomas!'"

He smiled at the memory. "Then, I was gone again to sea, and when I came again to the house, Marie was fourteen, taller, frightened, and skinny. Always she stared at me, and I brought her presents as before. Sometimes I took her to the theater, but to me she was a child. She was no longer gay, full of excitement and anger. She walked beside me very seriously.

"Four years then I was gone, and when I returned . . . you should have seen her! She was beautiful. Oh, I tell you, she was a woman now, and no doubt about it.

"I fell in love! So much that I could not talk for feeling it, but never did I think for a moment that it could matter.

"But did I have a choice? Not in the least! She had not changed, that one. She was both the little girl I knew first and the older one I knew later, and more besides. She laughed at me and said that long ago she had made up her mind that I was to be her man, and so it was to be whether I liked it or not! Me, I liked it. She was so much of what I wanted that she frightened me.

"Can you imagine what that did to me, m'sieu? I was a lonely man, a very lonely man. There had been the girls of the ports, but they are not for a man of soul, only for the coarse-grained who would satisfy the needs of the moment. Me, I wanted love, tenderness.

"I know." He shrugged. "I don't look it. I am a sailor and pleased to be one, and I've done my share of hard living. More than once, I've twisted my knife in the belly of a man who asked for it, and used my boots on them, too. But who is to say what feeling lives in the heart of a man? Or what need for love burns inside him?

"My parents died when I was young and the sea robbed me of my country. In such a life, one makes no close friends, no attachments, puts down no roots. Then, this girl, this beautiful girl, fell in love with me.

"Fell in love? No, I think the expression is wrong. She said she had always loved me even when she was a child and too young to know what it meant.

"Her mother and brother approved. They were good people, and I had lived long among them. Then the mother died, Pierre was away in the colonies, and Marie and I were to be married when he returned. So we lived together.

"Is this wrong? Who is to say what is right and what is wrong? In our hearts we understood and in France, well, they understand such things. What man is to live without a girl? Or a girl without a man?

"Then away I went to sea on my last trip, and while I was gone, the war came, and with it the Germans. When I returned, I joined the maquis to get back into France. Her letters were smuggled to me.

"Marie? She was a French girl, and she worked with the underground. She was very skillful, and very adept at fooling the *Boche*. Then, something happened.

"One of the men close to her was betrayed, then another, finally, it was her brother who was killed. The Gestapo had them, but they died without talking. One night I came to her to plead that she come away with me, it had been three years that I had fought in the underground, for her, almost six. But she told me she could not go; that someone close to her was working with the Nazis, someone who knew her. She must stay until she knew who it was.

"Yet try as she could, there was no clue. The man was shrewd, and a very devil. He finally came to her himself, after her brother was caught. He told her what he knew of her underground activities and of mine. He told her unless she came to live with him that I would be tortured and killed.

"He had spied upon her. He had even discovered her burning the candle before the dagger for Pierre after he was killed. He told her of it, to prove how much he knew—to prove he knew enough to find me—and she had admitted the reason.

"In the letter in which all this was told, she could not tell me who he was. He had friends in the underground, and she was fearful that learning who she was writing about, they would destroy the letter if they saw his name, and then she would be cut off from me and from all help.

"She would give me his name, she said, when I came next to Paris. He had not forced himself on her, just threatened. We had to plan to do away with him quickly. Marie said, too, that she was afraid that if the invasion came, he would kill her, for she alone could betray him; she alone knew of his activities for the Nazis.

"The invasion a secret? Of course! But when orders began

to come for the underground, come thick and fast, we knew it was coming. Then, the landings were made, and for days we were desperately busy.

"We rose in Paris, and they were exciting, desperate days, and bitter days for the collaborators and the men of Vichy. Their servitude to the Nazis had turned to bitterness and gall; they fled; and they begged, and they died.

"When I could, I hurried to the flat where Marie lived. It was near here, just around the corner. I found her dying. She had been raped and shot by this collaborator two days before and she had crawled to her apartment to wait for me. She died telling me of it, but unable before her last breath to give me his name."

"And there was no way you could figure out who he was?" I asked.

"How?" He spread his hands expressively. "No one suspected him. His desire for her was such that he had threatened her, and in threatening her he had boasted of what he had done. That was a mistake he rectified by killing her.

"Only one thing I know. He is one of our little group here. She said he lived in this neighborhood, that he was waiting here more than once when he accosted her. He thinks himself safe now. My girl has been dead for some time and her body buried. She is never mentioned here.

"Mombello? He is an Italian. Picard is a chemist, and has had traffic with Germany since the twenties. Matsys? An iron foundry owner who retained it all through the war, but who was active in the underground as were Picard and Mignet."

We were interrupted then by some others coming into the café, yet now the evening had added zest. Here was a deadly bit of business. Over the next two hours, as they trooped in, I began to wonder. Which was he?

The slender, shrewd Mombello with his quick, eager eyes? That lean whip of a man, Mignet? The heavy Matsys with blue and red veins in his nose, and the penchant for telling you he'd seen it all and done it all? Or was it dry, cold Picard who sipped wine through his thin lips and seemed to have ice water for blood?

Which man was marked to die? How long would Tomas sit brooding in his corner, waiting? What was he waiting for? A slip of the tongue? A bit of drunken talk?

None of these men drank excessively. So which one? Mombello whose eyes seemed to gloat over the body of every woman he saw? Mignet with his lust for money and power and his quick knife? Or big affable Matsys? Or Picard with his powders and acids?

How long would he wait? These five had sat here for months, and now . . . now there were six. I was the sixth. Perhaps it was the sixth to tip the balance. Here they were caught in a pause before death. Yet the man who killed such a girl, and who betrayed his country, should not go free. There was a story in this, and it had an ending, somewhere.

Over the following gray days, several in a row, the conversation ebbed and flowed and washed around our ears. I did not speak privately to Tomas again but there seemed an ongoing, silent communication between us. Then, in a quiet moment of discussion, someone mentioned the bazooka, and it came to me then that another hand had been dealt . . . mine.

"A strange weapon," I agreed, and then moved the tide of conversations along the subject of weapons and warfare. I spoke of the first use of poison gas by soldiers of Thebes when they burned sulfur to drive defenders from the walls of Athenian cities, then to the use of islands of defense; a successful tactic by the Soviets in this war, previously used by the Russians defending themselves against Charles XII of Sweden.

Then other weapons and methods, and somehow, but carefully, to strange knives.

Tomas ignored me, the spider in his web, but he could hear every word and he was poised, poised for anything.

Mignet told of a knife he had seen in Algiers with a poisoned barb in the hilt near the blade, and Mombello of a Florentine dagger he had once seen.

Tomas stayed silent, turning his glass in endless circles upon the table before him, turning, turning, turning. We locked eyes for a moment and before he looked away he seemed to sigh and give a nearly imperceptible nod.

"There was a knife I saw once," I said suddenly, "with engraving on it. A very old knife, and very strange. A figure of Christ on the cross rose above a fallen snake. The religious symbolism is interesting. I'd never seen its like before, the worksmanship was so finely wrought."

A moment passed, a bare breath of suspended time . . .

"It was not the only one, I think," Leon Matsys said. "Odd things, they were used in some custom dating back to the Crusades."

He looked up, about to say more, then slowly the life went from his face. He was looking at Tomas, and Tomas was smiling.

Jean Mignet's eyes were suddenly alive. He did not know, but he suspected something. He was keen, that one.

Leon Matsys's face was deathly pale. He was trapped now, trapped by those remarks that came so casually from his lips. In the moment he had certainly forgotten what they might imply, and could not know that it would matter. He looked to one side and then the other, and then he started to take a drink.

He lifted the glass, then suddenly put it down. He got up, and his face was flabby and haunted by terror. He seemed unable to take his eyes from Tomas.

I glanced at Tomas, and my muscles jumped involuntarily. He had the ancient knife in his hand and was drawing his little circles with its point.

Matsys turned and started for the entrance, stumbling in his haste. The glass in the tall door rattled as it slammed closed, leaving only a narrow view of the dimly lit street.

After a moment Tomas pushed his chair back and got up and his step was very light as he also went out the door.

A FRIEND OF THE GENERAL

I T BEGAN QUITE casually as such things often do, with a group of people conversing about nothing in particular, all unsuspecting of what the result might be.

My company was quartered in the château of the countess, as during the war she had moved into what had once been the gardener's cottage. It was the sort of place that in Beverly Hills would have sold well into six figures, a warm, cozy place with huge fireplaces, thick walls, and flowers all about.

The countess was young, very beautiful, and clever. She had friends everywhere and knew a bit of what went on anywhere you would care to mention. I was there because of the countess, and so, I suppose, was everybody else.

Her sister had just come down from the Netherlands, their first visit since the German occupation. There was a young American naval attaché, a woman of indeterminate age who was a Russian émigré, a fragile blond actress from Paris who, during the war, had smuggled explosives hidden under the vegetables in a basket on her bicycle. There was a baron who wore his monocle as if it were a part of him but had no other discernible talents and an American major who wanted to go home.

The war was fizzling out somewhere in Germany, far from us, and I wondered aloud where in Paris one could find a decent meal.

They assured me this was impossible unless I knew a good black-market restaurant. Due to the war there was a shortage of everything, and the black-market cafés had sprung up like speakeasies during the Prohibition era in the States—and like them you had to know somebody to get in.

Each had a different restaurant to suggest, although there was some agreement on one or two, but the countess solved my dilemma. Tearing a bit of note paper from a pad, she wrote an address. "Go to this place. Take a seat in a corner away from the windows, and when you wish to order, simply tell the waiter you are a friend of the general."

"But who," somebody asked, "is the general?"

She ignored the question but replied to mine when I asked, "But suppose the general is there at the time?"

"He will not be. He has flown to Baghdad and will go from there to Chabrang."

I could not believe that I had heard right.

"To *where*?" the naval attaché asked.

"It is a small village," I said, "near the ruins of Tsaparang."

"Now," the Russian woman said, "we understand everything! Tsaparang! Of course! Who would not know Tsaparang?"

"Where," the naval attaché asked, "are the ruins of Tsaparang?"

"Once," I began, "there was a kingdom—"

"Don't bother him with that. If I know Archie, he will waste the next three weeks trying to find it on a map."

"Take this"—she handed me the address—"and do as I have said. You will have as fine a meal as there is in Paris, as there is in Europe, in fact."

"But how can they do it?" Jeannine asked. "How can any café—"

"It is not the restaurant," the countess said, "it is the general. Before the war began, he knew it was coming, and he prepared for it. He has his own channels of communication, and being the kind of man he is, they work, war or no war.

"During a war some people want information, others want weapons or a way to smuggle escaped prisoners, but the general wanted the very best in food and wine, but above all, condiments, and he had them."

The general, it seemed, had served his apprenticeship during Latin American revolutions, moving from there to the Near and Middle East, to North Africa, and to China. Along the way he seemed to have feathered his nest quite substantially.

A few days later, leaving my jeep parked in a narrow street, I went through a passage between buildings and found myself in a small court. There were several shops with artists' studios above them, and in a corner under an awning were six tables. Several workmen sat at one table drinking beer. At another was a young man, perhaps a student, sitting over his books and a cup of coffee.

Inside the restaurant it was shadowed and cool. The floor was flagstone, and the windows hung with curtains. Everything was painfully neat. There were cloths on the tables and napkins. Along one side there was a bar with several stools. There were exactly twelve tables, and I had started for the one in the corner when a waiter appeared.

He indicated a table at one side. "Would you sit here, please?"

My uniform was, of course, American. That he spoke English was not unusual. Crossing to the table, I sat down with my back to the wall, facing the court. The table in the corner was but a short distance away and was no different from the others except that in the immediate corner there was a very large, comfortable chair with arms, not unlike what is commonly called a captain's chair.

"You wished to order?"

"I do." I glanced up. "I am a friend of the general."

"Ah? Oh, yes! Of course."

Nothing more was said, but the meal served was magnificent. I might even say it was unique.

A few days later, being in the vicinity, I returned, and then a third time. On this occasion I was scarcely seated when I heard footsteps in the court; looking up, I found the door darkened by one who could only be the general.

He was not tall, and he was—corpulent. He was neatly dressed in a tailored gray suit with several ribbons indicative of decorations. The waiter appeared at once, and there was a moment of whispered conversation during which he glanced at me.

Embarrassed? Of course. Here I had been passing myself as this man's friend, obtaining excellent meals under false pretenses. That I had paid for them and paid well made no difference at all. I had presumed, something no gentleman would do.

He crossed to his table and seated himself in his captain's chair. He ordered Madeira, and then the waiter crossed to my table. "Lieutenant? The general requests your company. He invites you to join him."

A moment I hesitated, then rising, I crossed over to him. "General? I must apolo—"

"Please be seated." He gestured to a chair.

"But I must—"

"You must do nothing of the kind. Have they taught you nothing in that army of yours? Never make excuses. Do what has to be done, and if it fails, accept the consequences."

"Very well." I seated myself. "I shall accept the consequences."

"Which will be an excellent meal, some very fine wine, and I hope some conversation worthy of the food and the wine." He glanced at me. "At least you are soldier enough for that. To find a very fine meal and take advantage of it. A soldier who cannot feed himself is no soldier at all."

He filled my glass, then his. "One question. How did you find this place? Who told you of me?"

Of course, I could have lied, but he would see through it at once. I disliked bringing her into it but knew that under the circumstances she would not mind.

"It was," I said, "the countess—"

"Of course," he interrupted me. "Only she would have dared." He glanced at me. "You know her well?"

It was nobody's business how well I knew her. "We are friends. My company is quartered in her château, and she is a lovely lady."

"Ah? How pleasant for you. She is excellent company, and such company is hard to come by these days. A truly beautiful woman, but clever. Altogether too clever for my taste. I do not trust clever women."

"I rather like them."

"Ah, yes. But you are a lieutenant. When you are a general, you will feel otherwise."

He spent a good deal of time watching the court, all of which was visible from where he sat. He had chosen well. The court had but one entrance for the public, although for the fortunate ones who lived close there were no exits, as I later discovered.

Not only could he not be approached from behind, but anyone emerging from the passage was immediately visible to him, while they could not see him until they actually entered the restaurant.

On our second meeting I surprised him and put myself in a doubtful position. I was simply curious, and my question had no other intent.

"How did you like Chabrang?"

He had started to lift his glass, and he put it down immediately. His right hand slid to the edge of the table until only his fingertips rested there. His tone was distinctly unfriendly when he replied, "What do you mean?"

"When I asked the countess if you would be here, she said you were in Baghdad—on the way to Chabrang."

"She said *that*? She mentioned Chabrang?"

"Yes, and I was surprised. It isn't the sort of place people hear of, being in such an out-of-the-way place, and only a village—a sort of way station."

His right hand dropped into his lap, and his fingers tugged at his trouser leg, which clung a bit too snugly to his heavy thigh. "You know Chabrang."

It was not a question but a statement. His right hand hitched the pant leg again. Suddenly I realized what was on his mind, and I almost laughed, for I'd been away from that sort of thing too long and had become careless. The laugh was not for him but simply that it seemed like old times, and it was kind of good to be back.

"You won't need the knife," I told him. "I am no danger to you."

"You know Chabrang, and there are not fifty men in Europe who know it. Am I to believe this is pure coincidence?"

He had a knife in his boot top, I was sure of that. He was a careful man and no doubt had reason to be, but why that was so I had no idea and told him as much.

"It was my only way out," he said. "They found me, but they were looking for a man who was carrying a great lot of money, and I had nothing but food, weapons, and some butterflies. They let me go."

"I believed it was a way out for me, too," I said, "but I was not so lucky. I had to turn back."

He turned to look at me. "When were you in China?"

"It was long ago." I have never liked dates. Perhaps because I have a poor memory for dates in my own life. "It was in the time of the war lords," I said.

He shrugged. "That's indefinite enough."

We talked of many things. He gestured widely. "This is what I wanted," he said. "I wanted time—leisure. Time to read, to think, to see. Some people make it some ways, some another. Mine was through war."

"It is no longer regarded with favor," I suggested.

He shrugged again. "Who cares? For ten thousand years it was the acceptable way for a man to make his fortune. A young man with a strong arm and some luck could go off to the wars and become rich.

"All the old kingdoms were established so. All the original 'great families' were founded in just such a way. What else was William the Conqueror? Or Roger of Sicily? Or their Viking ancestors who first conquered and then settled in Normandy? What does Norman mean but Northmen? Who were Cortés and Pizarro? They were young men with swords."

"Ours is a different world," I suggested. "Our standards are not the same."

"Bah!" He waved his fork. "The standards are the same, only now the fighting is done by lawyers. There is more cunning and less courage. They will sell you the arms—"

"Like Milton," I said.

He stopped with his fork in the air and his mouth open. "You know about Milton," he said. "I am beginning to wonder about you, lieutenant."

"Everybody in China knew that story. Perhaps I should say everybody in our line of business or around the Astor Bar. It was no secret."

"Perhaps not. Perhaps not."

Such stories are repeated in bars and tearooms, over bridge

tables as well as in the waterfront dives. Milton had been a well set up man in his early forties, as I recall him. A smooth, easy-talking man, somewhat florid of face, who played a good game of golf, haunted the Jockey Club, and owned a few good racehorses, Mongolian ponies brought down for that purpose. He had been a dealer in guns, supplying the various war lords with rifles, machine guns, mortars, and ammunition. As a machine gun was worth its weight in gold and as some European nation was always liquidating its stores to replace them with more modern weapons, Milton did well.

He reminded me of a first-class insurance salesman, and in a sense that was what he was. The weapons he sold were the kind of insurance they needed.

He might have become enormously wealthy, but he had an urge to gamble, and he had a blonde. The blonde, some said, was none too bright, but she had other assets that were uniquely visible, and nobody really inquired as to her intelligence, least of all Milton.

A day came when too much blonde and too much gambling left him nearly broke, and she chose that moment to say she wanted to go to Paris. She pleaded, she argued, and he listened. He was willing enough, but the problem was money.

At that moment an order came for six thousand rifles, some machine guns and mortars, with ammunition for all. Milton had only six hundred rifles on hand and insufficient cash. Such deals were always cash on the barrel head. He agreed to supply what was needed.

Long ago he had arranged a little deal with the customs officials to pass anything he shipped in a piano box, and as a piano salesman he seemed to be doing very well indeed.

Knowing the kind of people with whom he dealt, he also knew the necessity for absolute secrecy in what he was about to do, so with one German whom he knew from long experience would not talk, he went to his warehouse, and locking the doors very carefully, he proceeded to pack the cases with old, rusted pipe and straw. Atop each case, before closing it, he put a few rifles to satisfy any quick inspection. Yet the greatest thing he had going for him was his reputation for integrity. He supervised the loading of the piano boxes on a Chinese junk and collected his down payment of three hundred thousand dollars.

He had taken every precaution. Through a close-mouthed acquaintance he had bought two tickets on a vessel that was sailing that very night.

"Pack an overnight bag for each of us," he said. "Nothing more. And be ready. Say nothing to anyone and I'll buy you a completely new wardrobe in Paris."

Now, his rifles loaded on the junk, he drove at once to his apartment on Bubbling Well Road. He ran lightly up the steps carrying the small black bag. "Come! We've got to move fast! There's not much time to catch the boat!"

This, you must remember, was before World War II, and there were no airlines as such.

"Where are the tickets?" he asked.

She came to him, her blue eyes wide and wonderful. "Oh, Milt! I hope you're not going to be angry, but the Funstons are having a party tonight, and they are always such *fun*! Well, I turned in our tickets and got tickets on another boat, a much faster one, that leaves tomorrow!"

No doubt there was a moment of sheer panic; then what he hoped was common sense prevailed. It would take that junk a week to get to its destination. Well—four days at least. There was nothing to be done, and why not one more night?

The next morning was one I would never forget. I'd known Milton only to speak to, although we did have a drink together once. When a friend banged on my door at daybreak and told me he had something to show me, I went along.

What he showed me was what Milton might have expected, for the men with whom he did business did not play games.

There, standing upright in the parking lot outside his place on Bubbling Well Road, was a piece of the rusty pipe he had so carefully packed. On top of it was Milton's head. His complexion was no longer florid.

"Everybody knew that story," I repeated. "At least everybody of our sort. I heard it again a few days ago in the Casual Officers' Mess on Place St. Augustine."

"But you know about Chabrang," the general said.

The wine was excellent. "I see no connection," I said.

He gave me a sidelong glance, filled with suspicion. Why the mention of Chabrang disturbed him, I could not guess, as it was but an unimportant village on one of the routes out of Sinkiang to Ladakh. It was in no way noteworthy except that it was near the ruins of Tsaparang. The ruins represented about all that remained of a long-ago kingdom.

"Did you know Milton?" I asked.

"I knew him. If the Chinese had not killed him, I would have. Those munitions were consigned to me."

"To *you*?"

"They were consigned to me for the war lord, and the fraud put my head on the block. I was suspected of complicity."

"What happened?"

"I acted. Perceiving that I was suspected, and knowing the gentleman concerned was not one to dillydally, I made my move. You see, he already owed me money, a considerable sum. By disposing of me, he could make somebody atone for the fraud and liquidate his debt at the same time."

He fell silent while the waiter brought a steaming platter of seafood. When he had gone, the general resumed. "It was the time to move, so I acted. Remember that this is the first principle—*act*! Remember that, my young friend! Do not deliberate! Do not hesitate! Do not wait upon eventuality! *Act!* It is always better to do something, even if not quite the right thing, than to do nothing. *Action! Decision!* Only these are important!"

He toyed with an oyster, glancing from under his brows. "My mind, at such times, works quickly. He needed a scapegoat to save face. Not in Shanghai but there, before his men! At once! Instantly I perceived it was I who must pay."

He ate the oyster, and taking a bit of bread, buttered it lavishly. Many of the good people of France had not seen so much butter in months.

"You see, the commander himself did not yet know of the fraud, but immediately the discovery was made, an officer had left to report to him. He could reach him in not less than an hour, then an hour to return.

"The captain of the junk had seen none of what went on, so I went to him immediately, put money in his hand, and told him to sail to such and such a point upriver. The cargo would be received there.

"Then I went to the telegraph station, which was closed. I broke in to it and sent a message to another, rival war lord up the river, offering the guns to him for a fancy price. He was desperately in need of them, and I told him I could promise delivery if the money was paid to me in gold. A place of payment was mentioned.

"There was a charter plane at the field. You knew him, I think? Milligan? He would fly you anywhere for a price and land his plane on a pocket handkerchief if need be. Moreover, he could be trusted, and there were some, in those days, who could not. I placed five hundred dollars in his hand and said I wished to leave for Shanghai at once.

"'After I gas up,' he said.

"'Now,' I told him. 'Right now. There is petrol at—' I took his map and put my finger on the place. 'And you can land there.'

"'If you say,' he replied doubtfully. 'I never heard of—'

"'The petrol is there,' I promised him. 'I had it placed there for just such an emergency.'"

The general looked around at me. "You are young, lieutenant, and wise as you may be, you are still learning, so remember to trust no one! Prepare for every eventuality no matter how remote! Not even a mouse trusts himself to one hole only. That is an old saying, but it has remained in my mind, and can I be less wise than a mouse?

"We took off at once. Within twenty minutes of my realization I *acted*! And that night I was in Shanghai with *her*!"

"Her?" He had lost me.

"Of course! With Milton's blonde. What was her name? I've forgotten. No matter. I was there, consoling her.

"Of course"—he glanced at me—"I was younger then and not so— so—well, I am a little overweight now. But then, ah, I was handsome then, lieutenant! I was handsome, and I was, of course, younger.

"I found her in tears. She was weeping for him. For Milton. Or perhaps she was weeping for that lost trip to Paris. About women, lieutenant, one never knows. No matter.

"There on the floor was the black bag. It was out of the way, back against the sofa's end, but I recognized it at once. True, I'd never seen it before, but I'd seen others of the kind. In it would be the money! All that delightful, beautiful money! And she was crying? Well, as I have said, she was a woman, and about women one never knows.

"I consoled her. What else could I do? What does one do with a pretty woman who is sad and has a quarter of a million dollars, give or take a few? I told her she must not worry, that I—*I* would take her to Paris! And who knew Paris better? Who knew the nightspots, the cafés, the bordel—Well, who knew the town better than I? Even its history!

"Oh, I was marvelous that day! I told her exciting and glamorous tales of what the city was like, of living there, and I dropped names, names of all the famous and infamous. As a matter of fact, I actually did know some of them.

"She was consoled! She rested her head on my shoulder. As you have seen, they are very broad. She dried her tears; then she smoothed her dress, she touched up her makeup, and she said, 'I still have the tickets. We could go at once. I—there is nothing more for me here! Nothing!'

"'I know.' I took her two hands. 'It is tragic. But in Paris, my dear, you can forget. In Paris there is music, there is dancing, there is love, and there is beauty! And we shall be there—together!'"

He paused, refilling his glass. "She listened, her blue eyes very wide and wondering. She was a dear girl, no question of it. The black bag was at my feet. 'Look!' I took from my pocket a packet of bills and stripped off several of the thousand-dollar denomination. 'Take this! I shall meet you in Paris! Go to this place—' I wrote out the name of a small, discreet hotel—'and wait for me. I shall not be long.'

"Then I picked up the black bag and walked out. Once beyond the door with the bag I did not wait for the lift, but ran down the stairs. I had it, did I not? I had the black bag with the quarter of a million, and more to come from my own sale of the munitions! Ah, it was exciting, my friend, most exciting! It is always exciting when one is making money! And such delightful sums! Into my car then and away to the field where Milligan awaited me.

"Racing out on the field, I leaped from the car. Milligan was there, beside his plane, but he was not alone.

"Three men were with him, and one of them was the old marshal. He was the last person I expected in Shanghai, where he had many enemies, but here he was. One of the men stood guard over Milligan, and the other had a pistol directed at me.

"My eyes caught those of Milligan. He was a man I knew—a tough man, a ready man. Did I tell you that he was from Texas? Anyway, a lift of the brows, a small hand gesture—he knew what was coming. There was no doubting that he wished to be away as much as I.

"'Ah, Marshal Chang! How delightful to see you! And what a surprise to find you in Shanghai of all places! Once I knew what happened I flew here at once! At once, Marshal. It was my duty as your aide, your confidant, and your friend to rectify this error!'

"You see, one does what one can, and I had already given up on this money. True, what I was about to do would *hurt*! Hurt, lieutenant! But it was my only way out. The old marshal would be in no mood for games, and every second here was filled with danger for him, so he was desperate. As for me, it is a wise soldier who knows when to retire from the field.

"Anyway, did I not have money awaiting me at the other end? From my sale of the arms?

"'When I realized what had happened, Marshal, I flew to recover your money! It was the least I could do for one who has been my friend, my adviser, almost a second father!'

"'Recover?' he asked, puzzled.

"'Of course! It is here! In this bag! Now if you would like to fly back with me?'

"'Let me see the money,' he demanded.

"'Of course,' I said, and yielded the bag to his grasp. Yielded it reluctantly, you understand, for I had hoped to have that money somehow, someway. If I could just get the marshal into the plane—

"He gestured to one of his men, he who had been covering me, to open the bag. He did so. The marshal leaned over and peered inside; then he looked up at me, and his face was dark with anger.

"Looking into the bag, I knew why, knew that we had been cheated, that—

"The bag was filled with old newspapers, and there was a novel there to give it weight. And *that* novel? How could it have had weight enough? It was by a writer I have never liked—never!

"The old marshal was trembling with anger. 'You!' he shouted. 'You—!'

"It was a time, lieutenant, a time for decision! Never have I been more pleased with myself than what I did then! In an instant I should have been killed! And Milligan, also! It was a time for *action,* and like the old soldier I was, I *acted*!

"He who guarded me had lowered his pistol while he opened the bag, and for that reason he was holding the pistol but loosely. I struck down at the base of his thumb with the edge of my hand, and as the pistol fell from his hand, I seized it and fired!

"Not at the man I had disarmed but at the man guarding Milligan.

"Turning swiftly, I shoved the old marshal. He was a heavy man, and he tottered back off balance and fell. Milligan had leaped into the plane, and the man I had disarmed leaped at me. My pistol exploded, and he fell; then I leaped into the plane, and we were off—gone!

"Once again, lieutenant, I had snatched victory from the jaws of defeat. I do not wish to appear smug, but it is only the truth.

"In Kansu I received payment for the guns and told them where the junk would be. Then once more we took off. In the air I changed clothing, changed to such a costume as an English scientist might wear in the field. I had it always with me, for you know how the English are—one is apt to find them anywhere, in any out-of-the-way, godforsaken place, doing God knows what.

"I was to be a hunter of butterflies and a bit vague about all else. You see? It was an excellent cover.

"We landed—I shall not say where, for it is a field I have often used and may well use again. I have such places here and there. One never knows, does one?

"There I paid Milligan. Ten thousand dollars, more than he had ever seen before at one time, and there I left him, but with regret. He was a man, that one!

"I bought horses, and in a small town I found some equipment abandoned at some time by a scientific scholar before he attempted the Karakoram Pass. Have you tried it? If not, do not. It is—anyway, there is another older pass not far from there that is useful if one does not mind swinging bridges over gorges with roaring water beneath.

"It is a very remote country, yet it seemed by far the best and far from troublesome officials. Who would expect to find anyone in such a place. Yet when we reached Chabrang—"

"Yes?"

"We went to a place where we might find food, and I heard a merchant, a Kirghiz, complaining in a loud voice against the government! He had been stopped, searched, questioned. It seemed there were soldiers there looking for someone with a great deal of money. As if any merchant dared carry any money at all in such a place!

"You can see my problem. But again I refused to be defeated! It is my decision that counts! I decided, and I acted! Promptly!

"I inquired, and in a voice just loud enough that all might hear, as to the ruins of Tsaparang and which road must I take?

"I knew the road, and I had seen the ruins. Who could forget them, high in that yellow cliff? Built into the very face of it like some of your cliff dwellings.

"Of course I knew where the ruins lay, and we went to

them. The men I had hired to travel with me and who owned the horses were only too glad to lie in the shade and rest. I took a pack from a horse, some scientific instruments, and of course the money. Then I made my way up the steep slope. One too curious fellow chose to follow me, but I found heavy stones that must be moved from my path, so he soon lost interest.

"I hid the money, hid it securely, in a place only I shall find, and in its place I packed some broken bits of pottery, a few blue beads, bits of carnelian and such. I took measurements, and took pictures with an old camera I had wheedled from Milligan, and then returned to my horses.

"We were stopped, of course, and questioned. We were searched, and they found the shards of pottery, some butterflies collected long ago by that traveler, whoever he was, and some very smelly bottles.

"I had donned thick-lensed glasses with which I peered at them—I had to peer to see anything at all—and there, where they think much of the evil eye, they were pleased to be rid of me."

"And now you have been back? Did you pick up the money?"

He smiled. "One does what one must, lieutenant. Now I live here in Paris, and, I might say, I live well." He patted his stomach affectionately. "Even very well."

He sipped his wine. "Of course one must be careful when one has enemies. The old marshal—yes, he is alive and well—too well, altogether. He dislikes me for some reason. He would have me shot if he could. And regrettably there are others."

"What of the blonde? Milton's girlfriend? Did you ever see her again?"

"See her?" He smiled complacently. "In fact, I shall see her tonight. I see her quite often, in fact."

"And the money? Milton's money?"

"She had taken it out of the black bag and hidden it. But she was a fool! Did she spend it on beautiful clothes? Did she buy jewels and wine? She did not. She *invested* it, every centime! Invested it, can you imagine?"

He emptied his glass. "She invested in the black market. Somewhere she found truckloads of American cigarettes and tanks of petrol."

"So the quarter of a million is forever beyond your reach?"

"Did you say a quarter of a million? It is more than a million now, and only the good Lord knows where it will end! Given time, that stupid girl will own half of Paris."

I stood up. After all, I had things to do even if he did not, and as I turned to pick up my cap from an adjoining chair, there was a spiteful little snapping sound from beside me and a loud report from the door. Turning quickly, I saw the student, he who had been drinking coffee and working his sums at the outside table. The student had a Luger pistol that was slipping from his fingers, and as if by magic, the gendarmes were running into the court.

"Sit down, lieutenant." The general caught my arm, and holding it out from my body a little, guided me to a chair. "You cannot leave now. There will be questions."

Glancing out the door, I saw the student, or whatever he was, lying as he had fallen. Evidently he had spun when hit, for he lay face down almost in the doorway but headed the other way.

"Relax, lieutenant. It is nothing. The poor man! It is terrible, the kind of help one gets today! So inefficient!"

The police were there, questioning everybody, but of course nobody knew anything. We were the last.

The general spoke excellent French. "I am General—"

"We know, *mon général,* we know. Did you, by any chance, see what took place?"

"I did not, but you know how it is. The Free French are still finding pockets of resistance, and of course they are hunting collaborators. When they find them—" He held up his forefinger and thumb like a pistol. "When they find them—*ping!* And they deserve no better."

He stood up. "If you would like to search—?"

"Oh, no!" The gendarme was appalled. "Of course not, *mon général*! Of course not!"

When I reached my quarters that night, it was with some

relief that I pulled off my tie and then started to shed my trench coat. Something bumped my side, and I slid my hand into the pocket—an automatic, small, neat, and very deadly.

It was not easy to be a friend of the general.

AUTHOR'S TEA

"**I**'VE BEEN READING your work, Mr. Dugan, and like it tremendously! You have such *power*, such *feeling*!"

"Thank you," he heard himself saying. "I'm glad you liked it." He glanced toward the door where several women were arriving. They weren't young women. He sighed and glanced hopelessly toward the table where one of those faded dowagers who nibble at the crusts of culture was pouring tea. Now if they only had a steak—

"Mr. Dugan," his hostess was saying, "I want you to meet Mrs. Nowlin. She is also a writer."

She was so fat she had almost reached the parting of the stays, and she had one of those faces that always reminded him of buttermilk. "How do you do, Mrs. Nowlin?" He smiled in a way he hoped was gracious. "It is always a pleasure to meet someone in the same profession. What do you write?"

"Oh, I'm not a *regular* writer, Mr. Dugan, but I do so love to write! Don't you find it simply fascinating? But I just never have been able to get anything published. Sometimes I doubt the publishers even *read* my manuscripts! Why, I believe they just *couldn't*!"

"I imagine they are pretty busy, Mrs. Nowlin. They get so many stories, you know."

"Why, I sent one of my poems away not long ago. It was a poem about James, you know, and they wouldn't take it. They didn't even say anything! Just one of those rejection slips. Why, I read the poem at the club, and they all said it was simply *beautiful*!"

"Was—was James your husband?" he asked hopefully, glancing toward the tea table again. Still no steak.

"James! Oh, goodness no! James is my dog! My little Pom. Don't you just *adore* Poms, Mr. Dugan?"

Then she was gone, fluttering across the room like a blimp escaped from its moorings.

He sighed again. Every time chance caught him at one of these author's teas, he would think of Frisco Brady. He could imagine the profane disgust of the big Irish longshoreman if he knew the guy who flattened him in the Harbor Pool Room was guest of honor at a pink tea.

Dugan felt the red crawling around his ears at the thought, and his eyes sought the tea table again. Someday, he reflected, there is going to be a hostess who will serve real meals to authors and achieve immortality at a single stroke. Writers would burn candles to her memory, or better still, some of those shadowy wafers that were served with the tea and were scarcely more tangible than the tea itself.

He started out of his dream and tried to look remotely intelligent as he saw his hostess piloting another body through the crowd. He knew at a glance that she had written a book of poetry that wouldn't scan, privately published, of course. Even worse, it was obvious that in some dim, distant year she had seen some of Garbo's less worthy pictures and had never recovered. She carried her chin high, and her neck stretched endlessly toward affected shoulders.

"I have so *wanted* to meet you! There is something so deep, so spiritual about your work! And your last book! One feels you were on a great height when you wrote it! Ah! . . ."

She was gone. But someone else was speaking to him, and he turned attentively.

"Why do so many of you writers write about such *hard* things? There is so much that is beautiful in the world! All people aren't like those people you write about, so why don't you write about *nice* people? And that boy you wrote about in the story about hunger, why, you know perfectly well, Mr. Dugan, that a boy like that couldn't go hungry in this country!"

His muscles ached with weariness, and he stood on the corner staring down the street, his thoughts blurred by hunger, his face white and strained. Somehow all form had become formless, and things about him took on new attitudes and appearances. He found his mind fastening upon little things with an abnormal concentration born of hunger and exhaustion. Walking a crack in the sidewalk became an obsession, and when he looked up from that, a fat man was crossing the street, and his arms and legs seemed to jerk grotesquely. Everything about him seemed to move in slow motion, and he stopped walking and tried to steady himself, conscious it was a delirium born of hunger.

He had been standing still for a moment trying to work his foot free from the sock where it was stuck with the dried blood from a broken blister, and when he moved forward suddenly, he almost fell. He pulled up sharply and turned his head to see if anyone noticed. He walked on then with careful attention.

He was hungry.

The words stood out in his consciousness, cold and clear, almost without thought or sensation. He looked at them as at a sign that had no meaning.

He passed a policeman and tried to adopt a careless, confident air but felt the man looking after him. Passing a bakery, the smell of fresh pastry went through him like a wave, leaving a sensation of emptiness and nausea.

"You've had such an *interesting* life, Mr. Dugan! There must have been so many adventures. If I had been a man, I would have lived just such a life as you have. It must have been so *thrilling* and romantic!"

"Why don't you tell us some of the *real* stories? Some of the things that actually happened? I'll bet there were a lot you haven't even written."

"I'm tellin' you, Dugan. Lay off that dame, see? If you don't, I'll cut your heart out."

The music moved through the room, and he felt the lithe, quick movements of the girl as she danced, and through the smoky pall he heard a chair crash, and he looked down and smiled at the girl, and then he spun her to arm's length and ducked to avoid the first punch. Then he struck with his left, short and hard. He felt his fist thud against a jaw and saw the man's face as he fell forward, eyes bulging, jaw slack. He brought up his right into the man's midsection as he fell toward him and then stepped away. Something struck him from behind, and it wasn't until he got up that the blood started running into his eyes. He knew he'd been hit hard, and heard the music playing "In a little Spanish town 'twas on a night like this, stars were shining down . . ."

He was speaking then, and he heard himself saying, "There is only the personal continuity. The man we were yesterday may not be the man we are tomorrow. Names are only trademarks for the individual, and from day to day that individual changes, and his ways and thoughts change, although he is not always himself aware of the change. The man who was yesterday a soldier may be a seller of brushes tomorrow. He has the same name, but the man himself is not the same, although circumstances may cause him to revert to his former personality and character. Even the body changes; the flesh and blood change with the food we eat and the water we drink.

"To him who drifts about, life consists of moving in and out of environments and changing conditions, and with each change of environment the wanderer changes, also. We move into lives that for the time are very near and dear to us, but suddenly all can be changed, and nothing remains but the memory.

"Only the innocent speak of adventure, for adventure is only a romantic name for trouble, and when one is having 'adventures' one wishes it were all over and he was elsewhere and safe. 'Adventure' is not nice. It is more often than not rough and dirty, cruel and harsh . . ."

Before they screwed on the copper helmet, Scotty stopped by, his features tight and hard. "Watch yourself, kid, this is bad water and too many sharks. Some say there are more octopi and squids here than anywhere else, but usually they're no trouble. We'll try to hold it down up here." He slapped his waistband as he spoke. Scotty moved, and Singapore Charlie lifted the helmet.

"Don't worry, skipper, I'll keep your lines clear, and I can handle any trouble." Then Dugan was sinking through the warm green water, feeling it clasp him close so that only the copper helmet protected him. Down, down, still farther down, and then he was standing on the sandy floor of the ocean, and around him moved the world of the undersea. There was silence, deep, unfathomable silence, except for the soft hiss of air. He moved forward, walking as though in a deep sleep, pushing himself against the water, turning himself from side to side like some unbelievable monster that haunted the lower depths.

Then he found the dark hull of the old ship and moved along the ghostly deck, half shrouded in the weed of a hundred years, moving toward the companionway where feet no longer trod. He hesitated at the door, looking down into darkness, and then he saw it moving toward him, huge, ominous, frightening. He tucked his warm-blooded hands into his armpits to leave only the slippery surface of the canvas and rubber suit. It came toward him, only vaguely curious, and inquiring tentacles slipped over and around him . . . feeling . . . feeling . . . feeling.

He sipped his tea and avoided the eyes of the woman who had the manuscript she wanted him to comment on, nibbled impotently at those infinitesimal buttons of nourishment, and listened to the ebb and flow of conversation about his ears. Here and there a remark swirled about, attracting his momentary attention. He heard himself speaking, saying how pleasant it had been, and then he was out on the street again, turning up his collar against the first few drops of spattering rain.

AFTERWORD

OF ALL THESE volumes of the Collected Short Stories series this one is my favorite. Tales that for years have cried out to be presented together have now found a home in the same binding. An era in the life of Louis L'Amour is finally available in a manner where the work almost becomes an autobiography in fiction.

The first several stories in this collection are some of the most recently written, stories that Louis wrote from the early 1950s to the early 1960s; they show the end of an arc that also included "The Moon of the Trees Broken by Snow," a story published in *The Collected Short Stories, Volume One*. The rest of this collection, however, flashes back to Louis's very beginnings as a writer and, in fact, includes the first story he ever published: one recently unearthed and offered here for the first time.

"Death, Westbound" was actually mentioned by Louis in his memoir, *Education of a Wandering Man,* although he didn't mention the title. "I placed my first story for publication," he wrote. "It was a hobo story, submitted to a magazine that had published many famous names when they were starting out. The magazine paid on publication, but that never happened. The magazine folded after accepting my story and that was the end of it."

Interesting, but not exactly true. . . .

Fifty-five years *earlier* Louis had written to a girlfriend of his saying, "I have . . . managed to have one short story accepted by a small magazine one finds on the newsstands. It pays rather well but is somewhat sensational. The magazine . . . is generally illustrated by several pictures of partially undressed ladies, and they are usually rather heavily constructed ladies also. It is called *10 Story Book*. My story was a realistic tale of some hoboes called "Death, West-bound."

Now, I knew for a fact that Dad was trying to impress this gal like all get out. But it *seemed* like he was talking about the same story that he mentioned many years later. A check of his list of story submissions for the nineteen thirties revealed that he had continued to submit work to *10 Story Book* for the next several years. . . . Not what you'd expect if they had "folded." Much later in life, had Louis felt compelled to mention this early moment of triumph but at the same time deny his connection to the magazine's somewhat sleazy content?

A number of searches showed that very few copies of *10 Story Book* existed in libraries or public archives. So I began to put the word out to magazine aficionados, pulp collectors, and the fairly offbeat subculture of antique pornography collectors. About five years passed with little result other than occasionally calling or e-mailing various people and reminding them that I was still interested. But one day my in-box divulged a scan of "Death, Westbound" by Louis D. Amour. One of my contacts had finally come through. I don't know if the name, D. Amour, was a mistake or an early attempt at a pseudonym, but this was Louis L'Amour's first recorded sale.

Sensational photos (for the 1930s) aside, Dad seems to have been in good company; Jack Woodford is listed in the table of contents of the edition and I assume that this is the novelist, screenwriter, and short-story master of *Jack Woodford on Writing* fame. Other famous writers of the early twentieth century are also reputed to have been published here, too; *10 Story Book* following a model later used by *Playboy,* where the promise of unclothed women draws in readers who otherwise would never have bothered with literature at all; and the literature gave the magazine some class and protection from the opinions of moralists and pro-censorship types.

In this collection, "Death, Westbound" begins a cycle that will carry the reader through stories that relate to many actual events in Louis's early life. It should not be assumed that these stories are always literally true but they are a snapshot of the times—the 1920s and 1930s—and how Louis L'Amour experienced those times. Greatly influenced by Jack London, Eugene O'Neal, and later John Steinbeck, Louis began his career by trying to document the era that he lived in. Whether "Death, Westbound" is a "true story" or not, Louis did ride the side-door Pullman's of the Southern Pacific on many occasions; from Arizona to Texas and back again, and from Arizona to California even more often.

The stories "Old Doc Yak," "It's Your Move," and "And Proudly Die," soon followed, and were drawn from actual people that Louis knew in the time he spent waiting for a ship or "on the beach," as the sailors called unemployment, in San Pedro, California. Louis wrote of that time in an introduction from *Yondering:* "Rough painting or bucking rivets in the shipyards, swamping on a truck, or working 'standby' on a ship were all a man could find. It wasn't enough. We missed meals and slept wherever we could. The town was filled with drifting, homeless men, mostly seamen from all the countries in the world. Sometimes I slept in empty boxcars, in abandoned buildings, or in the lumber piles on the old E. K. Wood lumber dock."

The piled lumber Louis mentions often left gaps or overhangs, some well off the ground, which were shelter of a sort. But if you had a few cents, the vastly preferred place to spend the night was the Seaman's Church Institute, sort of a YMCA for seamen. "Survival," another story of that time, was based on a story that Louis had heard in his time around the Seaman's Institute, but many gaps in the narrative have been filled with his own material, and it is populated with mostly fictional characters.

Louis left San Pedro on a voyage that would eventually take him around the world and "Thicker Than Blood" and "The Admiral" are drawn from that experience. I don't know if the events in these stories are true in whole or in part, but buried in among Louis's papers I found the following photographs . . .

To the right is Leonard Duks, first mate of the SS *Steel Worker* and Louis's nemesis on a voyage that took them from San Pedro west to Japan, China, the Dutch East Indies, the Federated Malay States, Aden Arabia, the Suez Canal, and on into Brooklyn, New York. I don't know if Duks truly lived up to his fictional reputation in "Thicker Than Blood," but Louis didn't like the man and appointed himself as a spokesman for the crew's complaints about the unbelievably bad food and other various working conditions.

The ship did not call in Shanghai twice, so much of "The Admiral" may be fictional. However, the note on the back of the next photograph suggests otherwise. It reads, "Tony and Joe taken on the beach at Balikpapan (Borneo). Tony is the one in 'The Admiral.'"

Additional photographs from Balikpapan include one of the *Steel Worker* at anchor with much of what looks like their cargo of pipe in the foreground . . .

And the following, which reads, "Luflander, Malay barber, myself at eighteen, Balikpapan, Borneo."

"The Admiral" was originally published by *Story,* a magazine which was very prestigious at the time, and Louis's being included raised some favorable comment. Dad, more than anything, wanted to continue in this vein. He imagined a cycle of stories about San Pedro and another cycle that took place in

Shanghai, both utilizing loosely interconnected sets of colorful characters; hoboes and seamen, soldiers of fortune and gangsters, historical characters and working stiffs just trying to get by.

However, he also needed to get paid. The literary magazines paid on publication and while that was bad enough when the stories were scheduled months ahead of time, often they were not scheduled at all: the story was accepted but the editor had no idea when he would run it and thus no idea when he would pay. The pulp magazines, which published a far less literary fare, paid better and, more important, they paid faster, sending out a check the moment they accepted a story. Ultimately, Louis found this combination hard to beat. At times, though, he did wonder rather wistfully about what kind of career he would have had if he'd been able to keep writing in this more "personal adventure, personal experience" style.

"The Dancing Kate" seems to mix some of the more realistic elements of those "personal experience" stories with those of a pulp adventure while "Glorious! Glorious!" returns to the more antiheroic style. Louis could not have participated in the Riffian War where the forces of Abdel-Krim fought both the Spanish and the French Foreign Legions but the *Steel Worker did* sail the Moroccan coast during its final days. "Off the Mangrove Coast" has a plot similar to a story that Louis told about his own life, a story where he and several others unsuccessfully attempted to salvage a riverboat that was supposedly full of the treasure that a rajah from the Federated Malay States took with him when some form of uprising forced him from power. "The Cross and the Candle" is also based on an actual experience, though I do not believe that Louis was there for the climax of the story or that he played a part in solving the murder of the man's ill-fated sweetheart.

"A Friend of the General" is interesting because there is no indication of when it was written. I suspect that Louis wrote it quite late in his career, possibly in 1979 or '80, in order to include it in the collection *Yondering*. Louis's unit, a Quartermaster's Truck Company, *was* based out of Château de Spoir, home of the Count and Countess Dulong du Rosney. The count and countess had indeed moved into a gardener's cottage across the road from the château itself. The "cottage" (more appropriately, the home of the estate manager) was of a style and size that would have attracted notice even in Beverly Hills, so they were nicely housed even though first the German and then the American army had taken over the main residence. The Countess Dulong du Rosney has no memory of Lt. Louis L'Amour, Parisian black-market cafés, or the mysterious "General," but she still may have been the model for the countess in the story. When I spoke to her a few years ago it was obvious that she had that same sense of unflappable self-assurance. The story of the ill-fated arms merchant Milton is one that Louis told many times as if it were true, suggesting that he was teaching boxing at a fencing and martial arts academy in Frenchtown (a section of old Shanghai) at the time.

With "East of Gorontalo" we bid adieu to the group of stories based closely on Louis's life experience, and launch into three different series he created between 1938 and 1948 for Leo Margulies at *Standard Magazines,* a company that owned *Thrilling Adventures* and many others. Although there are few of Louis's personal experiences in the stories of tramp freighter captain Jim Mayo and the "pilots of fortune" Turk Madden and Steve Cowan, many of the locations were places that he had visited during what Louis called his "knocking around" period. In fact, in his collection *Night Over the Solomons,* Louis claimed that in the case of Kolombangara Island in 1943, a story of his had closely echoed reality:

> Shortly after my story ["Night Over the Solomons"] was published the Navy discovered this Japanese base of which I had written. I am sure my story had nothing to do with its

discovery and doubt if the magazine in which it was published had reached the South Pacific at the time.

My decision to locate a Japanese base on Kolombangara was not based on any inside information but simple logic. We had troops fighting on Guadalcanal. If the Japanese wished to harass our supply lines, where would they locate their base?

From my time at sea I had a few charts and I dug out the one on the Solomons. Kolombangara was the obvious solution. There was a place where an airfield could be built, a deep harbor where ships could bring supplies and lie unnoticed unless a plane flew directly over the harbor, which was well hidden. No doubt the Japanese had used the same logic in locating their base and the Navy in discovering it.

He went on to note that while his hero reached the island from a torpedoed ship, both an American pilot and John F. Kennedy had been stranded in the vicinity of Kolombangara under circumstances that would have fit his fictional story to perfection.

Louis's knowledge of the operation and layout of Mayo's ship, the *Semiramis,* came from the time that he had spent as an able-bodied seaman on similar ships and his years of working as a longshoreman and then a Cargo Control Officer at San Francisco's Port of Embarkation during the early days of World War II. The interest in aircraft and the appreciation of the freedom of a tramp flier was gleaned from his good friend Bob Roberts who had lived that life, though never in the Far East.

As Louis moved on through the next two stages of his career, writing crime stories and then westerns, many of the elements found in these early adventure stories continued to appear. His fictional Far East was crowded with types modeled on American gangsters, similar to the crooked sports promoters and gamblers in his stories of the boxing ring, and the *Semiramis* and its crew could almost stand in for a more racially diverse version of one of the beleaguered cattle outfits that his western characters later rode for. In a way his transition from one genre to another was more of a blurring of the lines or a recombining of elements.

For a more in-depth look at all of these stories and more information on this collection visit us at louislamourgreat adventure.com.

Over the next three years we will continue this program with the publication of *The Frontier Stories, Volume Five* in 2007. The following year we will bring out a collection of crime and boxing stories and then, finally, one last collection of westerns, *The Frontier Stories, Volume Seven.* I certainly hope you enjoyed this collection and that you find these next few equally pleasurable.

Beau L'Amour
Los Angeles, California
2006

ABOUT LOUIS L'AMOUR

"I think of myself in the oral tradition—as a troubadour, a village taleteller, the man in the shadows of the campfire. That's the way I'd like to be remembered—as a storyteller. A good storyteller."

IT IS DOUBTFUL that any author could be as at home in the world recreated in his novels as Louis Dearborn L'Amour. Not only could he physically fill the boots of the rugged characters he wrote about, but he literally "walked the land my characters walk." His personal experiences as well as his lifelong devotion to historical research combined to give Mr. L'Amour the unique knowledge and understanding of people, events, and the challenge of the American frontier that became the hallmarks of his popularity.

Of French-Irish descent, Mr. L'Amour could trace his own family in North America back to the early 1600s and follow their steady progression westward, "always on the frontier." As a boy growing up in Jamestown, North Dakota, he absorbed all he could about his family's frontier heritage, including the story of his great-grandfather who was scalped by Sioux warriors.

Spurred by an eager curiosity and desire to broaden his horizons, Mr. L'Amour left home at the age of fifteen and enjoyed a wide variety of jobs, including seaman, lumberjack, elephant handler, skinner of dead cattle, miner, and an officer in the transportation corps during World War II. During his "yondering" days he also circled the world on a freighter, sailed a dhow on the Red Sea, was shipwrecked in the West Indies, and stranded in the Mojave Desert. He won fifty-one of fifty-nine fights as a professional boxer and worked as a journalist and lecturer. He was a voracious reader and collector of rare books. His personal library contained 17,000 volumes.

Mr. L'Amour "wanted to write almost from the time I could talk." After developing a widespread following for his many frontier and adventure stories written for fiction magazines, Mr. L'Amour published his first full-length novel, *Hondo,* in the United States in 1953. Every one of his more than 120 books is in print; there are more than 300 million copies of his books in print worldwide, making him one of the bestselling authors in modern literary history. His books have been translated into twenty languages, and more than forty-five of his novels and stories have been made into feature films and television movies.

His hardcover bestsellers include *The Lonesome Gods, The Walking Drum* (his twelfth-century historical novel), *Jubal Sackett, Last of the Breed,* and *The Haunted Mesa.* His memoir, *Education of a Wandering Man,* was a leading bestseller in 1989. Audio dramatizations and adaptations of many L'Amour stories are available from Random House Audio publishing.

The recipient of many great honors and awards, in 1983 Mr. L'Amour became the first novelist ever to be awarded the Congressional Gold Medal by the United States Congress in honor of his life's work. In 1984 he was also awarded the Medal of Freedom by President Reagan.

Louis L'Amour died on June 10, 1988. His wife, Kathy, and their two children, Beau and Angelique, carry the L'Amour publishing tradition forward with new books written by the author during his lifetime to be published by Bantam.

FORGET
THE LAW
OF THE
JUNGLE...

The Worst
Drought In
Memory . . .

In Louis L'Amour's
classic tale
of loyalty
and betrayal . . .

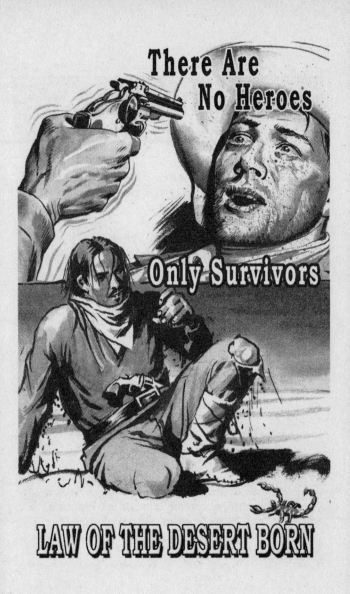

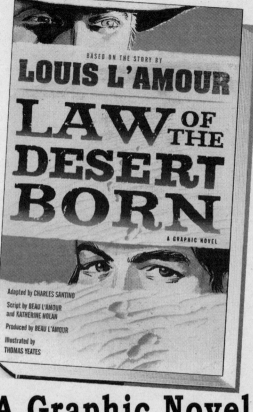